An Oathbound® Novel
Forged

Book 1 of the Queen's Blade Trilogy

Thomas M. Reid

A Bastion Press Book

Seattle

Dedication

To the Alliterates; here's to smooth prose, smoother Scotch, and the joys of having writers for friends.

OATHBOUND
Forged

Distributed worldwide to the book trade by Osseum Entertainment (www.osseum.com); distributed to all other markets by Bastion Press, Inc. (www.bastionpress.com) and regional distributors.

Cover art by A'lis
Cover design by Todd Morasch and Jim Butler
Edited by Brannon and Heather Hollingsworth

Original Oathbound concept by Greg Dent, Jim Butler, and Todd Morasch.

Bastion Press and the Bastion Press logo are trademarks of, and Oathbound is a registered trademark of, Bastion Press, Inc.

First Printing: July, 2003.
Printed in Canada

BAS-9000
ISBN: 1-59263-002-2

Bastion Press, Inc.
P.O. Box 46753
Seattle, WA 98146

www.bastionpress.com

An overview of the great city of Penance

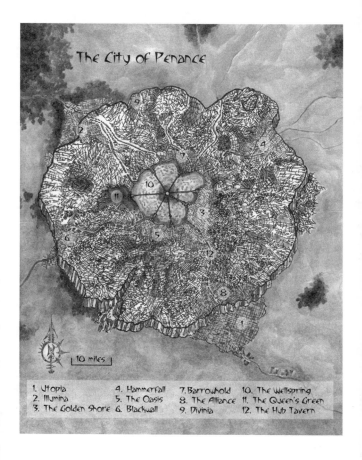

The City of Penance

1. Utopia
2. Illumina
3. The Golden Shore
4. Hammerfall
5. The Oasis
6. Blackwall
7. Barrowhold
8. The Alliance
9. Divinia
10. The Wellspring
11. The Queen's Green
12. The Hub Tavern

10 miles

The thread of your life on this world has run out. Take my hand and I shall give you a new one, and weave it into a beautiful tapestry of dreams and visions such that you have never imagined.

—Israfel, Queen of Penance

Prologue

To Iandra, Lyrien was little more than a shadow in the near-darkness of the muggy tent, but she didn't need to see his face—nothing more than a silhouette—looming over her own to lose herself in his presence. His breath smelled faintly of spiced cider, and of the morsels of chocolate she had hand-fed him earlier. He leaned in, his short dark hair and the stubble of his unshaven face faintly backlit in the predawn glow, and they shared a kiss. She grabbed at the back of his head, holding him there, wanting that kiss to exist forever.

It was what the queen needed right then, to let herself be consumed in the moment, the *now*, forgetting about the world beyond the inside of her tent. Instead, she concentrated on every tiny part of Lyrien, feeling the individual whiskers nudge against her face as he continued that kiss, knowing that he held it because she so desperately wanted him to. She closed her eyes and sank deeper into the embrace, sighed softly as he entwined his fingers with her own, pressing her hands down into the cushions on either side of her head and raising himself up again.

Iandra half-opened her eyes and stared up at that face she could barely see, the face of the captain of her guardsmen, her champion. She felt safe with him there, convinced that nothing outside those tent walls could get in, not so long as she alone could have his fierce, unwavering resolve to protect her. Merely summoning him to her bed could do that, could make everything right. She believed because *he* believed it.

So while the world outside was made to wait, Iandra tried to pull a hand free to draw Lyrien down to her again, and he wouldn't let her. She broke into a faint smile because she could sense that he was going to start teasing her then. She could feel him holding her hands down and not letting her go, could feel him shift, could feel him stir against her leg, and she knew that he would pause, waiting for her to try to wriggle beneath him to get *closer*, to force the issue. She giggled softly and opened her mouth, only her head rising up, working against his weight on her hands, trying to reach up and kiss him again, tease him right back.

"Wait," Lyrien whispered suddenly, holding perfectly still. "Did you hear that?"

Iandra ignored his words, drinking him in, the spiced cider and the chocolate blending with his own musky scent, which lingered in the still, heavy air. "No," she whispered, shaking her head and trying again to lean upward to kiss him. "Not yet," she said, imploring her captain to keep the world out for just a little while longer.

But Lyrien held himself still, listening, as his warm flesh pressed against her naked body where they were tangled together in the thin, damp sheets. The queen felt him nudging insistently against the inside of her thigh and wanted to pull him down to her, feel his mouth close over hers, run her hands through that short, coarse hair and across the scruffy stubble, but she knew not to disturb him. When her captain of the guard acted that way, she knew to trust his instincts. Iandra tried to still her own breathing, rapid with her need, to listen along with him.

A shout, a startled cry of anger, arose from somewhere outside, in the camp. Then Iandra heard the ring of steel on steel, faint, in the distance. The roar of a musket startled birds sleeping in the cattails on the shore of the swamp near the tent. They departed with a cacophony of honks and splashes. In the still, sultry air inside her pavilion, the sounds seemed to come from all around.

Lyrien was off her in an instant, scrambling on hands and knees toward the opening of the tent across the carpet that served as the floor. Iandra watched as he yanked aside the tent flap and darted outside, letting the glow of the early morning intrude into their sanctuary. Her heart was thumping in her chest, but it was no longer arousal that boiled her blood.

Lord De'Valen, she realized. She shifted to her knees and then stood, kicking away the damp cushions at her feet. How did he find us? Damn him!

Iandra stalked toward the tent opening. She reached the doorway and poked her head out. The air was slightly cooler outside, though it was no less damp. Lyrien had not gone far. He was crouched near the roots of a massive cypress tree, peering into the distance, a flintlock pistol in his hand. The pink light of dawn revealed the scar where a musket ball had skimmed the back of his shoulder, and she caught herself thinking of the countless times she had gently traced it with her fingers as he brooded after their lovemaking, his back to her. The glow also revealed the sad collection of tents belonging to what remained of her army, Ilnamar's army, though they were smothered by the heavy mist that cloaked the edge of the swamp, making them seem insubstantial, like the ghost of some long forgotten battlefield.

A commotion was pouring through the camp, soldiers wearing the black and red of Lord De'Valen's banner sweeping between the tents. A few of Iandra's own men stumbled forth, fumbling for weapons to defend themselves, but the surprise was complete. The black-and-red clad mercenaries serving the usurper put down anyone who confronted them, all the while making a line for her tent.

This wasn't just surprise, Iandra realized. It was betrayal. Even then she could see some of her own soldiers, men supposed to be on watch, working with De'Valen's thugs rather than against them.

"It's over," Iandra said softly, feeling bleakness wash over her.

"Not yet," was all Lyrien said, spinning back to her, heedless of his nakedness.

The queen ground her teeth to keep herself from trembling at the thought of Lord De'Valen, still chasing her despite already claiming and overrunning her kingdom. He would not be content until he had claimed her as well, it seemed. Only Lyrien seemed convinced that it was not a foregone conclusion.

"Into the swamp," the captain said, grabbing Iandra by the arm. "We'll hide there."

Iandra resisted for a heartbeat, knowing it was futile and wanting only to show some dignity in defeat. She was afraid, truly afraid, for the first time in a long while.

Lyrien tried to steer his lover around the side of the tent and toward the back, but still Iandra held her ground. "Wait!" she said, half-indignant, half-terrified. She tried to dart inside. "Not like this! My clothes!"

Lyrien yanked her back out and to him and gestured into the cattails with his other hand, the one that held the flintlock pistol. "There's no time!" he hissed. "Run now!" And he pushed her ahead of him. She gave one quick glance back at her captain and stumbled deeper into the swamp, feeling rather than seeing him behind her.

Back in the camp, the shouts and sounds of fighting grew louder. Despite her overwhelming trepidation, Iandra was surprised that there was not more gunfire.

She stumbled into the shallow water on the shore of the swamp, splashing and startling more birds, mostly loons but also a single great black bird. The creature went aloft awkwardly, screeching in irritation at her intrusion, and perched upon the blackened stump of a long-dead cypress not far away. It preened itself as it watched her, its head cocked sideways.

"That way," Lyrien said as he caught up to Iandra, gesturing with the flintlock toward a spit of land ahead and to their left. "Follow the path." Then he nudged her forward.

Cattails and vines slapped and scratched at Iandra's naked skin as she picked her way through the growth, crouching low in an attempt to stay hidden from the pursuit. She found the path Lyrien indicated, really nothing more than a game trail, and turned down it, pushing deeper into the moss-draped cypress trees, putting distance between herself and the shattered remains of her troops.

Iandra couldn't really blame her soldiers for the betrayal, she realized as her bare feet thumped along the muddy path. Deep down, even she had known her resistance had become a lost cause. Only Lyrien had seemed unwilling to admit defeat and had continued to lead her army with some grim, willful determination. The worse things seemed to get, the more driven he had become.

Still trying to prove something to his father, she supposed. But the troops had long since lost hope, the queen lamented. They were simple men, and in the end, none of them truly cared who ruled Ilnamar, when it came right down to it. One leader instead of another was better than death for a cause.

The path ahead of her turned, and as the queen rounded the bend, she saw that it split into two directions. "Which way?" she asked as she slowed a step. Three black crows went swooping by, cawing at her as they glided past to settle in a patch of thick brambles.

"Either," Lyrien grunted behind her, pushing her ahead again. "Just pick."

Without thinking, Iandra charged ahead and to the left, but her foot struck against a cypress root and she went sprawling, landing with a splash in the shallow water beside the trail. The black birds seemed to laugh at her as they cawed and crackled from the shrubs. Behind her, someone shouted, a sound that was too close. The pursuit was on.

With one arm, Lyrien hoisted Iandra back out of the water and shoved her ahead of him. "Go!" he insisted, still glancing back the way they had come.

Ignoring the mud and leaves that clung to her, the queen scrambled forward again, churning along the path and pushing the cattails out of her face as best as she could. She was stumbling along blindly with no idea where they were going.

Part of Iandra wanted to give up the fight, like her soldiers had done. She had grown so weary of running all the time. Surrender with honor and be finished with it, she had found herself thinking more and more often, but every time she had begun to lose hope, she had remembered her grandfather and his continued resistance to Lord De'Valen's conquests. She needed that image right then, of the defiant gleam in her grandfather's eyes—even when he was lying on his deathbed—to stiffen her resolve against those bleak thoughts. She was Ilnamar's queen and bore her grandfather's legacy. That responsibility had driven her onward when almost nothing else would, that and the icy chill she got each time she remembered the lust that gleamed in De'Valen's eyes whenever he looked upon her. He could take her lands, but he would never touch her. She prayed that Lyrien had a plan.

Around the next bend, the trail played out; on every side except the way the lovers had come, water blocked their path.

"Lyrien!" Iandra cried softly, pulling up once more. "We're trapped!"

The captain drew up beside her, turning one way and another, peering at the unbroken surface of the swamp. "That way," he said at last, pointing into the water and toward another peninsula of land yards away. He spun Iandra to face him, then drew her close. He crushed her into his arms, kissing her on the mouth, reminding her of the chocolate. Then her captain gave her a look with eyes of the darkest black. She could feel those eyes boring into her, to her core, to her very soul, every time he stared at her. She shivered, feeling so exposed to him, and she remembered why she loved him, felt herself falling for him all over again, but he only turned her away. "Go."

Iandra looked at Lyrien helplessly, fearing to leave him, fearing what might lie beneath the surface of the brackish water, but when he nudged her shoulder, she sighed and took the first tentative step. Her toes sank into rich, dark mud that came up to her calf before she found solid purchase. The next step found the water up to her waist. She shivered despite the sultry morning, as much from apprehension as from the chill of the swamp. The queen looked back to see if Lyrien was following her, but he stood peering in the opposite direction, watching for pursuit.

"Come on," Iandra urged her mate as she took another step and found herself up to her armpits in water.

"Don't wait for me," her captain replied, not turning around. "Swim for that spit; it's not far. And stay low, out of sight."

"Lyrien!" the queen pleaded, the fear making her throat feel thick. "Please, come with me!"

"I'm right behind you," Lyrien answered, still keeping watch along their back trail. "I won't leave you."

Iandra nodded, though she knew her lover couldn't see, then she took a calming breath, pushed off into the water, and began to swim across to the land on the far side of the narrow waterway. She took long, powerful strokes, like she had so often when she used to race her brother at the summer palace. Trepidation drove her to pull hard for the other side before something living in the water came at her. Her imagination conjured up snakes, alligators, and who knew what else, but the only living things near the waterway were more black birds, crows and grackles, chattering and cawing, all of them watching her. More of them arrived and settled into the thick moss that clung to the cypress trees as the queen reached the far bank and thrashed up out of the water onto dry land.

Iandra turned back, looking for Lyrien, but he had not begun the swim, yet. She wanted to call to him, urge him to catch up, but she was afraid her voice would give them away. Her captain looked back over his shoulder at her and motioned for her to keep moving, but she could not. She didn't dare continue; she would not let him out of sight, for his presence was the only thing keeping her from breaking down completely right then. She crouched low into the cattails, watching him.

At that moment, Iandra spotted movement in the underbrush just beyond Lyrien's position, further back on the trail they had followed. She swallowed in alarm and hissed at her companion, but it was too late. A shout rose up as men dressed in black and red came crashing through the cattails toward him. It was then that Iandra saw the skiffs on the water, flanking their position and coming toward her. They were filled with more men, armed and peering into the thick undergrowth of the swampland.

Lyrien rose up as the first of Lord De'Valen's mercenaries broke into his view, aiming his pistol. Iandra watched in dread as he pulled the trigger, but nothing happened. The sudden confrontation was enough to startle the foe, though, and Lyrien took advantage of the other man's hesitation to fling the weapon at his head. The pistol glanced off the man's temple, and Lyrien was at him in an instant. The thug swung wildly at Lyrien, but the captain simply bent smoothly out of the way, grasping his opponent's arm and carrying the thug through with his own momentum in the process. As the mercenary stumbled forward, Lyrien yanked the man's tunic up and inside out, over his head, shoving him into the cattails off-balance. Then Lyrien turned and dived into the water.

He was halfway across before the mercenary recovered, shrugging his tunic back down and drawing his own flintlock out of his broad sash. "Hold, Captain Ves'tiral," he called to Lyrien, sighting down the barrel of the pistol, "or I *will* shoot."

In desperation, Iandra snatched up a length of waterlogged wood lying at her feet and stood, flinging it as hard as she could at the mercenary. The wet branch spun in the air and struck the thug in the leg, not hard enough to injure him, but enough to startle him. The flintlock jerked and went off, the roar of its powder like thunder in the still morning. The ball skipped across the water less than a foot from Lyrien.

Surprised, the thug stared at Iandra, who realized that she had revealed her position. "They're here!" the mercenary cried out, waving one arm over his head. "This way!" The call went up all around, and Iandra realized the soldiers had fanned out and were working their way deeper into the swamp in hopes of surrounding the two of them.

Iandra turned and ran again as Lyrien reached the same embankment where she had climbed out of the water. Black birds swirled around both of them then, screaming and flapping in a mad dance as the queen ran past them, as though they were as upset as she. She could hear Lyrien's footsteps treading rapidly on the path behind her, and the shouts of their pursuers. A musket roared from out on the water, and the trunk of a cypress tree exploded into splinters near Iandra's head, making her flinch. She jerked away from the stinging fragments of wood and went sprawling to the spongy ground, at the same time spotting more of Lord De'Valen's troops ahead of her.

Lyrien reached the queen then, standing over her naked, mud- and leaf-covered form and holding a hand out for her to take. Iandra merely shook her head no, exhausted and disconsolate. It was over. She rolled to sit up, watching as more and more of the soldiers pursuing them appeared, some on the land, others paddling skiffs. Somehow, they had known exactly where to find the two of them.

Iandra watched as Lyrien stepped between her and the closest of the mercenaries, defiant until the end. He would hold that position until either he or their enemies were dead, she knew, but she wondered if the captain's unyielding principles, his absolute certainty that hers was the moral cause, would be his final undoing. And her own. A tiny part of her wondered if it might not be better to surrender and live. De'Valen might be everything terrible her imagination could conjure, but maybe, just maybe, it was still better than the death her captain promised her with his unwavering defiance. At that moment, she almost felt as trapped by Lyrien as she did by Lord De'Valen.

Iandra huddled at Lyrien's feet, reaching toward him, ready to tell the man she loved the one thing she knew would defeat him—that it was time to surrender, that she no longer wanted him to die in her defense. She took hold of his hand, tried to draw his attention down to her, but the damned black birds—ravens, crows, grackles, and even a pair of falcons—were everywhere, thrashing around them both, making him hold up his arms to protect his face. Iandra shrieked and clung to her lover's leg, closing her eyes to the hordes of flapping wings and scraping talons.

The sound of the birds was deafening and grew louder by the second. Iandra's stomach lurched in terror and she squeezed her eyes tightly shut, sobbing, as the fowl swarmed over the pair of them. She risked a single glance around, but there was nothing to see but a torrent of black feathers all around her. She quickly turned away, howling as talons and beaks raked at her bare skin and tore at her damp, bedraggled hair.

Out of nowhere, Iandra heard a voice rise up. It was a woman's, loud and clear and echoing through the cacophony of the mass of black birds.

"Your courage and defiance are admirable, Captain Ves'tiral, but your role in this play is at an end," the voice said, reverberating through the swamp. It was unreal, larger than life, and despite her terror, Iandra marveled at the warmth she felt inside when she heard it. "There is more for you to do, yet, but not here. It is time for you to come with me, where your passions will serve both of us."

Then Lyrien screamed, and Iandra did, too, crying out as a thunderclap bounced all around her, through her, jarring her bones and rattling her teeth. Even as the tremor rumbled and went silent, it took a moment for Iandra to realize that Lyrien was no longer there. Her arms were wrapped around emptiness. She crumpled to the ground in horror and despair, clearly hearing the sound of her own rasping sobs. The black birds were gone, along with her lover.

The queen, weeping softly, curled up in a ball upon the damp, black ground. The birds had taken her Lyrien from her. She could not understand how that was possible. Somehow, the woman behind the powerful voice had stolen her lover and left her alone, to die, or worse. She was going mad, she thought, or soon would be at Lord De'Valen's hands.

The queen opened her eyes to see a dozen or so of Lord De'Valen's men approach her warily, their eyes wide and their jaws hanging slack. Finally, one of them got close enough to Iandra to level his pistol at her. Miserably, Iandra sat up in a huddled crouch and stared at the man. One eye milky blind where a scar cut across it on his face, he looked unsettled, but whatever uncertainty he might have felt at the disappearance of half his quarry was pushed aside as he ogled the woman still there, licking his lips. His face broke into a smile as he motioned for her to get up. It was not a pleasant expression.

"Milady, if you please. Lord De'Valen would like a word with you."

Chapter 1

Captain Lyrien Ves'tiral kept his arms wrapped about his head and cowered, eyes clenched tightly shut against the blazing whiteness that engulfed him. His whole body throbbed with pain, and he truly believed that he was about to die. The soldier welcomed death if it meant escaping his madness. Only madness could explain the image that loomed over him of the winged woman, masked and horned, impossibly tall, with her resonating, overwhelming voice. Only madness could be responsible for the sensation of his very soul being wrenched from his body and borne away, into that terrible, searing whiteness. The whiteness must be causing this great pain Lyrien felt, burning through his flesh.

The pain increased but also became more focused, centralized, until at last Lyrien realized he was holding his breath. He let it go in one great, sobbing exhalation and, remaining curled up with his arms covering his head, he trembled. The whiteness still loomed, beyond his eyelids, and it took the man several more moments to understand that it wasn't the same all-pervasive glow from before. It now seemed to be simple sunlight. It seemed fantastically bright, but it was mere sunlight nonetheless. Swallowing the strong, metallic taste of fear that filled his mouth, Lyrien cautiously, fearfully, opened one eye.

The whiteness that glared back at the captain came from white stone, inches from his face. No, not just stone; it was smooth, white tile, warmed from a midday sun, and he was lying on a stretch of it. He peered around and found that he rested in a courtyard, a private garden, crumbling with neglect and age.

Suddenly, as his senses crackled and awoke fully, Lyrien realized he could feel the warmth of the tile beneath his naked skin and could feel rivulets of sweat trickling down his body. He smelled a dozen faint odors on the caressing breeze, and he could hear the cawing of birds. Birds! The black birds in the swamp!

"Iandra!" Lyrien cried out as he sat bolt upright, looking around desperately. As he realized the queen was not there, panic and cruel dismay washed over him like the surge of a river, driving him back down against the white tiles. He gave off another heaving, wracking sob. The sudden rush of sadness and loneliness was too much to bear. He had failed her, and he decided dismally that he would lie there and weep for his loss forever. Despite all his efforts and his absolute conviction that he would see her on the throne that was rightfully hers, somehow, Lyrien had come up short, and the queen would suffer for it. The mere thought made him want to stay right where he was and waste away.

Let me just die, the captain thought. Let the sun dry me to a withered husk, to simple dust, and I'll scatter in the wind. What does it matter? I wasn't strong enough and now I've lost her, forever. 'Forever' reverberated through his head, and Lyrien felt the whole *meaning* of it weighing down on him all at once, crushing the life and strength out of him, pressing him relentlessly into the warm tiles.

No, that is ridiculous, Lyrien told himself, sitting up suddenly. Stop whimpering like a child. You can find her. You *will* find her, the captain insisted silently, brimming with hope. He knew he would track her down, return to her, and nothing, no force in the heavens, would hold him back. He would not be defeated.

The captain half-rose to his feet, ready to set out at that very moment, but even as he scanned the crumbled and ruined building he found himself in, confusion washed over him. It was all too strange, too alien. He had no idea how he'd gotten to that place, or how he would return to her. Too many questions. Too much to work through, to many challenges to overcome. It couldn't be done.

Lyrien sank back down to the white tile a second time, his head in his hands. What's the matter with me? he wondered. I'm like a child, a weak babe. The tiniest thing upsets me. This isn't right! He screamed silently. Be a man! You're a soldier, fool! Act like one!

"Act like one!" Lyrien screamed aloud, pounding his fist against the stonework beneath him. He started at the clear timbre of the echo of his voice, radiating back to him. Then the pain of his bruised knuckles crashed over him as well, and he gazed down at the welling of blood in wonder. It shone bright and crimson in the fair sunlight, and when he sucked at it, the taste was sharper, more pronounced, than he had ever remembered before.

Suddenly a shape, something that had been camouflaged among the dappled shadows, shifted and moved. Even as the captain focused on the motion, a thing as wide as he was tall began scuttling across the tiles directly at him, impossibly fast for its size. The skittering thing was a giant wolf spider, all mottled browns and grays, with a body at least two feet wide and a leg span that carried it toward the captain in a heartbeat. The spider took a dozen lightning-fast strides and then launched itself through the air right at him.

Horrified, Lyrien rolled to one side on instinct as the brown arachnid settled lightly to the tiles where he had been sitting a split-second before. It turned to face him as he tumbled backward, gleaming black eyes and a pair of fangs, damp and shiny with venom, glittering in the dim light. Lyrien never stopped moving away, feeling in perfect balance, in total control of his fluid movements despite the fear clutching at his chest. He deftly shoved a half-rotted crate or something similar between himself and the thing as he retreated on all fours, still facing it. The box slid smoothly across the tiles, but a blink of an eye later, the spider had leaped atop the ruined item, bouncing slightly as it surveyed where its prey had retreated. Lyrien continued to roll himself across the tiles away from the spider, but it lunged forward again.

Desperately, Lyrien kicked out, trying to deflect the spider's body away from him. His bare foot struck solidly against the side of its abdomen, generating a meaty thunk as the kick drove the spider away a few feet. The attack felt good, the strength in his leg powerful. Lyrien grunted with the effort and reverse-somersaulted to his feet as the spider landed a couple of paces away, stunned for the moment. The captain took advantage of its momentary condition to dart farther away, seeking desperately for some sort of weapon. There was nothing of any consequence in the courtyard except for chunks of rubble where part of a wall had collapsed, the spot from which the spider had emerged. Lyrien snatched up two sizable pieces of the debris and spun back to keep his pursuer in view.

The wolf spider had shaken off its confusion and was skittering toward him once more, heedless of any danger its prey might present to it. Lyrien hurled the first chunk of rock underhanded at the thing, knowing his aim would be truer from low, on a line with the floor. The piece of rubble skipped once on the tile and glanced off the spider's abdomen, snapping a leg half-off in the process. The spider emitted a high-pitched hissing sound as it was wounded and danced away from Lyrien, dragging the useless leg with it. Even with only seven usable limbs, though, the arachnid was as mobile as ever.

The creature came at Lyrien again, though not directly that time. It seemed to be trying to circle around its prey, as though it thought it could outflank the captain. Lyrien spun in place, maintaining his facing directly at the thing, and when it suddenly darted toward him again, he flung the second chunk of rubble at it. The spider seemed to have anticipated the attack, though, for it leaped straight up into the air as it came forward, vaulting over the make-shift missile in the process.

Cursing, Lyrien scrambled backward as the spider hurtled through the air at him. He stumbled across more of the loose fragments of ruined wall and lost his footing, staggering into the rubble pile and finally going down in an undignified heap, sprawled out on his back, with several chunks of stone digging painfully into his back and rump. The spider landed mere feet away from him and sprang forward again, before he even had time to bring his foot up for another well placed kick.

As the arachnid landed atop his chest, its smaller fore-legs flailing eagerly toward him, Lyrien shrieked in panic and punched upward, slamming both fists desperately against the spider's head, trying to keep the dripping fangs from striking. The spider hissed again and raised up, either to avoid the blows or to strike, and in fear-induced madness, Lyrien flailed about for something to use to defend himself with. His hand closed on another fragment of rock. He swung the shard up without thinking just as the spider slammed down toward him again, fangs extended. The force of the captain's blow was enough to halt the spider's attack and crush one side of its head.

Dark ichor spurted from the wound and the spider shivered violently as it tumbled to the side, its legs spasming wildly in the air. Lyrien wasted no time, lunging up to his feet with a shudder to escape being so near to the thing. When he was certain it was no longer coming after him, Lyrien moved forward and loomed over the spider, bringing the hunk of stone down again, driving it with both hands into the soft underside of the spider's head, right where the menacing fangs flexed in and out. The resulting squishing sound and splatter of brown flesh left no doubt in the captain's mind that the thing was finally dead, though its body jerked and its legs wriggled for several more seconds.

Panting, Lyrien staggered away, afraid his heart would burst from beating so hard and so rapidly. The adrenalin coursing through him made his whole body ache severely. He had never felt such fear in his life, despite the number of fights he'd experienced.

You've never seen a spider that big before, though, Lyrien told himself. How is such a beast possible? he wondered, staring down at the half-crushed creature.

Every part of its body, from the coarse brown and black hairs that covered it to the shiny black orbs of its eyes, seemed somehow more real and defined than anything he had ever studied before. It was almost as if he and the spider were connected somehow. As if he had expanded his senses beyond the five he already knew to something deeper, more fundamentally a part of his essence, and the essence of everything—the spider, the stone, the sun shining down and the motes of dust that danced within its beams—was also a part of that connectivity. That sharper level of feeling was unnerving.

Lyrien spent several more moments recovering both his wits and his breath. Finally, when he felt he had calmed down enough, he turned his attention back to his surroundings. Everything was clearer and sharper. It all seemed more real than anything before. Every mote of light, every line, every color, every bit of motion stood out and drew his attention in an urgent and joyous manner. He was overawed by everything. And the words in his head, the mind's voice, were also crisper, more pronounced. Every thought, every raw emotion, reverberated through his whole body, making him ache in misery and shiver in delight in the span of a breath. In contrast, everything that had come before that instant, that time and place, seemed somehow less real. It was a distant memory, faded and diluted. He almost didn't believe it was real, except for the fact that every time he thought of Iandra, his heart wept.

Lyrien took a deep, calming breath. This place is affecting me, he realized. I've got to fight it.

He peered around once more, thoroughly studying the place. It was a courtyard, inside a building of white stone, perhaps limestone. The architecture was impressive and refined, but it was also strange and thoroughly unfamiliar. A fountain basin, dry and silent, rested in the center of the patio, and a sculpture of a creature unlike any he had ever seen in Ilnamar before stood atop a pedestal in the center. The creature had the body of a man, but its head was that of a dog, or maybe a fox. Regardless, the craftsmanship was exquisite, and Lyrien gazed at it for several long moments, drinking in every fine detail, every tiny imperfection in the stone that gave the thing such character.

No! He chastised himself, shaking his head. Don't get distracted! Lyrien steadied himself once more and drew on his military training. You are a soldier; stow those emotions right now.

When he had mastered his vertiginous passions once more, he continued his survey, determined not to become sidetracked. It was difficult.

The rest of the courtyard was enclosed by a building, two levels tall, with porches at each level running around the periphery of the atrium. Just beyond the edge of the roof along one side of the courtyard, a slender tower rose upward at least five more stories. Near the tower's apex, which flared in a domed shape, a walkway encircled the tower. At various points along the tower's length, windows filled with stained glass images decorated the white surface. Lyrien supposed that he might find the way inside that tower from an interior room.

Fluted columns formed the façade between the open plaza and the porches surrounding it. In addition to the fountain, planter boxes sat at each corner of the patio, and Lyrien could see more of them spaced about the porches at both levels, along with hanging baskets dangling from brass chains. Beyond these, in the shade, doorways led into the interior of the building. It had once been a beautiful place.

The plants now grew wild, creepers and vines tumbling out of the planter boxes, many of which were cracked, their soil spilled out upon the tiles. Several of the baskets were hanging askew, a chain missing or broken, while others had fallen completely, lying shattered upon the flooring below. The columns were stained black from rain and mildew, and a number of them were cracked. The balustrade that enclosed the upper porch was incomplete and toppled over. The stonework of the structure itself was listing, all of its angles imperfect, slumping and grim, as though the building, saddened at its abandonment, could no longer stand proudly. It was desolate and wild in that courtyard.

Lyrien drank it all in with his eyes, feeling a tumultuous collection of varying emotions pass through him as he studied his surroundings, willing himself to suppress the tidal wave of feeling that seemed to come unbidden at every new thought, every new sensation. It was both wonderful and terrible, and if he allowed himself to slip, even the slightest, it would wash away his logic and determination.

Climbing to his feet, Lyrien ignored the tingling of a gentle breeze drying the sweat upon his sun-warmed skin. Even his nakedness felt somehow more severe, and he fought the urge to both examine and cover himself as he planted his feet. The tiles felt good beneath them. He found his balance easily, shifted his weight, and was amazed at how sweet the simple sensation of standing felt. He curled his toes and took a step, then another, and on impulse, he deftly leaped up to land upon the basin wall of the fountain. The act was pure, the sensation phenomenal. He felt like a cat ready to pounce, a bird on the verge of flying.

Lyrien peered up at the sky overhead, squinting against the glow of the sun, and was astonished at how deeply blue it was. There were no clouds, but he somehow thought he could sense rain, a great roiling thunderstorm, seething somewhere out of sight, beyond the edge of the second floor.

A single black bird perched atop the roofline, its head crooked sideways, peering down at the captain with one eye. Lyrien frowned, remembering what had transpired prior to his arrival. The thought of Iandra made his chest ache, especially when he considered that by now, she was most likely Lord De'Valen's prisoner, but he forced that emotion down long enough to consider what might have happened.

Am I dead? he wondered. Is this the afterlife?

Lyrien wasn't a particularly spiritual man, but he had to consider the possibility. He remembered the swamp clearly, though dully, like a pale echo of what the reality must have been. The two of them had fled, stumbling through the cattails. He had sent the queen on ahead while he remained behind. He had tried to fire a shot at one of their pursuers, but the dampness had fouled the powder of his flintlock. Had he been shot in return? Was the rest of it just the ravages of death tricking him? The birds, the woman with the wings and horns, glorious to behold, standing over him, her voice reverberating through his thoughts. Was all of that merely an illusion, a tool of the mind to comfort itself during its final moments?

Perhaps, Lyrien decided, but he was skeptical. If the place was some sort of heaven, why was it in ruin, and why was he the only one there?

There was another possibility, but one that the captain was reluctant to consider. Heedless of his intense desire to repress it, the possibility crept into his mind unbidden. Known as The Taking, it might explain his predicament. The Taking was myth, though, pure fable designed to frighten children. Everyone in Ilnamar knew the stories of The Taking, tales of men and women, heroes and vagabonds alike, vanishing before the eyes of all those around them. No one really believed in them, except maybe in the dark of night when the shadows were deepest. He certainly had never given the legends any credence. His father would have scoffed at him for doing so right then.

Lyrien thought hard; had any stories of The Taking ever mentioned an impossibly tall woman, or scores of black birds? Perhaps. The stories had different forms, all mysterious and terrifying, but like any legend, the tales transformed with each telling, becoming more fantastic and yet more vague. Perhaps that was what had occurred, and there was truth in the old fables.

None of that, however, was going to help him right then, Lyrien realized. He had to find out where he was. If people built the place, then there must be more of them somewhere. He was determined to find them, determined to extract some sort of explanation from them about where he was and how he had arrived there—for he was certain that it was not Ilnamar. That was paramount to getting back home, back to Iandra. But first things first, he thought. I need clothing and a weapon.

Yet he hesitated, feeling completely vulnerable. He was naked, unarmed, and unsure of what threats like the spider might be lurking unseen nearby, and he had no clear notion of how to ascertain his circumstances. It made him quiver in doubt, in fear.

No, none of that, Lyrien insisted, clenching his jaw. You can't stay here. Survival is paramount, he reminded himself, his old sergeant's words echoing in his memory, flat and dull, like every other recollection of *before*. Everything you do must be geared toward survival. Then he remembered his father's words, taunting words: whatever worthless thing you're going to do, at least *do* it. For the first time in a long time, Lyrien actually agreed with the man's harsh comment.

The captain noted that the sun had moved well past its high point by then, and that most of the patio was in shadow. Darkness would follow soon, and he knew it would be much harder to traverse the grounds of the estate after nightfall. Still, he refused to relinquish caution. He peered up to the roofline, hoping he might find a way to scale the wall, reach the tower from there, and thus discover where he was, but there was no good place to try. He would have to venture further into the house and find another route up or out.

Grimacing, the captain moved forward, toward a portal along the same side of the plaza as the tower, a double-wide opening set into the wall. Beyond it, in contrast with the flaring brightness of the sun, was cool, impenetrable darkness. Each step felt heavy, but slowly, he worked his way closer. Once in the shade of the porch, the cooler air made his skin prickle, giving him goose bumps. He shivered at the sharpness of the contrast. He took another few steps, and then he was at the portal, peering inside. It was dim, but somehow, he was able to make out the interior with clarity, noting the tiniest, finest details.

There was a large, open chamber, which at one time had been decorated with frescos and murals on the floor, walls, and ceilings. The images were faded and cracked, though Lyrien could still make out bits of outdoor scenes, most prominently of the ocean. The only egress from the chamber was a darkened hallway at the rear, leading directly to the base of the tower. A faint blue glow emanated from there, seeming to shine down from above. It must be the light from the stained glass windows, Lyrien reasoned, feeling hopeful.

The room itself was filled with the remains of a number of tables and chairs, like some pub or inn, but in the same warm, airy style that reminded Lyrien of the tropical coasts of home. He supposed that it would have been a fine place to host a summer party, and he could almost imagine the mellow light from colored lanterns and the sweet smell of hyacinth and jasmine in bloom, as people sashayed in brightly-hued suits and gowns, mingling and flirting, while soft music wafted through the place as a backdrop to their merrymaking. Their laughing eyes and tinkling voices would be—

Lyrien shook his head, dispelling the enchanting vision. This is no time for fancies, he scolded himself. Get a firm hold, Lyrien Ves'tiral, or this place will swallow you in its . . . in its what? Magic?

No. Magic was just a part of the myths; stories told to make children's eyes grow wide in the light of a fire. He had liked the idea of magic when he was younger, but his father had banished that foolishness from his mind. Still, something was affecting him.

Its eeriness, he decided. Get a firm hold on yourself before this place swallows you in its eeriness. It's nothing more than a trick of the mind.

Setting his jaw, the captain reestablished his mindset and returned to the business at hand. He moved the rest of the way through the covered patio and into the hallway beyond. There was definitely a dim, bluish glow shining from overhead at the far end. He wasn't certain, but he thought he could make out the frames of more doorways flanking the passage as it receded before him. In the fading light, though, he could not be sure. He found himself trembling, wishing more than anything for a lantern. He resisted the urge to move back out to the patio and stay in the sunlight, stilling his out-of-control emotions once more.

Forcing himself to pick his way carefully, the captain began to move down the dim hallway toward the azure light. As he moved deeper into the gloom, the illumination from behind him revealed more detail than he had imagined it would, and after several yards and a number of closed doors to either side, Lyrien spotted a circular chamber with a spiral staircase ascending at the far end. It had to be the base of the tower. He quickened his pace, reached the staircase, and peered straight up the shaft of the tower. High overhead, he could make out light streaming through an opening. He prayed the stairs were solid enough to hold him and set out.

As he passed the stained glass windows, he admired their ornate construction, noting how tiny the fragments of glass were that made up the images. Of the images themselves, he was pleased to see that they depicted normal humans rather than horned women or dog-headed creatures. Their garb seemed odd, but he paid them no more mind than that, for the images were extremely stylized and simplistic.

By the time he was halfway up the staircase, Lyrien could feel it swaying with his steps. He passed bracing beams at regular intervals, but it was still unnerving, and vertigo threatened to overwhelm him at one point. He had never been leery of heights in the past. He forced himself to stop, clinging tightly to the railing, and then tried to calm himself with deep breaths before continuing on. The sensation of losing his balance had never been so strong as at that moment, but he fought it off and pushed onward. Finally, breathing hard from the exertion, Lyrien reached the doorway. Carefully testing his footing, the captain stepped out and gasped.

Instead of finding himself at a high point on some great estate, or perhaps peering down upon a common square in some village, as far as he could see in every direction, Lyrien spied a great city. There was no open space, no edge to it at all. Buildings were nestled next to buildings, as though some great giant had swept a set of play blocks into a mass, all jumbled together. Carefully, Lyrien circumnavigated the walkway that surrounded the tower. It was, indeed, one of the highest points, and in every direction, the city sprawled to the horizon's edge.

Staggering away from the balustrade and wedging his back firmly up against the wall of the tower, Lyrien gasped for breath. Filled with awe, despair, and a half-dozen other emotions he couldn't even name at the moment, he was overwhelmed. He knew of no place in existence such as that. He was trapped in an endless sea of urban blight and so finely attuned to it that if he wished, he could close his eyes and still retain the smallest details about it, and he had no idea which way to go to escape.

Out beyond the horizon, the captain could also see storm clouds building, thunderheads drifting toward the city. It was the rain he had somehow sensed before, when he had first found himself in the courtyard.

Senses so finely tuned, I can even feel the rain coming, he thought absently. *It's not natural. How is it possible?*

Something else caught the captain's eye at that moment, the sight of which made him blanche. In the far distance to his left, a second sun had just crested the horizon.

Lyrien gaped. It could not be. There should be only one sun in the sky.

This isn't real, Lyrien told himself, closing his eyes. I can't be here. I'm going mad.

A crow cawed nearby, and Lyrien opened his eyes, spotting the bird perched atop the railing near him. He wanted to throw something at it, knock it from its perch as it peered at him with only one eye, head cocked askew, but because the vertigo was back, he dared not move away from the comfort of the tower wall. A second bird joined the first, both watching him now.

"Get away!" Lyrien screamed at them, and the pair took off, cawing angrily, to float out over the city below.

Lyrien shook his head. I'm dreaming, he told himself. Or dead. This place is just wrong.

But he knew in his heart that he was both alive and awake. Steeling himself, he again looked over at the rising red sun, squinting against its glow. The strange way it lit the city along with the yellow light of the first sun made the shadows very odd, indeed. As he gazed down, studying the odd effects of the overlapping lighting, Lyrien at last spotted something that gave him hope; he saw smoke.

Where there's smoke, there are people, he thought. I can find them and they can help me get home. I hope.

With a most devout sense of renewed purpose, Lyrien began to descend the tower, hurrying down the steps rapidly, eager to find a way out of the building he was in. In his haste, he lost his caution, and when he reached the bottom of the spiral staircase and started to jog back through the darkened passage and into the chamber connected to the courtyard, he realized too late that the hallway was illuminated by a source of light.

In the instant Lyrien was hit with the realization that he was not alone, he saw a creature that was definitely not human. It walked like a man, and indeed, it was as tall as Lyrien, but like the creature that decorated the fountain in the courtyard outside, it had the head of a dog, a husky to be more precise. It was clothed like a man, and it held a lantern aloft to see by, carrying a slender sword in its other hand.

The creature seemed to have been sniffing the air, but when Lyrien appeared so suddenly and then nearly collided with it, the canine humanoid jumped and yelped, startled as well, and dropped the lantern with a crash, which promptly went out, engulfing both of them in near darkness. Lyrien was stunned by the effect the sudden darkness had upon his now heightened senses. The captain had little time to reflect on its ramifications, however, for in the next moment, the flooring beneath his feet groaned and gave way. Lyrien heard the canine humanoid cry out in surprise and then he tumbled into yawning blackness below.

Lyrien did not fall far. The hole became a chute or a slide of some sort, and he found himself sliding and tumbling down a steep angle, with dirt, rocks, and his impossible counterpart tumbling right along with him. The captain flailed about helplessly, trying to find some handhold to latch onto, anything he could grab to arrest his fall.

When he finally slid to a stop at the bottom of the incline, he could see nothing. Fighting panic, he cast a glance back up the way he had come and saw a faint bit of light perhaps twenty feet overhead, the dim glow of the sun shining down there through the hole in the floor above, heavily filtered through all the dust. Frantically, Lyrien scrambled to his hands and knees and tried to claw his way back up the steep slope toward that light, but the angle was too severe, and the loose rubble simply crumbled away beneath his churning. Coughing and choking, he gave up.

Beside the captain, something gave a stifled groan, and then he could feel a shifting in the loose debris, and something furry brushed against his leg. Lyrien shuddered and jumped away, his hands protectively out in front of himself. He waved them back and forth urgently, trying desperately to keep whatever the thing was at bay. He was just beginning to make out limited shapes in the dust-smothered light, and he saw the dog-creature then, moving slowly. It rolled over and sat up, coughing and wheezing.

Lyrien held his breath, fighting against what his senses told him was there. It was ridiculous. Dog-headed beings did not exist. He must have hit his head in the swamp, he now realized, must be hallucinating the city, the creature, all of it. He would wake up soon, he thought, since he recognized the delusions for what they were. He crouched quietly and waited, willing himself back to consciousness.

"By the gods," the phantasm across from the captain groaned. "I think I broke my muzzle."

Lyrien said nothing, fighting to stay calm. It's just a dream. Nothing more.

"Are you all right?" the thing asked in the near-darkness, turning toward Lyrien.

The captain still said nothing, though he began to feel around in the rubble now, wanting something in his hand to protect himself with. He closed on a large fragment of rock and hoisted it, ready to smash the creature in front of him, even though another part of his mind told him it was foolish to be afraid of something that wasn't there.

"Hello? Can you understand me?" The canine humanoid called, beginning to shift toward Lyrien now. "Are you conscious?"

"Don't," Lyrien finally said, backing away and holding his rock high overhead. "Get away."

"Easy," the creature replied, freezing in place at the sound of Lyiren's voice. "I'm not looking for a fight. Why don't you—"

Whatever the dog-creature had intended to say, it swallowed its words suddenly. A low growl emanated from the captain's left, from deeper in the darkness.

Chapter 2

Whatever imaginary thing had joined Lyrien and his illusionary dog-creature in that hole in the ground, it was not friendly. With a snarl, it leaped into the midst of the two of them, thrashing and growling wildly. Lyrien stumbled backward, trying to get away from whatever the nightmare was, until he felt his back press against cool stone. He flattened himself against the barrier and willed himself to awaken. Even being a prisoner of Lord De'Valen was far better than insanity.

The dog-creature yelped in sudden pain from a few feet away and then grunted in the darkness. Whatever the growling thing was, it had gone after the captain's counterpart instead of him. Lyrien was not sorry at all. He still clutched his rock and was ready to slam it wildly against anything he sensed was near him. He could barely breathe due to his anxiety, coupled with the choking, dusty air. He inched farther away, sliding along the wall that held him there, unhappy about the fact that his course was taking him deeper into the darkness and farther from the path back to the surface. However, he would not remain close to the frantic fight, blind as he was.

A sudden flare of light caught Lyrien completely off guard, and he blinked and jerking away, involuntarily covering his eyes with his arm. He heard a growl of frustration from one of the creatures, and a gasp of surprise from the other.

"Albine!" the dog-headed creature spat, and the tone of its voice plainly carried dismay. It grunted, and the captain heard the solid thunk of an impact, followed by another menacing snarl.

Lyrien let his eyes adjust and risked a look.

The captain saw that he was in some sort of low-ceilinged room, which reminded him of nothing so much as a bunker that was composed half of a stone wall and half dirt. The far side of the squat chamber was open to a yawning chasm of blackness beyond. There was one other tunnel leading out at an odd angle to Lyrien's left-hand side; it was a round passage that he might be able to crawl through on hands and knees.

The canine humanoid was sprawled out on its back, near the edge of the room opposite Lyrien, holding aloft something that might have been a smooth, rounded river rock. Amazingly, it was glowing with a pale white light, as brightly as a lantern would. Lyrien could see that the canine creature had a nasty gash on its arm, the fur peeled away to reveal the pale, bloody flesh beneath. It still held its slender blade in the other paw, even as it illuminated their surroundings, including the thing that crouched between the two of them.

Again, Lyrien did not want to believe that anything before him was real. He could not imagine how he might have conjured an image so hideous, so alien in form, but it just confirmed to him that he was delusional. He was caught in the throes of a fever-induced nightmare, most likely.

The beast crouching between the captain and escape was vaguely humanoid in shape and pale white in hue. Its skin appeared leathery and tough, and Lyrien doubted his meager rock would be much of a match for it. It had a huge, gaping mouth that was filled with dozens of long, sharp teeth, which jutted out at all sorts of odd angles. Its claws were equally as fearsome—thin, razor-edged talons as long as the captain's hand. It sat frozen for the moment, glaring at the dog-creature. Only its incredibly long, rat-like tail twitched and swished back and forth, like that of an irate cat. It seemed to be recoiling from the light.

"Beware the tail," the canine creature warned, shifting slightly to get up on its hind paws for better balance. "It can trip you if you are not wary."

The whitish beast lunged forward, swiping at the dog-thing's sword in the process, knocking the blade aside. It whipped its tail around itself and wrapped the end of it around the canine creature's right leg, then jerked hard and quick, yanking its foe from his feet. The dog-thing went down in a heap and a startled cry of fear. The white monster was instantly on top of it, snarling and slashing with its teeth and claws.

The husky-headed humanoid fought desperately, fending off the fierce creature's attacks as best it could with its bare paws, but two or three good swipes from the beast's sharp talons had the dog-thing yelping in pain and scrambling back, dangerously close to the precipice beyond. It was only a matter of time, Lyrien knew, before either the whitish beast got its quarry or the dog-thing went over the side.

It was time to choose a side, Lyrien realized; he was no longer truly convincing himself that it was a hallucination, but either way, he wasn't going to sit by while someone—something—needed help.

Hoisting the rock, the captain charged forward at the crooked-toothed beast, planning to dash the jagged stone against its head, as he had done with the spider. But the thing was far more cunning that the arachnid had been. It sensed him coming and let up on the canine long enough to turn its head back toward Lyrien. The creature snapped its tail out, slashing across Lyrien's ankles in a whip-like fashion.

The captain stumbled, throwing his aim off so that his strike with the rock missed the thing's head entirely and swung wide, out over its shoulder instead. As Lyrien staggered past, the monster slashed back at him with one clawed hand, dragging keen talons across the back of his shoulder. He grunted in pain, immediately feeling hot, sticky blood well up along the cuts. The additional force of the creature's blow also sent Lyrien tumbling ever closer to the ledge's edge.

Fortunately, the canine humanoid reached up and took hold of Lyrien, catching him by the arm as it tried to stop his forward progress. Unfortunately, it had to drop its glowing rock in order to claim a good hold on the man, and Lyrien stubbed his toe against the odd, shining stone, sending it tumbling over the precipice's side and out of sight. The three of them, man, dog-thing, and beast, were once again engulfed in darkness.

"Damn!" the dog-thing muttered, dragging Lyrien back from the precipice just as the captain detected the sound of the stone splashing into water below. "We're doomed, now."

Lyrien still held the rock with which he had tried to bash the monstrous thing's head, and he turned then and began blindly shoving it forward repeatedly, extending both his arms straight out from his chest, hoping to catch the beast with one of his two-handed rock punches. On the fourth attempt, he felt the stone hit something solid, and there was a grunt of pain that Lyrien knew did not come from his canine ally.

"That's it, hit it again!" the dog-thing said from beside Lyrien. "Can you see it?" it asked.

"No," Lyrien said, "but I'm keeping it away for the moment. What are we—" Lyrien's words stuck in his throat as the rat-like tail slung around his legs and nearly tripped him again. The captain managed to keep his balance that time, but in the effort to avoid falling, he had to let go of the rock, which bounced across the dirt floor and away into the darkness.

Lyrien's heart sank into despair. He had lost his weapon, and now there was nothing to keep the beast at bay. He began to cower, backing away slowly as another deep-throated growl issued forth from right in front of him. His heel found the ledge's edge. He knew that a drop of some substantial distance waited beyond that edge, and water below. The thought of tumbling down, down, into that black pit made his knees tremble.

He would rather die than fall, Lyrien decided, and he kicked out blindly, hoping to strike some part of the creature and drive it back. His foot sliced through nothing but air. Beside him, Lyrien heard a snap of flesh striking flesh, accompanied by a gasping grunt. The beast had attacked his companion.

The dog-thing howled, obviously in pain. "We're getting ripped to shreds! Over the side!"

"What?" Lyrien managed to say, just as he felt a paw wrap firmly around his arm. "No!" he tried to cry out, attempting to jerk his arm free. He felt a sudden tug, and he knew that his accomplice had leaped over the edge, but he steadfastly refused to go as well. He stood teetering on the very edge of the drop-off, his mind screaming at the thought of falling into the inky blackness. Already, he could feel himself slipping past his balance point, his arms windmilling to try to keep from going over.

The captain sensed the monstrous thing right behind him, could not help but imagine it slashing at his back with its claws, sinking its teeth into his shoulder or neck. The imagery made him shudder, and he realized he was going to topple over the side despite his efforts. At that same moment, the rat-like tail coiled around his ankles again and then he knew he was going to fall. Panic seized him. He flailed all the harder, but in the end, logic took control, and he leapt off, rather than allow the beast to trip him, knowing it would be better to hit the water feet first than to slam into it in an uncontrolled spin.

Jumping into that black void was the hardest thing Lyrien had ever done in his life.

The fall itself was far worse. The captain had the vaguest notion of moving, with an updraft of air whistling past him, but without being able to see the bottom, and the landing spot, he felt as though he were trapped in limbo, somehow hanging in space. It was a terrible feeling, and the anticipation of hitting stone instead of water made him lose his nerve. He began flailing again, hopelessly trying to claw his way up through the air itself, not wanting to strike whatever lay below him.

When he finally struck the water, it was such a shock to Lyrien that he jerked in fright. He felt his knee strike something hard with a glancing blow, something that gave way as he plunged into icy, cold depths. He sank well below the surface, blind and shivering. In the darkness, it was difficult to gain his bearings, and there was no way to follow the air bubbles. He thrashed about, unsure of which way was up, until he realized that there was something else in the water with him. It was furry and long, and Lyrien jerked away from it, certain that he was being attacked by a creature more terrible than the leathery monstrosity above. He then realized it was the canine-creature's arm, dangling loosely in the water. The dog-thing was floating beside him, and suddenly, Lyrien knew which way was up. He lunged that way and as his head finally broke the surface, he sucked in a great, cool lungful of stale, musty air.

Lyrien treaded water for a moment, gasping to recover his breath. The canine creature beside him did not move, but floated limply in the water.

"Hey," the captain said softly, nudging the dog-thing. "Wake up!" he said more insistently. His companion was out cold, or dead.

Lyrien looked around, trying to see, but it was pointless. He could not make out any edges to the pool, nor walls or any other structural elements. It might be a natural cave, or simply a rather large, deep basement. He had no way of knowing.

Suddenly, Lyrien realized that there was a faint light coming from below, a dim glow from under the surface of the water and it was drifting away, growing dimmer by the second.

No, the captain realized. It's still and *I'm* drifting on a current. As the faint light receded, Lyrien understood that it was his companion's glowing rock, lost in the fall and settled to the bottom of whatever body of water in which they had found themselves.

He could feel the sharp sting of the cuts along his shoulder, where the monstrous thing had managed to claw at him before he fell. It was a pain more keen, more precise, than he could ever remember. The clarity of the sensation was stunning.

Unable to determine any direction, nor how close the nearest shore might be, Lyrien instead grabbed hold of the canine creature and managed to get its head out of the water, letting it drift on its back to keep its face above the surface. They needed to get out of the water soon, he realized, his teeth already chattering. He began to swim crossways to the current, hoping he would bump against a bank of some sort where he could climb out.

Suddenly, Lyrien's fingers glanced off something solid in front of him. Tentatively, he reached out and felt himself sliding along stone, smooth and with regular joints, like a wall. He was moving at a pretty good clip, he realized. Then he began to detect a sound from ahead, drawing ever closer and getting louder. In the darkness, it was remarkably clear, if a bit distorted by echo—a waterfall.

He could not take another plunge over a precipice. Desperately, frantically, he began to feel for some top to the wall, sliding his hand along it, going higher, up, kicking with his feet to raise himself out of the water, his other arm releasing his unconscious companion only briefly, but he could not find a top to grab on to. His hand merely slid along the surface of the stone, and he only managed to jam and bruise his fingers against the crevices in the rock. Cursing, he tried again, hearing the roar of the waterfall growing ever louder.

With renewed panic, Lyrien tried again to find some sort of edge or opening in the water, bumping and scraping as he and his companion were pulled along by the swift current. The waterfall was very distinct then, not far away at all. They were going to go over the edge.

Lyrien was growing tired and the iciness of the water was sapping his strength quickly. He considered abandoning the dog-creature; it was weighing him down and draining his energy. He resisted the idea for the moment, but he knew that he could not aid the creature much longer. He willed himself to calmness; then he continued.

The next time Lyrien reached up overhead, feeling the wall, he found a change. The first time, he did not get a good hold on it, but the second time he lunged upward, he managed to hook his fingers over a ledge of some sort and hang on, feeling the drag of the water completely now. It felt like a window sill, though he could not imagine why someone would build a window into a wall below ground, right next to a flow of water. Still, he was grateful they had, and he tried to muster up the strength to pull himself up into it.

He was too tired; he could not do it with only one hand, and he sagged back down into the water, feeling his grip slipping. The captain shouted in frustration, listening as the echoes of his voice bounced all around him. It was disorienting. Drawing a deep breath, he let go of the dog-creature and locked his legs around it, under each shoulder, then lunged upward again, getting a grip on the sill with both hands. With a great grunt of exertion, Lyrien managed to heave himself through the window, or whatever opening it was, tumbling so that he was hanging across it. His legs, still locked around his companion, dangled on one side, his head, the other. The current still pulled upon the unconscious dog-creature, but Lyrien wasn't about to relinquish his hold on it.

You'd better still be alive, damn it, the captain thought.

For several long moments, Lyrien could do nothing but droop motionlessly there, his heart pounding and his breath short. He shivered, feeling the cold water running off of him in rivulets. Goosebumps formed on the captain's damp, naked skin, and though he couldn't see them, he could almost sense each individual bump. Much of the water dripped onto a flat surface directly below, at about the height a floor would be if it was, indeed, a window.

A floor, Lyrien realized, relieved. Not more water.

He knew that if he didn't get moving again, he would never warm up, so he dragged himself the rest of the way through the opening, turning to catch hold of his companion, then he pulled with the last of his strength until the dog-creature was on top of him, and they both tumbled down to the floor. Lyrien collapsed in a heap, trembling from exhaustion and relief, listening to the roar of the waterfall outside. Slowly, he relaxed and evened his breathing. He could hear the canine creature next to him, breathing as well.

Lyrien tried to still his shivering muscles. He had no idea where he was, how he was going to get out, or what the thing was that he had saved. He still wasn't convinced any of it was real, but the longer it remained the only focus of his consciousness, the more his doubts about it seemed to slip away.

As he rested, Lyrien thought of Iandra, trying to keep from letting the remorse and worry spill over him. As strange as his own circumstances were, the queen's had to be more perilous, he knew. Without him there to protect her, to keep her out of harm's way—he was angry with himself for failing her.

What was I thinking, going to her bed when De'Valen was so near? If I had been outside, dealing with the troops like I was supposed to have been, none of this would have happened! I should have been watching for the treachery. I should have seen it coming! Idiot!

Lyrien wanted to pound his fist into the floor, but he stayed his hand, remembering the bloody knuckles from previously, outside. Besides, he remembered, she had all but commanded him to come to her tent. He smiled at that thought, recalling clearly her smoky eyes and soft voice suggesting that the captain of her guard would serve her better inside the pavilion, where they could "discuss" strategy. He laughed aloud at that, feeling for a moment the sweet joy that came with the image. He ached to be by her side and vowed again to return to her.

But in order to do that, the captain reminded himself grimly, he was going to have to get out of there, back to the surface. He knew he must deal with that first and foremost and save the question nagging at the back of his mind, about who—or what—had brought him there, for later.

One step at a time, he thought. *It starts with the first small stride, so get moving.*

Lyrien got to his feet. He was surprised at how quickly his strength had returned. Leaving his companion lying by the window, the captain began to maneuver along the wall into which the opening was set, using his other senses to guide him, as his sight was thoroughly lost. By touch, he made his way through the strange subterranean realm, listening to the echoes of the sounds he made as he shuffled his feet and tapped on the wall. The place smelled old and decayed.

Shortly, Lyrien thumped up against a corner so he turned right and continued. A few feet further on, he came up against something that blocked his way. He ran his hand along its various surfaces and finally determined that it was a desk, shoved up against the wall he had been following. Mildly surprised, he carefully began to check it for contents, hoping against hope that he might find something by which to see.

The top of the desk, which was a tall one made for writing, was covered only in dust. Lyrien fumbled around until he found a drawer and pulled it open. Inside, what felt like paper disintegrated in his hands. There was also a trio of small stoppered bottles—ink, he presumed—and various other instruments of writing. He moved to the next drawer. Inside, he felt several long, thin cylinders of wax that he at first presumed were candles, excited that he might at last have light, but then he realized they were sticks of sealing wax. Then, reaching further back into the drawer, he nicked his finger on something sharp that turned out to be a thin blade—a letter opener, he realized.

Lyrien took hold of that firmly, thankful that he had at last found something that could serve as a makeshift weapon. Still, he was frustrated at not being able to see. In his anger, he nearly flung the drawer across the room, but his calmer instincts prevailed and he evened his breathing before continuing his search.

There was one last drawer in the desk and the captain pulled it open. The faint scent of tobacco wafted up to him. Curious, he felt around inside the drawer and found a soft pouch made of supple leather. The thing was half-rotted and as he disturbed it, he felt a thick dust sprinkle out. The odor of the tobacco instantly grew stronger, filling the dark room with its pungent scent. Shoving that aside, Lyrien dug deeper into the drawer, and his heart leapt into his throat when his hand closed around something small and curled in a 'C' shape. A fire-lighting steel! He continued his search, bypassing what was obviously a long-stemmed pipe, and found what he desperately wanted to be there: a chunk of stone, thin and sharp along one edge—flint.

His heart beating wildly in his chest, hoping against hope, he dug a little more in the drawer, but there were no candles. Lyrien groaned in disappointment and considered his options. There was no paper to be had, nothing to light a fire. He'd just have to keep exploring and hope he could find something soon. Picking up the letter opener, he moved around the desk and continued, taking the flint and steel along as well.

The captain's perseverance soon paid off. Not two paces past the desk, his tentative groping revealed the edge of a fireplace hearth. Carefully, he felt around, hoping to find some bit of kindling or charcoal from which he could coax a flame. He discovered several logs, but nothing so small that it could be considered useful for starting a fire. He kept moving, probing with his hands, feeling along the edge of the hearth to the other side. Finally, his fingertips brushed against a wooden box, and inside, in addition to more large logs, he felt what he was certain were wood shavings, scraps of bark, and twigs. Not enough to light a fire, but maybe . . .

On a hunch, Lyrien felt above the fireplace, seeking a mantle. It was there, as he'd hoped, and a quick inspection with his fingers rewarded him with a candle holder which still held a candle. It was not long, but it still had a wick. He hoped it would function.

Crouching down, Lyrien laid his weapon aside and gathered as much of the collection of wood shavings as he could. He piled them into a small mound and then took up the flint and steel. He gripped the curved metal in his hand and began to stroke the flint against it, aiming to where he knew the pile to be. The first few sparks flashed brightly in his eyes, causing him to flinch back. He had white spots in his vision. Shaking his head to try and clear the distraction, Lyrien tried again. On the fourth stroke, a spark landed true, and the tiny fragments of wood smoldered and glowed. Quickly, before he could lose the flame, he grabbed up the candle and held it close as he blew on the glowing wood, causing the flame to flare up. The wick of the candle suddenly blazed with a tiny flicker.

"Yes!" Lyrien crowed, squinting at his precious bit of light, seeming for all the world to him like the brightest blaze of the sun at noonday. His joy so overwhelmed him that the man simply knelt there for the first few moments, rocking back and forth, tears of happiness streaming down his face. He didn't even bother to try and control his emotions then, so happy was he to be able to see again.

Finally, when his eyes had grown more accustomed to the flame, Lyrien looked around. He was in what might have been a parlor, though the architecture was definitely different from the house he had been in before. The desk he had rifled through was next to him, and there was a nice collection of firewood in the wood box on the other side of the fireplace. The room also had a pair of overstuffed chairs, their cloth rotted away to reveal the framework beneath, a large armoire, and a buffet table against the opposite wall. There was also a single door, closed, that provided an exit from the chamber. In addition to the paneless window through which he had climbed—and it was a window, he confirmed—its twin sat in the same wall, albeit at the far end. Out beyond those two portals, all was still absolute darkness.

Ignoring the contents of the chamber for a moment, Lyrien crouched down and prepared some more bits of bark from the firewood, then very carefully lit it with the candle. Soon enough, he had a small fire blazing, and he put more logs on it to sufficiently build it to warm himself. Then he dragged his companion over by the fire. Finally, the captain simply sat and absorbed the heat from the flames, chasing the last chill of the water from his bones. Thankfully, the chimney and flue were not blocked, obviously still open at the other end, and he did not have to contend with the room filling with smoke.

After he was considerably warmer, Lyrien got up and strode over to the armoire, holding the candle before him. He hoped perhaps to find some piece of cast off or discarded clothing. Inside, he found a variety of garments, most of them dresses, but there were also a couple of pairs of pants and a shirt. Lyrien first used some of the fabric of one dress to blot at his shoulder. It came away bloody, but it was clear the gashes were already beginning to scab over; they were not very deep. He kept the makeshift bandage pressed against the wounds for a few moments, then quickly slipped the pants and shirt on. Lyrien noted with a mild smirk that the pants were made for a person a good half a foot shorter than he, as the cuff of each leg did not even reach the top of his ankle.

Lyrien found the sensation of being dressed as odd as he had of being naked. The clothing was itchy, and the captain felt as though he could discern every fiber that rubbed against his body. He was growing more tolerant of the heightened sensations, but their existence continued to distract him just the same.

Unfortunately, there were no boots; he would have to continue barefoot for the time being. He refused to let that dampen his spirits, though. Once he could see and had something to wear, he felt his confidence returning wholeheartedly. Real or imagined, this place would not keep him dejected for long.

Lyrien turned back and moved to check on his companion's condition. The canine creature was breathing easily, and it didn't seem to have any genuinely deep wounds, other than the gash on its arm that Lyrien remembered from before. Then the captain found the lump on its head, and he remembered the impact his knee had with something in the water when he fell. Apparently, Lyrien had fallen on top of it, knocking the creature unconscious.

Lyrien took the opportunity to get a better look at the creature. Its fur was dark brown in color with light brown highlights. Its forepaws were very human in shape and size, but its hind feet were still decidedly dog-like in form. Lyrien could not help but stare; he wondered if he was, in fact, dreaming the entire encounter, conjuring the figure before him from the long-buried memories of some forgotten fable or fairy tale.

Once Lyrien could get a more prolonged look, he saw that the creature was dressed oddly, with a cloak colored in drab gray and brown hues, the color of stonework. Beneath that, it wore a shirt and pants made of brown leather, which were obviously thick and protective, though still light enough as to not hinder its movement. It was armor, the captain realized, but not bulky and heavy, like the armor of which he was aware.

Ilnamaran soldiers who could afford it once encased themselves in extremely rigid and cumbersome suits of steel plating to defend against their enemies' weapon blows. But such protective gear had gone out of fashion many years previous. Muskets and pistols had become refined to the point where they could penetrate all but the heaviest of those suits, which created armor so burdensome that the men inside could barely stand, let alone move. Lyrien had not seen anyone dressed in armor that he could remember.

In addition to the cloak and armor, the creature lying before Lyrien had a vast array of belts that were strapped around it at waist, thighs, and across each shoulder like bandoliers, each of which had its own collection of pouches and odd tools clipped to it. The creature was some sort of explorer, the captain decided, and it wasn't in danger of dying immediately, so Lyrien thought it best to leave it alone.

The only way Lyrien's companion was going to recover, he knew, was to rest. So, making sure the fire was stoked high and that there was plenty of wood on it to keep the creature warm, the captain settled down next to the hearth in order to sample some of the heat, himself, and at the same time keep a watch out for anything that might come upon them uninvited.

A dozen notions flashed through the captain's mind as he maintained his vigil. There had to be a reason the city was so massive and also a reason why that section of it was abandoned. There also had to be some sort of explanation as to why portions of buildings, like the one in which he sat, had simply been buried beneath other structures. The architecture was just different enough that Lyrien never lost the sensation of visiting a distant land. The fact that the impression was both strong and constant was unnerving in and of itself, but Lyrien simply acknowledged it as yet another way in which that world—for, if he wasn't mad, he was surely on another world—affected him. And if he allowed himself the possibility that he had been magically brought to that world—for how else could he explain it?—then perhaps his overwhelming array of senses could also be explained as some sort of charm or sorcery.

Charms and sorcery don't exist, said that little voice he used to talk to himself. He could hear the echoes of his father's voice in it right then.

Lyrien nearly laughed aloud at himself as the ridiculousness of his train of thought hit home. It wasn't so much the fact that he was seriously contemplating wizardry as a solution to all of his unanswered questions that seemed absurd; it was more the case that his circumstances were outrageous enough to drive him to do so.

And yet, he was also examining his own thoughts at that very moment, Lyrien realized, questioning why he *wasn't* questioning how easily he had accepted magic as an explanation for his being there. That realization led to an even deeper realization that he was having a fundamental philosophical argument with himself. Then a third part of his mind wanted to step outside the rest of his consciousness and examine *that* in detail.

Each layer of self-examination spiraled deeper, to yet another layer, until the captain's mind was overwhelmed with myriad layers of consciousness, each pondering the previous layer of contemplation. As he sank deeper into that morass of deliberation, he got lost in it, trapped and consumed by it. Finally, Lyrien's eyes grew heavy and he unintentionally abandoned his intentions of keeping watch over himself and the strange dog-headed humanoid lying beside him.

Chapter 3

Lyrien sat bolt upright, blinking in confusion. A moment before, he had been adrift in a void, watching as millions of great black birds, each exactly the same as the others, spiraled around him. They circled and multiplied, each one watching him with one eye as they flew in lazy patterns all about him. And they were laughing at him in unison. It was terrifying.

Taking several deep breaths, Lyrien focused his thoughts only on his surroundings and his physical being, trying desperately to anchor himself to something real. And then he remembered where he was, and he realized he had been dreaming. At last, breathing more calmly and regularly, he focused, mentally examining the feelings of the floor beneath his half-numb rump, the dull throbbing of the healing cuts along his shoulder, and the weight of the letter opener in his left hand. Each of those sensations he examined in turn, until his mind no longer felt as though it were tumbling pell-mell down a slippery slope of endless, tangled contemplation.

"Hello there," the canine creature said softly beside Lyrien, catching him somewhat off-guard and leaving him feeling stunned, alarmed, and pleased. "Where are we?"

For the first time, Lyrien had a real chance to consider the creature's speech. The tone of its voice had a remarkably rich, deep, musical quality to it. The words were almost lilting and melodic, and they were delivered in an odd sort of accent, unlike anything Lyrien had heard before. His amazement that he understood the creature's words was forefront in his mind—it was his own language that had been spoken. He didn't know whether that made his being there all the more real or if it was actually an indication that he was, in fact, going mad.

"Hello yourself," Lyrien finally answered uncertainly, shifting to check on the fire, which had burned down to embers but was still putting off suitable heat. He kept one eye on his counterpart the whole time and a firm grip on the letter opener, too. Excitement or no, he was still leery of the beast's intentions.

The creature groaned. "My head is pounding. I must have struck it on something when I jumped." It looked over at Lyrien. "I see that you've managed to find some clothes," the creature said. "Though I'll wager you're still feeling more than a little lost, yes?"

"What do you mean?" Lyrien asked, still uneasy, but hanging on every wonderfully musical word the strange being uttered.

"It's pretty obvious you aren't from around here. You were hardly dressed in a fitting manner to be a rafter when we first, ah, ran into one another, so I guess you must be a seed." The strange being was working to sit up then, looking around. "Damn it," it said after a moment. "I seem to have lost my sword."

"Rafter? Seed? What are you talking about?" Lyrien asked.

"Nothing further need be said," the other said, barking a short laugh. "You didn't happen to recover my pack, did you?" The stranger paused. Then it eyed the small blade in Lyrien's hand. "Are you planning to slice me with that?" it asked warily.

Lyrien glanced down at the weapon in his hand and then shook his head. "Not unless you give me a reason to," he said at last.

The stranger answered, "I don't aim to. You've got no worries from me, Seed. You can trust me."

Lyrien couldn't suppress the flutters of excitement and apprehension that were passing through him. Sooner or later, he was going to have to trust someone, but still, he would gauge the stranger's behavior very carefully before he even considered letting his guard down. He swallowed nervously, then finally said, "And you, me."

The creature moved gingerly to stand, then, and Lyrien studied its face. Its ears were pointed forward, like any dog's might be when it was eager and alert. Its eyes, which held a look of bemused curiosity, were the color of sparkling amethysts. The creature was not quite as tall as Lyrien, though it was obvious to the captain's trained eye that it had a sure balance and a watchful gaze, like the snow dogs in the mountains along the northern border of Ilnamar.

Odd, indeed, Lyrien thought. But at least it—no, "he," the captain decided—he seems genuinely friendly.

"Now that you've sized me up," the stranger said after a moment, "I hope you've concluded what I already told you—you have nothing to fear from me." His voice still mesmerized Lyrien.

"You seem to be honest enough," the captain replied. "Though I've never seen the likes of you in my life. A talking dog?"

The creature bristled slightly. "Dover," he replied, sounding affronted, but then he visibly relaxed. "We are called dovers. Dogs run through the streets, sniffing at everyone's hind sides and licking themselves where the suns don't shine." He drew himself up. "we are a noble race that would never carry on like common dogs."

Lyrien had to stifle a chuckle. "My apologies, then. I've never run across a dover before. Well met, then."

"So, maybe you can tell me where we are. Obviously, we're in the undercity, but this is a long way from the albine's trap."

Lyrien frowned, unsure how to begin. "If by under-city you mean we're deep under the surface of whatever abandoned city this is and by albine you mean the creature that nearly shredded us to pieces, then yes to both." He pursed his lips in thought. "I think I accidentally struck you on the head with my knee when we fell into the underground river," he said finally, thinking the simplest explanation was the best. "I managed to pull us both out before we went over a waterfall, but beyond that, I haven't got a clue where we are."

"Ah, well, yes. That can happen. So my first assumption *was* correct; you *are* lost."

"More than you can imagine. Perhaps you can answer a few questions for me and help me find my way back to where I was before." Lyrien didn't see any reason not to get straight to the point.

"I'm sure you have a mouthful of questions," the dover remarked, obviously smiling. "And I'll be glad to answer every one of them, but first, I'm starving. Did you, by chance, put my pack somewhere?" The fellow eyed Lyrien's unusual outfit and added, "That's an improvement over wearing nothing at all, but I might have a change of clothing you can fit into, as well." Then he smiled again.

Lyrien smiled back, for he found that he liked the creature's easy-going manner and joyful demeanor. "What you have with you is what I pulled you out with. If there was a pack, it must have washed away, along with your curious glowing rock, I'm sorry to say."

"Ah, well," the creature replied forlornly. "That's a pity. There was food in there, and a map of this part of the maze." He shook his head and shrugged. "But at least you found something to wear."

"I found these in the armoire. I didn't have much with me when I . . . arrived here."

"Few seeds ever do, my friend."

"You've called me that three times, now," Lyrien said. "What does that mean?"

"Happy to explain," the creature said, peering out through the window. "But let's talk while we find a way back to the wrack. Maybe we can find some food along the way."

Lyrien nodded. "That's the way we came in," he said, indicating the window. There's a waterfall somewhere beyond. We were fortunate I managed to find something to latch onto."

"Indeed," the dover said, taking the lit candle and leaning out once more. "This may be trickier than I thought. It is going to be hard to retrace our steps. Incidentally, my name is Gade. Well, actually, it's Gadeile Damidion, but all of my friends just call me Gade."

Even as strange as the moniker sounded, Lyrien decided he liked it. He nodded and said, "I'm Lyrien. It's good to meet you."

"Just Lyrien?"

Lyrien shrugged. "Captain Lyrien Ves'tiral."

"Ah," Gade said as he pulled back inside the window and turned to face Lyrien again. "A military man. So tell me, Captain, what army did you command before you were so rudely pulled through by Israfel?" Gade cocked his head to one side, a quirky smile on his face as he listened.

Lyrien just stared at the dover. "You *do* know!" he blurted out at last. "Tell me what's happened to me!" A dozen questions popped into his head at once. "How did

I end up here? Who is Israfel? Is that the horned woman? Did she bring me here? Where *is* here? Is this your world, the world of the dovers? Oh, for the love of—!" Lyrien finally growled, throwing his hands up in the air in exasperation. "Listen to me! I'm a mad man! A babbling idiot!" He took a deep, calming breath and added, half to himself, "I never act like this. None of this can be real. It's not possible!"

Gade laughed out loud. "Easy, there, Seed. Slow down." He gestured for patience. "You're not the first seed who didn't want to believe what happened to himself. But I assure you, it's all quite real."

Lyrien took another deep breath and once more brought his thoughts into focus. "Again, why do you keep calling me that?" he demanded, still impatient for answers. "Why am I a 'seed?'"

Gade nodded sagely, as though he understood Lyrien's impetuosity all too well. "Because you are the seed of something much greater. You are the possibility of what might be, if you are strong enough. At least, that's the way Israfel views you, and the locals think that's an appropriate nickname. And yes, she is the one who brought you here."

"Why? Why would she do such a thing? Why would she rip me from my home, from the woman I loved? And how? How could she do what . . . what—no, there's no explanation for what I went through." Lyrien sighed, suddenly very tired. He stopped in the middle of gathering up his meager possessions, dropped down to the floor right there, and just sat. It was all too much. He was simply overwhelmed.

God, he thought, I could just waste away right here. And I don't care anymore. He set his chin in his hands and felt the emptiness wash over him. I'm never going to get back to her.

"Hey," Gade said, dropping lightly down beside him. "Don't let it get to you. It's always bad the first day or two, but you'll get used to it."

"What?" Lyrien asked glumly.

"The overwhelming feelings you've got. The raw emotion. There's joy and anger, confusion and sadness, all wrapped up and washing over you. It's not you, though; it's the Forge itself."

"The Forge? This place is called the Forge?"

"Yes. Well, the Forge is the whole thing: the world, the sky, and the suns—all of it. The city itself is Penance."

"Hmm," Lyrien said. "I saw both suns before, when I was on the surface. I thought I was dreaming. And this city—Penance, you call it?—Penance is so huge! I've never seen anything like it!"

"Yes," Gade replied. "Most seeds react that way when they first get here."

Lyrien nodded. "So what crimes did I commit that made this Israfel bring me to Penance? Why me?"

"Ah! Now you've hit on the crux of the matter."

"What?" Lyrien was getting more confused and despondent by the moment. Gade wasn't making much sense anymore.

"Israfel—all the Seven Feathered Fowl, for that matter—keep their own counsel. If anyone knows why she does what she does, I've never met them," Gade said, shrugging.

"Feathered Fowl? What in the hell are you talking about?"

"Israfel is one of the seven rulers of the Forge, known as The Seven Feathered Fowl. Israfel rules Penance, Haiel rules Wildwood, Orif'elle rules Anvil, and so on. Each has his or her own part of the whole, his or her own domain. They are immensely powerful beings who mostly keep to themselves and bring in seeds from other worlds to further whatever strange games they play."

Lyrien shook his head, unwilling to accept the fantastical story as anything other than nonsense. But every fiber of his being could feel that it was as real as anything he had ever known before. He considered what Gade had told him already. "What is she, some sort of a god?"

Gade shrugged. "Hard to say. Maybe, but I don't think so. Just immensely powerful."

"But you believe that she brought me here for some purpose?"

"Can we continue this while we walk? You must be starving, and the only food we're going to find is topside. If you'll let me, I'll take you out of here and to an inn or something."

The captain sighed and tried to regain his enthusiasm. When he felt like he could proceed without feeling totally despondent, he nodded and stood, gathering the flint and steel and his letter opener once more. "Yes. Let's go. Lead the way. I can't wait to get out of this maze down here."

Gade stood and adjusted his own possessions, checking his various belts and the strange items clipped to them. Then he approached the door, with Lyrien right beside him. "So, yes, you were brought here for some purpose. There's always a reason and that's what you have to find out. That's what every seed must discover once he or she arrives." He reached out and very tentatively pulled the door open, with Lyrien standing to one side. The captain wished he had more than the tiny letter opener for a weapon.

There was nothing beyond the opening but shadow. Carefully, Lyrien peered around the frame and saw that a hallway ran in either direction.

"I'm still searching for that reason, myself," the dover said as he peered in both directions of the hallway beside the captain. To the left, they saw that the hallway simply ended. To the right, the hall stretched away into darkness, though it was wide and featured many tall windows along the right side. If the building—definitely constructed in a markedly different style from the one in which they had begun their surreal journey—had ever seen the light of day, the hallway would have been open and majestic.

Lyrien looked over at Gade with a frown. "What do you mean? You're not from here?"

Gade shook his head as they began to move down the hall and said quietly, "Not even remotely. My home, my world, is known as Lumiar. When I first arrived, I was as overwhelmed as you are now, and just as despondent. I missed Lumiar terribly, and I couldn't imagine what had happened to me or why. But I managed to get over the worst of it, eventually figuring out that the Forge itself makes you feel this way."

"It's not natural," Lyrien insisted. "If I believed in magic, I'd say it was some sort of sorcery."

"Then you'd better adjust your thinking right quick, Lyrien, for the Forge is most magical. Still, it's an amazing feeling, isn't it?" And at that last, Gade looked wistful.

"It's unlike anything I've ever felt before in my life," Lyrien admitted. "It's like I was dreaming the whole time, and just now woke up."

"Exactly!" Gade said, jovial again. "And that's the part that you must grasp, must keep with you, draw on. The wonder of the Forge can be a powerful force, and if you learn to master it, direct your focus toward conquering its influence, you can do much with it."

Together, the man and the dover padded down one side of the walkway. Lyrien was leery of falling through any more holes in the floor, all the while keeping the letter opener ready. Beside him, Gade held the candle aloft. If something came at them from out of the darkness, he knew he would have to take the point. Gade was unarmed and perhaps still a bit woozy from the blow to his head. Lyrien fervently hoped it didn't come to that. Images of the spider and the albine kept forcing themselves into his mind's eye, though, giving him an involuntary shudder from time to time.

There were a number of doors on the left side of the hallway, but Gade explained softly that he suspected they all led into other chambers rather than a way out, so the pair bypassed them for the moment. "We're looking for a path—a staircase or something similar—leading upward," the dover explained, "and the best chance of finding one is to continue to follow the hallway itself. If that doesn't net any success, we can always backtrack and check the rooms beyond the portals."

The pace they set was slow but steady and they saw the end of the hall long before they reached it. It simply stopped, a jagged edge of stone that halted abruptly into a black void beyond. The two of them moved cautiously closer to the edge, trying to get some sort of visual reference by the light of the candle. It was as though the building simply ceased to exist there.

No, Lyrien realized, that's not quite right. He could see then that the hallway continued on the far side of the chasm. In fact, there was another entire hunk of the building there. It was more like a giant axe had split the structure in half, much in the same way a woodsman would split a log. The chasm sliced right down the middle, separating rooms, halls, the whole structure. Where the captain and Gade stood, the building was upright, apparently stable. But on the far side, across a gap perhaps fifteen feet wide, the other slice of building was slightly canted, leaning away from them. It disappeared both up and down, from side to side, into the darkness.

"What is this place?" Lyrien muttered, getting down on his hands and knees to peer over the edge, trying for a better look. "Why is this all here?"

"It's the undercity," Gade explained. "Penance has been here for hundreds of thousands of years. Rather than building outward, the inhabitants just keep building right on top of what's already here."

"Why?"

Gade shrugged. "That's a good mystery, but one for another time. We've got to jump across."

"We do?"

"Yes. I think I know where we are, now. I had some maps in my pack—which of course I lost, so I can't verify this—but this looks like a spot I remember from it. If I'm right, and we can get over there, I think we can make our way up to the surface by means of a staircase. Ready?"

Lyrien eyed the gap uncertainly and peered down into the gulf of darkness below. "All right," he said at last. "What about the candle?"

"Hmm," Gade said, thinking. "I'll jump first, then you toss me all the goods. I'll get the candle relit, and then you can jump."

For a moment, Lyrien felt suspicious, for it was entirely possible that the dover would simply walk away after receiving all the supplies, leaving the captain to die in the darkness. But he dismissed the fear as foolish. Gade had given the captain no good reason to doubt him thus far.

When Lyrien nodded, Gade smiled and backed up, farther into the hall in the direction they had already come. Then the dover took a deep breath, set himself, and finally started sprinting toward the edge. Lyrien stood off to one side, holding the candle as far out as he could to help light the way. When Gade reached the end of the hall, he lunged up and forward, kicking hard. The dover sailed easily through the air and landed on the other side, fading into the shadows beyond as he arrested his own momentum.

There came a cry from the darkened area beyond Lyrien's candle light.

"What?" the captain called, suddenly nervous. He still held the letter opener and now began to wonder if it wouldn't have been wiser to pass it along to Gade until they both got across.

"Oh, sorry," Gade called back. "Didn't mean to worry you. There's a corpse over here. Looks like he got crushed in some shifting stone. All is well."

Lyrien raised his eyebrows in doubt but realized that they were too far along their intended trail to back up then.

A moment later, Gade reappeared, looking none the worse for wear. "All right," he called. "Throw everything across. Carefully," he added as Lyrien prepared to fling the flint and steel, and then the letter opener, over the chasm.

Taking a deep breath, Lyrien underhand-tossed each item to the dover, who caught them all—with the exception of the letter opener, which he let hit the floor and then plopped his foot down on it as it slid past. Then, there was nothing left but the candle.

"You can get this relit, right?" Lyrien asked.

"Yes, I'll take care of it," Gade replied. "Just toss it across." Lyrien started to blow it out, but the dover frantically stopped him. "Leave it. It'll go out on its own when you heave it, but the longer I can see it, the better off I'll be."

"All right," Lyrien said, and very carefully pitched the candle over the chasm. As it sailed up and out of Lyrien's hand, it did indeed blow out, but the captain could see the glow of the wick for most of the arc across.

Gade grumbled as Lyrien heard a soft thump. "Damn it," the dover muttered.

"What happened?" Lyrien called again, peering nervously into the blackness.

"Oh, it hit me on the nose," Gade said in disgust, "and I got hot wax in my fur. But I'm fine, got the candle, should have it lit again in a moment." Lyrien watched impatiently as several sparks of light flashed on the other side, and then the candle was burning again. The captain let his shoulders sag in relief, only then realizing how tense he had been, waiting. Still, the light reaching his side was very dim, and he suddenly became worried that he wouldn't be able to see the edge of his leap clearly enough.

In the end, it took the captain three false attempts—he pulled up before committing each time, worried that he would miss the edge and plunge over the side—before he finally managed to leap across, yelling in desperation and flailing to try to give himself more distance. He tumbled to the floor on the far side, rolling a little way down the hall. He finally slid to a blessed stop right next to the corpse Gade had discovered.

The body was of a man, lying face down in the corner of the hall where it turned to the left. A wall had shifted and collapsed there, bringing a pile of worked stone blocks down atop the doomed fellow and pinning his legs. It appeared that the corpse had been lying there for quite a while, for the flesh was substantially desiccated, as was most of the man's clothing and gear. However, several metal items had survived, including a small number of gold coins spilling out of a rotted pouch, a grappling hook—the rope itself was partially disintegrated—and, perhaps the biggest prize of all, a decorative greatsword, partially pinned beneath the collapsed stonework, lying near one outstretched hand.

Gade began collecting the coins, dropping them into a small pouch of his own. "For that meal I promised you," he said.

Lyrien smiled and turned toward the sword. He would have preferred a pistol, or at least a more nimble blade, for a rapier would have felt most comfortable in his hand, but it was a weapon, and he knew that his days of working with the larger blades in the practice yard would come back to him soon enough. He reached for the weapon.

"Wait!" Gade admonished, reaching out and staying the captain's hand. "It may not be stable," the dover explained, gesturing toward the pile of rubble. "I don't want to end up like him," he finished, pointing to the corpse.

Lyrien nodded and stepped back. "We need it, though. What do you suggest?"

"Just give me a moment," Gade said, sounding distracted as he peered at the sword, and the stones surrounding it, from many angles. He grunted to himself several times, obviously contemplating whether it was safe to slide the weapon free without causing further collapse. Finally, nodding to himself, Gade leaned forward and, with considerable effort, shifted a block up and off the blade, holding it there. "Pull it out," he said, his voice tight with strain.

Quickly, the captain grabbed the hilt and pulled the greatsword free of the confines of the rubble, and Gade immediately laid the block down flat again. The pile of stonework shifted with a deep, resonating groan, and a trickle of dust sifted down from overhead. The groan reverberated for several seconds, and Lyrien could almost imagine the entire structure shifting and swaying slightly beneath his feet. He looked over at Gade worriedly, but the dover was standing very still and seemed to be holding his breath. Finally, the subtle shifting and accompanying noise stopped.

"That might not have been such a good idea," Gade whispered. "This part of the maze is not stable. We should get out of here while we can."

Lyrien nodded, taking a careful step away from the fallen stone. With the blade hoisted, he stood very still, listening for any further sounds of imminent danger. There were none.

Satisfied that the floor beneath his feet would not crumble away, he tested the balance of the large blade and was surprised at how well it handled. The grip felt perfect in his hands, and he could swing the thing almost effortlessly. It was a fine weapon.

Lyrien held the blade out toward Gade, offering it to him. "To replace the one you lost in the water," he said, smiling.

Gade shook his head. "I'm no good with one so bulky. You keep it."

Lyrien nodded, swinging the greatsword about a couple more times. He handed the letter opener to Gade. "Since you won't take the sword, at least keep this." The dover took the smaller weapon and nodded in thanks. "Let's go," the captain then said, motioning for the dover to lead the way.

Stepping carefully, Gade followed the turn in the hall, keeping well clear of the collapse, holding the candle high so they could both see clearly. The turn in the hallway wound up being the base of a staircase leading up. Before he would let either of them advance onto the first step, Gade examined it carefully for stability. Lyrien respected the dover's caution, though he had to assume that the corpse behind them had managed to come down that way before his fateful accident, and that it would support them, as well.

When Gade was satisfied that the stairs would hold, they began to climb. It took three flights, and as they rose, Lyrien began to detect another light source above. He initially hesitated, but Gade seemed eager to keep going, so the captain followed his companion the rest of the way up.

At last, the pair reached the top and could see clearly enough to make out another hall, identical to the one on the lowest floor, running off in the same direction. They were standing next to a doorway that was draped from the other side by a heavy, dark cloth. Sunlight, strong and white, seeped through faint gaps between the frame of the doorway and the cloth itself.

Gade sighed in relief and pushed his way through the gap and into the blinding brightness of daylight. Lyrien squinted in pain, fighting the flaring glow, protecting his eyes as he followed the dover into the brightness beyond. He felt uneasy, having to fight the glare and worrying about ambushes, but thankfully, nothing attacked them. Finally, as his eyes adjusted enough that he could see, he found himself standing in a solarium of some sort, and the light radiated downward from a domed ceiling in the center of the room. The rest of the place was tiled, with a large basin, like a pool, in the center. Lyrien imagined that the room once served as a great bath, and indeed, as he inspected the chamber more closely, he could see then that there was a great drain set into the middle of the basin, and the remains of some sort of wooden ductwork projecting out of the wall that appeared to have once borne water into the basin. The room was sweltering as the bright yellow sun must have shone directly into it most of the day already.

"Luck is with us," Gade said, pointing to a rope ladder that descended from the dome set atop the ceiling. "Our friend down below must have left this, hoping to return this way." The dome was a framework of clear panels, possibly panes of glass or some clear crystal held in place by lead bracing, but only perhaps half of it remained intact. The other half had broken away at some point, and the rope ladder that descended to the floor of the basin had been anchored to the framework where the dome was missing. Beyond the dome, the sky had turned as white as clouds, though it was obviously not overcast, at least not yet.

Lyrien moved to the ladder and tested it. It seemed sturdy enough, so he began to climb, hoping he would be able to finally escape the strange dwelling he had mysteriously invaded. With one hand holding the greatsword, he used the other to catch hold of the rungs of the ladder one at a time. Above him, a black bird settled on the edge of the remains of the dome, watching him. He found it vaguely unsettling, but he tried to ignore it, for he was eager to finally make progress beyond the confines of the abandoned structure.

As he neared the top, the black bird fluttered away with a faintly indignant squawk, and then Lyrien's head cleared the top of the roofline into blessed sunshine. What he saw stunned and confused him further.

From his vantage point, the captain could see that he was at the highest point of the dwelling he was occupying. Behind him, the solarium roof rose up at an angle, a long peak running for quite a distance. Somewhere beyond it lay the first building and the courtyard where he had awakened, for he could see the tower rising high above everything. Before him, though, the view was unnerving. Instead of finding himself peering down to the paved street a great distance below, he discovered that his head was only just at street height.

The roof of the solarium was only a step up from a paved road surrounded on every side by more buildings, all crowded in upon one another, and all in just as poor shape as the first. More buildings crowded in around the estate, blocking it in from a higher vantage point, as though someone had just kept building on top of old foundations. It would explain why so many windows existed that did not let in light, Lyrien realized. The whole place had been boxed in with other, newer construction. It even seemed logical that someone would eventually come along and build a newer story right on top of that dwelling, bringing it to a height in line with the rest of the structures. He wondered just how many layers had actually been added, and he thought of the river of water, far below him. Other darker layers might even then sit below that, long buried and forgotten. It was eerie and made his skin crawl.

Not your concern now, he insisted. Just find a way home. He climbed the rest of the way out and moved aside to allow Gade to join him.

Once the dover was standing beside the captain, they began to walk again. "So, now that you understand what's happened, at least some of it, are you ready to go find out why you're here?" Gade asked, leading the way.

"No," Lyrien said, feeling renewed determination once he had escaped the darkness of the maze, as Gade called it. "I'm not staying. I refuse to be a part of some other person's plans, a pawn in some game. I'm finding a way to get back."

Gade frowned. "That's much easier said than done, my friend. Many seeds have made similar boasts, but I don't recall ever hearing of one who succeeded. That certainly doesn't mean it's never happened, just that I never heard about it. Who knows, though? That may change at any moment. All right, keep a sharp eye out. You never know what you'll run into out here."

Lyrien shrugged but didn't answer. For a while, they moved together in silence, skirting buildings by way of broad boulevards, narrow alleys, wooden bridges that spanned crevices between buildings so deep the captain could barely see anything at the bottom, and by steps, ladders, and ramps. Lyrien kept a watchful eye ahead of him, expecting to spot some additional signs of life. Despite his eagerness, Lyrien felt the pangs of apprehension, fearful of the reception he would get.

Everywhere he looked, the captain saw the decay of the place. The stones of the buildings were gray and stained with mildew, and moss and weeds grew everywhere, sometimes overwhelming a particular spot where blowing dust had collected sufficiently to foster the growth. It all felt very lonely.

When it became clear that they weren't going to meet up with anyone for several blocks, Lyrien asked, "Why is this part of the city abandoned?"

Gade shook his head. "I don't really know. Actually, most of Penance is that way. The city—in fact the whole Forge—is ancient, beyond reckoning. As far as anyone knows, this is the way it's always been. There's just more city than there are people living in it. Maybe at one time, Israfel brought more seeds into the Forge than she does today.

"We'll reach a more populated section shortly. I'll warn you, though, today is a holiday; it's called Frenzy, and everybody has been celebrating as hard as they can most of the day already. It's going to be a madhouse."

As the yellow sun settled lower into its twilight and the red sun rose higher into the sky, the landscape slowly changed, gaining a ruddy hue that uncomfortably reminded Lyrien of blood. For a while, they walked in shadow, for the yellow glow from behind them touched only the tops of one side of the highest buildings, as did the red from ahead, shining on the opposite side of those structures. The captain also realized that the day was continuing to grow warmer, despite the fact that it was well past afternoon and into early evening, as marked by the yellow sun, at any rate. He supposed that that point, when both suns were in the sky together, must be the hottest part of the day. With the light of both suns merging together, the sky acquired a milky white hue, rather than the deep blue of before.

The other observance that interested Lyrien as they trudged onward was the fact that they almost continuously clambered over steps, followed steep paths that rose and fell, and slipped through narrow passages between high walls. When citizens did last populate the area, only foot traffic would have been viable as a way to move about, he realized. Coaches, carriages, and the like would have been useless in such a warren of tiny streets and thoroughfares.

"How long have you been here, Gade?"

"Six years."

"And you've been searching for a way home all that time?"

"No, not the whole time. Like I said, I've never heard of a seed returning home, but I sure tried to find out."

"Wait," Lyrien said, suddenly realizing something. "You're not native to this world, this Forge, as you call it. How many other kinds of creatures are there?"

Gade laughed, a true laugh that time, not a short, barking chuckle like previously. "A hundred-hundred or more."

Lyrien stopped and stared at the dover, dumbfounded. It only made sense, he supposed, but trying to wrap his mind around it was too difficult.

Gade slapped his knee and laughed again. "It's quite all right, my friend. I reacted much the same way you did when I first got here. The first thing you have to realize is that there are countless worlds, and each has its own species that can be brought through the portals that Israfel creates. Wait until you meet your first ceptu; you'll probably jump right out of your skin." And Gade laughed again.

Countless worlds? He would have been branded a heretic in Ilnamar for suggesting such.

Lyrien pursed his lips in a half-smile, wondering how many more surprises he was going to be privy to that day. "Hopefully, I can find a way back to Ilnamar before it comes to that," he said. "And I *will* find a way. But until I figure it out, you seem like someone I can trust, someone who can show me around. Will you accept my company?"

Gade nodded, smiling broadly. "Of course. For as long as you wish mine in return. But, let's see about getting you something decent to eat. I didn't count on—" the dover stopped abruptly, staring ahead of the two of them. A low growl rumbled from deep in his throat, a warning.

Lyrien looked to where Gade was staring. the pair of them had entered a narrow alley while they had been talking, and from the far end, a trio of men were approaching them. Actually, two men and something else entirely, Lyrien realized.

The third being was as tall as a man and stood on two legs like one, but that's where the similarities ended. Its body was all sinewy like corded muscle, and its head was strangely birdlike, complete with a beak and a row of horns, similar to a rooster's crown. It skin was a pasty white and in its oddly clawed hands, the thing held a pair of short, curved blades out and at the ready. Judging from Gade's reaction, those three were strangers.

Burying his incredulity at seeing such an outlandish creature for the moment, Lyrien opened his mouth to ask what was going on, but Gade cut him off.

"Run!" the captain's companion said, turning in the opposite direction. "Slavers!"

Lyrien snapped his mouth shut again in surprise, turning once more to look at the three strangers, who were very obviously fanning out to prevent him from slipping between them.

They're herding us, was the first thought in his head. It was instinct, really, a maneuver he had seen too many times on the field of battle. They weren't moving fast enough to prevent Gade and him from escaping them, just fast enough to make them want to run the other way.

"Wait!" Lyrien shouted to his new companion. "It's a trap!" But as these last words echoed across the thorough-fare, he saw that it was already too late. Gade had sprinted right into several more slavers who had been in hiding. They had him encased in netting which they had strung across the opening of the street leading back the way they had come. The dover flailed about, but there were enough of the other men that he was quickly subdued.

"Damn it!" Lyrien growled, turning back and sizing up the three who approached him. The tall thing that was anything but human looked to be the biggest threat, and he brought his greatsword up, stepping toward it lightly, ready for a fight. "Come on," he challenged, shifting the sword back and forth, watching for a chance to cut his way through.

The man on the far right of him laughed. "You might be worth sending to the arenas," he chortled as the sinewy creature moved forward, balanced lithely on its toes and swishing its curved blades through the air for effect.

Lyrien took another step in, ready to test the creature's defenses, when the one who had spoken produced a thin strip of wood from some inner pocket of his garments and gestured with it menacingly. At the same time, the stranger uttered a string of nonsensical syllables, mumbling those words in a chanting fashion, his voice rising in a crescendo.

As the man with the slender stick shouted the last incomprehensible phrase, Lyrien felt the oddest sensation wash over him. One moment he was ready to lunge at the rooster-headed creature, bring his greatsword through a sweeping strike at the thing's legs, and the next, he was standing perfectly still, for some reason completely unable to move. The sensation terrified him, for he felt completely helpless and vulnerable to his opponents' attacks.

He jerked his limbs in every conceivable way, but his body didn't respond; he was completely immobile.

"He's held," the man with the length of wood said, almost matter-of-factly. "Get the wagon down here."

The sinewy creature visibly relaxed, as though it had expected that outcome. It turned and trotted in the opposite direction.

Lyrien continued to strain against whatever invisible bonds seemed to be holding him, staring all about himself and panting in a near-panic.

Get free! a part of the captain's mind screamed silently. Do it!

But Lyrien could not. Soon enough, he saw a sight that made his blood run cold through his veins. From the far end of the thoroughfare, a large wagon appeared, pulled by four completely new and remarkable beasts. They were like overly large cats of some sort, but Lyrien ignored them for the moment. The wagon itself was what struck him with fear, for it was a very large cage, inside of which were a number of prisoners. The cage was being towed directly toward him.

Desperately, Lyrien once more began the futile exercise of escaping.

Chapter 4

The rain made Lyrien shiver as it tumbled from the distant red sky, a deluge from the thunderstorm he had spotted earlier. Down there at street level, it was nothing more than a thin strip of ruddy roiling clouds high overhead, the wind and light almost lost between the soaring walls of an endless series of very tall structures. The only real illumination came from the pale, opalescent glow of some strange plant—similar in appearance to a sea anemone—mounted in baskets at regular intervals on posts like street lamps. Still, the precipitation thoroughly soaked the captain and the other prisoners inside the wagon-mounted cage.

Lyrien stared out through the thick iron bars glumly, watching more of the strange city known as Penance drift past him. The slavers were maneuvering their wares through a populated area then, but there were few occupants out and about. Regardless, Lyrien no longer truly noticed the sporadic parade of exuberant, frenzied faces in the gloomy perpetual twilight of street level. When the smatterings of prancing, whooping passersby spotted the prisoners, their expressions grew somber and their gazes flinched away. Everywhere, those revelers gave the wagon a wide berth, studiously ignoring its occupants. No one really wanted to see those prisoners inside, doomed to become slaves. The few late-night pedestrians, most of them slaves themselves, simply averted their eyes and moved on, heedless of the rain that dumped down on them as they celebrated their strange holiday.

Only perhaps one face in five was even human, and each new creature that Lyrien spied had initially dazzled him, despite his predicament. Humanoid shapes of several varieties—a silver-skinned four-eyed man who seemed to glide rather than walk, an antelope walking on two legs, even a floating jellyfish as tall as Lyrien himself—the ceptu, Gade explained—came and went, occasionally crossing paths without a second thought to one another, as though their existences were the most natural thing in the world. Gade had told him about it, but hearing it and seeing it were two different things. Eventually, though, Lyrien grew somewhat numb to the wondrous variety displayed before him and ceased to care much after the first ten minutes. He barely paid any heed to the dazzling collection of creatures that wandered past his field of vision.

Observing it first-hand, Lyrien found himself standing on a most precarious razor's edge, delicately balanced between acceptance that it was real or admittance to his own insanity. To chose the former meant that everything he had ever known, every principle he had ever placed any faith in, was false, that his whole world had been a lie. To submit to the latter meant that he could no longer control even the tiniest part of what he perceived. He was not sure which was the more terrible scenario.

The strange, paralyzing phenomenon that Lyrien had experienced during their capture was magic, or so Gade had also claimed. The dover had repeated it several times, but still Lyrien wasn't sure he wanted to accept it.

Magic isn't real. It's all childhood stories. I don't believe in it.

But refusing to believe hadn't made it go away, and Lyrien didn't like what being insane implied; at least with the alternative, he could do something about his circumstances. Therefore he wanted—no, needed—it to be real. That insight caused a sharp, crystal clear feeling that was dangerously close to making him wretch. It was turning his whole existence upside down, and he was reeling from it.

Whether he had believed in it or not, the magic had made Lyrien as helpless as a newborn calf, and it had been a simple matter for the slavers to secure ropes to him, strip him of his newfound if meager possessions, and then drag him into one of the cells of the cage, which had been partitioned, each cell with its own locked door. All of it happened before he could twitch a finger to resist them. Gade had been tossed in shortly thereafter, stripped to his fur, as well. The slavers had laughed and cut up among themselves as they worked, ignoring their new prizes as though Lyrien and Gade were nothing more than crates at a wharf, waiting to be loaded onto a galleon.

Shortly afterward, the procession had departed that lonely stretch of street where the pair of them had been captured and worked its way in the direction Lyrien had been heading when he still had a choice, to a populated section of the city. It was Blackwall, so named by the immense ebony wall that surrounded it, built twenty feet high and ten feet thick in order to keep its enemies out and its inhabitants in. Overhead, more strange creatures flew about, patrolling the sky at the wall from an aerial point of view. Blackwall was a bloodhold, whatever that was, and once the wagon had passed through a heavily guarded gate, Gade explained, they were effectively trapped inside, subject to the laws of its bloodlord.

Lyrien had tried to follow the words of his newfound friend, though he didn't see much use in understanding any of what was happening; they were prisoners, headed toward some vast slave pits in the center of the place, and Lyrien was being pulled further and further from his goal of returning to Ilnamar. Gade had seemed particularly despondent over their destination, and it was infectious; Lyrien could sense the dire hopelessness of just about everyone there, and not just those trapped in the cage. Even for those out in the streets, their merry-making was forced, a temporary retreat from their grim lives. The rain splashing, trickling on his face was a suitable accent to his mood.

Occasionally, a luxurious coach rolled past, drawn by pairs of the same species of large feline creature that pulled the wagon. Kith, Gade had named them, and from his explanation, it seemed to Lyrien that the cat-creatures were as common as horses and used similarly. The occasional traveler on foot made way for the coaches, stepping aside as the kith, their golden brown coats slick with rain, padded past. The occupants of those coaches were the wealth of the city, the landed gentry who owned the property, including the immensely tall buildings and the bedraggled slaves who trudged in their shadows. And though those wealthy nobles were forced on occasion to pass among the labor upon which their empires were built, they made every effort to separate themselves symbolically. They kept the curtains of their coach windows drawn tight, and they were accompanied by disciplined escorts, soldiers sharply dressed in colorful liveries that either walked or rode additional kith alongside the transports.

"If I'm a seed, why isn't Israfel doing something about this? How can I be of any use to her locked in a cage?" Lyrien muttered to Gade, who was huddled beside him, raindrops glistening on his fur and soaking it through. The dover smelled just like a wet dog, the captain thought, though he would never insult his companion by admitting it. The light that shone weakly down from the rain clouds still held a harsh red glow, making the dampness seem like it was thin, watered-down blood. "How can this Mabon hold sway in Penance, if Israfel is the queen?"

"That's not how it works," Gade mumbled back, staring at his own toes and shivering occasionally. "Israfel rarely makes any sense. No one really knows anything about her, other than that she is the absolute authority in Penance. But all that means is that she sets up the laws that other people use to wield power. There are a whole set of rules, all set forth by Israfel, that allow others to stake a claim to sections of Penance. It's tradition and laws all wrapped up together."

"How does someone like Lord Mabon even come to power, though?" Lyrien asked, thinking of Lord De'Valen back in Ilnamar.

"The whole city is divided into cantons, and anyone with the strength to back up their laws can claim one or more cantons as their own, provided there are enough citizens living there. Once they do that, that section of the city is a bloodhold, and the leader a bloodlord. As long as they adhere to the procedures for claiming the territory, and as long as their own rules don't directly conflict with Israfel's own, the bloodlords can run their little fiefdoms pretty much any way they want. Lord Mabon is simply working within the system."

"That still doesn't explain why Israfel would bother to pull me through and then just leave me at the mercy of slavers," Lyrien said dully. He was growing angry at all of that foolishness, though he knew it wasn't Gade's fault just for explaining it.

"You're right," Gade said quietly, staring at Lyrien with those haunting, mesmerizing purple eyes. "But that's the way of things. No seed gets drawn through and then treated favorably; the only reason you were snatched away from your home was because she saw some sort of potential in you. It's up to you, and only you, to fulfill that potential. Or not. She doesn't help you along, and she doesn't tell you what to do. She just drops you in and watches to see how you perform."

"It's a crime," Lyrien said, shaking his head. "Some sort of sick zoo. A waste of so many lives." He spotted a young girl holding the hand of an even younger boy, both of them stopped and staring at the wagon as it rolled past. Lyrien stared back at them until a woman, most likely their mother, caught each of them by the shoulder and steered them away with a harsh whispered word in their ears. The three of them then danced as they trotted away.

"Perhaps," Gade replied, shrugging again. "But that's Israfel. No one yet has figured out a way to stop her, or what it is she really wants. Hell, she rarely says anything at all, much less explains herself. I only heard her speak one time."

"She spoke to me," Lyrien said, trying to remember the words he had heard the moment he had been swept away from Iandra, from Ilnamar. "She told me there was more for me to do, that my passions would serve both of us in time."

"Really," Gade said levelly, looking sharply at Lyrien. "Then you must have some potential. That's quite an honor." To Lyrien, the dover's words seemed to carry a hint of . . . what, jealousy?

"Some honor," the captain replied. "Destined for the slave pits. I have no idea what she meant, and I guess I didn't live up to my potential. Israfel must be grumbling over her wasted effort."

"Or else your potential has a chance of shining through because of the slave pits," Gade said, trying to smile. "There are worse fates, you know."

"Like what?"

"Like dying." Gade's stare was earnest then, and Lyrien could almost see a fire, a passion burning in those amethyst eyes.

Slowly, Lyrien nodded. "We'll find a way to escape," he said. "And then we'll go pay Israfel a visit."

Gade barked a short laugh. "I like the escape part," he said, smiling, "but let's not go overboard. It's not like you can simply walk up to her palace and request an audience to ask her what she had in mind for you."

"Why not? Surely she accepts visitors. If she spoke to me when she pulled me through, maybe she'd be willing to see me."

Gade shook his head, a bemused smile faint in the dim light. "You still don't get it. Like you suggested before, Israfel is like a god or something. She has ruled Penance for as long as anyone can remember, and she's just as mysterious and arbitrary as a god. No one has ever gone inside her citadel. In fact, no one really has any idea how it would be done."

"Then how does anyone figure out what they're supposed to do? How do any of you even know that she is looking for potential in those she brings here? How do you know I'm a seed?"

"You said it yourself; she told you." Gade turned away from Lyrien as he finished. "We're at the edge of the Pedestal. Now you can see how truly old the city really is."

Lyrien looked past Gade's shoulder and beyond the cage. The wagon had stopped and was waiting in a short line of vehicles for something up ahead. It seemed as though the city simply stopped, that there was an edge to it, and beyond was only open, red-hued sky. The captain could make out a long line of what appeared to be cranes ahead, moving ceaselessly. He realized those cranes where hoisting vehicles, bearing them into the air atop a very large platform, similar to a ferry. The slavers were waiting their turn for a ride on one. As he waited and watched, the crane nearest to them drew a large coach and its kith team into the air from the front of their line, swung out beyond the edge of the pavement and buildings, and then lowered it out of sight. Several minutes later, the platform reappeared, bearing three boxy wooden wagons, which the crane deposited at the edge of the street. Soon enough, the wagons were on their way, rumbling past the cage in the opposite direction.

"Where are we going?" Lyrien asked after watching the cranes for some time. "What's beyond the edge?"

"The new city," Gade replied. "And Lord Mabon's Grey District. That's where his palace is, as well as the slave pits and the coliseum. Our only chance at getting out of here is to submit ourselves for the arenas, fight as gladiators and win our freedom in the coliseum."

"You'll never make it that far," a slave in the next cell over chortled, its voice deep, rich, and resonant.

Lyrien shifted his position to get a better look at the occupant. A graceful, winged figure too large to fit well in the partition within its cage was huddled miserably, knees drawn up to its chest and arms wrapped around them tightly. It rested its chin on its kneecaps and just stared out through the bars. To Lyrien, the creature's face seemed remotely like a tiger's, though longer and more demonic because of the black horns that sprouted from atop its head. It was covered in gray fur and had very feline clawed hands and feet. The wings, however, resembled an eagle's, though they were folded tightly against the thing's back at the moment.

"Ignore him," Gade suggested. "Asherake lie just to hear the sound of their own voices."

"Suit yourself," the creature replied, shrugging as well as it could. It refused to look at either of them. "In the arenas, you don't last long unless you know the right folk; there's an art to setting up the matches, and those who know the right folk get matches they can win. Others get killed." The creature sounded both unfriendly and uninterested, which made Lyrien wonder why it was bothering to tell them that.

Lyrien looked at Gade, who shook his head, but the captain was intrigued, so he asked, "And how would we go about getting to know the right folk?"

"You don't, unless you can fight well enough to make things interesting," the asherake said. "That sword you had before they snared you; you know how to use it?"

Now it was Lyrien's turn to shrug. "Well enough, given the chance." The greatsword had been taken from him while he had been paralyzed, no doubt stashed away among the slavers' other valuables. Lyrien suspected that they would sell it on the side and get a reasonable sum for it, too; it was a well-balanced blade. "Doubt there's any way for me to prove it to you, though. Why? Do you know the right folk?"

The asherake growled low in its throat, a rumble more than anything. "This is the third time I've managed to escape the coliseum, only to be snagged again before I could get out of the undercity. I've been fighting in the arenas longer than I can remember. I might be able to arrange it so that you come fight with me in the coliseum. The team matches are particularly popular."

"Why would you bother doing that for us?" Gade asked, and Lyrien could see the doubtful look on the dover's face.

"Because if I don't have something interesting to offer the pit masters, they're likely to kill me just for causing trouble. You're my ticket to another chance to escape Blackwall once and for all. But you'd better know how to fight. If you're not up to snuff," the creature said, turning at last to look at Lyrien with baleful, glittering eyes, "and you make me look a fool, I'll drop you before they finish me off for disappointing them."

"I think we'll take our chances on our own," Gade said, trying to get Lyrien to turn away. "Thanks just the same."

The asherake sighed. "Suit yourself. But you'll never see the light of day again."

Lyrien leaned in close to Gade, noticing as he did so that they were next in line to be loaded onto the crane platform. "What's wrong? Why don't you trust him?"

"Askerake are the most ornery, deceitful creatures in Penance," Gade whispered back. "They're as likely to slash your throat as give you an honest answer about anything."

Lyrien nodded, but he felt dismayed nonetheless. It didn't seem that the two of them had many other options.

At that point, the wagon was ready to board the platform, and Lyrien moved closer to the outer wall of the cage in order to get a better view of whatever it was that Gade had wanted him to see. As the huge crane lifted the platform and its contents up into the air, the captain could feel everything sway slightly from side to side, and he wondered uneasily if there was any danger of the assemblage tipping or breaking apart. The crane swung out past the edge of the city, and vertigo washed over Lyrien as he beheld a drop of nearly a quarter-mile appear below him. The road where they had been moments before receded, abruptly stopping where the crane was mounted on the edge of the drop-off. He saw how the city seemed to be a great disk, an endless sea of buildings contained inside a massive wall that curved unevenly away in either direction. He understood then why he had been unable to see the edges of the city from the high tower before; Penance was enormous, miles across.

Where the crane lowered the cage, Lyrien could see more of the city below, still surrounded by the great black wall that held it all in. To his eye, it looked as though the old city was contained inside a great bowl, and a chip had broken off at that point. More of the city had somehow oozed out and spilled onto the plains below. Off in the distance, the captain could make out a thin waterfall that tumbled over the side of the old city and splashed into a pool, where it became a river and flowed away toward the distant horizon. More cranes operated there, raising and lowering entire ships from the new city to the old city and vice versa.

"Why is the city so high up?" Lyrien asked as he marveled at everything he could see. "Has it always been raised like that?"

"I told you, Penance is ancient," Gade replied, smiling. "For as long as the records show, it's been here. It's raised like that because the citizens just keep building right on top of the older parts. There are countless layers of older city underneath the surface. The deeper you go into the undercity, the older the construction. Of course, the bottom levels are long gone, crushed into a solid layer of foundation now by the weight of everything that's built on top of them."

"But why?" Lyrien asked, amazed. "Why not just expand, like Blackwall did down there?" he continued, pointing below them. The crane had them almost to the bottom, then, at the terminus of another road.

Gade shrugged. "Status, I suppose. There must have been a certain status to being close to the Wellspring in the center of the city, and where Israfel's citadel sits. No one wanted to expand the city farther away, so they just built right on top."

"Incredible."

"Look there," Gade said, pointing to one section of the side of the old city near where they were descending. "You can actually see some of the layers exposed."

Lyrien followed Gade's finger and saw where a section of the wall that surrounded the old city had broken free, exposing several layers of buildings, all stacked one atop the other. Those layers were low enough to the ground level that they were little more than strata of solid rock by then, but it was still clear that they had once been magnificent structures.

"So, what's down there?" Lyrien asked his companion, still gazing at the sight and remembering their detour into the dark depths of the estate where he had first arrived. The red sun was breaking through the clouds, then, and it was just a little before being directly overhead, casting everything in its rosy glow. As its light struck him, Lyrien enjoyed its warmth after the chill of the thunderstorm.

"Everything you can imagine," Gade said, almost beaming. "It's wonderful. Of course there's treasure to be found. Many times, people just had to leave everything behind when the foundation shifted and swallowed up their homes. There's also just a wonderful sense of history. You can see the changes in architectural style through the ages, and if you're lucky, you can find coins, jewelry, art, what have you.

"But it's also a dangerous place," Gade continued. "Besides being unstable in a lot of places, it's very easy to get lost. More rafters have disappeared into the undercity, lost forever, than have managed to come back, like what happened to our poor half-buried corpse. And there are plenty of nasty things creeping around in there, too, like the albine, and worse. You wouldn't believe the things I've seen down there."

"How many times have you gone into the undercity?"

Gade looked at Lyrien and just shook his head. "Haven't you been listening? That's what I *do*. I'm a rafter. That dwelling where I met you was once part of an affluent dover neighborhood."

"Never had much use for rafters before," the asherake interrupted. "Of course, I never had much use for the maze, either, except when I wanted to escape the coliseum."

Gade rolled his eyes where the winged creature couldn't see. "I heard your kind didn't like the maze much," he said, giving Lyrien a private, exasperated look.

"You heard right," the asherake answered. "Hard to maneuver with my wings. But when it's a choice between dying a slave or getting free, I'll tolerate it. You know, if you're half as good a rafter as he claims to be with a sword, we might be able to help each other get out of Blackwall once and for all. My offer's still good; come fight with me in the coliseum."

Gade shook his head. "No thanks."

The asherake growled but said nothing more.

The platform thudded to the surface of the street, then, and the reality of their plight came back in a rush to the two prisoners. Once more, Lyrien was reminded of just how easy it was to become lost in the moment in Penance; Gade's joyful exuberance while describing his explorations beneath the surface of the city had let them both forget their troubles. It made things that much more miserable when reality came rushing back. They were once again deep within the chasms that served as streets between the high edifices of the mansions, and Gade's expression grew glum again. The crane workers scrambled to free the tethers that had held the wagon in place. Eventually, the kith were towing the cage through the streets of the new city, which was remarkably similar to the old city high overhead.

Lyrien's stomach rumbled insistently, but the foul odor of urban filth that wafted through the cage from the street did little for his appetite. He was thankful that the rain had ceased, although with the return of the red sun, the air grew stifling and thick. All of this conspired to make him drowsy, lulled into a half-sleep by the droning rumble of the wagon wheels on the paved streets. Several times, Lyrien's head jerked awake as he slumped over in the beginnings of sleep. Each time, the streets seemed more and more abandoned, as though the last, die-hard revelers celebrating that strange holiday known as Frenzy had at last given up their carousing and had staggered off to recover.

At last, Lyrien was roused from his stupor by the wagon halting. Blinking, he peered around outside the cage to see where they had arrived. The wagon was stopped in front of a large gate set into the wall of a huge pavilion. The gate was open, but several more cage wagons were currently exiting, and Lyrien realized that the slavers who had captured the two of them were simply waiting for the traffic to clear before driving the transport inside the very large structure.

"The slave pits," Gade said quietly, still slumped against the bars of the cage where he, too, had drifted off into a nap. "Lots of traffic tonight. They always do a good business during the holidays. May the gods be willing to see us come back out of there."

Lyrien didn't answer, only watched morosely as the wagon team drove their cargo through the gate and into the darkness beyond.

Inside the pavilion, the stench of misery was palpable. The distant and not-so-distant screams of other slaves echoed everywhere, mingling with the creak and groan of the wagons and the surly shouts of the slavers. There was enough light shining through high, dirty windows to remind everyone inside just how dim and dreary the whole place was. The orange glow of torches and perhaps other fires flared high overhead against the ceiling of the great round structure. A pervading sense of absolute doom settled over Lyrien as he took all of this in, more devastating than any despair he had yet felt since his arrival.

The whole area was open, though divided by an intricate series of fences, netting, and walled enclosures that reminded Lyrien of an aviary. Dozens and dozens of wagons moved about a great circular path that hugged the outside wall of the pavilion. Along the inside of that path ran a second wall, perhaps fifteen feet high, and set into that wall was an endless series of gated openings. More of the caged wagons had been backed up through those gated openings and into some sort of enclosures beyond the wall. Over the top of the wall, Lyrien could see more cranes, similar to the ones at the edge of the old city, though much smaller in stature. He wondered what use they might have.

The wagon rolled around the perimeter of the pavilion until it arrived at one of the gates not currently in use. Carefully, the driver backed the wagon up until it passed through, and once it was in place, more attendants swarmed over the cage, attaching the cable from one of the cranes Lyrien had seen earlier to the top of it.

On the opposite side of the crane a massive hole opened into the ground. It was from there that all the anguishing cries of the forlorn welled up. Lyrien felt his blood run cold at the sight of that shaft, which he was convinced dropped into the bowels of hell itself. He wanted to wretch. He peered over at Gade, whose wide-eyed stare echoed Lyrien's own terror. They were both being hauled to their doom. The crane hoisted the cage up off the wagon and quickly swung its cargo out over the hole. For the first time, Lyrien could see what it held.

The vast shaft dropped down an immense distance, though it was divided into several increasingly narrower sections, like an inverted ziggurat. At each change in diameter, Lyrien could see innumerable bodies moving, swarming like ants along the ledge that surround the lower shaft. The crane carried them down past all those areas, three in all, until at last they were set down at the very bottom of the hell-hole, in the narrowest shaft, by far the darkest. In the faint gleam of a pitiful number of torches, he could see that the floor of the pits was lined with more cages, dozens of them, with narrow walkways passing between sets of four like miniature city blocks.

The cage was moved into place by more slavers, pale, bare-chested, muscular men and other creatures who sweated and sneered as they worked. When at last they were happy with its positioning, the crane dropped down the remainder of the way and the cage came to rest on the dirt floor at the very bottom of the slave pits. The crane's cable was then quickly disconnected and it disappeared, leaving behind the newly incarcerated slaves. As the single slender connection to the world above and the workers who had positioned their cage both disappeared, leaving the prisoners in near darkness, Lyrien felt like he had been buried alive.

Chapter 5

The bottom of the cage was softened by a thatch of hay spread liberally over the floor beneath the cells, and although Lyrien was thankful for the cushioning, the similarity to being an animal in a livestock pen was disheartening. He leaned against one corner of the cell and let his eyes adjust, afraid to contemplate his condition too much. Gade moved opposite him and settled down wearily.

"It's worse than the stories suggest," Lyrien's canine companion muttered dismally. "What you hear on the streets above . . . no one even knows."

"How long will they leave us here?" Lyrien asked, figuring that Gade had no more first-hand knowledge than he did, but hoping the dover at least knew some of what to expect.

"Hopefully not long," Gade replied. "We're not making anyone any gold down here."

"God, I'm starving," Lyrien mumbled, feeling his stomach rumble again. "Whatever they do, I hope they feed us soon."

"I doubt it," Gade said with a wide yawn. "It's almost Slumber by now. We won't get any attention until morning. You should get some sleep."

"Sleep?" Lyrien exclaimed incredulously, ignoring the stares of the other prisoners in the cell. "The sun was high in the sky when we were dragged in here. What is Slumber?"

Gade sat up again. "The cycle of the suns is different here. You can't judge day and night by the suns in the Forge. The yellow one stays constant, but the red one rises and sets at a different time of day over the course of the month. Here on the Forge, an entire season lasts a single week, and a month experiences all four seasons."

"So how can you sleep, or even keep track of *when* to sleep?"

"You get used to it. Like I said, the yellow sun rises at the same time every day, so you base your day around that and try to ignore the red sun. Some folks keep odd hours, like the slavers, I guess. And when there's a festival or holiday, folks tend to stay up as long as there is light, which sometimes can be the whole day long. Breakfast probably won't be for a few more hours. Get some sleep."

Lyrien nodded, but he didn't think he could actually drift off down there. He was wrong.

* * * * *

When the captain awoke, he was momentarily disoriented, blinding by a harsh orange light that seemed to shine right in his face. Then the memories of everything that had happened to him came crashing back, and he realized that he was staring into a lantern. Someone was passing a shallow bowl through the bars to him, and he took the offering in a daze. It was some sort of thin broth, with a wad of bread thrown into the middle of it. It didn't smell either familiar or terribly appetizing, but at the first whiff of its aroma, his stomach still growled loudly, and Lyrien wasted no time tearing off a hunk of bread. Across from him, Gade was stuffing broth-soaked chunks of the bread into his own mouth as fast as he could chew.

The first bite was stunning. Even though the broth was slightly bitter and way too watered down, the flavors Lyrien experienced made him feel like this was the first time he had ever eaten. It tasted so . . . real, so substantial. He savored every bite, even though he was so hungry he wanted to stuff it all in his mouth at once.

The meager meal was gone all too soon, but Lyrien spent several more moments lapping at the inside of the bowl, wistfully seeking even the tiniest remaining drops of flavor. When he finally gave up and set the wooden bowl down beside himself, he saw that Gade was watching him with a bemused smile on his face.

"What's really a shame is, your first meal here on the Forge had to be that wretched excuse for food."

Lyrien cocked his head to one side and looked at the dover, puzzled. "What do you mean?"

"Everything else you've experienced for the first time—the light, the colors, the textures, all of it—it's been dazzling, right?"

Lyrien nodded.

"Now imagine how good the first meal should taste. Imagine how it brings your taste buds alive with the very first bite, how every complex bit of spice, every blended fragment of flavor, creates a symphony on your tongue."

"You're a little melodramatic, but all right," Lyrien replied, imagining what Gade was talking about.

"With a meal that is worthy of being eaten, or something truly memorable on your plate, that experience would have been ten times as monumental as this refuse," Gade finished, tossing his own bowl off to one side with a clatter.

"And now the moment is spoiled," Lyrien said, completing the explanation, "and when I finally do get to sample some of Penance's finer fare, it won't be the same."

"Precisely," Gade said forlornly. "I wish it could have been different for you."

"My friend," Lyrien said, stretching out his legs as best as he could, "Make me a promise. When we get out of here—"

"'If,' don't you mean?"

"No; *when* we get out of here, promise me you will still take me to eat at your favorite pub. Promise me we will sample some of the finest culinary delights the city has to offer."

"Now who's getting melodramatic?" Gade asked, but he was smiling and finally nodded. "On my word, when we finally get out of this hole in the ground, I will take you to dine at one of the best places to eat I've ever been to. It's a place called The Hub Tavern, and the food there is unlike any I've ever had before. The owner is actually an old friend of mine, and if we can get him to cook some of his—"

"You seem awfully sure of yourselves, planning your next feast," the asherake rumbled next to them. "It might be a good long while before you even see the light of day again, much less enjoy any of Tiresias's spread."

"You know Tiresias?" Gade asked, seemingly genuinely surprised.

"Sure. But why he would consider a hound like you a friend, I can't imagine."

Gade stiffened momentarily at the asherake's words, but Lyrien cut in before the verbal exchange could get ugly. "Listen, you seem to want to make friends with us awfully badly, but then you go and say things like that. What assurances do we have that you're not playing us for some reason of your own?"

"You don't, though you're wise to consider the possibility. All I can do is make an offer, and all you can do is accept or decline. But when they come for us, when it's time to go to the testing level, I won't be sticking around. It's up to you whether you get to come with me or not."

By that time, Gade had turned his back on the ponderous creature, and Lyrien could see the muscles in the dover's jaw clenching and relaxing repeatedly. But the dover said nothing more, and the discussion died down at that point. Lyrien was soon lost in his own thoughts of home and soldiering when the slavers came to free them from the cramped confines of their individual cells.

"Time for the testing," the asherake said pointedly as all of them were released and herded into a group. "It's do-or-die time."

The prisoners were heavily outnumbered by their caretakers, many of the guards armed with hooked and pointed sticks that they used to goad the prisoners in the direction they needed. Lyrien didn't see much point in resisting, since he was about as deep in the ground as he could imagine and with no means of getting out, so he walked where his jailors directed. He still caught a poke in the shoulder or buttock for his troubles.

The prisoners were herded through the maze of other cages and into a larger holding area, all sectioned off by rope netting, even overhead, with the exception of one small opening that had a vertical pathway leading up and out of it, also confined by both netting and the side of the shaft. Once all the slaves from the cage had been steered into that area, Lyrien peered cautiously around at the prisoners. There were six other slaves besides Gade and himself that had been taken by that particular wagon. The asherake stood off to one side, stretching both his arms and his wings. The creature was a good foot taller than Lyrien, and his body rippled with clean, well defined muscles and was crisscrossed with more scars than the captain could count. Unlike most of the rest of the chattel imprisoned there, the asherake seemed confident, unconcerned with his fate. Lyrien almost envied the creature its vast experience in the slave pits. Almost.

In addition to the asherake, there were two other humans—one a male, the other a female—and a pair of what almost would have seemed human, though they were nearly a foot shorter, and their features were swept back and angular. Both males, they seemed almost angelic, surreal. Lyrien found them to be a beautiful species.

Without being prompted, Gade whispered, "Elves. Remarkable, aren't they?"

Lyrien gasped, drawing the attention of every one of the slaves, and he averted his eyes in embarrassment. So, his fanciful fairy tales of youth weren't without some truth, after all. The Taking, magic, elves, everything he had heard about in stories as a child were real on the Forge. He risked another glance at the two elves and just spent a moment marveling.

The last two creatures were reptilian, though obviously not of the same species. The first was very similar to a lizard, or perhaps a salamander, in appearance, with coppery colored scales and a darting tongue. Its fingers and toes had rounded pads, like certain kinds of frogs Lyrien had seen. It stood huddled with the rest of them, peering at the ground beneath its feet. The other reptilian creature was quite different. It was smaller and sported a pair of long, slender horns, and its snout was long and full of jagged teeth, like an alligator's. It also had a pair of batlike wings and a scaled, spiked tail, unlike the first creature. None of the prisoners had any possessions of any type, and Lyrien felt no small amount of sympathy for all of them; he could sense their despair mingling with his own, though he tried to keep his own anguish at bay, thrust down deep inside him.

The eight prisoners were guarded over by almost twice as many jailors, the same bare-chested men and creatures who had overseen the placement of their cage the evening before. Now, they simply stood in a relaxed circle around their new merchandise, keeping a watchful eye on their charges while they talked and chuckled among themselves quietly. Lyrien wondered what they were waiting for. Then, after a few moments, he realized what was going to happen next.

Another cage was lowered down the vertical chute from above and settled to the floor in the enclosure. Once the cage door was opened by a slaver, Lyrien and the others were forced to move forward and inside. The cage was a single large container, not divided into partitions like the one they had arrived in. He shuffled forward with the other prisoners until they were all crowded together inside the cage. The door was swung shut by one of the guards and locked, and soon enough, the cage was rising off the dirt floor, passing through the chute and ascending to what Lyrien assumed was the testing level.

When the cage arrived at the top of the smallest, deepest shaft and was swung over the edge and set to rest on the tier, Lyrien took the opportunity to get a good look around. If it weren't for the dark confines and the ample number of guards milling about, their hooked goads ready, Lyrien thought it looked a lot like a recruitment gang for the armies he once served in. Slavers moved among groups of huddled slaves, singling out individuals and sending them in one direction or another, sorting them through questions or simply eyeing them critically.

One slave, a broad-shouldered man with a thick beard who might have come up to Lyrien's chest were he standing on his tip-toes, began bellowing and shoving everyone around him, obviously unwilling to cooperate with the slaver questioning him. Quickly, a host of other guards swarmed in around the rebellious slave, using their goads to overwhelm him and pin him to the ground. Then he was quickly fettered in thick manacles and leg irons and dragged away, howling the entire time.

"Dwarves," Gade muttered next to Lyrien, shaking his head. "Never seen a more surly race of stubborn fools in my life."

Lyrien could only stare at the receding prisoner in wonder. A dwarf? "Where are they taking him?"

"To the training level," the asherake said, moving to stand beside Lyrien as the three of them continued to watch the dwarf being dragged away. "They'll torture him until he's docile as a baby kith," the winged creature added. "You'll want to be on your best behavior when it's your turn for testing, or that's where you'll end up, too."

Quickly enough, it *was* their turn. Slavers came to unlock the cage and shepherd the prisoners toward yet another net-enclosed area, where one of the strange, pale-skinned men with four eyes—a lunar, Gade had informed him during their ride through the city—stood with a bit of scrolled parchment in his hand and a quill pen in the other. He was accompanied by a stooped human with terribly bedraggled hair and a long beak of a nose, who continuously dry-washed his hands and smiled at no one in particular.

The pair of them paced around the group, staring at them, and the taller pale one occasionally muttered something under his breath to his hunched companion, who always seemed to nod eagerly and broaden his smile. Then, the four-eyed lunar would jot notes down onto his parchment and move on to the next prisoner in the group. When he came to Lyrien, he tilted his head to one side, muttered something the captain could not overhear, and then nodded in satisfaction and made a quick note.

Lyrien found the sensation of being scrutinized like a head of cattle particularly infuriating, and he nearly took a step forward toward the note-taker before he stayed himself. The guard nearest him must have sensed the captain's latent hostility, for he tensed and brought his hooked, sharpened goad up and leveled it at Lyrien, but the captain merely stared sullenly at the ground to keep his anger in check. The pale-fleshed man and his bobbing, smiling companion moved on to Gade.

When he made the complete circuit, the lunar moved off a little to consult with his stooped associate and made several more notes. Then, he stepped back in front of the group and gave them a mirthless smile.

"When you're given an instruction, move quickly and quietly to comply, and we'll have no problems. Otherwise, you'll be paying a visit to the training level. You won't like the training level. Are we clear?"

Lyrien simply nodded, but a couple of the other prisoners actually mumbled, "yes, Sir," which made him cringe.

I'll be damned if I'm going to give them the satisfaction, he thought, wanting once more to leap forward and throttle the arrogant slaver, but then he remembered the dwarf. Bide your time, he told himself. Your moment will come.

"Now, then," began the note-taker, "We'll start with—"

"You should start with me," the asherake interrupted. "You know what you're going to do with me, anyway, so why not get it out of the way?"

The pale-skinned overseer stopped and stared at the seven-foot-tall winged creature as though stunned at its audacity, then finally, with measured words, spoke. "What makes you think we're going to send you back to the coliseum again, Threlmak? Maybe we've decided to curb your efforts at escape by clipping your wings and hauling you to the mines."

The asherake seemed unfazed by this threat. "You know I'd never fetch you even a tenth of the price there that I will in the coliseum. My boys over there will make sure you get your due."

The overseer stared a moment longer, then finally nodded reluctantly. "Get him to the coliseum when we're done here," he muttered, then turned back to the rest of the group. Threlmak strolled off to one side, standing with a handful of the guards, who actually struck up a conversation with the asherake while they waited.

The overseer nodded toward the human female. "All right, we'll test you next," he said. "Come over here."

The woman, whom Lyrien had studiously tried to ignore for the benefit of her modesty, stepped forward two steps, her chin up in the air defiantly, seemingly unconcerned with her own nakedness. Lyrien gazed at her from behind, observing, not for the first time, that she was fit and trim, muscular enough that he suspected she had wielded a weapon a time or two. In fact, he realized, she had a few requisite scars along each arm and her back to support his notion.

"I wish to declare for the arenas," the woman said, folding her arms across her midriff and shifting her weight to one foot expectantly. "I will fight there."

Gade leaned over and whispered in Lyrien's ear. "That's what you want to say when it's your turn, too." Lyrien nodded. "And if we're lucky, they'll put us into the same cell with her," Gade added, smirking.

Lyrien glowered at his companion. "Stop it," he growled. "Show some respect."

Gade glanced at the captain with a look of surprise, then finally shrugged.

"You want to fight, huh?" the overseer said with a smug smile. "It would be a shame to destroy such a fine specimen in the arenas. You wouldn't last long, I'm afraid."

"Why don't you give me a blade and find out how long I last?" the woman said, taking a step forward, her hands now balled into fists. Immediately, two slavers were flanking her, holding her at bay with their goads. A murmur rolled through both the slavers and their prisoners at the woman's outburst. When she realized she was about to be restrained, she visibly relaxed and folded her arms once more.

"I think not," the overseer said at last, accompanied by fervent nodding and smiling of his counterpart. "You're much too lovely to send to the arenas. Much more value as a harem slave. We'll get a good price for you."

"But I've declared for the arenas!" the woman cried out. "You're required to let me fight!"

The overseer laughed out loud. "I'm sorry, did you say something? I just can't make out what you're mumbling. Take her up to Training, lads. I think she'll need a bit of seasoning before she's ready for a merchant prince's bedchambers."

"No!" the woman screamed, turning now to grasp at one of the goads a slaver nearby held casually. She got a hand on it and had almost wrestled it away, but she was quickly overwhelmed by several other guards, pinned to the ground, and placed in chains.

Lyrien had started forward the moment the woman began to resist. His vision filmed in red rage, he wouldn't stand by and watch her be humiliated and lose her dignity that way. It reminded him too sharply of what might have become of Iandra, and he couldn't bear it. But more slavers quickly surrounded the entire remaining group, as though they had expected trouble, and Lyrien realized that, unarmed and outnumbered, there would be little hope of winning through to help her. He felt a hand upon his arm, and in his fury, he nearly yanked himself free before he realized it was Gade.

"Easy," his companion whispered to Lyrien. "You can't help her. You'll only get yourself sent to Training, and she'll still be a slave. It's not worth it!"

"I thought you said that declaring for the arenas was a guaranteed way out of here!" Lyrien hissed back, still struggling not to lunge forward and beat someone sense-less. "What if they don't let us go, either?"

Gade looked at Lyrien helplessly. "I thought it was. No one's ever made a claim otherwise."

"Of course not! No one who got deceived by the lies ever managed to get back to the free world! I think it's time we took the asherake up on his offer, if he'll still let us."

Gade cringed, but Lyrien could see the fear in his eyes, and finally, the dover nodded. "All right," he agreed at last.

As the woman was hauled to her feet and dragged away, still kicking and screaming about her right to de-clare for the arenas, Lyrien tried to ignore her anguished cries and get the asherake's attention. He began to wave at the creature, motioning for it to come over.

"What are you trying to do, slave, go to the Training level with her? Step back!" a slaver snarled, turning and planting the sharpened end of his goad into Lyrien's chest.

Lyrien used every once of his willpower to relax and smile obsequiously. "My apologies, Sir," he said, trying hard not to clench his teeth. "The asherake made us an offer earlier, and my companion and I would like to take him up on it. Please, can we speak with him?"

"An offer?" The overseer said, returning his attention on his remaining charges now that the woman was prop-erly dealt with. "There's nothing a slave can offer you, human. He has nothing to bargain with. Now, you look like you're pretty strong. I think we can sell you to the docks as a laborer. Unless you want to spend some time in Training?" he asked, flashing that mirthless smile once more.

Lyrien tried again. "All I am asking is a chance for us to talk to him," he said plaintively, hoping he sounded suitably humble. He certainly didn't feel humble. "If you would speak with him yourself, he seemed to think there was some profit in it for you."

At the mention of a profit, the overseer paused, gesturing subtly for the two guards who were beginning to get forceful with the captain to back off. The pair glowered at Lyrien, but they complied with the pale-skinned lunar's wishes. "Threlmak, what sort of lies have you been telling the other slaves, here?" he finally asked over his shoulder.

The asherake perked up his head from where he had been animatedly talking with one of his supposed guards. "No lies, slaver. The coliseum could use them. We need more applicants for the team events."

"The coliseum? No one goes directly to the coliseum."

"They can fight. I saw them when they were taken. You'll get your gold for them, I promise. Just send them with me."

The overseer turned and looked back at Lyrien and Gade and scratched his chin for a moment. "Well, if I don't, it's your life, Threlmak." He jerked his head toward the asherake while looking at Gade and Lyrien. "All right, you two. You're with him."

Lyrien gave an inward sigh of relief and nodded with what he hoped was his most submissive smile imaginable and practically jogged over to where the asherake stood. Gade was right on his heels.

"Not so keen on trying it on your own, after all?" Threlmak said, laughing. "I tried to tell you."

"We won't let you down," Lyrien said, sounding grateful. And he knew he meant it, too, at least a little bit.

"You'd better not," Threlmak replied.

* * * * *

Lyrien was surprised at how nervous he was. He expected some degree of anxiety, like he usually was when

he was about to enter combat, but it was even more pronounced. He realized part of it was the fact that he *knew*
he was going to fight. Always in the past, even during
military campaigns, it was never a certainty that the battle
would come, or how it would unfold, or what form it
would take. The nervousness came from worrying about
all the uncertainties. He had been in command, then, and
so much could go wrong. At the arena, he had control
over nothing but the spear in his hands.

There was something else, though, too, something that
didn't feel right. He couldn't explain why that should be,
but it was definitely there, a sensation of wrongness. And
it seemed to be emanating from the collar around his neck.

The captain glanced over at Gade, who looked less
than pleased. The dover was examining his own spear,
but he seemed far less sure of it than Lyrien did of his
own. Of course, the thirty-foot length of chain that ran
between their collars probably did little to comfort him,
Lyrien mused, and he had to admit, it wasn't what he'd
had in mind when they'd decided to come to the coliseum with Threlmak. But then, the asherake had never
promised them they would get to fight a battle of their
own liking. Only that he would get them in.

The trip to the coliseum had been unremarkable. No,
Lyrien corrected himself, it had been downright boring.
The three of them had been taken straight back up to the
top level—the ground level—of the slave pits once the
overseer had finished processing his new property. Instead of reappearing at the unloading zone where they
had arrived, though, the trio had been taken to the opposite side of the pavilion, where the slave auctions were
conducted. Again, Lyrien had seen dozens of slaves being displayed at the blocks, species of every type. It had
been easy to see that a variety of different auctions were
going on, for slaves of every purpose had been on display. Pleasure slaves, laborers, specialized servants such

as musicians, scribes, and gardeners, and untold others had all been available for purchase. At first, Lyrien had worried that they would be auctioned as well, and possibly separated, but it was not to be.

Threlmak had seemed to know everyone there, and a quick word or two in the right ear had gotten the three of them taken back to an area behind the public auctions, where the arena dealers took delivery of the newly declared contestants. There had been no dealers for the coliseum itself, it turned out, for they only traded in seasoned merchandise, as Threlmak had explained. Still, there had been transports present willing to haul the three of them to the coliseum directly, for the right price. Money had changed hands between a transporter and the slavers—a considerable number of gold coins, Lyrien had noted— and then the three of them had been locked inside what amounted to a large wooden crate. It had been barely roomy enough for them, and of course, it had been hot and stifling, to boot.

After a long, hot, bumpy ride, they had arrived and were released, finding themselves inside a cool stone chamber decorated with military regalia. There had been guards there, but those were smartly dressed in matching uniforms. They had been no more friendly than the slavers at the pits, but they also hadn't unnecessarily poked and prodded their prisoners with their weapons. While Lyrien and Gade had stood around at a loss, Threlmak had quietly cut whatever deal he had intended to make, on the side, out of earshot of either of the two. Finally, they had been escorted out of the chamber, down a long hall, and into a smaller hall, where Gade and Lyrien had been placed in a comfortable cell of stone. Eventually, they had been given a chance to bathe, dress in a simple tunic, and eat, and then they had been left to wait.

The rest of an unremarkable afternoon had passed, and then they had been unceremoniously retrieved and prepared for their first appearance in the arena. As Threlmak had promised, it was a team event, and the rules, they had been told, were simple: kill the other team or be killed. Then they had been collared and chained together, each given a spear, and set to wait until their event started.

"Remember," Gade said as Lyrien continued to pace, "No mercy out there; the crowds hate it when you don't kill the other contestants."

Lyrien nodded curtly, walking to the limit of the chain leading to his neck without actually yanking it taut against Gade, and then turning and repeating the process in the other direction. "I don't like it, but ... "

"Exactly. Now, are you sure you know how to handle that thing?" Gade was gesturing to the spear in Lyrien's hands when the captain turned to look at him.

"Yes, I told you I did. It's not what I'd usually arm myself with, but I can hold my own." He tugged sharply at the collar, trying futilely to loosen it, growing more anxious by the moment. If the guards didn't summon them soon, he would start trying to tear it off his neck.

As if his thoughts had been read, the great door leading outside opened, raising up like a huge portcullis, causing harsh white light to stream in. Lyrien blinked, trying to adjust his vision, as a great roar erupted from beyond the glare. It was time to go.

"They would pick the hottest part of the hottest day of the month to do this," Gade muttered beside Lyrien, shading his eyes with one hand as he peered out beyond the doorway into the bright light beyond. "Both suns in the sky, and us right out in the middle of it."

Lyrien said nothing, only tightened his grip on his spear. As one, they trudged out into the brightness of day. Hot sand burned the captain's bare feet as he walked, but he ignored it and peered around, seeing for the first time the coliseum and its crowds.

The place was massive, easily as large as any building he remembered from Ilnamar. It was oval in shape, and tall rather than wide and flat. Like any arena, it had a central pit, where Lyrien and Gade now stood, and this was surrounded by high dun-colored stone walls, beyond which were stands filled with screaming patrons of every species the captain had seen and more. The stands rose up rapidly, so that the people sitting in the back rows had good views from lofty seats, looking down on the combatants. Great nets enclosed the arena itself from the outside world, obviously to prevent winged combatants from simply flying away.

"Israfel is watching us today," Gade commented, pointing to a handful of black crows perched along the top of the wall near where they had entered the arena. "To what do we owe such an occasion, I wonder?"

"What are you talking about?" Lyrien asked, turning this way and that, taking in the enormity of the coliseum.

"The birds. Israfel manifests herself through the black birds you see everywhere, watching what goes on in her portion of The Forge. Haven't you noticed how they seem to be everywhere?"

Lyrien only grunted as he surveyed the surroundings, but he had come to discover that any time he felt like he was being watched, there was usually a handful of black birds nearby. It unnerved him. Shrugging, he turned his attention back to the business at hand.

He realized that the floor of the arena had been partitioned into sections; he and Gade occupied only a portion, for he could see that the curve of the stands, and the people sitting in them, stretched well beyond the limits of their confines. So far, though, they were the only ones present in this little section. He wondered if there had been some mistake, or if the organizers expected the two of them to fight one another. Gade, too, peered around in apparent confusion, and then glanced at Lyrien, as though he also wondered if they would be expected to duel.

Lyrien began to get a rather uncomfortable feeling in his stomach at the prospect of being forced to slay the only friend he'd made in Penance so far, but his worries were quickly alleviated when a second doorway rose up. He and Gade turned together to face their opponents, and the captain forced himself to stifle any thoughts of remorse and sympathy he might have for those he was going to have to kill. If it meant getting out, getting home, then he would do it. That grim thought formed a coldness in his chest that he did not like the feel of, but he ignored it and adjusted the grip on his spear once more.

Any lingering thoughts of sympathy vanished the moment the captain saw their foes. The crowd roared even as he realized the betrayal. It was two asherakes, one of which was Threlmak, armed and armored to the teeth.

Chapter 6

Unlike Lyrien and Gade, who had been given only the spears in their hands, Threlmak and his partner were each armored in an ornate breastplate and each carried a massive two-headed axe. They also had no constraining chains running from neck to neck. As Threlmak strolled out into the arena, the crowd roared its approval, and the asherake soaked it all in, turning in a circle, his weapon upraised with both hands in acceptance and thanks.

"Damn him," Gade said, coming to stand close to Lyrien as the two of them watched their betrayer bathe in the limelight. "He was setting us up the whole time."

"You were right," Lyrien said grimly. "You didn't want to trust him, and I pushed. I'm sorry."

"No, it was the right decision. Let's just make him pay for misjudging us."

Lyrien looked directly at Gade now, and he saw a fierce determination blending with the fear that was already there. The captain nodded. "Keep close, back to back, and for God's sake, don't get tangled in the chain," he said.

"Which god would that be?" Gade asked, positioning himself to cover Lyrien's back. The two asherakes were now moving toward the pair of them, fanning out to try and outflank them. "We ought to pick one, and we'd better make it a good one, one who favors rats caught in a trap."

"What the hell are you talking about?" Lyrien asked over his shoulder, focusing his gaze now on the asherake that was coming toward him, a vicious smile on its face. It was not Threlmak.

"I mean, we ought to pick a god who'll do us some good, don't you think? It doesn't seem very smart to go into battle for the sake of a god of crop growing or arcane knowledge, does it?"

Lyrien realized that Gade's chattering was really just a way to stay loose, to mask his nervousness about their situation. He wouldn't mind it except that the dover was spewing nonsense that was making the captain's head spin. Gods? Just how many gods could there be?

The asherake feinted a charge and Lyrien crouched low, keeping the spear before him, wishing it was a long spear so that he could plant it into the sand or against his foot to absorb his opponent's momentum. The creature began to try to circle Lyrien then, watching more than testing, probably to see how well Lyrien could remain untangled from the chain.

All of Gade's mutterings had gotten Lyrien thinking despite himself. Lyrien had never been a very spiritual man and had never given Ohmal, the mother of the earth, much thought. In fact, until he had been pulled into the Forge and had briefly considered the possibility that it was some sort of afterlife, he had never given anything beyond the bounds of mortal life much thought. But there was Gade, in the midst of battle, prattling on about a whole plethora of gods like they actually did something that affected mortals, and Lyrien surprised himself by accepting it.

Why not? The captain thought as he circled to keep between his opponent and Gade's back. He could feel his partner moving directly behind him, shuffling his feet in the sand as he shifted to maintain their dual position. Everything else I thought I knew has been turned upside down, so why shouldn't there be a pantheon of deities out there somewhere? He swallowed hard and tried to force that revelation out of his head; it would only serve to distract him and get him killed.

When he realized that Gade was still muttering about the various pros and cons of picking a particular deity to venerate on this grim occasion, Lyrien sighed and said, "Shut up and concentrate on fighting rather than filling my head with nonsense about gods."

The asherake in front of him danced in and back a couple of times, obviously just feinting and toying with Lyrien while the crowd roared in delight. The captain continued to hold his own position, wondering why the creature didn't just come in and take a swipe at him. His weapon had better reach, and sooner or later, the chain locked onto Lyrien's collar was going to be his undoing.

Then Lyrien's eyes narrowed. They're waiting for something, he realized. Something else is going to happen.

As he kept one eye on the asherake before him, Lyrien began to scan the surroundings, looking for something that might give him a clue as to what surprise the coliseum had in store for them. There was nothing within their portion of the arena floor, and no sign that anyone else might arrive, though he had to admit that any number of foes could be led in through the doorways that both his team and the asherakes had used. There also didn't seem to be anything out of place in the crowds above, or on the walls. In fact, he noted, the crowds were getting restless, also waiting for something to happen. Boos were interspersed with the cheers now, and Lyrien could see some of them gesturing animatedly for their local favorites to get on with it. Still, the asherakes hesitated.

"Something's going on," Lyrien hissed to Gade behind him. "Be ready for a surprise."

"What do you mean?" the dover called back.

"They've got every advantage, but they haven't even really tested us, yet. They're waiting for something. Some surprise that will be to their definite advantage. So just be ready."

"As if they need any more help," Gade grumbled.

Lyrien took a couple of steps toward the asherake opposite him, gesturing aggressively with his spear, though he had no intention of separating himself too much from Gade's protective presence. Still, the asherake leaped forward and parried the captain's thrusts harshly, nearly knocking his weapon from his grasp. The crowd went insane, cheering wildly and urging them for more.

Lyrien retreated again and went back to his defensive crouch, and the asherake seemed content to wait once more. The captain shook his head in frustration, noting how the crowd resumed its booing with gusto. He was certain now.

The two enslaved gladiators didn't have to wait much longer to find out what was about to be inflicted upon them. One moment, Lyrien was crouching, ready to attempt another feint, and the next, he felt the collar around his neck tighten sharply, compressing against his throat and restricting his air.

Gade wailed in a strangled voice behind Lyrien. "Can't breathe!"

Lyrien lowered his guard and jerked a hand up to the collar in a vain effort to loosen it again, but the metal somehow, impossibly, kept tightening. The asherake before him, obviously expecting this turn of events, now strode forward boldly, twirling his double-headed axe in circles, practically dancing with eagerness to get into the fray. Lyrien reluctantly released the collar and brought his spear to bear again, barely holding the winged creature at bay. He felt light-headed and weak in the knees.

"What is this?" Lyrien tried to ask, but his words were barely a croak. He stumbled to one side as the asherake swung the axe high overhead and downward in a great arc, slamming the blade down into the sand where Lyrien had been standing only a blink of an eye earlier. Lyrien felt clumsy, uncertain of his footing in the loose sand, and he could do little more than try to evade the powerful swings of his foe and suck air in and out. Spots were beginning to form in his field of vision. All thought of watching Gade's back fled.

What a ridiculous way to die, Lyrien thought, strangely furious. He wondered if the crowds actually enjoyed such lopsided, foolish victories, but he couldn't tell whether they were cheering or booing because of the roaring in his ears.

Lyrien was down on one knee then, gasping and pulling at the collar. The asherake loomed over him and he twisted around for one last spinning attack. Feebly, Lyrien raised his spear up, knowing he could never hope to fend off the powerful blow. Then, in desperation, the captain scooped up a handful of sand and flung it at his enemy.

The oldest trick in the book, the captain thought, but it still works.

The asherake staggered backward, forgetting his attack as he clawed at his face. Lyrien ignored him and tried to work a finger up under the constricting metal. He couldn't imagine how it could be growing smaller. Then he realized. It must be more magic. He clawed at the hateful thing desperately, losing his spear as he started using both hands.

Suddenly, he was jerked backward as the chain connecting him to Gade yanked against the collar. He thought his neck had nearly snapped as he was dragged through the air and sand for several feet. He feared Gade had met his end, and he wasn't far behind.

Blasted magic! Lyrien silently shouted. The collar was tight enough now that he was completely cut off from air. He was blacking out. In his delirium, he imagined that he could feel the magic of the collar in his hands, that he could actually grasp it and reshape it. In a final, defiant act before he died, he simply imagined squeezing the arcane force associated with the collar with both hands, obliterating it. . . .

And felt precious air flow into his lungs. He sucked in a mighty breath, rasping and coughing. A shadow fell across him, and instinctively, he tumbled feebly to one side, not completely avoiding the blow of an axe blade, which grazed his arm painfully. He cried out and tumbled again, and again, not knowing which direction he was moving, and not really caring, so long as he could get far enough away from his attacker to regain his breath and maybe some of his wits.

After he rolled more times than he could remember, the captain tumbled right to his feet, peering in every direction to ascertain where the nearest threat was. He was breathing heavily, and his throat hurt, but at least he was breathing. One asherake was striding toward him, axe held loosely in both hands across his front. The other, Threlmak, was looming over the still body of Gade, his own axe dripping with blood. They were on the opposite side of the arena, more than forty paces away. Lyrien could never reach his companion in time, though he doubted it would matter.

The fact that he was so far away startled Lyrien. Somehow, in the confusion and suffocation, the chain connecting their collars had snapped loose. It was no longer attached to him.

No, that's not right, Lyrien realized.

His collar was simply no longer around his throat. For a brief second, he remembered the strange hallucination he had had, of crushing the magic of the collar, but then the asherake drew close, stalking toward him, and he was forced to retreat, sprinting for his life through the sand as the crowd went wild once more.

Lyrien thought he would be quick enough to reach his abandoned spear before the asherake could overtake him, but suddenly, when he was no more than five paces from it, the beast was settling to the ground with wings unfurled, and stood over the weapon, gazing at him. Lyrien drew up short and backed away, realizing he was going to have to account for their flying. They could out-maneuver him, the captain realized, and without a weapon, his situation was pretty dismal.

Threlmak had turned his attention to the fight between Lyrien and the second asherake now, strolling closer to gain a better vantage point, though he didn't seem too interested in actually getting involved in the contest. Lyrien then noticed that Threlmak was carrying Gade's spear with him, and when he reached his companion, the asherake tossed it down next to Lyrien's and had a quiet word with his partner. When the two winged beasts were finished with their private discussion, Threlmak positioned himself to guard both of the weapons, and the second asherake began to pursue Lyrien once more.

This isn't sport, Lyrien fumed. It's slaughter.

The crowd apparently agreed, for they began to boo again, and Lyrien could hear some members calling for a more even fight, while others simply wanted the two asherake to finish him so a more interesting spectacle could begin. He tuned them all out, concentrating on keeping both of his enemies in view. Even though Threlmak currently seemed content to stand watch over the spears, Lyrien wouldn't put it past the thing to attack him when his back was turned. In the meantime, the other one kept coming at him, taking to the air a couple of times in an attempt to corner the captain, but Lyrien was too deft at dodging out of the way of the larger creature's more cumbersome weapon.

"I can stay clear all day," Lyrien snarled as he darted to the side for perhaps the tenth time. "Your easy victory over helpless foes is ruined."

"Stand still, you jabbering runt," the asherake snarled right back. "Stand still so I can slice that gibbering head off your shoulders!" He lunged at Lyrien again, and again the captain spun free and retreated.

"Did you hear me?" Lyrien shouted, louder this time, raising his voice so as many members of the crowd as possible—as well as anyone responsible for controlling the fight, he hoped—could hear. "Your precious game is at a stalemate. How much longer will you let this mockery of a spectacle go on?" Just for good measure, he directed his final comments right at the cluster of crows still perched atop the wall. "Your entertainment is poor, and your audience grows dissatisfied!" As if actually understanding the captain's biting comments, the crows arose into the air and flew off in a cacophony of angry caws.

The boos grew louder, as if to punctuate the crowd's agreement with Lyrien's assessment. Lyrien raised his arms as if to say, "See? What do you expect?" before he was forced to retreat from his advancing opponent once more. The asherake was fuming, Lyrien saw, stalking toward him and swinging wildly every time he even got near to his target. Lyrien was careful to hold his position just long enough to make the creature think it could catch him, and then he darted away at the last moment. With every failed swipe, Lyrien could see that the winged creature was growing more and more enraged, which was exactly what Lyrien wanted. Sooner or later, the creature would slip up and do something foolish, and perhaps Lyrien could take advantage.

At that point, the crowd began to throw things from the stands. Even though the netting prevented either one of the asherakes from escaping the confines of the arena, the mesh had to be loosely knit enough that the audience could see, and bits of fruit, copper coins, and wadded up pieces of parchment—the handbills extolling the various contests for the day at the coliseum—came raining down into the middle of the arena. The boos grew louder, and some of the spectators even began to leave, streaming up the aisles toward the exits or to watch other parts of the fighting elsewhere in the coliseum.

This mass exodus just seemed to further enrage the asherake, which began to charge at Lyrien, who abandoned his last-minute escape strategy in favor of all-out flight. He was getting tired, and he imagined that the asherake was, too. Of course, his two opponents had the luxury of switching places, the captain realized. If they thought of it. And he knew they would, sooner or later.

At that moment, the flash of something metallic caught Lyrien's eye as it tumbled into the arena from the crowd. It was a dagger, and it fell into the sand near Gade's motionless form. Lyrien studied both of his opponents to see if either of them had noticed it, but they apparently had not, so he began to plan.

Feigning more exhaustion than he actually felt, Lyrien continued to stumble out of harm's way, gradually working his way over to where he had seen the dagger tumble. Finally, when he was close enough, he let his enemy lunge at him once more, and he dived away, pretending to stumble to his knees as he passed the dagger's position. As he went down, he snatched the small blade and kept it concealed from his pursuer. He made a show of crawling over to Gade's form, which he could plainly see now had been mutilated severely. There was no doubt in the captain's mind that his companion was dead, and he silently mourned his friend for a moment —as much of a friend as the dover could become in such a short and wretched time together—while waiting for the asherake to draw close enough.

Lyrien kept his head bowed, as though he were truly distraught and completely fatigued, hoping to lull his foe into a false sense of impending victory. The asherake stepped closer, and closer still. Lyrien was on the verge of lunging upward, hoping to get inside the other's reach before the winged creature realized what was happening, but at that moment, the doors leading into the arena floor opened, and a host of more guards dressed in the colors of the arena staff entered.

"No!" Threlmak roared from the center of the enclosed space, "you will not humiliate me!" he bellowed as the other asherake drew back his huge axe for a last deadly strike.

Lyrien sprang, lightning quick he hoped, up and at the asherake, who was overbalanced at the moment because of the severity with which he intended to deliver his killing blow. The creature's eyes widened in surprise and alarm, but he was too slow to react. Lyrien rammed the dagger home, slipping it just inside the collar of the breastplate, driving it to the hilt through the soft flesh of the beast's shoulder with the force of his lunge. The asherake grunted in pain and staggered back a step, dropping his axe behind him in the process. Lyrien's momentum was powerful enough to push his foe back, toppling him over, and Lyrien found himself sitting on top of the creature, staring down into his eyes.

"This is for Gade," Lyrien said coldly, yanking the dagger free and then drawing it sharply across the asherake's throat.

The combatant spasmed and gurgled, his eyes wide, then reached up with one clawed hand and grasped Lyrien around the neck. The claws sank into his already sore flesh, and he could feel his air being cut off again. The asherake squeezed, and the captain gasped, dropping the dagger and trying to break his foe's grip. Once more, Lyrien could feel his heart pounding, and spots swam in his field of vision, but his foe's hand trembled, and then weakened, and Lyrien was at last able to free himself. He staggered off and away from the asherake, who stared up at the sky overhead, blood soaking into the sand around his folded wings. But Lyrien didn't have time to savor his victory, because Threlmak was charging across the sand toward him, a snarl on his mien, his own double-headed axe dangling from one hand, and one of the spears raised high in the other.

Threlmak hurled the spear at Lyrien when he was still too far away for it to be effective. The captain watched the weapon approach and deftly stepped to the side as it whistled past him. He then retrieved the other asherake's huge axe even as the coliseum guards closed the distance, brandishing weapons of their own. Threlmak hesitated for a brief instant, then his visage hardened in determination once more, and he surged forward in full strides, hatred burning in his eyes.

Lyrien crouched, the axe grasped firmly in both his hands, and watched, ready to die if it meant taking the traitorous asherake down with him, but in the next instant, coliseum guards were around both Lyrien and Threlmak, a dozen or more of them, all trying to hold the pair at bay with spears or crossbows. The crowd's boos increased vehemently, but it was clear the fight was over for now, although Lyrien couldn't imagine why the coliseum would end it just when it had become a little more evenly balanced. He suspected they didn't want to lose their precious commodity in Threlmak the asherake.

Threlmak snarled and seemed on the verge of trying to slice his way through the circle of guards that ringed him, but something made him think better of it. Lyrien saw him relax at last and toss his axe to the sand. The asherake was quickly led away, although he cast one last glance back at Lyrien, who still crouched, ready to spring, his newly gained axe in his hand, and gave the captain a hateful grin that seemed to say, "Next time."

"You're finished if you don't drop that thing," said one of the guards, a human female with raven-black hair and a whitish scar on the bridge of her nose. She spoke with a strange accent, but the tone of her voice was clear enough. Lyrien turned in a slow circle, eyeing them all. Then, smirking at nothing in particular, he tossed the axe to the ground. It was at that point that he realized the crowd was screaming for him.

"All right," the woman said, gesturing, "get him inside. And get a priest to tend to that slice in his arm."

Lyrien looked down at where he had been struck by the axe, what seemed like a long time previous. A clean cut ran from the middle of his bicep down to his elbow. It had bled freely, but it was not terribly deep. He had forgotten about it during the heat of battle, but once his attention was drawn to it again, it hurt.

Lyrien didn't resist when several of the guards motioned for him to come with them, but as they neared Gade's body, the captain said quietly, "Wait." The guards paused, and Lyrien knelt down next to his companion's corpse.

It was certainly not the first time Lyrien had lost friends in battle, and he suspected it would not be the last, but still, he could feel a wistful sort of sorrow well up in him, and even though he knew part of the emotion was just being there in the Forge, he didn't try to suppress it. Instead, he merely bowed his head for a moment, paying silent respects to the one creature in Penance who had cared enough to befriend him.

Thank you, my friend. I'm sorry.

When he stood and was ready to move on, Lyrien silently vowed to pay Threlmak back somewhere down the line, and then to hoist a tankard in the dover's honor at the place Gade talked of with such fondness, The Hub Tavern. The captain was more determined than ever to find his way to freedom and eventually return home to Ilnamar and Iandra.

Another man, dressed in the same colors as the rest of the guards but in different attire, was holding the shattered end of the chain, as well as the remains of the collar to which it had been attached, and studying them with a look of incredulousness on his countenance. He looked up as Lyrien and his escort strode by.

"How?" he asked. "How is it possible?"

Lyrien merely looked at the man levelly as he walked past. The truth was, he had no idea what had happened. But whether Lyrien had somehow managed to destroy the collar or not, he knew that the man studying its remains had been part of the deception, in league with Threlmak and his plot of setting Lyrien and Gade up to lose the combat at his hands. In fact, the captain reasoned, the whole staff of the coliseum was well aware of the betrayal. Threlmak had been correct; the games *were* fixed. That thought made Lyrien seethe, for Gade was dead because of their deceit. But he knew that losing control, displaying his animosity, would only get him into trouble, so he simply glared and said nothing.

The man's words, however, echoed in Lyrien's mind. How *was* this possible? He kept wanting to believe that it had merely been a hallucination, that there was a much more logical explanation for the shattering of his collar, and the lack of air had tricked his mind into believing that he was somehow responsible for it. But he couldn't come up with another possibility for why it had happened, and the incredulity on this man's face told him that no one else could, either. So he wondered.

The crowd continued to cheer for him as he neared the doorway that led back into the bowels of the coliseum. Apparently, they had become enthralled with him, delighted in his unlikely survival. They chanted encouragement, called for more displays of his acumen and prowess, and flung copper and silver coins and garlands of flowers through the netting and onto the sandy floor of the arena in appreciation. He ignored them, finding them despicable as well, depraved souls craving the most decadent and cruel of entertainments. The people who witnessed these dissolute games were just as much at fault as those who catered to them.

The captain instead turned his attention on the half-dozen black birds that had returned to witness the end of the fight and discovered that they were ravens this time. They perched on the wall directly over the doorway through which he and Gade had entered the arena and through which he was about to be led back out. On impulse, he gave them a mocking salute as he passed beneath them. The ravens screeched and chattered and flew off, giving Lyrien a strange sense of satisfaction.

Once inside the confines of the coliseum's interior, Lyrien was quickly taken back to his cell. There, he was left to wait, alone again for the first time since he'd met Gade. It was eerily empty and quiet there, cut off completely from even the sounds of the crowds overhead. He considered again what he had experienced while the collar was choking him, but nothing seemed to make sense. It didn't help that he scarcely managed to accept magic's existence in the first place. But his inexperience with it only meant that he had no idea what was possible. What he did know, however, was that he was no magician.

Lyrien's musings were interrupted as the cell door opened and several members of the coliseum staff filed in. The first was an attendant, a human boy, who carried some small bundle in one hand and a basket of flowers in the other. Lyrien realized that the blossoms were the garlands that had been tossed for him in appreciation. The lad set both the basket and the other bundle to one side and left. The second bundle clinked as it hit the flagstones, and Lyrien guessed that it contained the coins he had "won" during his desperate fight.

Behind the boy strolled another human male, older and with a greedy gleam in his eye. He was round-headed, bald but with fringes of fine black hair around his ears, and when he grinned at Lyrien, his crooked teeth were yellow and cracked. He was dressed smartly, in fine robes the colors of the coliseum, and a number of gem-encrusted gold rings adorned his fingers and his ears.

"There," this visitor said, pointing to Lyrien but looking over his shoulder at the next visitor in the procession. "Tend to him." Then to Lyrien himself, "You, my friend, have become quite a stir with the public. We're going to make you one of the most popular exhibits in the show. We'll—"

Whoever was supposed to "tend to" Lyrien didn't get the chance. An exceedingly tall, thin man pushed past and strolled imperiously into the room. Lyrien gaped at him for he was oddly beautiful, though his head was completely shaved. He wore robes even more rich and refined than the first man's, though these were of a cool blue color, and they were interwoven with thread-of-gold and adorned with sapphires. The fabric perfectly matched eyes the color of icicles, which flashed at him once, and he could sense the distaste they exuded. Then he ignored Lyrien and directed his haughty gaze fully on the bejeweled man.

"Lord Mabon wants the slave." The word 'slave' rolled off his tongue like he had tasted bitter medicine. "I am to deliver him immediately after he is presentable. He spoke to me on this matter personally." He then handed the coliseum manager a small pouch, spun on one slippered heel, and drifted from the room, leaving behind shocked silence. Everyone was looking at Lyrien in awe.

Chapter 7

Lyrien's mind reeled. Lord Mabon. The bloodlord of Blackwall. Lyrien still had no idea exactly what that meant, but he was being summoned to meet this bloodlord. Lord Mabon had asked for him personally. A dozen thoughts raced through his mind—he was going to pay for ruining Threlmak's little game; Lord Mabon and Israfel had watched through her black birds and were angry at his insolent salute; Threlmak was more highly connected than the captain realized and this was simply a ruse so the asherake and his friends could exact their revenge on him. All that and more crossed his thoughts, but the actual truth would have never occurred to him.

"L-Lord Mabon?" the bald-headed fellow with the covetous mien mumbled, staring after the already-departed man. "But—but, my games! The profits!" Then, shaking his head as though clearing his thoughts of such selfish notions in the face of obviously superior requirements, the man examined the pouch, and his eyes bulged as he guessed what must be inside. Turning the pouch on end, he emptied its contents into his palm. A handful of cut rubies spilled out, more gems than Lyrien had seen in his entire life. The man turned back to Lyrien, his smile as wide as his face, and said, "By Sestyrr, you made a bigger impression than I thought. Well, there's nothing for it but to get you ready. Gertroll, tend to him, like I told you before. Quickly!" And then he was replacing the rubies in the pouch, which disappeared into a pocket of his robe soon after.

The person who had been about to enter the cell before Lord Mabon's representative created such an uproar proceeded in then, moving directly toward the captain, and Lyrien recoiled slightly. The creature was humanoid, and could have been a very ugly man, were it not for the tusks protruding from its mouth and the sickly green shade of its skin. Its beady eyes glowed a feral red as it saw Lyrien's reaction, but it didn't seem to exhibit any other response. Instead, it crossed the distance with purpose from the door to where Lyrien reclined on the stone bench.

Lyrien was stunned. The notion that he had just been bought for a handful of rubies was beyond his comprehension. He had a sudden urge to flee, though he had no idea where he could go. He stood and retreated to one side, planting his back firmly in the nearest corner, a sensation he positively dreaded. He longed to have that short spear from earlier in his grasp.

For its part, the creature paused, raising one sharply protruding green eyebrow ridge in surprise, and said, "What's wrong with you?" in a surprisingly smooth and elegant manner, though its voice was guttural.

"Leave me alone," Lyrien said, glaring at all of them in turn. He felt like a cornered rat, and he wanted neither Lord Mabon's punishment for his victory, or whatever sweet praise and rewards the mysterious bloodlord might bestow. He could imagine both, but he presumed neither.

"I'm just going to heal that gash on your arm," the creature said. "Gods! You act like you've never been healed before."

"I can wrap my own wound," Lyrien said sullenly. "Just leave the bandages and water and I'll do it." The captain knew good and well that he was in no position to make demands, and though he realized his words sounded very much like one, it was really more of a plea. He wanted them to leave him alone, for he suddenly felt out of control, like everything that had happened to him since arriving in Penance was being directed from elsewhere, and he was simply being led along his path like a bull with a ring through its nose. He hated the feeling, and he felt helpless to do anything about it, at least until he could have some time alone to sort it out.

"Nonsense," the richly dressed man said. "Gertroll here is a fine priest, and it's a simple matter for him to heal your wounds for you. And then you will bathe and I'll have something to eat brought in. You can't appear before Lord Mabon on an empty belly." Then he added, mostly to himself, "although I suppose he might wish to let you feast with him, and it won't do for you to be full." He began to dry-wash his hands as he fretted over whether or not it was a good idea to let the "honored guest" eat before being presented to Lord Mabon.

Lyrien winced at the notion of being presented like some sort of an exhibit, as though he were a valued prize.

But I *am* a valued prize; a handful of gems says so.

The captain began to pant as a sensation of vertigo overwhelmed him. The heightened emotions were cascading through him, and he was unable to rein them in. Gade was dead, Iandra was lost, and he was trapped in this stone chamber with a man who wanted to display him like some treasured piece of fine art. It was too much.

"No!" he screamed, putting his hands to his head. "No! No, no, no!" It was all his mind could think of to say, for though a dozen dozen ideas swam in his head, though a hundred feelings wanted to come out, he couldn't get control enough to remember the words. So he just shouted the same thing over and over again, thrashing in fury and terror and despair and panic and helplessness and losing track of where he was or who was with him.

Then, without warning, a cool calm settled over Lyrien. It was unexpected, but he welcomed it. His equilibrium righted itself, and he was no longer screaming. In fact, he was no longer standing, either. He opened his eyes and found himself lying across the stone bench, and the green-skinned creature with the tusks was kneeling beside him, running a beefy hand across his forehead and in a surprising and somewhat disconcerting manner. Behind him, the human with the avaricious mien worriedly stared down as well.

"Easy, friend," the creature, Gertroll, said. "Just take it easy." His breath stank of fish.

Lyrien blinked, then moved to sit up. Gertroll extended a hand and helped him. "I—uh, I don't know—"

"It happens sometimes to seeds, especially in here. Not to worry, though, I cast a calming spell before you could hurt yourself."

"You cast a . . . you did what?" Lyrien said, remembering the cool sensation of calm. "A priest who deals in wizardry?" He had thought that he had somehow managed to regain control himself. He was . . . disappointed.

"Hardly," Gertroll said with a smirk. "My wondrous works are divinely granted through the grace of Ozri'beye the Twelve-eyed. I would not taint my soul through the foul use of mere arcane puppetry."

"This Ozri'beye is your . . . your god? And you talk to him?" Lyrien didn't know why he was asking those questions. He was very much afraid of the answer.

"Of course. What, aren't there even priests in your world, Seed?"

Lyrien shook his head, then nodded it, then shook his head again, still sorting through everything.

Gertroll chuckled. "Well, which is it? Yes or no?"

Lyrien sighed. "Yes, there are priests in my world, but magic of any type is really only a myth. They don't go around . . . what did you do to me?"

"You were about to bash your head against a wall. I simply instilled in you a serene calm. It's a minor spell, really, nothing to get worked up about. It's over, now; everything you feel at this point is purely your own. Now, let me do a quick healing on that arm of yours."

Lyrien didn't want any more magic worked on him. He hated to admit it, but it scared him. The fear of the unknown, he knew, but knowing it didn't change the fact that he felt the fear. He began to scoot away, holding up a hand to ward off Gertroll before the creature could do . . . whatever he was going to do.

"No," Lyrien said, though this time, the word didn't ring in his ear like an agitated cry of desperation. "Leave me alone."

"Nonsense," the other man said again. "Even if it weren't totally unacceptable to have you bleeding in Lord Mabon's palace, I can't risk having your arm fall off from disease. Now, stop wasting time, slave. Gertroll, heal him now."

The creature gave an exasperated glance back over his shoulder at the man, then turned and looked at Lyrien and shrugged helplessly. "I must do it, friend, so why don't you just relax? It won't take long, and you'll feel much better."

Lyrien wanted to bolt again, so desperately did he want to evade the magic, but he willed himself to hold still and watched as the green-skinned creature took hold of a strange symbol wrought in silver that hung from a sturdy chain around his neck. Gertroll began to mutter in some harsh, clipped tongue under his breath, closing his eyes and laying his other hand on the blood-encrusted gash on Lyrien's arm. The captain watched, holding his breath, apprehensive and yet strangely mesmerized by the proceedings.

As Gertroll's words rose in pitch and volume, Lyrien began to see a strange glow forming beneath the creature's palm, where he was touching Lyrien's arm. The glow grew stronger, and Lyrien fancied that he could actually feel the energy. It was just like before, he realized, with the collar, though without the minor inconvenience of choking to death to distract him, it was clear to him that he could affect it if he wanted.

Tentatively, Lyrien reached out and pressed the tip of his finger against the edge of the glow and found that he could nudge it. Gertroll's eyes fluttered open at this first gentle pressure, staring at Lyrien in mild confusion even as he continued his chant. Smiling back and feeling emboldened, Lyrien pressed harder, and Gertroll's chanting ceased. Lyrien wanted to laugh. He drew his hand back the slightest bit and swatted at the glow, and in an instant, it had shattered, fragmenting into a million motes of bluish light that radiated in every direction. Gertroll stumbled back and fell on his rump, staring up at Lyrien in amazement.

"By Ozri'beye, I've never—how in the hells did you do that?" Gertroll asked, slowly standing. "You just said there was no magic in your world."

"What happened?" the bald man asked worriedly, scrutinizing Lyrien warily.

Lyrien shrugged. "I could see the magic, and I pushed it away."

Gertroll pursed his lips, staring at Lyrien in deep thought. "Perhaps you have a latent bit of magic in you after all. You've just never been exposed to it to know it."

"Is he dangerous?" the greedy man asked. "Should I summon more guards?"

It was Gertroll's turn to shrug. "You'll have to bring in a wizard—" he said that word with some distaste, "—

to find that out. All I know is, I can't heal him unless he lets me."

"What? No, we must heal him!" The bald man fretted, dry-washing his hands once more. He turned to Lyrien directly. "Please, Lord Mabon will be most displeased if we don't present you to him suitably prepared. You *must* let Gertroll heal you."

Lyrien gave the man a knowing smile. "Will Lord Mabon be displeased with *me,* or with *you?*"

The bald-headed man blanched, his eyes growing wide. "N-No! You must not do this! I have children! There must be some way to convince you. What can I offer—"

Lyrien's smile was gone, then. "You will bring me soap, hot water, and clean bandages, and I will clean my own wound," he said forcefully. "No more magic. That's my price for cooperating."

The bald-headed man's eyes grew even wider, if that were possible, but then he finally seemed to get control of his faculties and began nodding vigorously. "Yes, yes, of course. Gertroll, fetch him whatever he needs. He must be bathed. And food! Whatever he wants to eat."

Gertroll shook his head, though he was still looking at Lyrien. There was amazement in that gaze, but the captain also thought he saw a hint of grudging respect there. "I'm not one of your servant boys, Frennot. Have *them* fetch for him." And with that, the green-skinned creature stood and left the cell.

Frennot's jaw dropped at Gertroll's outburst, and he did nothing but stand and watch as the priest walked out. Once he was gone, though, Frennot blinked a couple of times, coming back around to the matter at hand, and went charging out of the cell, loudly calling names and demanding half a dozen things immediately. The bald-headed man departed so hastily that he didn't even bother shutting the cell door, and Lyrien moved to see how feasible escape might be, but he barely even got his head through the doorway before four guards arrived—only one was human; the other three were more of the sinewy, bird-headed creatures, the same species as the one who had originally enslaved him—insisting that he accompany them to the baths.

Sighing, Lyrien trudged through the stone halls with them to a tiled chamber replete with several stone basins for bathing in. More of the servants were there, only some of them human boys, ready to assist him with his washing, but he resolutely refused to even dip a foot in the steaming water until they all cleared out and left him in peace. It wasn't so much that he was self-conscious; he was simply taking a delightful pleasure in getting Frennot's goat. And besides, he wanted a little peace and quiet to consider everything that was going on without a bunch of attendants fawning all over him.

The required bandages and a salve had also been brought, so Lyrien cleaned his wound first and then settled down for a soak. The warmth of the water felt incredibly good to him, soothing all of his tired, sore muscles. He realized that he hadn't actually bathed since the day of his arrival in Penance, when he had fallen into the dark river of water with Gade, and that hardly counted. He sighed contentedly and sank down to his chin in the water and just let his body relax.

The captain had absolutely no idea what was going on with the magic, or rather more specifically, with his ability to affect it. It puzzled and intrigued him, and at the same time, he feared it. Some latent ability that had lain dormant in his body all these years, only able to manifest itself once it was actually exposed to the presence of magic? That just seemed so . . . ridiculous, he heard his father say. And he would have agreed, except that very little else he had accepted as normal all his life was, in fact, reality any longer. So this explanation would have to do for the time being.

Once he gave up trying to understand why he was able to sense and control magic, Lyrien's thoughts drifted to home, and Iandra. *She would be laughing at me right now,* he thought. *Soaking in a bath like one of her pampered lady friends. The next thing you know, she'd be trying to talk me into letting her sprinkle some sort of oils or flowers in the water, "to make it smell nice," she would say.*

Lyrien smiled at the thought, but the smile clouded over as the events of her separation from him came flooding back. The truth was, Iandra had been in exile—on the run with him leading her tattered army—for a long time, and he doubted she had enjoyed a hot bath in quite a long while. He could barely stand to think of where she was right then. His imagination had a way of cruelly conjuring up all sorts of unpleasant images, images fueled by the slavery he had witnessed and been subjected to. He ruthlessly tried to banish them from thought, but that was easier said than done, and they lingered, lurking, just below the surface.

Finally, knowing that this idleness was what was making him dwell on his lost queen, Lyrien finished the bath and wrapped his wound with dry bandages. Then he dressed. Gone were the tattered and bloodstained white trousers and tunic he had worn during the arena combat. The outfit that had been left for him in their place was not really to his liking.

A pair of tight pants in a deep shade of purple with gold highlights and made of some thin, sleek fabric like silk was accompanied by a very loose-fitting robe of the same material that hung down to just above his knees. A pair of slippers finished out the garb. There was no shirt, and the robe had no ties, so it hung open, leaving his chest bare. Lyrien felt like some sort of primped up nobleman strutting for the ladies, and he would have much preferred his normal attire of breeches tucked into good fitting boots and a plain blousy shirt with a doublet that kept his sword arm unhindered, but that would have to wait for another day, he supposed.

The captain wondered if he could browbeat Frennot into fetching him more comfortable clothing, but his bath had mellowed him somewhat and he didn't feel like pushing his luck with the greedy, bald fellow.

I've got him dancing on strings enough already, Lyrien decided, tug much harder and they might snap.

Not that he really had any sympathy for the man; Frennot was undoubtedly just as involved with the unfair set-up for the combat as anyone, and Lyrien could just as easily hold the man responsible for Gade's death as Threlmak. No, the truth was, Lyrien just didn't find toying with the man to be all that satisfying.

Revenge should be short and to the point, for it seldom accomplishes what you wish, Lyrien's father used to say. When you've exacted it, you rarely feel any better, and you've just exhausted your energy for nothing. Better to pour that energy into righting the wrong done in the first place.

One of the few things he ever said that made any sense, Lyrien mused. Though his notion of exactly what righting the wrong meant was far different from mine. How could he be so cold and uncaring about so much?

Lyrien dismissed that silent conversation almost as soon as it began. He had worked through it often enough and had never reached a satisfactory conclusion to it. He had just accepted that he was never going to understand his father, any more than his father had understood him.

At that moment, four servant boys—again, only one of which was human, the boy from earlier, who had carried the flowers and coins inside—appeared, followed by Frennot.

"Please, you have had ample time to prepare yourself. We must go. A carriage is waiting already," Frennot said, bustling about and checking the cut and fit of Lyrien's outfit. "You have no time left to eat, I'm afraid, but that shouldn't be a problem. There will be feasting; there always is."

Lyrien stood still and let Frennot fuss with his robes for about two seconds, then gestured for the man to leave him be. "I'll be fine," he said. "Just get me to where I'm supposed to go."

Frennot nodded and gestured through the door, where Lyrien's four guards were still there, waiting for him, it seemed. The guards escorted him through more halls of the coliseum, taking several sets of steps down, rather than up, which Lyrien found odd.

"Are you sure we're going the right direction?" he queried the human as they proceeded. "I thought Frennot said a carriage was waiting."

"It is," the guard replied. "We're going there now."

Lyrien shrugged but kept silent for the rest of the walk. Eventually, the five of them arrived in a chamber that Lyrien was certain was well below the surface of the city, and then he understood. The chamber had a broad opening on one side, connected with a wide tunnel that led off into the distance, lined at regular intervals with more of the odd glowing plants he had seen on the streets above. Waiting in the chamber itself was a very fine open carriage, all in black, pulled by six kith. A pair of coachmen—both of them the slender, copper-scaled reptilian creatures he had seen before in the slave pits—waited patiently, dressed identically in black livery. Seated inside the carriage itself was the imperious man with the shaved head.

Upon seeing the procession of guards and their charge arrive, the icy fellow gave Lyrien one quick cold stare, sniffed, and looked away again. At the same time, one of the coachmen stepped smartly to the side and opened the door of the carriage so that Lyrien could climb in. As he ascended the pair of steps that had been lowered for his benefit, he saw that the seat opposite the man had been outfitted with a set of stout chains with manacles at the ends of them.

Lyrien sighed. "Are those really necessary?" he asked.

"Shut up and sit down," one of the guards barked and, when Lyrien complied, locked the thick metal cuffs on each wrist and ankle. He then proceeded to string together additional chains between the various restraints, so that, when he was finished, Lyrien could sit comfortably with his hands in his lap, but he could not move his arms or his feet more than a few inches in any direction.

"Well?" the man said to the coachmen once the guard had made sure the chains were secure and had exited the carriage. "Proceed. Lord Mabon doesn't like to wait." One of the coachmen shut the door and climbed up onto the back, the other reptilian creature took its place in the driver's seat, and then they were off. Lyrien watched the chamber recede behind them as they entered the tunnel, saw the four guards standing and watching him, and realized the utter futility of escape. He began studying the walls of the tunnel as they went by, wondering if there were ways to get back to the surface from there, assuming he could somehow free himself from the restraints.

"If you're thinking you might break free," the man said, "don't bother. Those chains are made of adamantine; an ogre could not shatter them. Besides, Lord Mabon has made certain that the only ways in and out are at each end." He smiled frostily at Lyrien when his reaction must have made it clear that he had read his mind.

Lyrien chuckled once, thinking perhaps to throw this unfriendly creature off-balance, while continuing to examine their route. "The Lord's hospitality is well thought out," he replied. "But why would he want to meet some poor slave fresh from the pits who got lucky in his first and only fight in the coliseum?"

The man sniffed again, refusing to look at Lyrien. "Lord Mabon never wants to meet anyone; it's *my* responsibility to procure slaves *for* him. I don't bother him unless I think there's a good reason. So first you'll answer to me, and then we'll see what my lord thinks."

"And you are … ?"

"You will refer to me as Master Salas."

Lyrien frowned and looked away at the rows of glowing plants that whisked by as the coach made its way through this interminable tunnel. The route had taken a couple of turns at various points, but in general, it was straight, unusual compared to what he had seen of the rest of the city, both above and below the surface. The captain had pretty much already assumed that he was still merely a pawn in some larger game, that Lord Mabon's sudden interest would have repercussions, but the callus way in which this disdainful creature defined his role in the larger scheme was still biting. Plus, the man sitting opposite him had just confirmed that he had lied to Frennot about Mabon speaking with him personally on the matter of Lyrien's purchase. He wasn't sure whether that made him feel better or worse.

The rest of the trip was made in silence, and after a short time the carriage rolled into a wide chamber. It had been decorated to appear as the front entrance to a grand estate, with a circular drive before a broad set of steps leading up to a wide porch. The walls of this chamber had been decorated to appear as an expansive lawn, and the ceiling, a night sky filled with stars. It had a remarkable realism to it, and Lyrien did a double-take when he realized that the stars were twinkling. Was this more magic?

The two coachmen were down an instant after the vehicle stopped moving, opening the door and lowering the steps so that Master Salas could disembark. He waited impatiently as they unlocked a portion of the chains, leav-

ing the manacles on Lyrien. At the same time, a pair of
massive, hulking guards, creatures that towered eight feet
or more in height, appeared at the top of the steps and
approached. They were similar to Gertroll, the priest from
the coliseum, though they seemed more monstrous and
savage. Each wore a simple loincloth and had a great
curved sword strapped to its back. They came attentively
to stand before the bald-headed Salas, who muttered some
instructions to them, then proceeded toward Lyrien while
the captain's frosty escort made his way inside.

Lyrien gawked at the pair of guards, remembering
tales from his childhood designed to frighten children
into behaving. There was always a scary monster that
looked as the two guards did, some foul beast hiding
under a bridge or in a dark cavern. He found himself feeling anxious and frightened all over again, just as he had
during his youth.

The two monstrous creatures waited, looking at the
captain expectantly, and finally, Lyrien made his way out
of the carriage. A length of chain ran between his ankles,
long enough that he could walk or take steps one at a
time, but no more. A similar chain ran between his wrists,
and a third chain ran around his waist, keeping his hands
pinned close to his body. Once he was off the last step of
the carriage, each guard took a shoulder in one meaty
hand as big as his head and began to guide him up the
steps and inside the "estate."

The first room just inside the doorway was an entry
hall, all marble and gilt. Columns ran from floor to ceiling, and a great hallway proceeded back from there. A
staircase ran up each side of this high-ceilinged chamber
to a second-story balcony. Several doors led off into other
parts of the palace. But the centerpiece of the whole affair
caught the captain's attention, filling him with amazement and horror.

In the center of the entryway, positioned on a white marble pedestal, was a work of living art. It appeared as a nude human woman, though she had both a pair of small red horns protruding from her brow and a set of black, leathery wings flaring out from her shoulders. Slender circlets of gold were locked onto her body at various joints, and a slender golden rod extended down from each of these manacles to the pedestal below, holding the creature in position like some sort of inverted marionette. She had been posed to appear to be down on one knee, her arms extended as though making an offering, and a silver bowl that held fresh fruit had been set upon her upturned palms. Lyrien could only imagine how uncomfortable this creature must be, forced to hold such a position indefinitely. He wondered how long she had been left like this.

Lyrien's escorts stopped him front of this depraved display while Salas strolled up to the living statue and extracted a small clump of what appeared to be yellowish grapes from the bowl. He then returned to stand by Lyrien's side and admire the work of living art.

"She's still in training," the man explained, gesturing with the bunch of grapes in his hand. "She hasn't quite figured out her role in Lord Mabon's harem, yet, so until she does, I've decided that she must greet guests arriving from other parts of the Grey District."

Lyrien shook his head, staring into the face of the cruelly imprisoned creature. "So, if I don't figure out my role, does a similar fate await me?" he asked, letting the sarcasm roll thickly and clanking the chains around his wrists for emphasis. The winged woman looked at him with obvious pleading in her eyes, but she never opened her mouth to speak. Whether she was forbidden from talking on penalty of some further punishment, or if some sorcery prevented it, Lyrien didn't know, but he was thankful, in a way. He didn't know if he would be able to resist trying to aid her if she had actually asked for it.

Without batting an eye, Master Salas said, "Oh, I'm certain we can come up with something else unique and clever, but no less encouraging." He turned away to continue their journey.

Lyrien tore his gaze away from the slave on display and followed his guide, fearful of what he would see next. Salas led them up the stairs, and Lyrien was actually thankful that the guards flanking him had such a stout hold on him, for he feared that he might trip over his chains and would have no way to halt his fall. At the top, they found another slave on display. It was a dover, though unlike Gade's brown fur, its coloring was white with patches of gray. It, too, was devoid of any clothing. The creature was simply anchored to the wall, like some sort of organic bas relief sculpture. It couldn't even turn its head to look at them as they passed, though Lyrien saw it follow them with its eyes. His stomach in knots as he thought of his companion, Lyrien hurried past.

At last, after winding their way through a veritable maze of halls and chambers, all extravagantly decorated with both traditional appointments and living displays—some of single slaves, others of whole collections forming complex exhibits—Lyrien's guide led the procession down a rather long hallway that contained a series of arched doorways set into both walls at regular intervals. Each archway was covered with heavy curtains. Finally, Salas stopped before one and motioned for the captain to step forward. He said, "This is it," Then ordered one of the two guards to remove Lyrien's restraints.

Once the shackles had been unlocked, Master Salas gestured for him to pass through the doorway, where Lyrien found himself in a small sitting room, part of a suite, it appeared. Beyond this front chamber were two other rooms, both separated by arched doorways draped with gauzy curtains. In one, he could see a bed, while in the other, he could see a large basin, steaming with warm water. The wall opposite the doorway through which the captain had passed was open to the outside, and Lyrien could see a colonnaded balcony there, warmed by the rays of both suns, though the two were canted at odd angles to one another at the moment. Beyond the balcony he could see the tops of orderly rows of trees, and he suspected the patio looked out over a garden of some sort.

It took Lyrien a moment longer to realize that he and Master Salas were not the only two in the room. He caught motion out of the corner of his eye, and when he looked over into the corner, the most beautiful creature he could imagine was rising up from a cushion where she had been lolling and approached demurely.

"Ah, Ezeria, my dear," Salas said to the woman, "You arrived ahead of us. Good girl. You are both to remain here in the suite until I tell you otherwise." The bald-headed man tilted his head forward, giving the woman named Ezeria a very meaningful stare. "See to the gladiator's every need." The woman nodded and turned to Lyrien. And with that, Salas was gone, passing back through the curtains and out into the hallway beyond.

Ezeria had the swept-back features he had seen on the two creatures Gade had called elves, but it seemed to Lyrien that she was of mixed blood, for she wasn't as fine-boned and diminutive of stature as those others he had seen, and her elven features were not quite so sharp or prominent. Still, from her almond-shaped eyes to her slender, pointed ears, she favored the elves. Her jaw was narrow and delicate, and her skin was creamy and smooth. Lyrien could see every inch of that skin, too, for she was dressed in diaphanous loose black silk pantaloons and a matching halter, an outfit that added fashion while hiding nothing. She had lustrous blonde hair that hung down in waves to her waist, which she had draped over one shoulder. She met Lyrien's lustful gaze with a slight smirk.

"Well?" she said at last, extending a hand for him to take. "Come on. I'll show you the rest." Unlike what he had expected from such an angelic throat, her voice was low and sultry.

Lyrien hesitated, struggling between lust for this unearthly creature and a need to resist anything that Master Salas would use to hold over his head. Besides, he felt some level of betrayal to Iandra. He struggled to keep his gaze focused on the elven woman's face, rather than the rest of her sensuous body. It wasn't possible. "I should just get some sleep," he said dully, hoping she would take the hint and make the decision easier for him.

But Ezeria only shifted her weight to one leg, resting her hand on her hip rather provocatively, "Sleep! It would be such a waste. How disappointing."

Lyrien shook his head again even as he took her hand and let her lead him into the room with the basin. "I appreciate the Lord's hospitality, Ezeria, but all the same, I should rest. I fought at the coliseum today, and I need to sleep."

The woman pouted the tiniest bit, but then gave up the seduction game for the moment and said, "You don't think you really have a choice, do you? I can see the desire on your face."

It took Lyrien several moments to realize what Ezeria was implying as he struggled not to get caught up in her deep green eyes. They seemed to sparkle with a mischievous joy as she stared back. "So you're telling me I can't resist you?" he asked, trying to affect a cool demeanor.

It was Ezeria's turn to chuckle. "You catch on quickly, Tempest."

Lyrien raised his eyebrows in confusion. "Tempest? What does that mean?"

"Ah," Ezeria replied, giving his hand a gentle but affectionate squeeze as she passed out onto the balcony. Sure enough, there was a vast garden stretching out on the grounds below. "That's what everyone has taken to calling you, since no one bothered to find out your actual name. I suppose they didn't expect you to live long enough to make it worth anyone's while to get to know you, but your name is upon the lips of nearly all the powerful and prosperous in Penance now. Tempest the Gladiator. Tempest, who shatters iron with his bare hands. Tempest, who defiantly defeated two of the coliseum's best veterans in a wild display of weaponry and guile. Didn't you know?"

Lyrien shook his head. "I guess no one thought I would live long enough to be bothered with telling me." He was finding it more and more difficult to concentrate on what the nymph next to him was saying. He could smell a musky aroma radiating from her now, and the soft brush of silk on silk as she walked was mesmerizing. He could feel himself stirring with desire. He had to fight it. "Please, I don't know what you're used to doing with your charges, but I shouldn't. I can't."

The elven beauty laughed. "You really are a foolish man, Tempest," she said, then backed Lyrien against a column and leaned in to kiss him.

The last vestiges of his resistance melted away with that kiss, and he realized after a moment that she was pushing away. "Come on," she said, flashing that enchanting smile once more. She truly was an angel, he decided.

"Lyrien," he mumbled as Ezeria pushed past the gauzy curtains separating the balcony from the bedroom, leading him back inside. "My name is Lyrien, not Tempest."

"Of course it is," Ezeria said, letting go of his hand and taking several steps more, then loosening the diaphanous silks that clung to her perfect frame. As the flimsy cloth dropped away, she stepped out of it and sashayed back toward Lyrien, her eyes smoldering. "Now, kiss me like you did before," she said, embracing him and pressing herself against him.

Chapter 8

"How long have you been in Penance?" Ezeria asked. The pair of them were entwined on the bed, her head resting atop Lyrien's chest as he lay on his back. He was adrift on a sea of exhausted sensation, drowsy, completely spent.

Of all the ways in which the Forge heightens the senses, the captain thought, that has to be the most . . . stunning. Yes, that was how he felt at the moment as he mulled over the last several hours in his mind. Even later, in retrospect, it took his breath away.

Lyrien had to count back to answer her question. He could see beyond the shimmering curtains leading to the balcony beyond that it was dark outside. The yellow sun—Crux, he knew it was called by then—had vanished shortly after his arrival in the chambers, and the red one, Storm, had crossed the sky all during their lovemaking. It was gone, too, replaced by the faint bluish glow of a crescent moon. He had no idea what time that meant it was. "A little more than a day," he finally answered. It seemed like a lifetime. "I've spent most of it locked in cages and cells, so it's hard to tell for sure."

"A whole day?" Ezeria said, laughter in her voice. "Well, that explains a lot." And she raised up and kissed him.

He began to return the kiss, but then he pulled away, staring at the gilded ceiling overhead. Even then, he was locked in a cage, though his cellmate was extraordinary. She shrugged and kissed his chest, instead.

"What am I doing here?" Lyrien asked, half to himself. "Why would this bloodlord, the ruler of an entire section of the city, have me brought here and then dumped into a room with a harem girl?"

"What, are you complaining?" Ezeria asked as she let her kisses move lower, to Lyrien's belly.

"Stop it," he insisted quietly, looking down at her.

The half-elven beauty stared up at him with those enticing emerald eyes, but she pulled away and sat up at the foot of the bed, watching him. She didn't bother to cover herself. "Is there something wrong with me?" she asked softly, forlornly. "Do I not please you?" The tone of her voice was sad, but there was something . . .

"Quit with your seduction games," Lyrien said, rolling to the edge and getting up. "It's getting insulting." He started for the balcony.

Ezeria snorted, causing Lyrien to stop in mid-stride and turn back to face her, incredulous. She wasn't exactly glaring at him, but her mien revealed an honesty he hadn't seen from her, yet. "Insulting?" she said derisively. "You want to talk about insulting? You seemed happy enough to get what you needed from me last night, and this morning, you treat me like I'm leprous. So you tell me . . . who's the one being insulting?"

Lyrien sighed softly. "All right," he said, holding his hands up to placate her. "I am being an ass. But if that's what it takes to get you to drop the pretensions, I'm not completely sorry."

Ezeria shrugged. "Fair enough," she said. "No more games. So what's the problem? What did I do?"

Lyrien shrugged and began to pace. "It's not you I'm angry with, it's me. I shouldn't be flopping around here, mating like a rabbit. None of this makes any sense."

"Well that's *much* more complimentary," Ezeria said wryly. "You really know how to make a girl swoon, you know that?"

Lyrien stopped pacing and turned to face her again. "Look," he said, "I'm sorry I'm not being a gentlemanly companion right now, but I need to understand. One of the bloodlord's top men buys me from the coliseum and hauls me here, then sticks me in a room with you for the night. I wasn't locked in a cage, and there are no chains around me." He began to pace again, continuing animatedly. "So what am I? A slave? A guest who can leave if I want to? Something else entirely?"

"Lyrien," Ezeria began, but the captain continued on, talking right over her.

"See, nobody pays a handful of rubies for me just so I can be dropped into a life of luxury without another care in the world for the rest of my days. This Salas character has plans for me, and you're here to sweeten the offer." Lyrien turned again and sat down beside Ezeria, who at last had drawn the sheet up around herself and was staring down at her own lap. "Believe me, you made me feel amazing last night, and I won't even pretend I didn't love every minute of it. But you're the bribe, Ezeria. Salas, or Lord Mabon, or somebody wants something from me, and you're here to make sure I give it to them."

"You think I don't know that?" Ezeria asked softly. "You think I don't realize just what my purpose in this scenario is?" She shifted to her knees then, angling herself so that she was now behind the captain. "Yes, I am a tool for others to use. That's the reality of my life. I make the best of it. Why don't you?" and with that, she let the sheet drop away again and pressed against his back, wrapping her arms around his waist. She kissed him gently on the back of his neck and then pressed her cheek to the back of his head.

"I'm sorry," Lyrien replied, disentangling himself from her and standing. "You're any man's dream, Ezeria, but I can't do this." He took a deep breath. "There's someone I care very much about. I need to get back to her. She's in trouble."

Lyrien expected Ezeria to smolder at that, but instead, the woman just shrugged and climbed off the bed toward him, letting the sheet trail off her body. "Yes, and?" she said, closing to him again. "You think I didn't once have someone else? You think I never had another life, where someone needed me? But that was then, and this is now. This is the reality. I serve at the whim of others, but I make the best of it." And she leaned up and kissed him, beginning to wrap her arms around the captain's neck.

Lyrien returned the kiss momentarily, but then he took hold of her arms and pulled her off of himself. "No," he said. "I won't be bought. I'm not staying here any longer." He began to get dressed.

"What are you doing?" Ezeria asked, genuine concern in her voice, now. "You can't just leave. You heard what Master Salas said. We're to remain here until he comes for us."

"Too bad," Lyrien replied, slipping the foolish lavender trousers on, followed by the slippers and the robe. "I won't be . . . whatever it is he wants me to be. I have to find a way back to my own world, and I'm starting right now." He moved toward the curtained door that led out to the hallway.

"No!" Ezeria cried, jumping off the bed and running to intercept him. "You can't get out! Don't you understand? There are guards out there. They won't let you leave." She moved in front of him, holding both hands up as he approached the door, trying to make him stop. "Listen to me," she said, and when he tried to move around her, she moved with him. "It may seem like you're a pampered guest, but if you cross them, things will get bad for you in a hurry! No one is going to let you get twenty paces beyond this room! Do you understand?"

Lyrien turned away and headed toward the balcony. "Then I'll climb down into the garden and go that way," he said. "There's a way out; I've just got to find it."

"Damn it, Lyrien, stop it!" Ezeria yelled, loudly enough that Lyrien was certain anyone standing out in the hall could hear and would come through to investigate. He continued to move toward the porch, intent on getting over the railing and down before anyone noticed he was gone. But Ezeria caught up to him, grabbed his hand and pulled hard enough to turn him around to face her in mid-stride. "Don't you understand?" she said, and the captain could see real fear in her eyes. "You must not leave," she said, emphasizing each word. "The repercussions are—" and she faltered, her lip trembling, and she lifted the back of one hand to her mouth to suppress whatever terror she was feeling.

"Are you so self-centered?" Ezeria whispered finally, swallowing hard. "This isn't about you! You think this is some sort of test, or bribe, something Master Salas is doing to you, but it's not."

Lyrien looked at her, bewildered. "Then what else is it?" he asked doubtfully. Nothing else could explain his circumstances.

"It's about *me!*" the woman replied. "It's *my* test! And I'm failing it, because you have some noble quest you have to follow. And if you try to leave, *I'm* the one who's going to be punished."

"What?" Lyrien asked, still unwilling to really accept what she was saying. "Why? What are you talking about?"

"Because *I* didn't do a good enough job to convince you to stay!" Ezeria said, her voice thick with emotion.

She turned away, moving to sit on the bed, grabbing the sheet up and wrapping herself tightly in it. "My usefulness to Master Salas is limited by how effective I am at keeping you here," she said, tears shining on her cheeks. "So, if you rush out of here, bent on this holy mission of yours, *I'm* the one who pays for your transgressions. *Me!*"

"Damn," Lyrien said, feeling helpless and angry all at the same time. Hearing that was the same as having a shackle around his own ankle. "I didn't know." He wanted to go to her, to wrap his arms around her and comfort her, but he kept seeing Iandra's frowning face, so he instead stood rooted to the spot.

"But you weren't *supposed* to know," Ezeria said, regaining her composure. She turned away and wiped her face with the back of her hand. "Telling you would ruin the test. It doesn't matter now."

Lyrien rolled his eyes. "Why not? I'm not going anywhere, now. Not if it means that you get hurt."

"That's very noble of you, but it doesn't work like that. By now, Master Salas is on his way—"

As if to prove Ezeria a prophet, the thin, shaven-headed man appeared, wearing a brand new and differently decorated—but just as ornate—blue robe. He stepped through the curtains, a smirk on his face, followed by the two towering humanoid guards. "Indeed, Ezeria," Salas said, smiling coldly. "And here I am."

"How did you—?" Lyrien began to ask, but knew just as soon as the words began to tumble out of his mouth. "Magic. You eavesdropped with magic."

"Indeed," Master Salas answered, nodding and smirking. "Ezeria, my dear, I'm afraid that didn't go well at all."

"Look," Lyrien said, stepping between the man and Ezeria, "Whatever it is you want me to do, I'll cooperate, but don't punish her for this. It wasn't any shortcoming on her part, I assure you."

"Indeed?" Salas remarked, apparently fond of that word, cocking his head to one side with that bemused grin still on his face. "If that's so, then why were you trying to leave?"

Lyrien clenched his hands, wanting to smack that smirk off Salas's face with a nice right cross, but he ground his teeth and simply said, "I need to return to my own world. There's someone there who matters a great deal to me, and she's in trouble. Ten more like Ezeria wouldn't keep me here in the face of that."

"Ah, but my protective gladiator, that's precisely why we have her here. And if she can't overcome your delusions of duty, then she's not much good to us, is she?" Master Salas turned his head slightly and gave a quick nod. "Confine her to her quarters," he said, "I'll deal with her later." One of the guards moved to obey.

Lyrien stepped in front of the guard. "I said, leave her alone," he insisted evenly, wondering how much it would hurt to be hit by this creature, which was half again as tall as himself.

The humanoid growled, an almost subsonic rumble in his chest. He reached forward with both hands, ready to grab Lyrien by the collar of his robe, and the captain smacked at them, knocking them away—barely a foot.

The captain was blindsided by the fierce backhand strike from the other guard, which sent him sprawling halfway across the floor. Spots filled Lyrien's vision, and his head rang from the impact. Before he even had a chance to collect his breath, two sets of huge, meaty hands had seized him, one holding him down, pressing him roughly into the floor, the other yanking his arms up his back painfully. Ezeria let out a yelp of fright.

"My foolish Tempest," Salas said from somewhere across the room as Lyrien felt a set of manacles snapped onto his wrists, "This is really no time for your heroics.

You don't really think you can best two ogres, when you yourself are unarmed, do you?"

"Lyrien, don't," Ezeria pleaded, moving closer to him, putting a hand on his shoulder. "Please. You're only making it worse."

"I'm not going to let you punish her," the captain said, thrashing around until he felt a knee pressed into his back. "She never stood a chance, and your test was doomed to failure," he growled over his shoulder at Salas.

"You seem so full of opinions today. Not very becoming of a slave, you know. Nevertheless," Salas said, his smile gone now, "You are in no position to make those sorts of decisions. And she is right; the more trouble you cause, the worse it will become—for both of you. Now, relax, or I will have Bruhark and Friest truss you up completely and carry you to more appropriate quarters." Salas tilted his head down slightly to stare pointedly at Lyrien. "Something a little more confining," he finished, emphasizing each word coldly.

Lyrien tensed, ready to kick and roll, anything to try and win his freedom and stop Salas and his thugs from hurting Ezeria, but the soft pressure of her hand on his shoulder finally changed his mind.

"Please," she said again, quietly, "Don't do this. It's not worth all this fuss." He turned to look up at her, not understanding how she could surrender so cavalierly like this. "I'll be all right," she added, forcing a smile that Lyrien didn't buy for a minute.

He shook his head. "It's not right," Lyrien said. "I can't just . . ." but he didn't know what else to say.

"Shhh," Ezeria said, putting a finger on his lips. "You can, and you must. For me. I can't stand the thought of what they'd do to you—to both of us—if you don't settle down."

"You should listen to the slave," Salas remarked casually, his tone superior. "She has experience in these matters, and her wisdom could save you lots of grief."

Lyrien spun his gaze back around to look over his other shoulder, wanting so badly to pop the nasty bald man right in the mouth, but he drew a long, slow breath and said, "Tell me whatever it is you want from me, I grow tired of these games."

Salas inclined his head once in apparent acquiescence. "You're finally making sense, Tempest. You," he said to one of the ogres, "let her get dressed, then take her to her quarters," the ogre nodded. "And you," The blue-robed man said to the other, "help him to his feet." Then, gloating as he looked at Lyrien, he said, "It's almost time for you to meet Lord Mabon. But first, I want to show you something. Bruhark, watch him carefully. I doubt you'll surprise him again."

Lyrien gave one last, desperate glance back at Ezeria, who simply gave him a smile to reassure him, then he allowed the ogre to lift him up. Once he was standing, he followed Salas out of the quarters and into the hallway, the ogre right behind him with a massive fist locked onto the back of the captain's neck, steering him along. Lyrien could not shake the distinct feeling of being a prisoner led to his own execution.

They walked together in silence for a time, moving from one section of the palace to another. The various chambers and passageways they passed through were all constructed of a dull gray stone, as his room had been, but the décor varied widely from section to section. There were lots of tapestries, plush carpets and rugs, and numerous fountains and pools, as wells as plants and baskets with a wide variety of blooming growths. And, everywhere they went, there were slaves. Some were on display, as he had seen the night before, but others were free, moving about, intent on their own errands. Some were clothed, and some were not. All who could bowed deeply at Master Salas's approach. Those who could not tended to stare at him with fear-filled eyes.

In addition to the slaves, numerous guards either stood stoically at attention, occupying corners or flanking doors, or they hurried along their own way, every one of them in the same red and black livery with an unsettling symbol embroidered on the right breast. Some of the traveling guards moved in groups by themselves, laughing and talking softly, or escorted slaves—some relatively willingly, others remarkably reluctant, or in cages on wheels. Many of them gave Salas a quick salute as they passed.

As the trio made their way through the palace and Lyrien could see just how heavily guarded the whole place was, he slowly found some balance to his emotions, gradually calmed down enough to realize that he was never going to succeed at gaining his freedom as long as he overtly resisted Master Salas. The only way he would succeed in extricating himself from the bloodlord's clutches would be to lull them into believing he was not going to be a problem. Yet every time he saw a slave suffering, every time he thought of what might be happening to Ezeria—or the winged woman at the entryway, or any of the slaves they passed along their route—his anger welled up in him. The captain just could not abide seeing such cruelty, and he silently vowed he would put an end to it eventually. A foolish promise, he realized, but one that he had to make, for his own peace of mind.

Eventually, Master Salas led him outside, into the gardens. The soft bluish glow of the crescent moon, slowly rising in the evening sky, was joined by the ruddy light of a second rust-colored moon, nearly full at the moment, which sat almost directly overhead. Together, they faintly illuminated the route Salas followed. The three of them passed through an area of well tended beds, trees, and shrubs, much of them in full bloom. Scattered between these beds were pools, many of them with fountains and cascading waterfalls that babbled and tumbled in a pleasant, musical way. The beds and pools were separated by grassy paths that meandered among them. In one area, Lyrien could see a large open area of manicured grass, and several slaves were running and laughing in the moonlight, although under the watchful eye of a number of guards positioned about the periphery of the open field.

Once they were past the gardens, Salas led the three of them along a path of crushed stone to a large, sweeping building that was all unusual angles and high, sweeping buttresses. The most extraordinary thing about this structure, though, was that it was made almost entirely of a frame of steel inset with large panels of colored glass. Lyrien couldn't imagine how it could remain standing without more stone and mortar.

Magic holds it together, he decided, mildly surprised that he no longer really questioned the existence of such.

As they entered the front doors of this odd building, Lyrien had a momentary sense of foreboding. He feared that the structure might collapse down upon them. He tried to shake off his unease and followed the bald-headed man into the first chamber. It became obvious immediately that this was some sort of a holy place.

Salas moved through the outer room and to a second set of doors, and Lyrien followed him inside. This was the inner temple. The chamber was circular, with an altar in the middle and rows of seating, wooden benches, encircling it on nearly every side. It appeared that there was some sort of spiral staircase leading down from the central dais into the sub levels below. The ceiling of the temple soared high overhead, great curving beams that curled upward to a point, like a pavilion, rather than flattening toward the top like a normal arch. He could imagine the great panels of colored glass filling the place with a light and energy during daylight hours. The whole place glowed with the fire of thousands of candles. Lyrien felt no small amount of awe, both at the physical structure and at the sense of radiant power that permeated the place.

Lyrien peered around and noted that it was richly decorated. There was an abundance of gold and gems adorning every surface, every item of religious significance. Images adorned columns that supported the ceiling, and a large fresco was set into the floor in gems and covered over with a layer of some clear material to protect them.

Several creatures: three humans, two different reptilian species—a chromithian and a picker, Lyrien knew by that point—and a valco, one of the goatlike humanoids, all stood about the altar, talking quietly among themselves as they prepared for something. Each of them wore a set of identical tan robes embroidered with strange symbols in a dark brown color. The robes were further decorated with a number of amber and yellow gemstones.

Priests, Lyrien decided.

As the three newcomers entered the temple, the priests turned as one and bowed to them. They then returned to their preparations at the altar. It was at that moment that Lyrien looked more closely and realized there was a body there, draped in black cloth.

"Are you ready?" was all Master Salas asked, his voice echoing sharply through the vaulted, round room, and one of the robed men nodded. "Then get on with it," the bald-headed man commanded.

The priests moved eagerly, lighting candles that had been positioned along the periphery of the altar. Lyrien could see other accoutrements positioned in regular spots around, as well.

"Come on," Master Salas said, heading toward the center of the chamber. The trio arrived at the front row and settled there, Bruhark making it a point to sit behind Lyrien. The captain struggled to find a comfortable position in which to sit, since his arms were still manacled behind him. It was a losing battle.

One of the human priests clapped his hands together as the rest of the robed clerics began a low, somber chant. Then, two more priests appeared, rising up from the staircase in the center of the chamber. They were accompanied by a cadre of guards escorting a prisoner. It took Lyrien only the blink of an eye to recognize that prisoner as Threlmak.

The asherake seemed taken aback at this presentation, and it was only through considerable effort that his escort managed to force him into the center of the dais. Threlmak looked around the chamber, eyes wide with concern.

"You!" the asherake spat as he spied the captain. He lunged forward, extending his claws and spreading his wings, but he was immediately restrained by both chains and goads, all held fast by the guards escorting him. Threlmak snarled. "I don't know what lies you told to save yourself, but they will not serve you long!" Then the asherake turned to Master Salas, and his tone changed considerably. "My lord, my master, you know I have served you faithfully, as you have instructed. Do not be fooled by this traitor's lies. He speaks evil of me that cannot be true!"

Master Salas snorted. "He's not the one who informed me of your attempt to escape, slave. What was this, the third time this year?" Threlmak snapped his jaw shut, chagrined. He began to say something more, but the blue-robed man cut him off. "Get on with it," he said to the priests, and the asherake, realizing his pleas were to go unanswered, began to struggle all the more violently, howling and pleading.

"His time has run out," Salas commented to Lyrien, who wondered what, exactly, they were planning to do with his foe from the previous day. He feared that it would be very unpleasant, and he actually felt some sympathy for Threlmak.

The priests began to chant in an unknown language as Threlmak was forced down on his hands and knees near the altar. The asherake fought every step, but there were too many keepers around him. He was eventually driven down to his knees, his head and hands forced into a bowing position and locked into place with chains connected to stout rings anchored to the floor. Apparently, this was not the first time such a presentation had been made. Even after Threlmak was secured, he continued to buck and strain to get free.

"Oh, for the love of Israfel, Threlmak, show a little backbone," Master Salas called out. "You brought this on yourself."

But the asherake continued to thrash and pull, alternating between pleas for his freedom with promises to obey and vile invectives at anyone and everyone present.

The human priest's chanting rose in volume and became some sort of beseeching litany as he took up a huge curved sword and moved to stand near Threlmak's head. Threlmak's struggles reached a desperate level, and the asherake howled once more in terror, and then in one swift motion, the priest swung the sword down. The blow was quick and clean; the priest lopped Threlmak's head off.

Lyrien saw it coming, knew the fate of the prisoner even before it happened, and he still blanched. Master Salas intended for him to see this. Was it a warning? "What sort of dark ritual is this?" he asked, moving to stand and flee before he was forced to witness any more. "I won't be a part of some evil magic!" he said.

"Sit down," Master Salas commanded. "There was no magic there, just an execution."

Lyrien stared at the callous man, but he sat just as Bruhark arose as though to force the issue. "How can I know that? To which god do these priests pray?"

"To their own god."

"Why did you make me watch that?" Lyrien asked, more quietly this time. "Is that your subtle threat for me to behave?"

"Hardly," Salas replied, smiling that infuriating smile of his. "We just thought you'd enjoy watching him get his punishment. He was the one who caused your friend's death, after all."

Lyrien shook his head. It wasn't that he was sad the asherake was dead, exactly, but the circumstances of the execution were more than a little disconcerting. A religious ritual made him uncomfortable.

"If you think that killing my enemies is supposed to endear me to—" Lyrien began.

"Shh," Salas said. "This is what you have been brought here for. Watch."

The priests who had been chanting continued, and they began to encircle the altar. Each of them took a position at even spots around it, continuing their droning. The human one who had killed Threlmak stood at the apparent head of the corpse, and once more, his speech became louder, more pronounced. He raised his eyes up to the rafters overhead, as though beseeching whatever deity he honored for some aid. Then, he produced a pendant that hung from a chain around his neck, presented it firmly to the body, and finally stepped forward, moving his hands over the corpse and continuing to chant. At regular intervals, the priest pressed his palms against the fabric that covered the body, touching places where the flesh must have been rent, for whenever he pulled away, there were blood stains soaking the cloth. The priest completely circumnavigated the form lying there, occasionally touching it, letting blood seep through. Once he was back around to the head of the corpse, he presented his pendant once more, then reached down and yanked the sheet away from the corpse atop the altar. It was Gade.

"God!" Lyrien cried out before he could stop himself. "What the hell?" was all he could think of to say.

As if in answer to the captain's breathless query, the dover's body stirred atop the altar, feebly coughing and trembling. Lyrien nearly choked on his own shock.

Chapter 9

The captain watched open-mouthed as a body that looked for all the world like Gade coughed and spasmed then finally sat up.

It can't be. Gade is dead. This is a trick, a cruel joke being played on me. The 'body' has been alive the whole time, simply lying still until the appropriate moment.

The priests who had been chanting were no longer droning on, and a couple of them helped the dover to swing his legs over the side, then one of them handed him a skin. He took a long drink, though he was shaky and spilled some of it.

"I don't—" the captain began, but he had no idea what to say. "That's not real."

"Oh, rest assured that it is," Master Salas replied, giggling softly. "Those high priests are quite good at resurrecting folks from the afterlife, don't you think?"

Lyrien reeled. *Resurrected? Brought back to life? That is simply impossible.* He said as much, shaking his head, feeling like he would become ill.

"Trust me, it's imminently possible," Salas said. "And expensive. And I wouldn't go to the trouble if I didn't think it well worth it. You see, I wanted to make it perfectly clear exactly where things stand. I have the power of life," and he gestured toward the dover, "and death," and pointed toward Threlmak's body, "over any and every slave in Blackwall. I operate with the full approval of Lord Mabon himself. In your case, I wanted you to see just how beneficent I can be. But since it was such an expensive undertaking, I'm sure you'll understand that your friend must remain here in the palace as Lord Mabon's guest for a while."

"Basically, you're telling me he's your hostage to ensure that I don't resist you."

"'Hostage' is such a troublesome word." Salas replied. "But I think you do understand the situation well enough. Thus, it really does behoove you to give me, and anyone else here, every cooperation."

Fury burned in Lyrien, fury at what Master Salas was threatening. The fury was coupled with disbelief, though, and it left him unable to respond. Gade was alive—if it was really him, and not some elaborate trick—but the hateful man had Lyrien right where he wanted him. One wrong step, one refusal to acquiesce, and the dover would suffer, or they might even kill him again outright. He stared across at this creature that was supposed to be his friend, caught his eye. The dover—Lyrien refused to admit that it really was Gade, yet—seemed to grow excited for a moment, but the captain saw a distinct look of unease in his eyes. Unease, and something else: a profoundly haunted stare. It seemed clear to Lyrien that he really only had one choice.

"All right," Lyrien said, grating his teeth. "You leave me little choice, it appears. But first, I want to talk to Gade. I want proof that it's really him."

"Of course," Master Salas answered. "I wouldn't have it any other way, actually. But he's really in no condition right now. You can visit with him tomorrow, if you like," the man said, rising from his seat. "But regardless, I'm so pleased you understand our position now."

Lyrien merely grunted, unsure of anything. The man had played him well, he realized. Master Salas knew just what his weakness would be and then exploited it. He wanted to slam his fist against something, preferably Salas's face. He jerked uselessly at the shackles binding his arms behind him.

"Well, come on," the bald-headed man said, gesturing. Bruhark stood too, then turned and waited for Lyrien to join them. "I think it's finally time to meet His Lordship."

Lyrien sullenly turned and followed Master Salas out of the temple and back into the evening, casting one last look back at Gade, or the likeness of him. The dover gave a quick but forlorn wave. The captain was at the point of despair and had no idea how to extract himself from this mess.

The three of them made their way back to the main building, passing through the gardens once more. Then Master Salas took Lyrien in a new direction, up several flights of broad stairs to a level higher than he had been thus far. Finally, they ascended one last spiraling staircase that deposited them in an anteroom, open and airy, with many wide windows looking out onto the cool night sky, with just a tint of blush to indicate that one of the suns might be rising soon.

Lyrien shook his head in confusion. "What time is it?" he asked his escort.

"About Tenth Shroud," Master Salas replied. "Crux will be up soon. You slept late," he added with a knowing chuckle.

Lyrien shook his head again, still trying to understand the hours of the day and the normal course of activities that followed them. "How can I have slept so late when it is still dark out?"

Salas cast a quick glance toward Lyrien as he led the captain past another hulking pair of ogre guards and toward a wide, curtained archway. "It's midway between breakfast and lunch," he said with some disdain. "When Crux rises, it marks the midday meal."

"I see," Lyrien replied in mild surprise. "On my world, we get up with the sun and eat our midday meal when it is directly overhead."

"Then you lived in a strange world, indeed," Salas remarked as he parted the curtains and gestured for Lyrien to precede him inside.

The room beyond was like something out of a ribald tale of old. Immediately beyond the curtained doorway was a spacious area, dimly lit and lavishly decorated all in red, from the heavy drapes that hung from every wall to the thick, plush carpeting that hid the floor. Even the lamps were screened in red, casting an eerie crimson tone to the whole place. The air was smoky from braziers and incense burners, filling the chamber with a sweet-smelling haze. Columns filled the room and helped to divide it into different areas, like individual conversation nooks in a parlor. Beaded curtains further delineated those private alcoves, though they did not completely hide the spaces beyond.

Lyrien could see collections of furniture, broad couches and cushions thrown together in piles, and he could see forms, dozens of them, lounging on the cushions and couches, coupling or sleeping or perhaps talking in low, murmuring voices. Again, there was a wide variety of species, every type of creature he had seen thus far, and several more besides. The whole sensual essence of the place made his head swim, on the verge of losing his self-control. He felt overwhelmed with desire, even as he was appalled at his own reaction.

God! Last night wasn't enough?

Lyrien shook his head, trying to clear it of the dizzying feeling of eroticism that was tantalizing him. He tried not to look too closely at anyone as he passed them, concentrating instead on simply following where the guide in front of him went.

Master Salas led him past the den of hedonism and through a second curtained doorway. In the center of the chamber beyond, which was circular, there was a raised platform, with the largest round bed the captain had ever seen atop it. Sprawled on the couch were several creatures. They were intertwined with one another, though they seemed to be dozing or sleepily observing some of the other creatures spread out on the floor around the platform. Around the perimeter of the smaller, more intimate chamber, a host of muscled, naked guards stood, eunuchs perhaps, somehow ignoring the whole display before them. They watched Lyrien with sharp expressions, but they didn't move.

Salas strolled right to the platform, knelt on the edge of it and bowed to a creature, a demon if Lyrien had ever seen one. Skin that was black as coal was stretched tightly over its skeleton, and its lips were peeled back in a perpetual devilish grin. Long, yellow claws extended from its bony fingers and toes, and a pair of swept back horns protruded from its ridged skull. Currently, it had its head propped up with one arm under its head, watching as Lyrien and his escorts approached.

"Hello, Oderic," the ebony creature said to Master Salas, its voice as harsh as gravel on a washboard. Lyrien realized that was the first time he had heard the bald-headed man's first name. He stared with a mixture of horror and fascination at the creature in front of him, already certain he knew its identity.

"My lord, I've brought the gladiator to see you," Master Salas said, rising to his feet once more and stepping back. He motioned subtly with his head for Lyrien to step forward, presenting himself to the black beast. Reluctantly, the captain did so.

The creature sat upright, nudging a naked, green-scaled humanoid woman gently aside. She rolled over onto her side and propped her head in one hand, looking back at Lyrien with a smug smile on her face. "Ah, yes, the gladiator. I am Lord Galak Mabon. Welcome to my harem."

Lyrien merely gazed at the black creature levelly, wondering what was expected of him now.

"When I arrived, he was arguing with the harem slave I sent to his bed last night," Salas said casually. "She was trying to convince him of the folly of attempting to escape, but he was having none of it."

"Oh, really?" Lord Mabon replied, looking Lyrien up and down critically. "Then I suppose it's quite a surprise that you have joined me this morning," he said.

"Hardly surprising at all, considering that Ezeria and Gade would pay for my 'transgressions,' even though neither would be guilty of anything," Lyrien said, carefully keeping his gaze on the foot of the bed. Around the three of them, the carnal revelry had continued unabated. "I won't make them suffer for something they can't control."

"He's quite the chivalrous fellow," Salas offered. "He actually threatened Bruhark earlier; I had to have him restrained before we could visit."

Lord Mabon pursed his lips in an expression of surprised admiration. Lyrien wasn't sure whether it was genuine or derisive. "Well, that's good to know," the demonic creature said thoughtfully, tapping a finger against his lips. "Very good to know. Well," he continued, shifting forward and rising from the bed, "first, I want to introduce you to someone, and then we can enjoy some repast." The bloodlord turned to a dover standing nearby. "Titus," he said, "I want to see Jezindi. Have someone bring her to me." The dover nodded and trotted off. The bloodlord of Blackwall then donned a robe and sat examining the claws of his hands while they waited.

After a time, a sinewy haze approached, a naked human female in tow by means of a thick chain that was attached to a very stout iron collar around the woman's neck. The slave would have been pretty, Lyrien thought, again self-consciously trying to avoid gazing at her entire form, if her short, dark hair wasn't matted and filthy and plastered to her head. The slave seemed in a daze, her large, dark eyes half-closed, her hands draped loosely over the chain in front of her as though she were using it to steady herself. She stumbled as she followed her keeper toward the table, swaying and weaving.

The haze brought the slave toward Lord Mabon, who took hold of the chain very near to where it was attached to her collar. "Thank you, Fairblood." Using the collar as leverage, the bloodlord forced the girl down to her knees, which to Lyrien seemed to be a relief for her.

"There," Mabon said, pointing to Lyrien. "Take a look." The slave blinked a couple of times then turned to stare at Lyrien. Her eyes might have widened the tiniest bit, might have flickered in recognition for an instant, but she merely nodded and let her head droop as much as the collar would allow. "What do you see, Jezindi?" Mabon demanded.

The slave mumbled something that the captain could not make out. "Louder," Mabon insisted, yanking upward on the chain in his fist, drawing the girl's face up close to his own.

She cringed as she slid forward on her knees, her neck strained at an awkward angle. "As strong as steel, yet as supple as a reed in the marsh," she said, her voice soft, and thick with slurring. "He cannot be broken, and his death would bring your downfall."

Lyrien blinked, confused by these cryptic words. Broken? Downfall? What was going on?

"Is there anything else?" Lord Mabon asked, drawing her even closer to him and staring at her balefully.

The slave named Jezindi flailed helplessly, her small hands fluttering in fists near where the bloodlord had a hold of her, as though she wanted to tear herself free but was afraid to do so. "No, Master!" she sobbed, shaking her head as much as his grasp would allow. "No other visions about him."

Somehow, Lyrien knew the slave was lying and was trying to conceal it from her master. He wanted to leap across the open space to stop Galak Mabon from further tormenting this poor slave girl. He clenched his fists tightly where they were locked behind him and reminded himself of the futility. Letting out a long, slow breath, he eased his taut muscles. Even though he hadn't taken a step, he realized with a start that three of Mabon's concubines were standing between him and the bloodlord, who was still seated on the bed. At the same time, he felt a heavy hand grab him by the shoulder from behind. Lyrien knew without looking that it was Bruhark.

Lyrien was impressed. One moment, everyone had been lounging on plush cushions, and the next, they were alert, wary, apparently ready to take him down if he made even a single threatening step toward anyone there. The ogre didn't pull him back or push him down to the floor, but it was obvious from the guard's grip that Lyrien would not get a chance to reach the bloodlord without a struggle. Somehow, they were well attuned to threats, even potential ones, to their master.

Lord Mabon didn't seem to notice the sudden protective barricade, or if he did, he didn't show it. He shoved the slave girl away with a snort of derision, and she collapsed at the foot of the haze who had brought her to the patio. "Get her out of my sight, Fairblood," the bloodlord growled, his voice raspy. "We'll see if she has anything else to tell me about our new addition in a couple of weeks."

The haze nodded and yanked the girl to her feet by one arm, taking hold of the chain and pulling her along. Jezindi stumbled helplessly behind the haze, still seeming to be groggy and unbalanced, as the two of them left.

Lyrien watched the guard half-drag the girl out of sight. The concubines returned to their lounging, apparently believing the potential threat was over.

"So, you have a soft spot in your heart for poor Jezindi, eh, gladiator?" Lord Mabon said casually as he stood up.

Lyrien said nothing, but he hoped his glare made it plain that he disapproved of everything the bloodlord was about.

"Ah, well. We can continue this discussion over some breakfast. I have a business proposition to make to you, gladiator. Come on, Oderic, there's a place set for you, too."

Lyrien suspected his eyes must have betrayed his feelings upon hearing Lord Galak Mabon's revelation, for the smile that crossed the bloodlord's face was one of amusement. The captain still felt no small amount of anger, though it simmered just below the surface of his thoughts for the moment. Instead, confusion roiled through him; he was stunned at the bloodlord's offer.

Lyrien looked at Master Salas askance, but the bald man merely smiled and gestured for the captain to follow Lord Mabon. Bruhark fell in behind them, his hand still resting upon the back of Lyrien's neck.

The quartet moved through several other rooms of the inner harem until they passed through an archway onto a large veranda, an upper-level patio that looked out over the endless stretch of gardens that Lyrien had been able to view from his own chambers earlier. From that vantage point, Lyrien could see a large hedge maze. The gardens sprawled off into the cool pre-dawn air as far as

Lyrien could see by the light of the two moons. He briefly noted with mild surprise that the ruddy-hued moon had moved higher overhead in the sky just since their visit to the temple, and that its phase had changed to one-quarter illumination. The other moon was near to setting.

Glancing back down into the gardens, Lyrien could easily imagine inhabitants of the harem consorting and chatting in secret places all through the grounds. In fact, he could see several figures moving about down there, and he had to remind himself that darkness had very little connection with the time of the day there. On the veranda, a number of additional harem concubines lounged on soft cushions and couches around the perimeter of the patio. Others swam languidly in a crystal-clear pool of water that sat adjacent to the patio, also overlooking the gardens.

The bloodlord himself sat down at a table laden with a delightful assortment of foods, beverages, and even a collection of powders, serums, and tobaccos that the captain assumed to be stimulants and aphrodisiacs. Lyrien took advantage of the bloodlord's stillness to study him further. In addition to the simple robe, several gold rings and other bits of jewelry adorned Lord Mabon. He placed an ornate dagger on the table near at hand, which he occasionally reached for and caressed fondly, regularly, almost subconsciously. Then Mabon turned and regarded Lyrien. "Release him, Bruhark," the bloodlord said. The ogre moved to obey at once, although Salas raised a single eyebrow in surprise.

Once the manacles were gone, Lord Mabon gestured to the empty seat across from him. "Please, have something to eat," the bloodlord said.

Lyrien stood frozen, rubbing his wrists, and shook his head. "Thank you, but no," he replied, finding his voice at last. Though the aromas of the feast laid out before him made his mouth water and his stomach growl, the captain was not much in a mood for pleasantries. Besides, he had no idea whether the food was safe to eat or not. For all he knew, the bloodlord might be intending to drug or poison him. But then he saw Salas take a seat to one side of the black creature and immediately begin filling a plate with food.

He might know which things to avoid, Lyrien tried to convince himself. Or maybe something will be slipped into my drink after it's been poured.

Lord Mabon looked at Lyrien. "Few refuse me," he said casually, giving his head a subtle shake, looking past Lyrien to something unseen. The captain turned around and saw that Bruhark, as well as several other of the ever-present guards, had started forward, toward him, but were now retreating once more, retaking their places along the periphery of the patio. "Or rather, few refuse me and live long afterward," Lord Mabon continued, returning his stare toward Lyrien.

Oderic looked at Lyrien, who saw a sort of desperate gleam in the man's eyes. "For you, that quality can be valuable, to a point. It will serve you well for what I have planned. But seriously, when Lord Mabon offers you a place at his table, it is not wise to refuse. And I know you haven't had a decent meal since you were captured, and possibly not even for a while before that. It's perfectly wonderful fare, and I'd hate for it to go to waste. Now, why don't you come have a seat?" the bald-headed man said, gesturing to an empty chair.

"Or, if you don't want to eat," Lord Mabon added, holding up an ornate silver bowl, "you could at least enjoy a fine smoke with me." The bowl's lid was off, and Lyrien could see it contained a rich, aromatic tobacco. With his other hand, Lord Mabon extended a clean pipe, similar to the one resting at his own elbow, toward the captain. He gave an expression that Lyrien assumed was a smile, his feral mouth widening the slightest bit.

Lyrien wasn't sure how to deal with the figure before him. He had expected a man, and the reality was a surprise, but more puzzling than that was the bloodlord's agreeability. He wanted to hate the creature in front of him, and he could easily remind himself of all the cruelty he had experienced and witnessed since arriving in Blackwall, but the pleasant conversation was breaking down his resistances. Anyone responsible for the enslavement and merciless torture of so many should not be so . . . respectable. Or perhaps the fiend was using some sort of magic to persuade him.

On impulse, Lyrien tried to focus his thoughts on the presence of magic. He peered at the black creature before him, concentrating on . . . he didn't know what. There was a flicker, maybe, a brief glow that surrounded the bloodlord, or rather some of the jewelry he wore, and there was something that he suspected was a complex pattern of sorcery, but it faded again almost as soon as it appeared, and Lyrien could not bring it back. He wasn't even sure he had seen anything at all.

Finally, Lyrien sat, letting his sudden ravenous hunger get the best of him. He mentally shrugged at his fear of duplicity, figuring that the civility was either genuine, in which case the creature in front of him didn't mean any harm to him for the moment, or it was a charade, in which case the bloodlord was going to inflict whatever cruelties he had in mind upon Lyrien whether the captain let himself be drugged or not. Ultimately, eating or not eating wasn't going to change the circumstances appreciably, and it just smelled too good.

"Ah, that's better," Lord Mabon commented as Lyrien took a plate and began to load it with food. There were eggs smothered in a spiced cheese sauce, and some sort of black sausage that smelled of sage and mild chilies, Pan-fried fish drenched in butter cream, mushroom caps stuffed with glazed liver pate, a vegetable soufflé, and a dozen other things that Lyrien had never seen before, but which smelled wonderful. When he couldn't get anything else on his plate, the captain set it before him and began shoveling bites in his mouth with gusto. The flavors were magnificent, each one dancing on his tongue and blending together, just as Gade had told him they would. Thinking of his companion only reminded Lyrien of what he had witnessed only a little while previous, which caused him to cringe. Whether the rafter was alive, as Salas asserted, or still dead, the captain felt no small amount of guilt at his enjoyment of this meal without Gade by his side. But not eating wouldn't do the dover any good, regardless of his condition, and if he was still dead, Lyrien wasn't so sentimental that he would abstain just for the sake of a friend's memory.

A small reptilian serving slave stood nearby, and at a gesture from Mabon, the creature leaped forward and poured a steamy cup of some sort of spiced wine for Lyrien, who sipped at it when it was set before him. His eyes widened in surprise, and he gulped several mouthfuls just to savor the richness of it.

For a time, Mabon watched Lyrien eat, content to sit back in his chair and smoke his pipe. Somehow, the aroma of the tobacco smoke that wafted past Lyrien made the flavors of the food even more delectable, blending with them in just the right way. Until he had begun to consume the fare piled on his plate, Lyrien hadn't realized just how hungry he was, but once he got started, he found he wasn't satisfied until he had gone through two helpings and half of a third.

Finally, he pushed the plate away, not exactly stuffed, but somehow knowing that another bite would only diminish the experience in some way. Mabon nodded and passed the pipe and tobacco toward Lyrien again, and that time, the captain accepted them. He had never smoked much, finding it difficult to take the time to truly enjoy the pastime, but right then and there, it seemed like the perfect way to finish the meal.

The captain filled the bowl of the pipe with some of the shredded leaf from the silver container, then lit it. He held a burning taper to the bowl, drawing some of the flavorful smoke and swirling it around inside his mouth. He took several long pulls from it, savoring the taste of the tobacco, which was quite good, he decided. For several minutes, no one spoke. The three of them just sat at the table, enjoying the aftereffects of the meal and blowing smoke rings into the air between them.

After a while, Oderic cleared his throat. "Since you seem sated for the time being, perhaps we could get down to the business at hand." Mabon made a noise that Lyrien assumed was a chuckle, though it was raspy and grating.

Feeling calm and content for the moment, Lyrien nodded in easy agreement. He still felt some level of caution about what, exactly, they would want from him, but he was willing to hear them out. He imagined that it wasn't every day that the ruler of Blackwall offered to negotiate, instead of simply imprisoning and torturing his guests.

"Yes," the bloodlord said. "I trust you found our little ceremony at the temple pleasing? Always nice to see the return of a long-lost friend, yes?" When Lyrien said nothing, Lord Mabon shrugged and continued. "Based on Jezindi's earlier revelations, it seems I would be better served by working out an agreement with you."

"You see," Salas began, "Lord Mabon has specialists in his employ who are well suited to delve into this unique talent of yours."

"Talent? What talent?" Of the several things Lyrien had guessed at, this was not among them, and he had not expected Master Salas to serve as spokesman. He looked first at Lord Mabon and then at the thin man. "I don't know what talent you're talking about."

"Of course you do. This odd ability to shatter magic. I witnessed it yesterday at the coliseum. It's my understanding that you have no prior experience in the use of magic, though, correct?"

Lyrien gaped at Oderic. "How did you know—?" Then it dawned on him. Salas had been aware of the conditions of the match yesterday. The captain's eyes narrowed and he said in his coldest voice, "The only way you could know that was if you knew the properties of the collars. Gade died because of those collars."

Salas chuckled and nodded. "Indeed," he said. "And now he's alive again." As Lyrien continued to glare, the clean-shaven man waved his hand in dismissal. "Oh, don't look at me that way," he said, still smiling. "It's not as if *I* set the match up. The collars are common knowledge, anyway. You don't think you and your dover friend were the first two to ever wear them during a match, do you?"

Lyrien shrugged, hating this man more and more. His callousness appalled the captain. "I have no disillusions about my worth in your world," he finally muttered.

"Oh, but on the contrary, this gift you possess may prove most valuable. And your lack of denial only tells me you are aware of it. So I wish to put it to good use."

During all of this conversation, Lord Mabon had said little. Lyrien looked over at the bloodlord now, wondering who really ran Blackwall. The black creature seemed to be intently studying one of his concubines at the moment, completely oblivious to the revelations at the table.

"Put it to use for what?" Lyrien inquired. "How long do you need my services?"

"You will learn that when the time is appropriate. And *that* will be determined by how quickly you demonstrate your ability to control your gift," Lord Mabon said. "It all depends on you."

Lyrien's eyes narrowed. "That's too open-ended," he said. "You could deem me to never be ready and keep me here forever."

"I have no need to create elaborate deals if I wanted to do that," Mabon replied. "My offer is forthright."

Lyrien shook his head, still wary.

Salas, apparently sensing Lyrien's reluctance, said, "Trust me, there are many ways we could make this work, but I would much prefer your cooperation. I'm willing to make the whole experience most pleasant."

Lyrien raised an eyebrow. "What, by sending a harem slave to my quarters every night? You think that's enough to convince me to let you poke and prod me like some animal in a cage in your laboratory?"

"Well, I hardly think it will be that unpleasant," Salas said with a dismissive laugh, "but certainly, that and more. Remember, your companion's well-being is in our care. But why stop our generosity there? You can have your pick of just about any slave in the harem." At that point, Master Salas turned to the bloodlord. "Provided that Lord Mabon has no objections," he finished.

Galak Mabon waved a hand in agreement, his concentration on a morsel of food lodged in his teeth. "As long as I don't have a personal need," he said in his gravelly voice.

"See there? Most generous, in my opinion," Salas concluded.

"And if I still refuse?" Lyrien asked finally. "If I choose to abandon Gade—assuming it really is him—and simply leave?"

"You won't refuse," Galak Mabon said, still looking away. Lyrien started to ask how the bloodlord could be so sure, but before he got his mouth open, Mabon continued. "In return for your cooperation, I will see to it that you and your friend both find your ways back to your home worlds."

Lyrien gaped. "How can you—?" he began.

"It can be done," Salas said. "And we will make it happen. Now, do we have an agreement?"

Lyrien considered the possibility. It sounded too good to be true, and yet, it was his best chance to get back to Iandra. He was still not sure he believed any of it. "Any slave in the harem as my own?" he asked.

"Any but Jezindi," Mabon said. "She's not to be touched by anyone but me."

"Yes," Salas said. "And a handful of others who are some of Lord Mabon's personal favorites," he said, turning back to Lyrien. "Or who serve him as his bodyguards. But you wouldn't know them, anyway, nor would you particularly enjoy their company, I'd wager, and there are still plenty of others."

The captain nodded. "Then I want Ezeria."

Salas chuckled. "But there are so many to choose from, and you've hardly had a chance to see—"

"I made my choice," Lyrien said, interrupting. "If you're going to honor your offer, she's the one I want."

Salas opened his mouth as if he intended to argue or even deny Lyrien his request, but then he snapped it shut again in a most unbecoming frown. "Very well," he said at last. "I will have her prepared for you. Now, if you are certain you're done with your meal, then I would like to get started. With your permission?" the bald-headed man inquired of Lord Mabon. The bloodlord seemed to be thinking about anything other than the conversation at hand, but at his henchman's words, he dismissed them both with a wave. Salas rose quickly and gestured for Lyrien to follow. "Come along," he said.

Chapter 10

"Again," Samos insisted, watching Lyrien carefully. "Try it again."

The captain sighed in exasperation and began to feel his way along the invisible wall that the half-elven sage had erected in the middle of room. Even as he focused his attention on trying to see the magic, trying to discern its presence, another part of his mind was reflecting on how an invisible, magical barricade could exist in the first place. As his hands slid along the glassy smooth surface of this wall of force, Lyrien tried to imagine that he could see it, that he could perceive its energy as he had done with the collar in the arena, and the efforts at healing that Gertroll the priest had attempted. For a brief moment there was a flicker, a sort of reddish glow that matched what Lyrien could feel with his hands, and he felt the surface of that invisible barrier flex the slightest bit. Then that glow was gone, and Lyrien might as well have been pushing on steel.

"I felt something," Samos said excitedly. "Tell me what you did!"

Lyrien threw his hands up in the air. "I don't know!" he growled and stalked across the room to sit down on a bench. "Yes, yes, there was something. For a moment, the blink of an eye, I could actually see some sort of power emanating from your magic wall, but then it was gone. I don't know how I saw it. I don't know what I did differently before!"

"That's all right," Samos said, pulling his ear and pursing his lips in thought. "Something must trigger it. We'll figure it out soon enough."

The captain studied the sage on the other side of the room, dismayed at the half-elf's singularity of thought and purpose. The two of them had been at this for a number of hours, and Lyrien was growing weary, both physically and mentally. The spectacled sage with the curly white hair simply paced as he thought, heedless of the toll his studies were taking on his subject. Lyrien would have happily slipped out the door and fled, except for the fact that Bruhark was standing near the only exit from the room. The captain had no doubt that the ogre's single responsibility was to keep him there, cooperating. As if Gade's life wasn't already riding on that very cooperation.

"Try again," Samos said, breaking Lyrien out of his thoughts. "Try to sense the magic with more than just your sight."

Lyrien rolled his eyes, exasperated, but he stood up and crossed the room back to the wall, his hands extended outward to try and find it, as before, initially by touch. When he finally bumped against it, he jammed his finger into its surface slightly. "Damn!" he snarled, yanking his hand back in pain and pulling on his finger to straighten it. He shook his hand to try to throw off the ache and then slammed both palms against the hidden surface, tired of testing.

The reddish glow materialized almost immediately, and Lyrien punched his fist through it in a near rage before he realized what he had succeeded in doing. The wall—or rather, the reddish glow—seemed to shatter into a million motes of light that vanished like shooting stars as they sprayed through the room. Lyrien was left standing there, his fist hovering in mid-air. The wall was gone.

"What did you do?" Samos asked quietly, his eyes wide, staring at where the wall had been a moment before. "You just obliterated it," the sage muttered.

"I don't know," Lyrien said again, though without the previous vehemence. Even he felt a twinge of excitement at the revelation. "I just smacked my hands against it, and when I sensed its energy, I just punched at it."

"So you thought about destroying it, and it appeared?"

"Actually," Lyrien said with a half-smile, "I was wishing it was you and not the wall that I was hitting. I'm more than weary of these tests and games, sage."

"That's excellent!" Samos said excitedly. "Anger! You were angry! Maybe that has something to do with it!"

"Perhaps," Lyrien said doubtfully, mentally going back over the circumstances of the other two incidents. "But I wasn't angry when the priest tried to heal me; I was panicking. The same with the collar."

"All right, then, it's not just anger, but any strong emotion. You need to be emotionally riled up in order to sense the presence of magic." Samos quickly pulled open a drawer at his work table and removed a thin straight piece of iron from it. "You told me before that you had experienced a magical force when the slavers captured you," Samos said as he walked closer to Lyrien. "Was it something like this?" and he waved the piece of iron in Lyrien's direction as he uttered a few unintelligible phrases.

The captain, upon hearing the sage's last question, raised his hand in alarm and opened his mouth to shout a protest, but before he could get the words out, Lyrien was stuck fast, unable to move any part of his body at all, save for breathing. He couldn't even blink his eyelids or change his line of sight. The sensation reminded him strongly of the moment when he and Gade had been taken

in the abandoned streets of Penance, what seemed a lifetime ago.

"Now, I know you can't answer me," Samos said, pulling a stool around and sitting casually on it. "So I want
you to try to eliminate the magic. I'm not releasing the
spell; you'll have to free yourself."

Lyrien wanted to snarl, to leap forward and throttle
this idiot sage. Instantly, he began to tense his muscles,
trying to shove away whatever was holding him fast, but
he couldn't change his position in the slightest. The in-
ability to control his own movement drove him to try all
the harder, growing more and more anxious as the moments slipped by.

I'm suffocating! the captain thought. Damn you, wizard, dispel it!

"Come on, now," Samos said, leaning forward eagerly
to watch the captain's efforts. "It must be getting claus-
trophobic in there. Find it! Find the emotion and break
the spell! I'm not letting you out!"

Lyrien struggled, the panic rising, and then suddenly,
there it was. A greenish-yellow energy seemed to surround him, seemed to cloak his body, and then it was a
simple matter to jerk himself free, to yank on that field of
energy and tear it to shreds. The whole thing disintegrated
as it fell away from him.

"By god!" Lyrien screamed, taking several threatening steps toward Samos, ready to strangle the smug wizard. "What the hell were you doing?"

Bruhark took two large steps and placed his strong,
unyielding fist on Lyrien's shoulder, pulling him back,
away from the half-elf. Lyrien half-turned, ready to go
toe to toe with the brute, but Samos was clapping in delight.

"Excellent!" the sage exclaimed. "You did it! I knew if
you got anxious enough, you'd be able to affect the magic
of my holding spell. Well done!"

"You're crazy," Lyrien muttered, jerking free of the guard's grip but moving away from the sage, rather than toward him. "Don't ever do that again," he added, sitting down on the bench once more.

"But how are we going to learn about this gift of yours if we don't study it from every angle?" Samos asked, apparently genuinely shocked that Lyrien did not share his exuberance over this revelation.

"Enough," Lyrien answered, standing in order to leave. "I've had enough for today." *Just let him try to get in my way,* he thought, eyeing Bruhark balefully.

"Indeed, for today, you have," Oderic Salas said, stepping into the room as though he knew exactly when Lyrien had reached the end of his patience. "You've been at it for nearly twelve hours. I'm sure you're ready for a little rest and relaxation."

"But we're just making headway!" Samos wailed, wringing his hands. "I'll have to get him all riled up again next time," he added. "It'll just waste time."

"That's enough, Samos," Master Salas said, gesturing for Lyrien to join him. "We can't wear our new guest out so quickly, so you'll just have to cease for the day. He'll be back tomorrow."

As Salas turned to exit the room again, Lyrien on his heels and the ogre following behind like a constant shadow, the captain wanted to mutter under his breath, "Like hell I will." Lyrien knew, however that he would return, for Gade's sake. If the dover was, in fact, still alive.

Again, as though the blue-robed man was reading his thoughts, Oderic said, "I've made arrangements for you to spend a few moments—a few moments only, mind you—with your friend the dover, just so you can confirm for yourself that it really is him."

Lyrien nodded curtly, his heart beating heavily in his chest. The thought that he might actually get a chance to come face to face with someone who had died and was brought back to life was more than a little intimidating. But as soon as the notion filled his head, Lyrien wanted to dismiss it, to deny the possibility that Gade had truly been resurrected.

The bald-headed man led Lyrien through several new passages and into the bowels of the palace. Lyrien practically stalked as they went along, still feeling put out with all of his trials and tribulations of the day's research. He was in such a foul mood after that last trick of Samos's, he even considered simply grabbing Master Salas around the neck and dashing his head against a wall so that he could get out of there once and for all. The two problems with that plan were Bruhark's presence and the fact that he really didn't know where he was. Even if he dealt with the ogre first—a big assumption, the caption admitted silently—he was bound to be caught by others who knew better than to allow him to prowl the halls unescorted. Lyrien doubted the bloodlord's generosity would hold over if the captain attempted to escape. He clenched his teeth and willed himself to calmness as they walked.

"Oh, I almost forgot," Master Salas said, turning and handing Lyrien a key. "For you," he said, smiling.

"What's this for?" the captain asked.

"You'll see," was all his escort replied.

The three of them walked the rest of the way in silence, Lyrien brooding over the situation and Salas seemingly content to stroll and study the surroundings of the palace. The blue-robed man led Lyrien into a passage that he at first mistook for the corridor that ran past his own rooms, for the tapestries and rugs were similar, and the length of the hall was lined with the same arched doorways, colorful curtains carefully concealing whatever was inside. But he soon realized that he was on another side of the palace. Oderic led him around a corner to a second hall, and this one, Lyrien realized, was slightly different. The arched doorways contained barred gates in addition to their draped coverings. At one of these doorways, a little further down, Lyrien could see two guards lounging around a small table, apparently playing cards.

As Salas neared the two soldiers, one of the guards stood and gave a casual salute. "Sir?" he inquired crisply, eyeing Lyrien with mild interest for a moment before turning his attention back to the bald-headed slavemaster.

"We're here to see the dover that I had brought here earlier today," Oderic said, dismissing the salute with a wave of his hand.

"Yes, sir," the guard replied, fetching a ring of keys from his belt. He turned and unlocked a padlock that secured a large sliding bolt set into the iron gate covering the archway. The bolt itself prevented the gate from opening without first being slid back. Once the lock was off, the guard slid the bolt back and pulled the gate open, making an ushering motion with his free hand to the two visitors. Lyrien ignored the guard as he pushed through the curtain and into the chamber beyond.

In many ways, the suite was identical to Lyrien's, though the decorations were distinct. The main difference the captain noted immediately was that the balcony was completely enclosed by more iron bars. Beyond them, he could see that both suns were in the sky, though Storm was rising and Crux was setting. At least, he thought they were.

"Well?" Oderic said, bringing Lyrien out of his thoughts on stellar timekeeping. "You said you wanted to see him." Lyrien turned to see Salas pointing to the bed, and when he turned in that direction, he saw what appeared to be Gade sitting on its edge. "I'll be outside. Don't be too long," the slavemaster said, then stepped back through the curtains. Lyrien heard the barred gate clink shut a moment later.

"Gade?" the captain asked softly, stepping forward, approaching the figure on the bed. "Is that really you?"

As soon as the words were out of his mouth, Lyrien thought they sounded ridiculous, but he didn't know what else to say.

The dover looked at him, and Lyrien could see that that same haunted stare was prominent on his face. "Lyrien?" the dover asked. "Is that actually you?"

Lyrien almost chuckled then, realizing how similar the dover's words were to his own. He nodded and sat down beside his counterpart. "Yes. It's really me. How are you feeling?"

"I'm feeling . . ." the dover's attention seemed to drift away for a moment, then came slowly back. "Strange," he said at last. "I'm so confused."

"I can imagine," Lyrien replied. "What do you remember?" He decided to keep his questions vague, to just let the dover talk. He wanted to avoid leading him as much as possible in order to see how accurate the answers to his queries would be. He still wasn't certain this wasn't an elaborate trick of some sort.

"Oh, I remember it all clearly," the dover replied, blinking and staring at nothing. "The coliseum, the choking collar, the . . . the . . ." He stopped, swallowing, and Lyrien could see that he was trembling. "The feel of the axe, slicing into me," he finished with a whisper.

"Then what?" Lyrien prompted.

"That's the part that's confusing me," the dover replied. "And I can't really tell you why. I know I was someplace . . . else, and it doesn't seem real now, but that's not even it." The dover looked directly at the captain. "The thing that's confusing me is that there was no pain there, no sadness, no worries about the future, and yet I still wanted to come back here. I could remember what it was like here, and I wanted to be here."

Lyrien sat back, studying his counterpart. "Why in the world would you want to return to a life as a slave?" he asked.

The dover shrugged. "Because here, even though I'm trapped in a cage, even though my choices aren't my own, I can feel." And he turned to Lyrien, staring earnestly into the captain's eyes. "It's so vibrant, you know? The colors, the textures, the taste of the food. Everything just makes you feel so much more than just alive."

Lyrien nodded. "The world has a certain pull," he admitted. Then, on an impulse, he asked, "What were you and I talking about at the beginning of the match? Right before you . . . you know."

The dover gave Lyrien a penetrating stare. "You mean, when we first found out just what a rotten deal we'd been given by that accursed asherake?" Lyrien nodded. "We were talking about which god we ought to be praying to," the dover said. "Not that it did much good in my case," he finished wryly.

Lyrien smiled, because he knew. Then his smile grew a little bigger, and suddenly, he was laughing out loud, and he clapped Gade on the shoulder. "It's good to see you again, my friend. I don't know how it's possible for you to be back among the living, but I'm damned glad of it." Gade smiled back, and for the first time, Lyrien noticed how tired the dover looked. "Listen," the captain said, "Things are not perfect. We're both guests of the bloodlord. I have promised to do some things for Lord Mabon in exchange for keeping you out of harm's way, if you know what I mean. Once I've fulfilled my obligation, we're both leaving here. I have a promise."

"Get out," Gade whispered fiercely. "Don't trust him; he's a faust! Don't trust any of them! They're going to turn on you the minute you're no longer useful! I know Blackwall. You don't! Don't stay here!"

"I can't leave you here," Lyrien protested. "If I run, they'll . . . do things to you."

"They'll do them, anyway," Gade insisted. "It's not worth it. Find a way out, and go!"

"No," Lyrien said, shaking his head vehemently. "I'm not abandoning you."

Gade opened his mouth to argue further, but at that moment, the curtain parted and Oderic Salas entered the chambers. "Flee!" the dover hissed under his breath.

"All right," Salas said. "You've had plenty of time today to verify his authenticity. It's time we left him to rest for a while."

Lyrien stood. "Listen, Master Salas. You don't have to keep him locked up in here. I gave you my word that I would cooperate, and I will. Let him go."

"I think not," Oderic replied, a hint of a smirk on his face. "Your friend here is too valuable to be set free."

"Valuable? How?"

"As insurance," Salas replied. "Now come on."

With one long look back at Gade, Lyrien followed Salas out the doorway and back into the hall. As they strolled away, Bruhark shadowing him as usual, the guards shut and locked the gate once more.

"So, obviously you're convinced," Salas said. "I told you."

"And I told you," Lyrien replied, perhaps a bit more snappish than he wanted to reveal, "you could trust me. I don't know why you need to keep him locked away."

"He's far better off in there than in many other places in the palace," Salas replied, and when Lyrien recognized the threat hidden in the words, he snapped his mouth shut. He wouldn't push the point if it meant seeing his friend stuck on a pedestal or platform as living art somewhere. He spent the rest of the walk back to his own rooms silently ruminating on his situation.

Finally, they reached the curtained archway that led into the quarters where Lyrien had spent the previous evening. Salas simply gestured for the captain to enter and turned and headed away back down the hall, whistling softly. Bruhark moved to take a position on the opposite side of the hall from the archway, resting against the wall. Lyrien looked at the ogre for a moment, realizing the guard was going to stand there to make sure he didn't try to leave. Finally, shrugging, Lyrien stepped through the curtain and into his rooms.

The captain found Ezeria huddled, naked and miserable, at the foot of the bed, a cumbersome iron collar fastened around her neck. The collar was thick and wide enough so that she could not even turn her head more than a small distance in any direction. A chain was locked to the collar, the other end of which was bolted to a ring set into the stone floor. The half-elven woman had maybe four feet of play in the chain, but she hadn't strayed far from the cushion-strewn throw-rug that had been tossed down next to the fastening point. She looked up as Lyrien entered, and her eyes brightened slightly at the sight of him.

"Please tell me you have some way to release me," she said, getting to her knees and jingling the chain.

Lyrien considered the key Master Salas had handed him a while ago. "I suppose that is what this is for," he said, holding it out for the woman to see, trying to focus just on her face and not the rest of her curvaceous body. "But why did they do this to you? How long have you been here?"

"Since Spark, I guess," Ezeria replied, more than a little exasperation in her voice, "and because I have been given to you," she added, looking at the key with hope in her eyes. "Apparently, you requested me for your very own. I guess I must not have done a half-bad job of convincing you last night, after all."

"I still don't get it," the captain said as he moved closer and examined the collar and chain. "Master Salas said I could have my very own companion from the harem; we never spoke about locking you up here while I was gone." There turned out to be two locks, not one. The first held the collar shut about Ezeria's neck, while the second one connected the chain to the collar. The chain itself was permanently connected to the ring on the floor.

"Because I was *given* to you," Ezeria said, sounding like an impatient parent explaining something to a child. "I belong to you, now. It's up to you to decide what becomes of me at any point of the day or night. I was delivered here the moment you chose me."

Lyrien paused in his examinations. "Keep up with that tone, and you can just stay right there," he said, keeping his face carefully neutral.

Ezeria's eyes widened at the implication, and she looked directly into Lyrien's, perhaps seeking some sign of his demeanor. At last, the beginning of a smile cracked the captain's façade, and when the half-elf saw it, she sighed loudly and playfully punched him in the shoulder. "You're mean!" she said, laughing. "Now please, master, unlock this poor slave girl so she may better serve you," she added, her voice growing instantly more sensual.

Lyrien grunted at the soft blow to his arm as he inserted the key. It fit, and he quickly released the lock on the collar itself. As the iron semicircles swung apart, Ezeria gave a thankful sigh and slipped free, rubbing and stretching her neck. "Oh, thank the gods that's finally off."

"So where are your clothes?" Lyrien said, looking around for them so she could dress. He wasn't about to make her spend any more time as she was, for his sake as much as for her own modesty. While he could see nothing for her to wear, he did note with both satisfaction and relief that an open wardrobe cabinet in one corner of the room held several sets of clothing for him—loose shirts and breeches with a matching doublet and nice supple leather boots, much more practical than the foolish outfit he'd been wearing since the coliseum.

"I don't own any," the half-elven beauty replied, standing and stretching in such a way that Lyrien had to make himself turn away again just to avoid staring. "Not until you deign to allow me to wear some. Even then, they belong to you, and you can take them away again as you see fit." The tone in Ezeria's voice was still playful, and as Lyrien considered this, she walked around to where he faced, sashaying into his field of view with a saunter that left no doubt of her intentions.

"Well, how am I supposed to get anything for you to wear?" he asked, trying desperately to keep his gaze directly on her face, though even that didn't help, for her emerald eyes glittered suggestively. "I have nothing to buy any with, nor would I know where to steal some from. Not to mention that I'm confined to the room, myself."

"Then I guess you'll just have to keep me as I am," Ezeria purred, walking toward him now. He opened his mouth to protest, to tell her that he wasn't ready to do this again, to tell her anything he could think of to get her to stop with the teasing. But somehow, he could sense that that time, she wasn't pretending. Somehow, he knew that that time, she wasn't auditioning for some test. The protestations died in his throat as she closed to him and took him by the hand.

"Come on," she said, smiling demurely at the captain. "Why don't you enjoy a hot soak? I'll wash your back," she said, leading him toward the basin, where a steaming bath was waiting.

Lyrien opened his mouth to ask how it stayed hot all the time, then snapped it shut again as Ezeria began to undress him. Once she had him disrobed, she guided him into the steaming water and slipped into it behind him.

Magic, he decided. It must be magic.

* * * * *

"Are you content being a slave?" Lyrien asked Ezeria, wondering why he was so willing to break the mood with such a pointed question. They were lying on the bed again, though he was on his stomach and Ezeria was now straddling him, kneading the muscles in his back. They had coupled several times since his return to the room, and he was both exhausted and relaxed.

"There are worse ways to spend my days than this," she said, a smile in her voice. "Lord Mabon treats me well enough. And I am not a mere slave; I am a harem concubine."

"Yes, of course," he said sarcastically. "You're hiding behind semantics. You're locked up, but you don't notice because it's with a golden chain." He didn't bother to hide the bitterness.

"What difference does it make to you?" Ezeria asked. "I'm happy enough."

"I can't believe that. Mabon and his toady Oderic Salas are both despicable."

Ezeria rolled off the captain and he sat up to look at her. She stared at Lyrien worriedly. "Not this again," she said. "You are too new to understand. This is just the way it is. It's not Lord Mabon's fault. He was a slave once, too, but he rose to his position through cleverness and cunning. He didn't create our society, he only excelled within it."

"That's nice." Lyrien muttered. He doubted he could ever accept the act of committing atrocities as simply working within the system. Whether Mabon had created the slavery or not, the system was wrong, and he burned with the desire to break it. He wondered why she was so quick to defend the creature that had enslaved her. "He may have started out a slave, but he's not one now, and he has the means to change it if he wants to."

Ezeria laughed, a melodic noise that he would have found enchanting at some other time. At that moment, though, he could hear his father's own laugh in there, though his father would not merely be amused; his father would be belittling him.

Always standing up for lost causes, he could hear the man saying; always fighting the crusade that no one else cares about. Questioning his practicality was one thing, but ridiculing his values made Lyrien wonder how he had ever managed to grow out of the man's shadow at all.

Lyrien blinked, realizing that Ezeria had said something and was now watching him expectantly. "I'm sorry?" he said, embarrassed that he had let his thoughts wonder.

"I said, You don't believe it, do you?"

"Not for a minute. I'd be fighting my way out of here in a second if they weren't holding threats over my head."

"What do you mean?"

Lyrien shook his head in disgust, thinking on the situation. Then he told Ezeria about Gade, about how they had met and been captured, and about the dover's death in the coliseum. Then he told her about witnessing the resurrection earlier in the day, and the conversation with Gade right before returning to his rooms. "The thing is," he said when he had finished the tale, "they didn't just imprison me, try to force me to do their bidding. Instead, they've used other people against me. Like Gade. Like you."

"Of course," Ezeria said, sitting cross-legged on the bed next to the captain, drawing a surprised look from him. "You're too willful for them to try to force anything on you directly. But they know your weakness, and they're exploiting it."

"Well, it's not just that, I don't think," the captain said, flopping back to the pillows and staring up at the ceiling, his hands behind his head. "Lord Mabon had someone 'read' me today. A slave named Jezindi. She made some wild claim about me being unbending and unbreakable, and the downfall of anyone who tried to kill me, or some such nonsense."

"Ah-hah," Ezeria said. "That makes even more sense."

"Who the hell is this Jezindi?"

"A pathetic creature with a very valuable gift," Ezeria answered. "She can know things about people just by looking at them. But she's very sad. I think she would find a way to kill herself, if Lord Mabon didn't take great pains to prevent it. I've heard that when she first arrived as a seed, she went crazy, screaming and crying about something that had happened. No one really knows what it was, though, because afterward, she just sat and stared vacantly. If it wasn't for her gift, I'm sure Lord Mabon would have had her killed already."

"So, whatever it was that she told the bloodlord, he firmly believes."

"Because it always seems to come true. Somehow, she always tells the truth, although often, you don't realize what it was until after the fact. Anyway, if she said all those things about you, then Lord Mabon isn't about to try to force you to do what he wants. He'll use blackmail instead, just like you described. Like I said before, he and Master Salas know your weakness and they're exploiting it; you're very idealistic." She began to play with the hem of the sheet as she continued. "Not that I'm not grateful, believe me. Still, I haven't met such a strong idealist in a long time. It's refreshing."

Lyrien smirked. "I'm glad *someone* appreciates it. It hasn't really served *me* too well so far."

"I said it was refreshing, not that it was wise." She leaned in now, her mouth close to Lyrien's ear. "But if you really do feel that way," she whispered, "then there's someone you should meet." She unraveled herself from the bed linens then and stood up.

"What, right now?" Lyrien asked. Just seeing her beauty before him again was stirring his thoughts to another round of coupling. He lowered his voice at her wordless admonition to be quiet. "It's the middle of the night."

"That is precisely why it should be right now," she replied. "Get dressed," she whispered, and then sighed in resignation as she took up the sheet. "He's going to think this is the only thing I ever wear to come visit him," she muttered as she wrapped it around herself.

Lyrien frowned and came to Ezeria. "Wait a minute," he said softly, taking her by the arm and turning her to face him. "What's going on?"

The half-elven woman looked at him, pursing her lips. "I'm not just a concubine in Mabon's harem. I also work for another. If you really want to escape Blackwall, be free of Mabon's rule, then you should meet him."

"Why should I trust this 'him?'"

"That's for you to decide, once you meet him."

"Then why should I trust you?"

"I've got nothing to gain by deceiving you," she replied, running her fingers down his chest, "and so much to gain by making you happy." Then she pulled away. "Hurry, now, and get dressed; there's not much time."

"How are we going to get past the guards that are everywhere?" the captain asked, even as he began to dress, thankful that, wherever she was taking him, at least he could dress appropriately.

"Leave that to me," Ezeria replied. "But first, a little enchantment to keep suspicious folk from peeking in on us." And she moved toward the doorway to the room with the basin. Standing very still, she began to weave her arms in a complex pattern, while at the same time muttering a lilting string of nonsensical phrases. When she finished, she made one last gesture, and suddenly, Lyrien could see an image of the two of them sitting in the bath, could hear the sounds of gentle splashing, and two sets of playful laughter. It made him blush.

"You can wield magic," he said, no longer surprised by anything.

"Quite so," Ezeria replied. "And I'm about to wield it again, so ready yourself," and before Lyrien could open his mouth to protest, the elven beauty began again, weaving her hands through the air and mouthing more of the strange sing-song language.

There was a sudden flash, and Lyrien had a moment of unbridled panic, for it reminded him of his arrival. But in the blink of an eye, he was simply standing somewhere else, Ezeria right beside him.

The pair of them were in a rather small chamber, an office, it appeared. In addition to a large desk of a rich, dark wood and a matching ornate chair behind it, the entire place was filled from floor to ceiling with bookshelves of the same material. The whole room was warmly lit by lamps on lamp stands.

Seated behind the desk was a middle-aged man with a salt-and-pepper beard and moustache, hunched over a very large book. He was scribing something into its pages, and he didn't seem to flinch or start in the slightest as Lyrien and Ezeria arrived. Instead, he kept at his work for a moment longer, leaving Lyrien feeling a little intrusive.

Finally, the man put his quill down and looked up at the two of them, a smile on his face. "Ah, Ezeria," he said with a deep, mellow voice. "You convinced him. Excellent." The man stood and walked around the desk to stand before Lyrien, his hand extended. "I'm Effron Cadmus. I'm sorry for the clandestine nature of my methods in setting up this meeting, but you will understand once you hear what I have to say."

Lyrien shook the man's hand, though he said nothing.

"Please, sit down," Cadmus said, gesturing toward a comfortable-looking set of overstuffed chairs across from his desk. He then returned to his own chair and dropped into it, leaning back with his fingers interlaced behind his head. "I know you probably have innumerable questions, but let me get to the point, and maybe I can answer some of them.

"First, let me make it clear that Ezeria has risked her life tonight bringing you here. In fact, both of our lives. It's your choice whether to accept what we tell you and keep it to yourself, or to reveal what you learn tonight to Galak Mabon. But Ezeria wouldn't have convinced me that it was all right to have her bring you here if she didn't think you're a man worth trusting, so we're going to proceed as though we can."

"Fair enough," Lyrien said, settling into the chair.

Cadmus nodded and continued. "I know a little bit about your predicament. Mabon has you jumping through a number of hoops, yes? I'm sure there's also a promise of great reward if you cooperate."

Lyrien nodded, wondering how the man could have found that out so quickly.

"He's a cunning one, that Galak Mabon," Cadmus said. "He's also not to be trusted. The minute you let down your guard, he'll stab you in the back. But I can solve your problems. In fact, I want to. If you'll let me, I will arrange your escape, yours *and* your dover friend's. But in return, I'd like you to perform a task for me."

Here it comes, Lyrien thought. "What would that be?" he asked suspiciously, already knowing he was going to dread the answer.

"I want you to kill one of Mabon's concubines."

Chapter 11

Lyrien nearly laughed out loud. "What?" he asked, trying to recover. "You honestly believe I can kill someone in Lord Mabon's palace and get away with it? He has the palace more heavily guarded than you can imagine! Even if I could get through all of that without getting caught, I am no assassin." The thought of eliminating someone purely for another's gain made him ill.

"Oh, I absolutely believe it," Effron Cadmus replied, staring at Lyrien directly without even the merest hint of humor in his own visage. "At least, with a little help from us. You see, I want to see Galak Mabon's reign ended. I want to topple him from his perch as the bloodlord and bring about a better way of life to the people of Blackwall. And I'm not alone. There are a number of others who feel as I do, but we're fighting a difficult battle. By doing this, you would be helping the whole population of the bloodhold."

Lyrien shook his head in incredulity. "Why should I trust you?"

"Why shouldn't you?" Cadmus stood from his chair and began to pace behind his desk. "I've trusted that you'll keep this meeting a secret. I've put my life—both Ezeria's and mine, in fact—our lives into your hands by bringing you here. So I'm trusting you."

"That didn't answer my question," Lyrien replied, smiling faintly.

"Because I know that, should you find out I've betrayed you in some way, you'd simply tell Lord Mabon about me."

Lyrien grunted noncommittally. "Maybe, but doing so would also confirm my own complicity in the whole affair. And what if you're actually in league with Lord Mabon, working to try to trick me into betraying him, just to see if I will? He and I have an understanding, but I wouldn't put it past him to test me. He seems fond of those," the captain added, looking over at Ezeria, who had moved away and was browsing some of the tomes on a shelf across the room.

"I can't prove that I'm not," Effron answered. "But I would ask you to consider that Ezeria believes in me. Do you trust her?"

Lyrien didn't answer the nobleman as he sat and watched the half-elf thumb through some pages. *That's a very good question*, he thought. *And I don't know the answer.*

"In any event," Cadmus continued, "if saving the population of Blackwall from the depraved appetites of Galak Mabon is not enough reason to convince you to do this—and I think it is, based on what I've heard about your impeccable morals—then the other part of my offer should; succeed, and I can provide you with your freedom."

"I'd need several weeks to plan, at the very least," Lyrien began, already trying to piece together the tactics necessary to accomplish the task. "I'd need to know where this concubine was at any given time, determine where the guards were and when the most opportune time would be to get past them, and a dozen other particular bits of information that I would have to research firsthand. Unfortunately, I have an ogre shadowing me all the time. And I don't even have a weapon. It's a suicide mission." He sat forward in his chair. "Besides, why would you want me to kill a concubine? How does that help your cause?"

"Valid points, all. And I can give you all the answers you want. But understand that I am no happier about this solution than you are." Effron leaned back in his chair, staring at the ceiling for a moment as if collecting his thoughts. Finally, he continued. "The harem slave is a girl named Jezindi."

Lyrien started. "I've met her," he explained when Cadmus raised a quizzical eyebrow. "Mabon forced her to do some sort of reading on me."

"Then you understand how she can be a threat to me and the rest of my supporters. We're a part of Lord Mabon's court, advisors and land owners in our own right. It's a position we've worked long and hard to obtain. But we fear to plan any specific, detailed action so long as she is around to expose us."

"Ah," Lyrien said, understanding at last. "She can read your true colors and would tell Lord Mabon."

"Precisely," Cadmus said, nodding. "And if there was any less lethal way to remove her, we would have done it already. In fact, we've tried to extract her from the palace three times now. Each attempt has ended in utter failure. No, worse than failure; each one has put Mabon on guard, caused him to tighten his security around her."

"But if I could get her out rather than slay her . . ." Lyrien began, seeing a possibility that was much more to his liking.

"I would welcome it, of course. In fact, try that first, if you wish," Cadmus said, nodding earnestly. "By all means, make the effort. But, if it becomes untenable, if you should run into difficulties that make that impossible, then fall back on my plan."

"It won't be necessary," Lyrien said firmly. "There's no way I'm killing this woman."

"Nevertheless, I will provide you with a weapon. Don't use it unless you have to, but if there's no alternative, use it. We can't move until we eliminate this threat to our secrecy."

"There's another problem," Lyrien said, pursing his lips. "Assuming I am forced to resort to your backup plan, how will you keep her dead? Lord Mabon has the ability to resurrect people. I know; I watched it first-hand."

"Another good question. You are astute, and it makes me confident that we've recruited the right man for the job. The dagger I'm going to give you is enchanted. It's going to take care of that little problem for us. And let me add that, if you are discovered before you ever reach her, use it on yourself," Cadmus Effron said quietly, leaning forward across his desk to emphasize his point. "If you are caught, your punishment will be dreadful, I assure you. You may think you can withstand whatever the bloodlord and his slavemaster have to inflict upon you, but you would be deluding yourself. I've seen some of the most strong-willed individuals try to hold up, but all of them failed in the end. Eventually, you will be begging Lord Mabon to let you tell him everything you know. Despite your best intentions, you will expose my companions and me, and I think you know we can't have that."

Lyrien nodded slowly, digesting the nobleman's words. If it came to that—but he was going to make sure it didn't.

"All right," Lyrien said. "Let me think about it. After all, I don't have anything but your claim that Lord Mabon will renege on his promise. I need some time to weigh my options."

"Well, don't weigh too long," Cadmus replied. "We must act soon; my cohorts grow restless. If we are to succeed in supplanting Mabon and his sick, perverse rulership, we must begin now. Once you've made your decision, Ezeria will bring you back here at an appropriate time."

Lyrien nodded once more. "I understand your urgency," he said. "I just want to really mull over everything I've heard so far."

"I respect that," Effron replied. "Until next time, then."

Lyrien and the nobleman shook hands again, and then the captain moved to stand beside Ezeria, who was now returning from her far corner of the chamber. Somehow, Lyrien thought as he stood near her, she manages to make a bedsheet look amazing. "All right, let's get back," Lyrien said.

"If you follow through with what he asks," the half-elf said, her green eyes flashing, "Many who suffer under Mabon's rule would be freed."

"It's easier said than done," Lyrien replied, "but I'm considering it."

Ezeria nodded somberly, and then, without further comment, began to weave her magic again, and in a quick flash, they were standing back in the suite from where they had departed.

The images and sounds of her little enchantment still carried on in the bath alcove. Both the companions looked around quickly, but there was no sign that anyone was or had been in the suite of rooms during their absence. With a snap of her fingers, Ezeria dismissed the sorcerous magic, then turned to Lyrien. "Come to bed, master," she said, her voice sultry. She turned and sashayed toward the bed, unwrapping the sheet from her body and letting it trail off and onto the floor. She gave Lyrien one glance over her shoulder as she raised a knee and slipped onto the bed.

Lyrien sighed but shook his head. "Not right now," he said, surprised at how hard it was to turn Ezeria's advances down. "I need some time to think."

Ezeria pursed her lips in a frown, but she nodded in understanding. Grabbing the sheet again, she pulled it atop herself and curled up on the copious pillows with a yawn. "Wake me if you change your mind," she said, smiling. Then she laid her head upon her hands and grew still.

Lyrien sighed again, softly, and headed toward the balcony. As he pushed through the gauzy curtains and out onto the tiled patio, he could see the red sun, Storm, sinking low into the western sky. To the south, the rust-colored moon glowed oddly, due to the way both suns shone upon it. It sat perhaps halfway up the sky, lower than the previous night. Lyrien had learned by then that it traveled a different path than the suns or the other moon, for it moved perpendicular to the rest of them and changed its phase over the course of a single night. It was odd, to say the least, and he had long since given up trying to predict where he would see it or how full it would be.

The captain moved to the railing and leaned his arms upon it, looking down into the gardens below. Everything had a crimson hue, and the residual heat of earlier, when both suns had been in the sky, made the air warm and sticky. He could tell, though, that the height of the summer was already fading.

Lyrien quickly forgot his contemplations of the weather and the heavenly bodies drifting through the sky as he pondered all of the choices, all of the dilemmas, before him. There seemed to be no easy answers to this.

Why should I risk my situation here? Or Gade's, for that matter? So far, Lord Mabon has kept to his word, and I'm not suffering much for my cooperation. So why?

Because Cadmus Effron is absolutely right, he told himself. The institution of slavery in Blackwall is a terrible crime against the people here and should be obliterated. He swelled up with his indignation, feeling very strongly at that moment that he should remain true to his convictions and do whatever was necessary to stop the atrocities being committed by the bloodlord. The very next moment, he winced, though, for he imagined he could hear his father ridiculing him for once more taking the high but untenable stance.

Always fighting the noble but lost cause, Lyrien could hear the man say. *Fool-headed notions of justice and righteousness.*

They aren't fool-headed! Lyrien wanted to scream at the mental spectre of his father. *They were your convictions too, once! Why did you abandon them?*

The captain realized he was clenching his fists, his fingernails digging into the palms of his hands, and he relaxed his muscles and slowed his breathing to calm himself.

You're letting your emotions get the best of you tonight, Lyrien silently and ruefully told himself. *No time for emotions in the heat of battle. The question is,* he replied, carrying on this mental debate with himself, *which battle do I choose to fight?*

He spent several hours standing at that balcony, long enough to watch Storm set in the western sky, long enough to see the stars begin to twinkle overhead, and long enough to watch Anahita, the blue moon, rise in the east, nearly halfway to full. When he finally turned to go back inside, to crawl onto the bed beside a faintly snoring Ezeria, to settle atop the covers because it was still too hot and muggy to get under them, he was no closer to an answer. When he finally fell asleep, he dreamed of Iandra.

* * * * *

Streams of sweat rolled off Lyrien and cascaded down his face and body as he studied the footpath before him. He squinted against the late afternoon glow of Crux, the yellow sun, shining in his eyes. The glare made it difficult for him to try to look for the presence of magic, and he was growing ever more frustrated in the sweltering heat. Overhead, Storm shone down unmercifully; with both suns in the sky, the day was unpleasantly warm. Cautiously, he took another step, and then another, staring intently at the ground.

It was the third day of his testing and training with Samos, and the captain and the sage were in the gardens on the grounds of Mabon's palace. They had been joined by two others, individuals who said little to Lyrien directly but who spent a great deal of time privately conversing with one another and with Samos. For the whole of the previous two days, they had conjured up strange magics that trapped, threatened, and even injured him— he had been forced to ingest some rank-smelling substance on two different occasions after suffering wounds from these fools' spells, and both times, he was amazed at the healing power of the liquid—so he was in a particularly foul humor. For the afternoon's activities, they had insisted that Lyrien attempt to move through a cordoned-off area of the gardens, trying to spot their hidden traps.

Despite his anger and resentment over Samos's testing methods, Lyrien had to admit that he was developing a much better rapport with his gift. Although it still didn't manifest itself at will, the captain was learning little by little how to coax it along. He was secretly pleased with the skill he was attaining with it. He hoped that Samos was a pleased as he was, for he didn't know how much longer he could stand to suffer the half-elven sage's maniacal methods. Lyrien was ready to be done with the tests and serve whatever purpose Lord Mabon and Oderic Salas had in mind.

The captain shaded his eyes with one hand as he checked the path again. He willed himself to see the magic, looked everywhere he could think of that might conceal some hint of the glow, and when he was satisfied that there was nothing, he proceeded down the path. On his third step, something coiled tightly around his ankle and jerked him into the air, lifting him up off the ground to hang upside down, flailing helplessly.

"Damnation!" Lyrien snarled, swinging gently back and forth. He hunched his head up to get a better look at what had a hold of him, and saw a shimmering glow of deepest blue emanating from a length of creeper. The creeper itself was wrapped tightly around his leg, with its other end wrapped around the branch of a large shade tree. That creeper had not been dangling from the air before, he was sure.

Lyrien heard the telltale sounds of individuals approaching. Silently cursing himself for letting his emotions get the better of him, he arched his back briefly to gain some momentum, then swung himself up fully, trying to double over so that he could reach the vine with his hand. He grabbed hold of his leg and held tightly, feeling the burn in his stomach muscles. If he didn't make it on that attempt, his pursuers would catch him before he could get free and, upon Samos's orders, would attempt to cloak him in a handful of additional spells, just to see how he would react. Every other time it had happened to that point, he had not taken it very well. He resolved not to let it occur again.

Tugging hard on his own leg so that he would not fall back upside down, Lyrien strained upward, reaching out with his arm to where the vine was binding his leg. He could still see the blue emanations, and with a tiny thrust of his finger, he managed to poke it hard enough to dissolve it. In that instant, the vine released its tension, rapidly uncoiling from his ankle. The captain grunted as he dropped to the ground, landing unceremoniously on his rump and back.

He wasted no time lamenting the pain, instead rolling into the bushes along the side of the footpath. He had only just managed to settle in and hold still when one of the two observers strolled past, peering this way and that. Lyrien had come to understand in a rudimentary way that the fellow, Persold by name, dealt exclusively in nature magic. Everything he had done to the captain up to that point had involved plants, the soil, insects, and water from the pools scattered throughout the gardens. Samos had referred to him as a druid. He was the one who had created the magical snare, Lyrien was sure.

Persold reached the spot where Lyrien had been caught by his magical trap and stooped down to examine the now limp creeper vine. The captain could see a smile play across the man's face, and the druid immediately stood up and began turning his head back and forth, studying the bushes to either side of the path.

To Lyrien's dismay, Persold seemed to have spotted him, and he took out a thin length of wood and began to mutter. With a shout, Lyrien leaped out of his hiding place, charging toward Persold, hoping to reach him before the druid could produce the magical effect of his wand. The captain was a step too slow.

The ground cover all around Lyrien immediately wriggled to life, flailing and undulating around him. He tried to leap over the last bit of ground, to vault across that distance and catch hold of the druid, but grass, shrubs, and more tendrils of the creeper vine entangled him, jerking him short of his goal and slamming him to the ground with a thud, knocking the wind from him.

He groaned as more of the animated plants wrapped him up, pinning him to the ground.

As the captain became firmly imprisoned by the effects of Persold's wand, the druid gave a shrill whistle. But Lyrien refused to give up so easily. He tried to free one of his arms and banish the magic that was animating the growth all around him. He could certainly see the glowing emanations of the sorcery that Persold had produced, but he could do little more than free his hand; the growth was dense enough that the rest of Lyrien's arm remained in the firm grasp of the greenery.

"I think that's enough for today," Samos commented as he strolled up to Lyrien's position, joined by Stevacal, a diminutive man-like creature known as a gnome and the other practitioner of magic working with the sage. "He looks weary," Samos added, cocking his head and peering down at Lyrien with a grin on his face. The captain merely scowled and waited for Persold to release the plants holding him down.

"At least we know he can detect and affect all types of magic," Persold commented, holding up the strand of vine that was still in his grasp. "I think he missed seeing my snare, but once he was caught in it, he still managed to free himself."

"Hmm," Samos replied, nodding. "And you still haven't been able to notice any sort of magical presence around him when he does this?" he asked Stevacal.

The gnome shook his head in answer. "So far, none of my detection dweomers have been able to catch even a glimmer of arcane energy manifesting around him. Whatever he's doing, it's not magical."

"Then perhaps it's mental energy," Persold suggested, folding his arms. "Some sort of psychic phenomenon."

"Yes, that's my thinking as well," Samos agreed, pulling at his ear. "He must be a psion. Or rather, his gift is some sort of latent psionic ability that he really doesn't understand, yet."

"That would definitely explain why I can't sense what he's doing," Stevacal said, nodding in agreement. "I know someone who might be able to assist—"

"Listen," the captain interrupted, "It's all well and good that you're so excited about your various theories, but while you're collectively mulling them over as though I'm not even present, I'm becoming food for these accursed plants. Do you think you might see your way clear to *release me?*" he finished with a shout. "I'd like to stand upon my own two feet if you please."

The three sages turned and looked at Lyrien as though they were, indeed, surprised to discover him still among them. Finally, with an apologetic shake of his head, Persold waved his hand over the region where Lyrien was sprawled out at their feet and muttered something under his breath. As the captain climbed to his feet, brushing the dirt, leaves, and twigs from his body, the druid cracked a small grin. "Sorry," he said, then turned back to the continuing discussion.

Lyrien merely shook his head in bemused disgust and made his way down the path toward the palace proper. He knew from the brief experience he had already gained that the three sages would probably debate their notions about his gift for a good hour, perhaps longer. He had no intention of standing around, waiting for them.

They'll banter on until after Crux sets and night falls, he thought, snorting at the absurdity of that mental image. Tomorrow's another day, he told himself. No more testing for this soldier today. And if Samos doesn't like it, then a bucket of dung to him.

Lyrien paid little attention to the environment around him as he approached the door that would take him inside the great stone structure of the palace. Bruhark was no longer shadowing him constantly, for which he was very thankful. He didn't have any idea why that change had been made, and he certainly wasn't going to inquire. As he followed the steps up to the door and slipped inside, Lyrien also noted that the guards paid him little attention. The captain could only assume that the guards had grown accustomed to him moving freely through the complex.

Not sure what's convinced them to trust me, he thought, but it seems Lord Mabon is keeping up his end of the deal. The circumstances were making him more and more reluctant to agree to Effron Cadmus's pleas for aid. It wasn't that he didn't agree with the nobleman that changes had to be made. He really couldn't stand to see all of these slaves suffer, and he could see no flaws in Effron's story. He had to admit that the nobleman seemed on the level. But the truth was, he still wasn't sure he could afford to trust the man.

If it turns out he's lying to me, setting me up, then I'm not just risking me, I'm risking Gade. And it means that either Ezeria is lying to me, or she's in as much danger as I am.

Unlike the time following their initial meeting, now, thoughts of the half-elven beauty who was sharing his quarters made him flinch. He had become more and more withdrawn from her over the last couple of days, and he knew it was bothering her. But the sense of guilt he felt over his own weakness to resist her was catching up to him. He couldn't stop thinking about Iandra, kept trying to convince Ezeria—and himself—that the only reason he had named her as his personal slave to Oderic Salas was to spare her any punishments she might have received due to his own circumstances. He wanted to protect her, to keep her safe, but sharing his bed with her was making him ashamed of himself.

The captain knew that the growing tension between himself and the concubine was only compounded by the fact that he had yet to make up his mind about rescuing Jezindi. Every time Ezeria brought the issue up, Lyrien tried to change the subject, and he could tell that the half-elf was growing more and more disappointed at his reluctance. She just didn't understand what she was potentially asking him to do, who she was asking him to risk by betraying the bloodlord. He wasn't sure if he wanted that responsibility right now. Placating Galak Mabon and Oderic Salas wasn't the only way to protect everyone around him, but to the captain, it was the safest way.

And every time he considered that he was taking the safe route, Lyrien felt selfish and grew even more ashamed, which was why he hadn't told Cadmus no, yet. He needed someone else to talk to, someone who wasn't caught up in the circumstances. But there was no one. Still, he wasn't quite ready to face Ezeria. It was then that he realized that he was making his way toward Gade's chambers, rather than returning to his own rooms.

The captain slowed, wondering if this was such a good idea. Master Salas had not forbidden him from visiting the dover, but he had also made a point of being with him the previous time. Shrugging, Lyrien pressed on. The worst that could happen, he reasoned, was that the guards would not let him through to Gade's room.

As Lyrien rounded the corner and closed the distance to Gade's doorway, he saw that only one guard sat at the table, rather than the two of the previous visit. When the red- and black-clad man saw the captain approaching, he cocked his head inquisitively and stood up. Lyrien tried to put on his most disarming smile as he sidled up to the guard.

"I just wanted to drop in and see how he's doing," Lyrien said, gesturing casually toward Gade's gate. "See if he has recovered since the . . . well, you know."

"Master Salas didn't say anything about allowing visitors," the guard said, a bright-eyed young man with curly blond hair and the beginnings of a goatee. "I'm not sure you should be here."

Lyrien shrugged. "Master Salas didn't say I couldn't drop by to check in on him, did he? I'm not trying anything," he added, desperately attempting to appear as disarming as possible. He leaned on the wall, just to seem relaxed and self-assured. "He's my friend, and I just want to make sure he's all right. He's eating, isn't he?" the captain inquired, hoping that changing the subject would put the guard more at ease.

The young man nodded. "Like a horse," he said and grinned slightly. "He keeps asking to go for a walk, but I've got strict orders not to let him out of there."

"Of course you do. And I wouldn't ask you to disobey any orders. If you don't feel comfortable letting me visit him, I'll just go find Master Salas and get him to approve it. I just hate disturbing him, as busy as he is." Lyrien turned on his heel to go.

"Wait," the guard said, reaching for his keys. "I wasn't told that you couldn't go in," he said. "It's all right for a little while, I guess."

Lyrien nodded eagerly. "Thanks," he said. "Like I said, I just want to find out how he's doing and maybe bring him something good to eat."

"Yeah, he'd probably like that," the guard said, unlocking the gate. "Like I said, he's eating like a horse. Hey!" the guard called out a little louder, toward the interior of the room, beyond the privacy curtain. "You have a visitor!"

"That's all right," Lyrien said, pushing past the guard. "I'll find him." And with that, he stepped through the curtain and into Gade's chambers.

The dover was sitting on his bed, staring through the gauzy curtains that separated the interior from the cage-enclosed balcony. He looked over sullenly as Lyrien entered, then his face brightened immediately. Almost as quickly, though, Gade frowned again. "I thought I told you to flee," he said in a low voice, standing and moving close to Lyrien. "Get out of here! Run! Get to the Oasis. You'll be fine there."

"It's good to see you, too," Lyrien said, trying to smile. "So, you're glad to see me, huh?"

The dover growled, a low, rumbling sound. "Damn it, Lyrien. It isn't that; you know I am. But you're a fool to stay here and try to protect me. Why won't you listen?"

"Because I'm a fool. A fool who isn't going to abandon you, no matter what you say. But leave it alone for a moment," Lyrien said. "How are you feeling?"

"Bored out of my mind. They won't let me out of here for anything. I get fed plenty, and the room's comfortable, but it seems like I'm going to be stuck in here forever."

"Well, at least until I do whatever it is Mabon and Salas want."

"Don't do it."

"I said, leave it alone." Lyrien sat down on a chair that had been brought into the room. He could see that a writing table had also been provided, and there was a collection of notes and maps written up on some sheets of parchment. "What are you writing, your memoirs?"

"Something like that," Gade replied, waving his hand in dismissal. "Not that anyone who matters will ever see them, but they are some notes on some of my most recent expeditions into the maze."

"I see." Lyrien shifted back to the dover. "Listen, Gade," he spoke in a low voice. "I've been contacted by a nobleman who has offered to free both of us if I perform a small service for him. So far, he seems on the level, but I'm leery. Besides, Salas and Mabon have stayed true to their word. I wanted a second opinion."

"Who's the nobleman?" Gade asked.

"I'm not going to tell you," Lyrien answered. "If there ever came a time when the slavemaster tried to torture it out of you, I would rather ignorance become your ally."

"Oh, that's very reassuring," the dover said, snorting. "Well, what does he want you to do?"

"He wants me to kill one of Mabon's concubines. She has the ability to see things, sort of a fortune-teller or oracle. The bloodlord keeps her close, and this cabal of nobles who want to overthrow him can't act for fear of being exposed."

"So they're members of the bloodlord's court?" Gade asked.

"Right. But they claim to want to end slavery in Black-wall."

"I seriously doubt you're hearing the whole story," Gade replied. "The nobles stand to gain a lot by seeing Mabon deposed, but they stand to lose a whole lot more with the abolishment of slavery. I'd be wary."

"That's been my thought, too. I've been reluctant to agree."

"I think that's wise. Instead, you should sneak out, tonight, and get as far away from here as you can!"

Lyrien sighed. "You're not going to let this go, are you?"

"No." Gade got very still, looking pointedly at the captain. "Listen. I'm not kidding. You can't imagine how flattered I am that you want to stick around on my behalf. A part of me is so very grateful. But my fate is sealed. If the lord of Blackwall is known for anything at all, it's for his unbridled cruelty and capricious nature. He changes his mind on a whim. The only thing he does consistently is go back on his word and torture slaves. He is feared throughout Penance for his ardent brutality." The dover took a deep breath, and then, emphasizing every word, said, "You must get out."

"I can't."

"Can't? Or won't? Because if you won't, then you're only killing us both." Gade hung his head. "I don't want to die. I'm terrified that Lord Mabon will somehow sit up and take some notice of me. The stories . . . But I can't do anything about it. I *can* do something about you. Except you won't let me. Why won't you listen?" Gade was growing more and more agitated as he spoke, rising from the bed at last and stalking back and forth. "Please, for the love of all things good, run!"

"I'm not leaving you. I think that's enough visit for one day. I'll come back tomorrow." And with that, the captain stood to leave.

"Gods!" Gade exclaimed, throwing his hands in the air in exasperation. "Most hardheaded . . ." he shook his head. "Fine. I can't convince you, then you'll have to learn the hard way."

"I'm sorry," Lyrien said earnestly, moving over and taking his friend by the shoulder. "No matter how much wisdom there is in your words, I can't leave you behind. It would haunt me the rest of my days."

"Well, despite my pleas, I'm kind of glad." Lyrien turned to go. "Hey," the dover called, prompting the captain to stop and look back over his shoulder. "Thanks," Gade said.

Lyrien nodded and turned back to the gate. "Guard," he called as he neared the doorway. "I'm ready to leave."

Chapter 12

"So, if I fail to spot and neutralize all of the different enchantments you've used to protect the 'gem,' I could be harmed, even killed?"

"Precisely," Samos answered, nodding to Lyrien's question. "Simulating the threat doesn't seem to work as well; you're emotions are not so strongly tied into the reading, it seems. So we're going to make these threats real."

Lyrien shook his head, sighing. "You never send a novice swordsman into the practice yard with a sharpened blade until he's got total control of it. This is ridiculous. What good am I to you dead or maimed?"

"Not much," Samos admitted, "But if something happens, we'll bring in the priests to restore you." The sage inclined his head for emphasis. "It would be much better if you didn't let anything happen, though. Some of our little surprises will be quite painful if you don't dispel them."

Lyrien merely pursed his lips in consternation. You don't have to convince me, he silently grumbled. What a fine continuation to an already *wonderful* day.

The captain had been awakened early that morning by Bruhark. The ogre was simply standing over the bed, staring down where Lyrien and Ezeria lay entwined in the damp sheets, sleeping off the previous evening's pleasures. After he had finished his visit with Gade, Lyrien had returned to his own rooms to find Ezeria in a forlorn state. He could tell she had been weeping, though she pretended otherwise. It hadn't been difficult to coax the truth out of her, though, and soon enough, the half-elven harem slave was sobbing gently against his shoulder, claiming not to understand why he would not lie with her any more.

Lyrien had tried to explain his conflicting feelings, but that only seemed to make it worse, and before he knew it, they were kissing. He had let his arousal get the better of him, then, succumbed to the fierce burning desire he had for Ezeria that was only heightened by being on the Forge. Their lovemaking had been frantic at first, a release of the tension that had been growing between them, and then it had settled into a mellow sort of coupling that happened lazily, off and on, throughout the small hours of the night.

Discovering the ogre guard looming over the two of them, leering at their half-covered forms, had ignited Lyrien into fury. He and Bruhark had almost come to blows when the guard simply announced that it was time to visit Samos. Ezeria had managed to shoo the ogre out of their chambers and calm the captain down sufficiently, but guilt over his weakness from the previous evening only threw up a wall of tension between them once more, and he had left his companion huddled on the bed, looking miserable.

Lyrien was in a section of the palace he had never visited before, some sort of inner sanctum that was normally not in use but that was being utilized that day by the sage as a makeshift treasure vault. It was going to be Lyrien's job to sneak into the vault, extract a worthless piece of quartz that was serving as a valuable gem, and escape, all without tripping any of the magical protections that

Samos and Stevacal had erected around it. Persold had not joined them that morning.

"You may as well get started," the spectacled sage said, gently pushing Lyrien through a door. "We'll be watching from above." With that, the half-elf with the curly white hair shut the portal and the captain could hear it being barred from the outside. He grimaced and turned to survey his surroundings.

The vault was a sort of simple maze, Samos had told Lyrien, and indeed, he found himself standing in the middle of a hallway running to either side of his current position, lit periodically by torches set into sconces on the walls. Each direction ended with a turn about twenty feet from his position. Overhead was a sort of gallery where spectators could watch the proceedings. He could also see a sheet of thick meshing, similar to what he had experienced at the coliseum, that prevented escape from the maze. The captain began to realize that the area had been constructed for entertainment purposes. He imagined slaves being thrown into the maze, perhaps hunted by opponents or wild beasts. The spectators could watch from overhead while the contestants pursued or fled through the twisting, turning passages.

Although he had learned much of the talents and abilities of the two sages currently testing him, Lyrien still felt no small disadvantage at his inexperience in the uses and forms of magic. If he was to succeed in the test without suffering any injuries, he was going to have to prepare for the unexpected, wipe his mind of any preconceived notions, and simply go slowly. That in and of itself was a difficult proposition. His military mind wanted to formulate contingencies, to plan for multiple possibilities; it would be hard to avoid anticipating the traps and protections that he faced.

The captain knelt down and studied both directions of the hallway, wondering if there would be any clues to reveal which path he ought to choose. The floor was smooth stone there, very finely worked blocks that fit well together with almost no seams. The walls were the same. Despite his normal desire to stifle his emotion, Lyrien felt his heart pound with nervousness and let that fear wash over him. He used the emotion to focus his thoughts, tried to look for telltale signs of magic. He could see none. That was worse than finding something, he realized.

Unsure of himself, the captain finally decided to take the left passage. He began a cautious walk in that direction, keeping to one side of the hall, rather than treading down its center. When he reached the corner, he halted, knelt down, and only then peered around the edge of the stone wall to the right to see what lay beyond. The passage simply continued, making another right turn further on. He sighed, wondering how long that was going to continue before he found something.

It would be clever to drag this out, make me impatient, Lyrien thought. *Just when I get hasty, the first trap is sprung.*

Willing himself to avoid that impatience, he prepared to stand up when he caught a glimmer of aura. Oddly, it was around the torch nearest to him. He could feel the adrenalin coursing through him, making his limbs ache, as he studied the torch more carefully. Once he could focus his attention on something specific, he realized that every torch had a similar glow. He turned to look back the way he had come and saw that he had already walked past three such lights.

Damn it, the captain snarled silently. *Pay attention!*

Carefully, worried about what might be triggered, Lyrien reached out and gently poked at the magical emanation that surrounded the closest torch. He pressed it until it popped like a bubble, scattering the afterimages of the aura like tiny purple sparks—and every torch in the maze went out, leaving the captain immersed in darkness.

God, Lyrien groaned in dismay, realizing what he had done. The first trap had been designed to trick him. Instead of improving his situation by dispersing the magic, he had just made it far more difficult. From then on, he would be forced to feel his way blindly, hoping that he would see magical auras before he stumbled into their effects. Shaking his head, he began to creep forward again, following the new tunnel all the way to its end.

At the next turn, Lyrien repeated his careful safety precautions, kneeling before peering around the corner. The captain realized that a magical aura was present along a large section of wall a little way down that new hall, again to the right side.

A doorway, Lyrien surmised as he stood up to move closer. He reached the point and discovered that the red glow revealed one of the magical, invisible walls that Samos had tested him with on the first day. The wall of force blocked an arched doorway that led into a dark space beyond. The captain started to smack the wall from existence and continue on, then changed his mind.

Better to be thorough, Lyrien told himself, and passed up the blocked doorway, moving the rest of the way along the hall by feel. He reached yet another turn to the right, and at that turn, he continued, moving all the way back to the first passage, where the door that had let him into the maze in the first place was. He nodded in satisfaction, content in the knowledge that it was a pair of concentric squares, a four-sided hallway surrounding an inner chamber. That way, he was certain nothing could come at him from behind. The captain turned back and approached the magical barrier.

Before he prepared to dismiss the magic, Lyrien tried to peer through it and into the space beyond. However, the only way to make that work was to concentrate on *not* seeing the aura itself, which only served to make everything pitch black. He was just going to have to take his chances. Focusing his will, he hesitantly placed his hand against the barrier and pushed. He could feel the resistance of the wall, but as he became more forceful, the magic bowed, then broke, the aura scattering wildly as it had every time before.

Quickly, Lyrien ducked back around the corner, fearful of new magic assaulting him. When nothing immediately occurred, he peered back around the edge of the doorway into the area beyond. The whole place glowed with magic, he realized. He could clearly see a place in the middle where some sort of pedestal rested, holding aloft a small box. He assumed that was the gem, guarded by multiple wards. In addition to that feature, he could see that the floor of the chamber radiated a magical aura in several circular areas surrounding the pedestal, each one shining particularly brightly right in the center, where there was an unusual symbol the likes of which he had never seen.

These two are just drunk on the power their magic gives them, Lyrien thought, rolling his eyes in the dark. Let's see just how difficult this is going to be.

The captain moved cautiously forward into the room and toward the first symbol on the floor, careful not to move over the edge of the perimeter of the emanations. Crouching low, he examined what he could see of the symbol. Then, he reached out and tried to nudge the magic at the edge of the glow. Unlike his other efforts, this seemed to have no effect. There was no resistance; it was simply a matter of not being able to physically affect the magic.

Swearing softly, Lyrien backed away and sat down to think. The magic was obviously centered on the symbol in the middle of the area, he reasoned. Therefore, that would have to be what he needed to manipulate in order to destroy it. But he couldn't reach it without passing through the outer glow, something he was reluctant to do unless he had no other alternatives. He could not pass between the glowing zones, as they overlapped slightly, completely encircling the pedestal. He supposed he would have to leap over, then.

Standing and retreating as far back from the center of the room as he could, the captain was just about to take a running start and jump across the glow when he realized how foolish that would be.

For all you know, he scolded himself, *there's a pit surrounding that magic, and you're about to jump right into it.* Judging the physical presence of the room by the glow of magic was a mistake he had made several times during Samos's testing already. Sighing, Lyrien sat back down.

"Giving up?" came the sage's voice from somewhere overhead, in the darkness. "I thought you'd be more innovative than that," Samos added.

Lyrien shrugged, wondering how the two of them could see what he was doing in the darkness. "Just thinking," he replied. "The torches were very clever."

"We were just trying to make you think, rather than simply shattering magic without thought for the potential consequences."

The potential consequences are, I'm stuck, Lyrien silently fumed. He scooped up a handful of sand and tossed it onto the symbol in a fit of anger. It did nothing, of course, but it gave him an idea. Rising quickly, he went back out into the hallway and removed one of the torches from its wall sconce. Then, returning to the chamber, he moved as close to the edge of the magical barrier as he dared, then tossed the torch over the area, listening. The torch clattered against stone flooring right next to the pedestal.

Well, there you go, Lyrien thought. *No pit.*

With that, the captain backed up and charged forward, leaping over the magical zone to the dark space on the opposite side. Even as he stretched his leg out, ready to land firmly on the clear space beyond, his mistake became apparent. The magic of the strange symbol did not merely expand outward horizontally, across the floor, but it radiated upward, too, like a bowl turned upside down, and Lyrien passed right through the emanation as he crossed over the symbol. A wave of arctic cold shot upward from the symbol, sending waves of bitter chill through the captain. He cried out in aching, muscle-cramping pain as he continued his arcing leap.

The blast of cold air made Lyrien convulse abruptly in mid-leap, and he lost control of his landing, flailing and twisting as he hit the floor, losing his balance and toppling down in the process. He skidded up against the pedestal with a thump, sensing despite his pain-induced haze that he had triggered that magic as well. He groaned and tried to sit up, still feeling the effects of the frigid blast making his muscles quiver. He blinked several times, trying to clear his head. Beside him, there was a strange clicking sound, followed by a flash of brilliant blue-white light.

Damnation, Lyrien thought, even as he rolled to the side and heaved himself to his feet. Something snapped at him and clicked again, and he could see sparks flashing from whatever was there. The captain stumbled backward, away from the thing, and realized too late that he had passed into the area of effect of another of the magical symbols. Another wave of biting cold coalesced around him, staggering him and driving him to his knees. The thing before him, whatever it was, pounced forward, crackles of electricity cascading across the surface of its back. It reached Lyrien in a single bound, biting into the flesh of his leg with sharp pincers.

The captain howled in pain and swatted the thing off of himself, giving himself a shock for his troubles. The jolt made his arm numb and useless. Groaning, he tried to stand and see what had become of the thing that was attacking him.

"Enough!" Lyrien yelled as he retreated from the creature, which he could see was a large beetle, perhaps half as long as he was tall. He was shaking from the cold, his skin ached from frostbite and energy jolts, and he just wanted the test to end. There was no answer from above. "Damn you!" he cried as the beetle came scurrying toward him again.

Desperate to avoid another crackling shock from the thing, Lyrien turned and fled out into the hallway beyond the central room. He stumbled around a corner and ran to the end, where the hallway turned. The beetle skittered out into the hall and began to scamper after him. Growling in frustration, the captain took off again, racing to the next corner, feeling his way along the wall with his good hand. The next time, he didn't wait for the thing to appear, but instead kept going, right to the door where he had entered the test.

Lyrien tried to force the door open, but it had been securely sealed shut somehow from the outside. He threw his weight against it a couple of times, but the portal was solid and wasn't going to crack any time soon. With another growl of despair, Lyrien turned just as his pursuer rounded the corner and came at him again. He retreated in the opposite direction, furious with Samos even as he was desperately trying to figure out a way to fight the beetle off.

Suddenly, the captain had an idea. He turned the corner twice more and found himself back before the doorway into the central chamber. He darted inside and tried to focus on the magic still present in the room. It came easily that time. He could see two more of the symbols on the floor, plus the magic emanating from the box atop the pedestal. Everything else was no longer present.

Lyrien ran around to the far side of the room, navigating by feel and instinct alone. He positioned himself on the back side of one of the symbols, so that it was between himself and the beetle. Then he took a deep, calming breath and waited.

A moment later, the beetle came into the room, taking tentative steps as though searching carefully. Lyrien could see it only by the glow of the crackling energy that arced every which way across its back, but it was enough. The thing must have sensed his presence, for it immediately charged forward, directly toward him. Lyrien waited and watched. When the huge insect passed into range of the symbol, a pulse of cold air throbbed into existence, bathing it in frigid waves of energy. The beetle reacted instantly, leaping straight up into the air with a mad clicking sound, its legs flailing wildly. It came down hard upon the floor, on its back, and twitched and scrabbled around, electrical sparks bouncing wildly about it. It spun in place as it thrashed, not dead and trying to right itself.

Lyrien took advantage of the delay to reposition himself, moving so that the last remaining symbol was between him and his foe. Soon enough, the beetle managed to flip itself back upright, though it seemed to weave uncertainly. Still, it could sense its potential prey and rushed forward toward the captain again. True to form, the last symbol blasted the insect with its magic, and that time, when the beetle hit the floor, its was reduced to a few spasmodic twitches before finally growing still.

Lyrien sighed in relief and sank down to his rump, exhausted and close to passing out from the pain of feeling returning to his frozen extremities.

"Well done," Samos called from above. "Now *that* was innovative."

"This test is over!" Lyrien shouted hoarsely at the darkness overhead. "I'm through playing these games!"

"Not yet," Samos replied without the barest hint of emotion. "You still haven't recovered the gem."

"And I'm not going to," Lyrien spat. "You can just let me out, because I'm not going any further."

"That's not the agreement," Samos said, and that time his voice was hostile. "You're not coming out until you finish or fall unconscious. So which is it going to be?"

With a snarl, Lyrien stood up, moved to the box, and reached out. He was so angry, it was a simple matter for him to flick a finger and shatter the magic that surrounded the container. When he realized the box was also locked conventionally, he simply raised the whole thing high over his head and dashed it to the stone floor as hard as he could. He could hear the fragment of quartz bounce off into the darkness.

"There," he said, directing his bitterness upward. "I got your damned stone. You'd better be at the door by the time I reach it." And with that, he moved to where he had heard the quartz chunk tumble. It took him perhaps half a minute of feeling around before his fingers brushed the mineral. He snatched it up and stalked out of the room, through the square hall, and to the door. Just as he was about to raise his fist and begin pounding on the portal, he heard a latch being drawn back, and then the door opened, allowing light to flood in and daze him.

Lyrien shoved the quartz into Samos's hands. The captain was just about to tell him precisely what he could do with the hunk of quartz and then stalk off, but the sage interrupted him.

"Well done," Samos said. "I think you're ready."

"Ready for what?" Lyrien asked, taken aback. He scowled, still angry, but the sage's words stilled him for the moment.

"Why, to begin the next step, of course," Samos replied. "Certainly you realized that Lord Mabon has a specific plan in mind for you once your training is complete."

Lyrien shrugged uncertainly. "I had no illusions to the contrary. What does he want from me?" he snapped.

"That," Oderic Salas said as he strolled into view, "is what you and I are about to go discuss with His Lordship." The slavemaster wore yet another finely woven and decorated blue robe. Lyrien wondered if the man ever wore any other color. "Come along," Salas said, motioning, pausing only long enough for Lyrien to down one of the awful-tasting healing draughts. "He's waiting."

Lyrien looked back and forth between Samos and Stevacal, then back at the slavemaster. He was still seething, but he realized things were coming to a head, and an outburst then would only make them more difficult. Taking a deep breath, he turned and followed Master Salas.

The pair walked in silence as they moved through the halls toward the inner harem. On the one hand, he felt a sense of eagerness to be getting near the end of these arrangements. He was growing restless to finish and get out of Blackwall. On the other hand, he felt a rising sense of dread, trying to fathom what Lord Mabon might want from him and his peculiar talent. Although the captain had grown more comfortable with both the concept of magic and his effect on it, he still wasn't too keen on being in contact with it on a regular basis. In those last few days of exposure to it, he had found the arcane art to be too unpredictable and potentially lethal. He thought it would feel good to be out in the open with a blade in his hand again for a change, far away from sages and magic.

But there was more to Lyrien's concern than unwanted contact with magic. He knew too well the bloodlord's disposition, and he harbored no illusions that the faust was going to expect something fairly drastic from him. Whether or not he thought he could survive the encounter was only a small part of the captain's concern, he realized; his greatest fear was whether the task was going to force him to compromise his morals.

Can I do something repugnant, even if it means earning my freedom? And Gade's? What am I willing to sacrifice in order to gain that?

Before he could give himself a true and honest answer, Lyrien and Salas arrived at the patio where they had dined with Lord Mabon previously. There was yet another extravagant spread laid out on the table, and the faust was already busily consuming a heaping plate of delectable fare, servings of dishes whose aromas made Lyrien's mouth water.

Lord Mabon glanced up at the pair without stopping his consumption. Master Salas and the captain waited quietly for a few long, increasingly awkward moments, until the bloodlord finished off his first helping. Then, as he began to serve himself some seconds, he gave them another glance. "I understand that your training has gone well," Lord Mabon commented as he ladled another scoop of some thick whitish stew over a wedge of bread. "Oderic tells me that he thinks you have a strong enough handle on your ability that we can proceed."

Lyrien glanced at Oderic, wondering if these were rhetorical questions or if he should actually answer. Salas saved him the trouble.

"Samos is confident that our gladiator here has enough mastery of his gift that he is capable of succeeding."

Succeeding at what? Lyrien wanted to ask. But he kept his mouth shut and just waited. He had a sense that he was balanced on a very precarious pinnacle of rock, very close to the end of a long and treacherous ascent, and if he could maintain that balance for just a little while longer, he was home free, but the slightest misstep, one wrong word or deed, would find him plummeting down into ruin.

"Well, are you?" Mabon asked, sucking grease from his fingers.

Lyrien gave a noncommittal shrug. "I have no idea what you want from me, Your Lordship," he answered, using the honorific he had heard Master Salas employ only moments before. "But I feel confident, and if Master Salas and Samos think I'm ready, who am I to argue with them?"

"You never shied away from making your true feelings known before," the bloodlord said with a raspy snort. "Why so acquiescent now?"

Lyrien was taken aback at the faust's candor. He grimaced, trying to come up with a suitable answer. "Let's just say that I want to complete my end of the bargain as quickly and as smoothly as possible," he finally replied. "I have a lot invested in making you happy."

The bloodlord laughed out loud, shoveling another bite of food into his mouth when he had regained his composure. "You have no idea what you've got at stake," he said and flashed a wholly mischievous grin at the captain that made him actually flinch with its malevolence. "So much more than you know." Then Lord Mabon turned to Oderic. "I think you're right; he's ready."

Lyrien felt more unsure of himself than ever, then, but he stayed quiet.

"Very good," Master Salas replied. "In that case, we can go ahead and tell you what you are to do." Lyrien blinked, bracing himself for what was coming. "You're going to help Lord Mabon kill another bloodlord."

Chapter 13

At that moment, Lyrien realized he had been half-consciously convincing himself he was willing to take a fairly big step over the line that defined right and wrong in order to get himself and Gade out of bondage and escape Blackwall. But right then, he knew that he had deluded himself, that his notion of how far he could tolerate bending the rules was so shortsighted it was almost laughable. To think that he would be willing to aid in the murder of one of Lord Mabon's enemies, even with Gade's life hanging in the balance, showed just how badly the bloodlord and the slavemaster had misjudged the captain.

It took Lyrien several moments to realize that he was gaping, and he shut his mouth and relaxed his face the second it occurred to him. Taking a deep breath, he refocused his attention on Oderic Salas, who was apparently waiting for him to answer. He wanted to tell the man how utterly ludicrous his request was, but he simply looked at the blue-robed man with that ever-present infuriating smile on his face and asked as calmly as possible, "How am I supposed to do that?"

"By destroying something very dear to him," Master Salas replied. "Lord Flollo of the Oasis has a very fine suit of armor that has served him well in his defense of his position. It gives him considerable power and protection in battle, and he is formidable with it on. You, my gladiator, are going to kill the magic inside it."

Lyrien nodded, struggling to maintain a composed demeanor while he really wanted to scream in rage and throttle the man. He could sense that his hands were trembling with his emotions, anger that threatened to wash over him despite his efforts at calm. One part of his thoughts already drifted to the task of figuring out a way to get Gade out of his imprisoned state. With Ezeria's help, he might be able to succeed, though once he had the dover free, he wasn't sure where they would go. He knew it was time to take Effron Cadmus up on his offer.

"I see," the captain finally replied, trying to make his words soft and agreeable, despite the fury seething just beneath the surface of his expression. "And of course, this armor is well-protected, with a number of magical wards, right?"

"You catch on so very quickly!" Salas beamed. "That's precisely why your unusual talent is going to be so handy."

"How soon must I do this?" Lyiren asked, trying to fake a good balance between willingness and resignation so as to appear genuine. He only cared about the answer for how much time it gave him to escape.

"You will set out tomorrow," Lord Mabon said, finishing his meal and shoving the plate away. "We will have the necessary documents to allow you to leave Blackwall. From there, you will make your way to the Oasis, get inside Flollo's court, find where he keeps the armor, and destroy it. Once you have done these things, if you are alive and manage to escape, you will come back here to inform me. I will take care of the rest." That devilish grin reappeared on the faust's face, and it sent an involuntary shiver down Lyrien's spine.

"Tomorrow?" Lyrien asked, genuinely surprised. He had assumed the bloodlord would want him to refine his training for a few days, first, once he knew what it was he had to accomplish. "That soon?"

"Wasn't it you who just said you want to complete your end of the bargain as quickly and as smoothly as possible? Yes, tomorrow. If we wait to act, Flollo might catch wind of my plans. It's time for him to surrender his bloodhold to me," Mabon finished in a chilling tone.

Lyrien shrugged. "Yes, Sir," he said, trying to sound matter-of-fact. He prayed that neither the bloodlord nor the slavemaster could see his clenched fists. He had to grit his teeth to keep from sneering in disgust.

Lord Mabon scrutinized the captain intensely for a long, awkward moment, his gaze making Lyrien begin to fear that he had somehow given away his true feelings. His heart thumping wildly, Lyrien wondered for a split-second if he was going to be accosted by guards at the bloodlord's command. He silently vowed to go down fighting and even glanced about to see if he could swipe a weapon from one of the unsuspecting soldiers standing nearby, but in the next heartbeat, Galak Mabon nodded.

"All right, then," the bloodlord said, making it obvious from his tone that he was dismissing both of them. As the captain and Master Salas turned to go, Mabon called after them. "Oderic, make sure he has everything he needs."

Oderic Salas turned back and bowed deeply, then strolled off, his robes swishing crisply.

Lyrien followed the man as far as the outer hall. There, the slavemaster turned to him and said, "Return to your room. It's late, and you will want to get plenty of rest before you set out tomorrow morning. I will permit Ezeria to remain with you only for the night."

Lyrien started to protest that she was supposed to belong to him, but he thought better of it, nodded, and turned to go back to his chambers. Salas went in the opposite direction. As soon as the bald-headed man was out of sight, Lyrien slumped against a wall. He wanted to hit something.

Gade warned me. Cadmus warned me, too. I got complacent. Too comfortable with the gray area between right and wrong.

Enough kowtowing, the captain vowed, feeling ashamed. He wasn't sure where the willingness to compromise his sense of right and wrong had come from, but it had crept in slowly, subtly, in much the same way that his indiscretions with Ezeria had happened. He had bent too many times. It was one of the less desirable symptoms of being on the Forge, he decided. It was changing him in more ways than he had realized until now.

It's time to put a stop to that, Lyrien swore. *It's time to tell Gade and get out of here.*

The captain turned down a side hall that he knew would take him in the direction of the dover's quarters. On the way, Lyrien tried to bring his swirling, chaotic thoughts in line. He had so little time. He wanted to begin planning some sort of escape, but first, he needed to get Ezeria to take him to Effron Cadmus so they could finalize the deal with the nobleman. He had no idea how he was going to manage to get to Jezindi and free her, but it would have to be that night, he realized. That was definitely how he would play it, he knew; he kept the notion that he might just be forced to kill her firmly at bay, refusing to give it consideration.

Lyrien rounded the corner and saw that there were no guards outside the barred archway leading to Gade's quarters. A lump rose in his throat.

Am I too late?

Quickening his step, the captain called softly to Gade when he reached the iron gate. From inside, he detected a soft, plaintive sort of whimper, and nothing more. Swearing under his breath, Lyrien yanked on the barred portal and found that it was unlocked. Slamming it open, he darted inside.

Gade occupied the middle of the chamber, his mouth currently stuffed with a thick wad of leather. The dover had been suspended by his wrists from the ceiling, dangling several feet off the floor. Suspended in turn from his ankles was a black kettle or cauldron that hung just above the floor. A pair of flumes drained into the cauldron, their high ends placed beneath two massive blocks of ice that were melting steadily. As the runoff from the ice dripped into the flumes, it was borne down and into each of the cauldrons, slowly filling them up. Little by little, drip by drip, the dover was being stretched to death.

At the sight of his friend, Lyrien lost all sense of reason. Almost blinded by white-hot fury, he bounded forward, determined to free the dover. Quickly, he tipped the cauldron over, dumping its contents onto the floor. Gade gave a relieved groan and closed his eyes. Lyrien then unhooked the cauldron from the chains that connected it to the dover's ankles, but he then discovered that that was as much aid as he could render. The chains themselves were locked on, both at ankles and wrists. He looked about the room, desperate to find something, anything, that would release the shackles. There was nothing.

Lyrien wanted to howl in frustration, pound his fists on something. Of course, he thought in despair. Mabon knew I would want to back out. Damn it! He took a deep breath to calm himself and refocus. "I'm sorry, Gade," he said softly, his voice filled with anguish. "I can't get you loose, yet. I'm going to go get Ezeria. She'll know how to free you."

Gade closed his eyes again in resignation but nodded in what Lyrien presumed was thanks nonetheless.

Hating himself for his ineffectualness, Lyrien turned to slip away, knowing that once a palace servant or guard discovered what had been done to the insidious torture device, They would begin to hunt him down. He would have to hurry.

He found it difficult not to run as turned and hurried back out into the hall, heading for his own rooms. He almost smacked right into Bruhark, who stood there with a wicked grin on his face. Two more ogres stood to either side.

"Master Salas knew you'd try to run," Bruhark said, his scimitar in one hand. He reached forward to grab Lyrien by the scruff of the neck with the other.

At the sight of the ogre's huge, meaty hand closing in on him, Lyrien spun around and kicked out, letting his blind rage power the blow. He first knocked the guard's weapon out of his hand and then, spinning again and snapping the heel of his boot back, he struck against the side of a second ogre's knee. If it had been a mere man that Lyrien had attacked, the blow most likely would have crippled him for life. As it was, the ogre simply grunted in pain and dropped down as his knee buckled.

"You'll pay for that," Bruhark said, backhanding Lyrien. The blow snapped the captain's head back and sent him flying across the hallway. The back of his head bounced against the stone wall and he slid down it, dazed.

The two unwounded ogres moved toward him, Bruhark reaching out to grab him bodily and haul him up. The look on his face told the captain that he had pushed the guard too far.

Lyrien tried to kick out again, but the monstrous guards were ready for him that time. Bruhark punched Lyrien in the jaw, snapping his head back into the wall again. The captain saw spots. The second guard gave him a blow to his gut that took his breath away. He doubled over, unable to speak. Then Burhark kicked Lyrien in the ribs, and the captain heard—and felt—one or two of them crack. He cried out in pain.

Lyrien winced as his body shifted and his ribs sent shooting pains through his chest. He threw up his hands in supplication. "Wait," he begged in a raspy whisper, unable to draw a good breath. "Please. I'll stop."

"Too bad, slave. Next time, you'll know to obey." Bruhark said, smacking the captain with another backhand. The other two ogres, one of them limping, closed in around him again, raining kicks and punches all over his battered body.

Lyrien thought he would pass out from the pain. "Wait!" he croaked in desperation, but with a sudden inspiration. "You can't kill me!"

The three guards looming over him paused very briefly, eying their would-be victim warily. "Why not?" Bruhark asked, already drawing his arm back for another vicious punch.

"Because the prophet-woman said my death would be my slayer's doom!" Lyrien answered earnestly, curled up in a fetal ball.

Apparently, the three ogres knew enough about Jezindi's talent to give Lyrien's claim serious consideration, for they held their attacks, Bruhark going so far as to step back, his eyes glittering dangerously.

"You remember that?" came a voice from behind the captain, a raspy voice that made Lyrien's skin crawl. He rolled over, one eye already swelling shut, and squinted to see Lord Mabon imperiously strolling down the hall toward them, accompanied by a host of personal bodyguards, palace guards, and serving slaves. Galak Mabon closed the distance between them until he loomed over Lyrien, staring down with eyes narrowed in obvious anger. Lyrien could see cold malice in that visage, and he was amply afraid.

"I gave you an honest deal, a chance for your freedom, and you repay me by trying to escape," the bloodlord said venomously. "You do realize I don't have to actually kill you to bring you great pain, slave."

* * * * *

Lyrien groaned and wanted to let his head droop, let his chin settle against his chest. The sound he made was muffled by the thick, leather-wrapped bar wedged far back in his teeth. He had long since given up the possibility of spitting it out; the sour-tasting bit was held firmly there by a strap locked around his head. He wanted only to lie down, to curl up into a ball and drift off into unconsciousness, but he was going nowhere. The captain opened his one good eye and studied his predicament once more, futilely searching for some means of escape or relief.

Lord Mabon's sense of irony was not lost on Lyrien, though he saw little humor in it at the moment. The bloodlord had ordered him strung up in the same cruel device that the captain had discovered Gade in. Lyrien had no idea what had become of his friend, but he was more firmly convinced than ever that he had made the right choice by trying to free the dover, for his whole body was in agony. He doubted seriously that he would live long enough to find out. He prayed he wouldn't even remain conscious much longer.

Lyrien was stretched taut, suspended naked and spread-eagled in mid-air in a round chamber that served as the terminus of four hallways. It was decorated in a garish style, with black wall hangings and carpeting serving as a backdrop to a variety of torture instruments that lined the walls around the perimeter of the room. The whole place was dimly illuminated with lanterns that had glass panes glazed in red, purple, and green, further heightening the surreal atmosphere.

Iron bands locked around the captain's wrists held him aloft, while similar manacles locked onto his ankles bit into his flesh from the pressure of chains pulling relentlessly down. Those chains ran through a handful of pulleys until they were attached to, not one, but three cauldrons each. The cauldrons were hung in a series, one suspended to the next, in order of increasing size from top to bottom. The weight of those three iron pots alone was enough to prevent Lyrien from even drawing his legs up, but the weight was growing. As before, a flue allowed water from melting ice to trickle down into the top cauldron. As that cauldron filled and began to overflow, the runoff dripped into the next cauldron, which in turn would drip into the last one. Currently, the first cauldron was full and had just begun to drip into the middle one.

That was not enough punishment to suit Lord Mabon, though. The bloodlord had also personally thrust scores of barbed hooks through little pinches of Lyrien's skin, snagging folds of flesh across the entirety of his body and face, each hook trailing a length of twine that was in turn tightly tied off to the bars of a sort of fence that surrounded the point where he had been suspended. He couldn't even move his head to inspect the dozens of wicked puncture points, for both of his earlobes and both cheeks, as well as the septum of his nose and both his eyebrows, had been impaled. But he could certainly feel the harsh tug all across his flesh, from the webbing between his thumbs and forefingers all down his arms and torso to the webbing between his toes. Not even his genitals had been spared. The slightest motion on his part, the gentlest of shifts, painfully distended the flesh where the vicious hooks were embedded.

The ache in the captain's arms, shoulders, back and legs was beyond mere pain then. Even with the growing numbness, he could sense that his muscles were cramping and spasming from being stretched taut for far too long. He wriggled his fingers and toes in desperate frustration, but all he got for his efforts was a tingling pain in those extremities. He groaned again and stared beseechingly at the set of guards that had been placed in the chamber to watch over him.

Lyrien had not wound up in that position right away, of course. First, Galak Mabon had insisted on questioning the captain, trying to find out what part of their deal Lyrien had misunderstood. The bloodlord calmly explained that the terms of the agreement were not negotiable, nor was Lyrien going to be permitted to back out of the deal. It was obviously not acceptable to allow the captain to leave until both Lord Mabon and Master Salas were satisfied that he would not attempt such a stunt again, nor would he try to run to Lord Flollo and reveal the faust's plan once he was outside of Blackwall.

The captain had no idea how long prior that conversation had been. It seemed like ages to him. He had to fight against the urge to shift his position the slight ways in which he could, resist twisting his arms and legs in hopes of quelling even a tiny portion of the shooting pains stabbing through his chorded muscles, for that only caused the hooks to tear at his flesh mercilessly.

He sobbed, unable to even let his chin drop to his chest in misery. He imagined that before long, he would be babbling incoherently through the bit in his mouth, begging the guards to free him so that he could tell Mabon anything the bloodlord wanted to hear. Galak had even suggested as much at one point during his conversation, but he calmly explained that it would be a while longer before Mabon believed him.

Lyrien began to let his head loll against the pull of the hooks in his face now, no longer able to hold it upright. He whimpered from the burning sting and began to drift in and out of consciousness, entering a strange half-dream state that carried him away from the pain aching in his body. In his stupor, he began to see Iandra, standing in front of him in his bound position, smiling at him, though the smile turned feral when Ezeria appeared, too. The women stood side by side in front of him, laughing at him and sharing some secret. Their smiles were not warm.

"Hey! No sleeping, now!" the captain heard in the distance, immediately followed by a wrenching pain that shot through him and jerked him awake again. As he literally howled through the gag, he saw that one of the guards had strolled close and had given the two sets of cauldrons a good shove, setting them both to swaying and sending small tremors through the chains that ran back to his legs. Of course, to Lyrien, those small tremors where like iron spikes being driven through his leg muscles. He stared through tears at the guard, who only sneered and returned to his post. Then his body began to spasm again, muscles everywhere tensing and vibrating, elevating the pain so much that he drifted into merciful blackness.

Lyrien drifted in and out of that blackness over an indeterminate amount of time. When he became aware at all, he hallucinated, drifting through dreams where his body was stretched so much that it began to split in two, or dreams where he simply became longer, his flesh and bones stretching and growing until he was the size of an ogre. Then there was the most bizarre dream of them all, where the guards positioned around him in the rounded intersection somehow began to die, one after another, from an unseen attacker.

Lyrien began to laugh at that dream, throwing his head back and cackling at the absurdity of it, knowing that he was close to death and his mind was freeing itself of the inevitability of that event by creating punishments being visited upon his tormentors. But despite his humor, the images wouldn't go away, merely transformed into other dreams.

"Lyrien!" his father shouted at him, "Stop that non-sensical daydreaming and get back to work!"

Lyrien sighed and tossed the wooden practice sword he had been playing with to the ground and ran across the yard toward the well. Lito ran along beside him, panting and nipping playfully at his heels, tongue lolling out of his mouth in what Lyrien was certain was a mischievous grin.

"When did he lose his faith, Lito?" Lyrien heard himself ask his companion, wondering why he was pondering such philosophical questions at only twelve years of age. "He used to believe in what he did. He used to tell me that the only things in life that mattered were loyalty and devotion to duty. And I believed him. I really worshipped him. He was the captain of the king's guard, after all." The boy grabbed up the pail and lowered it by the rope tied to its handle down into the well, fetching water for his mother to use to cook supper with.

Lito ran around the well, barking at Lyrien as the boy worked. "Stop being naïve," the dog replied as it cavorted on the grass. "You know very well his derision and scorn were aimed at himself as much as at you. When the king just gave up, just quit fighting to save Ilnamar, it was the ultimate betrayal to your father. He couldn't find it in himself to believe in anything again. And he just couldn't stand to see you get hurt the way he did."

"Couldn't stand to see me get hurt, or couldn't stand that I was a better man?" Lyrien asked, then paused in the middle of hauling the bucket up from the well, dismayed by what he'd just said.

"Ah, so that's what this about," Lito said as he frolicked about. "Your sense of justice in the face of overwhelming odds, the way you throw yourself at causes that all reason says are lost. It's all about being the better man. About punishing him."

"Maybe," the boy said, resuming his pull on the rope. "Maybe I just don't want to be like him."

"You don't?" Lito asked. "But you sacrificed your sense of right and wrong for the easy way out, and told yourself it was for the sake of everyone else," Lito said, jumping up and down and putting his paws on Lyrien's chest. "You convinced yourself that serving the bloodlord was better than fighting his oppression, being his puppet and crossing into that gray area between good and evil rather than standing up to him was the best way to protect your friends. You don't want to be like him? You *are* like him. *Now* who should you be punishing?"

Lyrien looked sharply at his canine companion as the bucket reached the top. As he poured the cool water into an iron cauldron, he wanted to tell Lito to shut up, that it wasn't nearly the same, but it was time to take the water inside to his mother. As he tried to lift the cauldron, though, it grew in size and became six cauldrons, three in each hand. He struggled to move the cauldrons into the house, but they were too heavy, and he just made his arms ache trying.

"Lyrien," Lito said, jumping in front of the boy and making him slosh the water in the cauldrons, "Just take it easy. Don't try to move too fast." The dog was right in front of the boy, now, standing up on its hind legs and talking to Lyrien, resting its paws on his shoulders. "We'll get you to a healer as soon as we can," Lito added, "but you've got to hang on."

Lito's face dissolved into Gade's then, and Lyrien found himself back in the chamber with the multicolored lanterns. The guards were all dead, and the dover was in front of the captain, holding him up while someone worked to unhook him from the chains that held him aloft. He could tell that the hooks were still in his body in most places, but there was no more pull on their lines. The fencing that had surrounded him had been shoved away so that Gade could get to him. As soon as the tension left his right arm, it dropped lifelessly down across Gade's shoulder, and Lyrien nearly screamed in agony from the movement.

"Gods, we got here just in time," Lyrien heard another voice say. He turned and saw through a half-closed eye that it was Jezindi. She stood off to one side, next to Ezeria, and the captain could see tears streaming down their faces as they watched his rescue. Then there was the feeling of thousands of hot needles sliding through every muscle, and of icy cold in every one of his joints as he completely collapsed onto Gade, who lowered him gently to the floor.

"Drink this," Gade said, pressing the rim of some cup or flagon to Lyrien's lips. "Just sip it," the dover commanded.

Lyrien caught a whiff of a rancid odor from the container and tried to jerk his head away.

"No, no," Gade said, gently but insistently holding the captain's head up and still while tipping some of the contents of the bottle—it was a bottle, Lyrien realized—into his mouth. "You've got to drink it all," Gade said as he poured. "No sloshing. I know it tastes awful, but it'll help. Now, drink up."

Lyrien wanted to wretch, both from the pain and from the taste of the stuff Gade was force-feeding him, but he gulped the liquid down. Almost immediately, he felt a lessening of the pain that wracked his body. Some of the chorded muscles in his arms and legs began to relax, and a good amount of normal feeling was restored—enough so that Lyrien suddenly felt exhausted. He just wanted to curl up right then and there and go to sleep.

Gade pressed the nozzle of a skin to the captain's lips then, shaking the captain gently to keep him from dozing off, and Lyrien tasted cool, blessed water trickling into his mouth. He drank several deep gulps, amazed at how parched his throat felt, vaguely remembering the horrid leather-wrapped bit and a great deal of muffled screaming on his part as his body was slowly drawn in two. The soothing water chased the residual taste of the first liquid away.

"That's right," Gade was saying gently, still supporting Lyrien's head. "Drink as much as you need."

Lyrien looked up at the dover and smiled, but then Gade's face faded away, and the captain was still suspended in the chamber, suffering Lord Mabon's punishment. Choking back a sob, he knew that the other cruel punishment, the one his own conscience was inflicting on him, was far from over, either. Lyrien floated off into blackness once again.

* * * * *

Lyrien came to as he felt slack growing in the chains connected to his wrists. Bruhark was lowering him to the floor and as he touched the stones, he slumped down in pain and exhaustion. It was the third—no, the fourth— the fourth time he had been released . He didn't even move as the ogre pulled the gag free of his mouth.

"Are you ready for a healing drought?" Master Salas asked, and Lyrien merely looked at him, in too much pain to say anything. "Well, when you are, you just let me know," the slavemaster finished and set the small stoppered vial down next to him while he sat in a chair across from where Lyrien was crumpled.

The captain groaned, knowing his muscles were too injured to move. The damned man was going to make him ask for the healing again. Beg for it, in fact. Groaning, he rolled over, every small motion an agony. "Yes," was all the captain said, the word coming out in a croak from his parched and swollen throat. He tried to reach out for the potion.

Master Salas snatched it up. "Yes, what?" he asked, looking meaningfully at Lyrien. The captain saw that the slavemaster shot a quick glance over at Bruhark, who had the handle of the winch firmly in hand. At a nod, the ogre would simply crank Lyrien back up into the air and reset the cauldrons.

Lyrien closed his eyes, swallowing his pride in favor of relief. "Yes, please," he whispered through gritted teeth, and Salas immediately handed the captain the vial.

"Drink up," the slavemaster said warmly, even deigning to smile at Lyrien. The captain grimaced, remembering what had happened the last time Oderic had given the vial for him to drink himself. He had spilled most of it and the remains had been ineffectual. The next time, he was more careful, waiting until he was sure he could hold it steady before unstoppering it. As the nasty fluid slid down his throat, leaving behind a bitter aftertaste reminiscent of blade oil mixed with chicken liver, he felt soothing warmth seep into his aching bones, felt the sharp, throbbing pain in every muscle melt away, and felt the stabbing tenderness of his hundreds of puncture wounds fade into oblivion.

As the healing potion did its work, Lyrien closed his eyes in blessed relief, although he knew that respite was short-lived. Soon, Bruhark would simply crank the chains, hauling him into the air for another round of torture. The notion of it made him sob out loud. "Please," he begged. "No more."

"What was that?" Master Salas asked, leaning down. "What did you say?"

"I said, no more, please. I'll do it. Exactly how you say. No trouble from me." Every word coming from his mouth was an anathema to his ears, but Lyrien could no longer withstand the punishment.

"Oh, excellent! That's what I thought you said. Haul him up, Bruhark," Salas said, motioning for the ogre to crank the winch.

Lyrien's cry of anguish echoed through the round chamber for several moments, at least until the bit was forced between his teeth and strapped tight again.

* * * * *

The next time Lyrien was let down from his suspension, Master Salas had him released completely. This time, however, the captain was denied the requisite healing drought. Instead, Master Salas lectured him.

"Lord Mabon was very disappointed that you were so recalcitrant regarding upholding your end of the bargain before," the slavemaster commented as Bruhark and another ogre lifted Lyrien to his feet. They began to stroll along beside Oderic, following him down the hall as he scolded. Every bit of motion, every jostle sent stabbing pains through Lyrien, and he nearly blacked out several times. The gag had not been removed, and he knew it was to prevent his torturous cries from being so loud.

"You've set his timetable back substantially, and therefore, he believes further compensation is in order," Master Salas continued. "He no longer sees fit to send you back to your home world, should you complete the assignment he has given you. Your freedom, and that of your friend, will be the only thing granted. Is this clear?"

Lyrien nodded profusely despite the torment he was feeling at being half-dragged through the corridors. He knew where they were going; he was being taken to his chambers. He sobbed in relief, not caring what anyone thought of his appearance.

"Wonderful. You have one day to prepare," Oderic said. "You will set out tomorrow."

As the two ogres dragged him through the archway and dropped him to the floor just inside his room, Master Salas bent down and got right in Lyrien's face. "You understand, of course, that a small taste of your own punishment has been administered to your companions, don't you?" Lyrien looked at the bald-headed man, knowing his eyes had grown wide.

No! he silently screamed, sorrow filling him at what had been done to Gade.

"Keep that in mind, my gladiator. If you resist in any way again, they will receive a far worse sentence than even you experienced. That will be the price of your failure." And with that, he spun on his heel and strode out the doorway, the two ogres right behind him.

Chapter 14

Lyrien heard a sobbing from deeper in the room and turned to see Ezeria, once more collared and chained to the ring in the floor. Her face was wet with tears, and she had a trembling hand pressed to her mouth as she stared at the captain. Her glittering green eyes were filled with such sadness, it almost broke his heart. Then he realized her compassionate gaze was for his benefit.

Lyrien groaned and sat up. He reached up and found the clasp on the gag and unbuckled it, then removed the thing from his mouth and threw it across the room. Slowly, every movement an exercise in willpower, he crawled over to where Ezeria knelt. When he reached her, she flung her arms around him and hugged him tight.

"Look what they did to you," she cried softly, over and over, rocking him gently in her arms.

"I'm all right," he mumbled, knowing full well that she wasn't going to believe him for a moment. As she held him, Lyrien could see that there were abrasions, though fading now, on her ankles and wrists, marks from manacles. He narrowed his eyes and swore silently to himself.

"They will pay," he said softly to her, bending his mouth close to her ear. "They will pay for what they have done to you, and to Gade."

Slowly, Ezeria pulled back from him and stared. "What happened?" she asked, sniffling. "Why?"

Lyrien forced himself to rise to his knees. "I refused to do Mabon's dirty work for him," he said, resisting the urge to grimace from the pain. "I wouldn't help him slay another bloodlord. Someone named Flollo."

Ezeria sniffed again, her eyes weepy and red, but she smiled. "Of course you wouldn't," she said, her voice cracking in sorrow and compassion again. "Not my idealistic Lyrien." She shifted her weight and ran a hand along his face. "But they will kill you. And Gade." Her eyes glowed with both admiration and fear.

"Not if we get him and get out of here," Lyrien said, determination making his voice stronger than he intended.

Ezeria pressed a single soft finger against his lips, shushing him. "How?" She asked in a near-whisper. "Effron?"

Lyrien nodded. "We must go to him. Can you do it?"

Ezeria stared at him for a long moment, her eyes searching his. Finally, she nodded. "Right now?" she asked.

"Yes," Lyrien replied. "Tonight. Salas expects me to set out tomorrow. We don't have much time."

Almost immediately, Lyrien could see her eyes brighten. But then she said, "I won't go with you. I can do more good by staying here."

"Are you crazy?" Lyrien asked, his jaw dropping. "Once they realize I've managed to escape, that you helped, you're finished. You can't stay here. How could you possibly want to stick around?"

"It's not that I want to," the half-replied. "But there are more slaves who need my help. I'll be all right."

Lyrien shook his head. "No. Absolutely not. It's suicide. Besides, I need you to help me free Gade. I need to know where he is. If you do that, your cover is blown. Let's just go see Cadmus; I'm sure he'll agree with me."

Ezeria frowned, but she nodded. "All right, we'll see what he says."

"First, we have to get you out of this," the captain said, yanking helplessly on the chain that bound her to the floor. "I have no key this time," he said. "I have no way to free you."

Ezeria pursed her lips. "Can you pick a lock?" she asked. Lyrien shook his head. The harem slave nodded resolutely. "I had hoped to save this for when it was needed more," she said, shifting up onto her heels. "But I guess I have no choice." She began to mutter softly, speaking what Lyrien by then recognized as arcane words of power. The half-elf reached up and gently touched her finger to the lock on the collar, and with a soft click, the lock fell open. She removed the collar and tossed it aside.

Lyrien nodded in appreciation. "It would be good to have that later," he agreed, lamenting the loss of her spell. "But one step at a time."

Quickly, Ezeria stood up and went to the wardrobe where Lyrien's sets of clothing were still stored. She donned one of his shirts and a pair of the pants hanging there. As he had been given only one pair of boots, she stayed barefoot. She grabbed up a second set of clothing and the boots, then returned to the captain, who was still kneeling wearily on the floor. Even in his exhausted and wounded state, Lyrien had to admit that Ezeria was fetching wearing his clothes.

The half-elven beauty knelt down and gently ran a hand across his brow. "Effron will be able to heal you," she said softly. "We'll wait to get you dressed until after then." When Lyrien tilted his head to one side, revealing his confusion, she pointed to the myriad puncture wounds on his flesh. "The blood," she explained. "Don't want to ruin your clothes." Without waiting for him to answer, she then laid the clothes on the foot of the bed.

Ezeria next wove the spell that would create the illusory images and sounds of the two of them. That time, she made it appear that they were asleep in the bed. Then, taking the captain's hand, she began to chant once more, and instantly, they were standing in the nobleman's study in a quick flash of light.

Effron was not there, but when the pair of them arrived, they were nonetheless not alone. A huge dog, a mastiff, was sleeping near the hearth. At their appearance, the beast immediately got to its feet and advanced slowly, fangs bared and a low growl in its throat.

"Don't move," Lyrien commanded Ezeria, who had already frozen in place at the sight of the hound. "Just stand still," the captain said, turning slowly to face the creature.

The dog took another step forward, on the verge of barking. Lyrien longed for a weapon, but all he could find within reach was a large paperweight on the desk. He reached up, closed his fist around it, and waited, sitting as still as possible.

A set of double doors leading into the study opened then, and Effron Cadmus stalked through, a staff clutched in one hand. When he saw who was there, he visibly relaxed. "Down, King! Sit!" he ordered, and immediately, the dog dropped to its haunches and began panting. Cadmus strolled over to the mastiff and scratched it behind the ear. "Ezeria, you know better than to come at odd hours like this," he scolded. "If I had been elsewhere, King here might have taken off a few arms."

"I was just about to put him gently to sleep," the harem slave replied, wriggling her fingers in a suggestion of casting a spell. Lyrien unobtrusively replaced the paperweight, feeling chagrined.

"Well, whatever brings you here unplanned must be pretty urgent," Cadmus said, eyeing the captain, naked and bloody on his floor. "I take it you've finally seen the error of your ways," he added, moving around his desk and sitting in the chair. He was looking at Lyrien as he said this. King moved back near the fireplace and plopped down in front of the hearth once more.

"You were right," Lyrien began, then corrected himself. "Or rather, I was wrong. I can no longer in good conscience serve Lord Mabon in exchange for our freedom. The asking price is too high."

Cadmus smirked. "And you've already paid so much," he said sardonically. "Both of us tried to warn you. And now, I'm sure time is precious. Am I correct?"

Lyrien nodded. "I got complacent, comfortable in that gray area between right and wrong. I came to my senses a few days ago. I paid for my refusal, and right now, Lord Mabon thinks he has broken me. I have one last chance to make amends. If the offer is still on the table to help me free Ezeria and Gade, I will fetch Jezindi for you."

"You think you can pull it off tonight, on such short notice? And in your condition? Just the other day you were complaining about how it would take you a month or more to plan."

"I know," Lyrien admitted, chagrined. "But I don't have a choice. Mabon is trying to send me away tomorrow. If I don't act now, I might not get the chance later."

"Effron," Ezeria said, "He needs healing. Look at him," she added piteously. "Please help him."

"I can do that," Cadmus said, pulling a desk drawer open. He extracted a small box, from which he produced a stoppered vial. He handed the vial to Lyrien, who took it and, with Ezeria's help, managed to quaff the contents. Immediately, all the injuries he had sustained during his torture faded. He closed his eyes and sighed in relief.

When Lyrien opened them again, Effron Cadmus was shaking his head. "I think this is too risky now. You're being watched. The bloodlord knows you've tried to bolt once, and you may do so again. No, I think we wait for a better time. I'm sorry."

Lyrien stared at Cadmus in stunned silence. He opened and shut his mouth several times, searching for something to say, some way to convince the man that he must reconsider.

"Effron, you can't do this," Ezeria chimed in. "You can't abandon him like this, when the situation has gotten so desperate."

"Can't I?" the nobleman replied. "It didn't seem to bother him to avoid my request, when I first asked for his help." Ezeria looked down. Cadmus turned back to Lyrien. "If I send you in there to try to reach the harem girl now, the chances of you getting caught are too high. And if you don't make it, if you don't at least put her out of her misery, then I've only set myself back further. Mabon will increase his security around her, and I'll never be able to reach her. I'm sorry, Lyrien, it's just not in my best interests to attempt it. I wish you had listened to me initially."

"Look," Lyrien said desperately, leaning forward in his chair. "I can do this. I can reach her. Trust me, I can at least get to her. I want to free her, but if I can't do that—" He paused and swallowed hard, regretting admitting what he was about to say. "If I can't bring her to you, I will make sure that Mabon never exploits her again. Please," he pleaded. "Give me a chance."

Effron Cadmus sat back in his chair and steepled his fingers in front of his mouth, considering. He frowned as he studied Lyrien, who felt like he was using force of will to try and convince the nobleman to agree. Finally, Cadmus sighed and nodded. "All right," he said, although he sounded reluctant. "I'll do this against my better judgment. Some of my compatriots are growing restless to see movement on this issue, at any rate." He pulled open his desk drawer and removed a dagger from it. The scabbard and the hilt were of black leather. He slid it across the table to where Lyrien sat. "You know what this is for," the nobleman said.

Lyrien took hold of the dagger and felt a mild wave of revulsion wash over him. He scrutinized the weapon, sliding it out of the hilt. The blade was forged of a black metal and was finely honed. As he looked at it, Lyrien could see an aura surrounding it. He had to stop himself from reaching out and crushing the emanation. "I won't need this," he said, for his own benefit as much as for Cadmus's.

"Nevertheless, you will take it," Cadmus replied. "Avoid using it for as long as you can. But if you can't free her, or if you get caught before you manage to reach her, use it. Don't let either one of you remain in Mabon's clutches."

Lyrien slid the dagger back into its sheath and nodded. Then he stood up, Ezeria rising right beside him. "Where will you meet us after I extract Jezindi and Gade? How will you know when we're ready?"

"Ezeria knows how to summon me," Cadmus replied. "Work out the details with her, and she'll know what to do."

Lyrien looked over at his counterpart, who smiled at him and nodded. "We'll get them both out," she assured the captain. "I know we can do it."

"And you," Lyrien said sternly, looking from Ezeria to the nobleman. "Tell her she can't remain behind after this. Mabon will flay her alive, once I escape with the other two. Make her see reason."

Cadmus looked at Ezeria and nodded. "He's right. Once we pull Jezindi out, your safety is suspect. You can't stay."

Ezeria hung her head briefly, but then she nodded. "All right," she agreed. "When I send you a whispering spell, we all leave together."

"Good. It's time for you to go, then," Cadmus said. "Good luck."

Lyrien and Ezeria stepped back into the center of the room and moved close to one another. King raised his head and sniffed at them once, then yawned widely and settled his head back down. Cadmus stood and watched as Ezeria summoned her magic and whisked them back to Lyrien's chambers. The chamber was empty so the half-elf dismissed the illusion and turned to the captain.

"Bathe quickly and get dressed," she said, motioning to the steaming basin. "When you're finished, I'll tell you how to get to her. There's a back way into the throne room, where Lord Mabon keeps her safely locked away at night," Ezeria said. "It's not too hard to reach from here."

"What about Gade? Where will I find him?" Lyrien asked, slipping into the magically heated water. The thought of soaking in it for several hours appealed to him, but he knew he had no time. Quickly, he began washing the blood and sweat from his body.

"Leave that to me," Ezeria answered, smiling. She began to unbutton the shirt she had borrowed from Lyrien's wardrobe, then slid it from her body and let it drop to the floor. The pants followed soon after. "I'll get him and meet you back here," she said.

"Like that?" Lyrien asked, staring at her despite himself. He climbed out of the basin and began to don his clothing. He thought it strangely funny that the two of them were reversing their states of dress. He chuckled, eliciting a strange look from his counterpart.

"What harm could a poor, naked slave girl do?" she asked demurely. "Now go get Jezindi," she said, pressing herself up against Lyrien and brushing his lips with her own. It wasn't a sensuous kiss, but one of genuine affection nonetheless, gentle and tender. "I'll bring Gade back here. Come back, gladiator," she said, the urgency in her voice obvious.

"I will," Lyrien answered, pulling her close in a hug. There was no lust at that moment—well, it simmered below the surface, at least—only warmth and concern. "You're sure you can get Gade out?" the captain asked, pulling away at last.

"Yes," Ezeria replied. She stepped back and motioned for him to get going. "Be careful."

Lyrien examined the weapon once more, pulling it free of the scabbard. Holding the thing gave the captain an eerie, uncomfortable feeling. "What will it do?" he asked Ezeria, slipping the blade carefully back in its sheath.

The woman shrugged. "I learned a long time ago not to ask questions. Just use it like he told you. I'll be here by the time you return."

"But what about guards? And other protections? What should I expect?" Lyrien asked, feeling suffocated at that moment, fretting about all the details, all the points he hadn't yet contemplated regarding the crazy scheme but that he knew he would think of later—after it was too late.

"You shouldn't have any trouble; the guards aren't looking to stop you; they think you've been cowed, or else you wouldn't even be wandering free. As for Jezindi, during the day, he keeps her chained beside him while he receives important visitors, but at night, when he's elsewhere, Lord Mabon has her locked in a cage there. He long since stopped trying to bed her. The throne room should be empty at this time of the night."

Lyrien nodded. "I'll be back soon," he said, tucking the blade into the waistband at the small of his back, concealing the weapon. He gave one final look at Ezeria, then glanced out past the diaphanous curtains to the balcony. The fading sunlight of Storm told him that it was past midnight. He stepped out through the curtained doorway and into the hall beyond.

In the small hours of the morning, before much of the palace would be stirring, there was no one around, and many of the lamps had been dimmed or shuttered, leaving the passages in deep shadow. Lyrien didn't know whether the dearth of wanderers was a blessing or a curse; few would see him slinking through the hallways, but he feared that anyone who did might become immediately suspicious.

Stalking from shadow to shadow, from balustrade to column, the captain made his way in the direction Ezeria had indicated, praying he would encounter few guards. His heart pounded in his chest, and that metallic taste of fear had returned. With each stealthy step, he listened for any signs that there were others in proximity to him.

The first guards he encountered were two ogres standing before a doorway, slouched against a wall, self-absorbed in their obvious boredom. Lyrien wondered briefly if Gade might lie beyond that curtained portal, and contemplated if he should try to find out, but he dismissed those musings again quickly. He and Ezeria already had their plan in place, and altering it now would only lead to disaster. Besides, he had enough to do figuring out how to get past those two behemoths without making them suspicious. He briefly considered finding a way around them, but he wasn't sure he could track his progress through the winding maze of hallways, stairwells, and blind passages that made up the palace.

Finally, Lyrien realized he was just going to have to bluff his way past, and taking a deep breath to calm himself, he strolled out from the shadows as though he were on a casual walk. Immediately, the two guards grew alert, peering at the captain warily as they fingered the great curved swords they held, points down against the floor. Lyrien simply smiled as he sauntered by, pretending that he had no worries in the world. But he thought it odd that they would behave so warily.

Unless they heard about Mabon's treachery and expect me to try something, he thought uneasily. Or unless Gade *is* inside there. No! Stay on task! he ordered himself. Don't blow it now.

"Can't sleep," the captain said finally as he got close to the pair of ogres, but they said nothing in return, merely continued to stare at him as he moved on by.

At least they didn't challenge me, he thought.

Whatever they were guarding, that was the limit of their duties.

Once he was around the next corner, Lyrien exhaled in relief, leaning against a wall for a moment to regain his composure. Guided by Ezeria's instructions, Lyrien continued his trek toward the throne room, taking the route she had suggested in hopes of minimizing his contact with others. Thus far, her directions had been accurate. He reached a point about halfway down one passage and found the doorway she had claimed would be there. Unlike most of the portals in the palace, it was actually a door, thick wood bound by metal. He pushed on it and found it locked.

Lyrien growled in frustration and peered in either direction, checking once more to see if anyone was coming. When he was certain he was alone, he removed the black dagger from the waist band of his trousers and slipped the scabbard off. The blade seemed to gleam, even in the deep shadows where he stood at that moment. Shaking off the feeling of dread he was experiencing, he slipped the blade into the crack between the door and the doorframe and began to feel for a latch on the other side.

After several frustrating moments of failure, Lyrien finally managed to wedge the thin dagger against something on the opposite side and felt it give slightly. Carefully so as not to lose his positioning, the captain nudged the blade upward, feeling it stick against the stone, trapped because of the angle. Exasperated, he stuck a toe underneath the door and pulled it to the limits of its catch, which freed the blade enough to let it slide the rest of the way up, at last releasing the latch. The door swung silently open, away from him, and Lyrien slipped inside and shut it, leaving himself in darkness.

From there, Ezeria had claimed Lyrien could take a narrow spiral staircase upward two levels in order to reach the throne room. This staircase let out into an alcove behind the throne, hidden by curtains. It was one of many routes Mabon could take to flee his throne room unseen, if necessary. Lyrien had not counted on finding it darkened, though he realized it was not illogical. Nonetheless, he could faintly make out the winding steps ascending in front of him, and he realized the dagger still in his hand was glowing with a faint purple hue, illuminating the area ever so slightly.

Keeping the weapon out as a light source, dim though it was, Lyrien was able to climb the stairs quickly and quietly and reached the top after only a few moments. There was a second door there, identical to the one below, though the second one was not locked. The captain cracked it open a tiny bit and peered out, but there was little to see other than a heavy drape only a couple of feet from where he stood. In fact, the curtain was so close that there would barely be enough room for him to stand between it and the closed door without disturbing it.

That's exactly what Lyrien did, though, maneuvering himself to the edge of the shallow alcove in which he found himself after pulling the door shut behind him. From there, it was easy to peer around the edge of the curtain into the room beyond.

The throne room was vast, a high-ceilinged chamber with columns running down the center of it in two parallel rows. The close end of the room was raised higher than the rest of it, with a massive chair carved of a single chunk of a translucent black stone, possibly some sort of quartz. A pair of balconies ran along either side, well up off the ground, but down on the floor level, there was nothing but stone flooring. A banister cordoned off the majority of the room from the dais at the near end, a reminder to the audience that they must maintain a respectable distance between themselves and their ruler. Several lanterns hanging on large iron stands would maintain a bright glow when turned up, but many of them were currently out, and the few that still burned had been dimmed considerably, so that the light they cast was quite faint, accentuating the murk of the shadows between them. Still, after the near-absolute darkness of the stairs, Lyrien had little difficulty spotting the cage.

The cage was held aloft, high above the floor and beyond his reach, like a bird cage, and indeed, it had a similar shape, round and domed, although it was substantially larger, sizable enough to contain a human being, which it did at that moment. From that distance, Lyrien could only make out the silhouette of the figure, curled up and lying on its side, apparently asleep. In the half-light, he could not see how the apparatus was anchored, nor how to lower it. He would have to move into the chamber and get closer in order to ascertain this.

Lyrien hesitated for a few moments, peering into every darkened corner and shadow of the room, looking for some telltale sign of guards. Effron Cadmus had been adamant that Lord Mabon had the slave well protected, and Lyrien had assumed that meant plenty of guards. But he saw nothing, even when he tried to spot magical emanations. That almost made him more nervous. He waited a moment longer, listening, watching. There was no one else there.

Stepping carefully, Lyrien brushed past the curtain separating the small alcove from the rest of the chamber and began to creep across the floor in the direction of the cage. He peered about, still staring into the shadows, trying to spot anyone or anything that had eluded his search previously. He had the most uncomfortable feeling that he was being watched as he drifted across the open space between the alcove and the cage, but every time he stopped and stared, there was still nothing. Nevertheless, the feeling would not go away.

Finally, Lyrien was close enough to the cage to see that it was connected by a long chain that ran up into the gloom at the ceiling. A second chain ran back down from the same point and at an angle, attached to a large winch mechanism there. The captain closed the remaining distance to the winch and crouched down to examine it.

The winch itself was geared such that Lyrien felt reasonably confident he could operate it himself, but his heart fell when he noticed that it had been locked into place with a thick iron bar that itself was held in place by two padlocks as big as his hands. He had no skill in picking such locks, even if he had the proper tools. Silently groaning in frustration, he stood, studying the chain that ran from the winch to the ceiling, ascertaining whether or not he could climb it and reach the cage that way.

He had just shrugged out of his shirt and was about to remove his boots when a small, feminine voice called from above, "Watch out!"

Chapter 15

Instinctively, Lyrien dived forward and to the side, but his boots, still new, got poor traction and he ended up sprawling in place, instead. Still, the sudden movement probably saved his life, for a blade whistled over his head as he fell in a heap.

Instantly, Lyrien rolled over and kicked out, catching his assailant across what he hoped was one knee. As he spun, he tried to get a good look at his attacker, but the form was shadowy and indistinct. The impact of his foot against the knee joint was solid, though, and Lyrien heard a resounding crack. The assailant grunted, but the sound had a strange echoing sort of resonance that made Lyrien's skin crawl. He scrambled backward and to his feet, wishing desperately for a weapon besides the dagger pinned against the small of his back, which he knew he could not use.

The assailant leaped forward with surprising speed, though he had a limp, and Lyrien was forced to dance back as a scimitar slashed at him almost out of nowhere. His foe was utterly silent as he advanced, and the captain noticed that he was hunched over, as though he were deformed in some way. Lyrien stared hard into the shadows, trying to get a clearer view. He could see that his foe was dressed in dark wrappings from head to toe, covered by a light suit of leather armor. In addition to the scimitar he wielded, the assailant also had a small buckler shield to protect himself with.

As the scimitar flashed toward him again, Lyrien noticed that the hand that was clamped around the hilt of the weapon was desiccated and clawed, inhuman in appearance, and suddenly he was very afraid. He continued to back away from the death-shrouded enemy, looking around the chamber for anything at all he could use to defend himself. He noticed again that the lanterns were hooked onto large iron stands, and he backed his way to one, watching his adversary close the distance with that awkward limping gait, tilted slightly to one side to compensate for its deformity.

How can it move so quickly when it's crippled like that? Lyrien wondered absently, knowing already that the thing he fought was unnatural.

The captain reached one of the lantern stands a moment before he was forced to duck to avoid another slash, then took hold of the heavy device and swung it around, trying to swat the black-clad creature full in the torso. The lantern that had been hanging from the stand was flung off into the darkness, shattering with a horrific crash in a distant corner. Lyrien winced at the noise, but his foe merely dodged backward, spun, and made a quick, flicking cut that drew blood across Lyrien's forearm.

Lyrien stifled a snarl of pain and brought the iron stand around, holding it like an unwieldy quarterstaff, ready to block any further blows. Whatever he was fighting, it was too fast for him to stay on the offensive with his own cumbersome makeshift weapon. He was running out of time, especially with the commotion he was making. The rescue attempt seemed doomed to failure before it had really gotten underway. But quitting was not an option, so he fought on, hoping for some sort of a miracle.

The hunchbacked creature launched another series of attacks, and Lyrien was forced to focus all his energy on blocking the well placed blows. The speed with which the thing moved was stunning, and when Lyrien overdefended on a high slice to his outside shoulder, his opponent spun back in low and cut him across his thigh.

"Damn it!" Lyrien hollered, staggering back and knocking away another swipe at his head. "I need a blade!" He caught another scimitar slice squarely with his lantern stand and shoved with all of his might, sending his foe stumbling back a couple of steps.

"Burn it," came that same feminine voice from above, in the cage.

Lyrien glanced up, nearly losing some of his fingers in the process as he badly parried another attack, and saw a form half-lounging within the confines of the prison, watching the combat. He blocked another strike and retreated again. "What?" he called out, watching his foe advance.

"I said, burn it. Use a lantern." If it was indeed Jezindi, she sounded drowsy, her speech slightly slurred.

Lyrien pursed his lips as he deflected attack after attack. The thing coming at him didn't seem to tire in the slightest, for it just continued to rain blows down on him from every angle. For him, on the other hand, the lantern stand was growing heavier by the minute. "What is it?" he asked, trying to conserve his energy now as best as he could. Each strike was knocked just enough off the mark to keep from injuring him, but no more.

"Something that should have been left dead," came the reply. "Some poor, wretched thing that Mabon's wizards brought to unlife. Every night they let it loose in here to keep everyone out. It should be destroyed; burn it."

Lyrien backed away from another onslaught and steered his retreat toward another lantern stand, one with a light that still burned. Once he was there, though, he realized his difficulty; in order to grab at the lantern, he would have to lower his guard, for the iron stand was too heavy to hold in place with just one hand. His opponent would be able to strike at him while he was defenseless. Several times, he staved off an attack and began to reach for the lantern, but each time, the iron stand drooped, and the undead thing in front of him tried to take advantage of his sagging defenses to initiate a new strike. Each time, Lyrien jumped back and grabbed hold of the stand just in time.

This isn't going to work, Lyrien thought, desperately yanking the stand back up a third time. I can't do both at the same time. Then the captain's eyes narrowed in resolution. So be it, he decided.

When the next strikes at him came, the captain deflected them back, then dropped the iron stand completely, grabbing at the lantern as he did so. The undead assailant took advantage of the opening to lunge in with its scimitar, but Lyrien was ready. He spun just enough to let the blade of the creature's weapon graze him across the ribs, rather than taking the blow squarely, and grabbed hold of the hilt with his free hand, pinning the weapon under his arm and holding the creature close to him. He could feel the edge of the scimitar crease his flesh, winced as the hot trickle of blood began to run down his flank, but he ignored the pain.

With his free hand, Lyrien swung the lit lantern up and overhead in a wide arc, bringing the light crashing down atop the hunchback's shrouded head. Just as his makeshift weapon connected, the sentinel gave one last, near-soundless snarl, and the captain could see sightless eye sockets, glowing faintly with a sickly green light, peering at him from behind the black wrappings on its head. Then the lantern impacted, spilling burning oil all down the creature's body, and instantly, it was ignited.

Lyrien released his hold on the undead thing's weapon and jumped free of the flames, and immediately, heedless of the fire that was consuming it, the sentinel advanced, raising its weapon up for another strike at him. He fell back steadily now, dodging the last half-dozen blows from the thing, and then it collapsed, silently crumpling to the floor, emitting thick clouds of black, foul-smelling smoke. Lyrien watched it burn for a moment, wanting to make sure that it was not going to move again, before sagging to his knees in exhaustion and pain.

Can't rest now, the captain insisted. A small part of him wanted to flee, to forget about the rescue, but he was through running. The vertigo of panic was creeping in on the edges of his mind, and he fought it with all of his will.

Whatever happens, he decided, I'm not going down without a fight.

Lyrien grabbed up the scimitar the thing had been fighting with. He swished it through the air a couple of times, testing it. It was a good blade.

Quickly, painfully, Lyrien did a visual inspection of himself. Blood slicked his body in several places, the most serious wound of which was the cut across his side. All of the cuts stung from the sweat that poured off his body, but none of them were so severe that they needed immediate treatment.

Can't go prowling the halls like this, he realized. The blood is too noticeable.

The captain rose to his feet, grabbing at his shirt. His luck had held out so far, for no one had come running at the sounds of the battle, but he knew that he had little time left. He could feel the dagger pressing into the small of his back, briefly thought of the fall-back option.

No. She saved my life. I won't take hers. Not unless there's no other chance.

"Hey," the woman in the cage groggily called out. "What happened to the rescue?"

Lyrien chuckled softly as he began to remove his boots, planning to climb up the chain. "Who says this is a rescue?" He called up. "Maybe I'm supposed to kill you. You *are* Jezindi, aren't you?"

"Yes, and you're not going to kill me," she said.

Lyrien turned to look up at her. "Oh? How do you know this?"

"Because I'm supposed to go *with* you."

Lyrien had one boot off and was working on the second, but he halted with one foot in the air. He glanced up over his shoulder at the woman in the cage. "What?" he asked quietly, unsure if he understood.

"That's how I know you're not going to kill me. So whatever you do," Jezindi added, sitting up and making her cage sway. "Don't leave me here."

"Don't worry, I'm getting you out of there. You saved my life. But I was sent to kill you if I couldn't get you out," Lyrien acknowledged. "Without your warning, I'd be dead, though, and the irony's significant, don't you think?"

"The what?" Jezindi said, sounding drowsy again.

"Never mind. Just hang on. I've got to get you out of there before Mabon's thugs find me."

"I'm supposed to go with you," Jezindi repeated, less clearly, as though she were fighting off sleep and could barely succeed. "Something . . . important to do . . . but can't . . . without . . . me. . . ."

Damn, Lyrien thought. He moved back under the cage. "Are you still with me?" he called. No answer. "Jezindi?" Still nothing. Fine, he thought, tossing his shirt down again and moving to the winch after redonning his boot. Can't carry her and climb down at the same time. Guess we'll try the winch again.

The two locks were thick and stout. Lyrien knew he was going to have to break them. It took him only a heart-beat to think of the heavy lantern stand. He snatched it up and began methodically striking the locks, wincing with each loud, resounding clang. After perhaps a dozen blows each, the locks were a mangled ruin.

The captain yanked the restraining bar free and re-leased the winch, letting the cage freefall. He ran over just as it settled with another loud clank to the floor. There was, of course, another lock on the cage door. He had it shattered in three strikes.

Inside, Jezindi had apparently passed out. Whatever nasty potions Mabon had been feeding her, they did their job well, for she was a sorry sight. The captain could see how dazed and unkempt she was. Naked except for the thick metal collar that was not merely locked but bolted around her neck, she had very short dark hair that was plastered against her head, damp and dull. Her equally dark eyes were glazed over, and she stank of old sweat and bodily filth. She was certainly in no condition to walk.

The collar will have to wait for later, Lyrien deemed. *Of course, she's too far out of it to explain her cryptic comments.* Then again, he thought, *maybe she just lied to me to get herself out of there.*

Lyrien draped his shirt around her and hoisted her over his shoulder, then staggered out of the throne room. He made his way down the spiral stairs and back into the lower levels of the palace, hearing the sounds of an alarm being raised as he proceeded.

Someone heard me, all right. I guess the word is spreading.

To his consternation, the halls were crawling with guards running one way or another, and Lyrien was forced to go a different direction than he wanted to. He hoped initially to find a way around and back to his own rooms, but each time he thought he had his route figured out, either the passageway turned the wrong direction, or he almost encountered more of Mabon's thugs. Soon, he was lost, kicking himself for not being more patient and just taking the route he knew would get him back where he needed to be.

After a time, Jezindi regained her awareness a little more. "I can walk," she informed Lyrien softly, squirming to get down from his shoulder.

Thankfully, wearily, the captain set her down. "Are you sure?" he asked.

Jezindi nodded, but her eyelids fluttered or remained half-closed. Sighing, Lyrien helped her slip inside the shirt and buttoned it up for her, then he took her by the arm and led her along. Their progress was no faster than when he had been toting her, but at least he wasn't exhausting himself with her weight.

Soon, though, Lyrien wanted to howl in frustration. Jezindi just couldn't move fast enough to keep ahead of the pursuit, and it was making him crazy. But he knew it wasn't her fault, so he bit his tongue and quietly urged her to hurry as best as she could. They stumbled along together, him supporting her with an arm around her back.

Several shouts echoed from the hallway ahead, emanating from around a corner. Lyrien took hold of the half-dazed woman and pulled her by the shoulders into a side hall, a narrow passage—that led into a barracks, Lyrien realized in dismay.

God, I've led us right into the teeth of the enemy, he silently lamented.

The captain no longer had any idea which way he was going. His only focus right then was keeping them out of harm's way, but it appeared that he had done just the opposite. The sounds from out in the main hall were growing louder and, with no other choice, Lyrien steered Jezindi deeper into the barracks area, poking his head through multiple doorways, desperately seeking a good hiding place.

Finally, just as the pursuit seemed to be right outside the hall, the captain discovered an empty bathing room and shoved Jezindi inside, following right behind her. The woman staggered over to one side, where a bench had been built against the wall, and slumped down, her chin drooping and coming to rest on her chest. Lyrien stayed near the door into the room, watching the hallway outside. He gripped the scimitar, ready to engage anyone who thought to check in that particular chamber.

A clump of guards strolled by, but they seemed at ease, talking low among themselves. They weren't searching for him, Lyrien realized with relief. They must just be off duty. The flock of guards moved by, heading deeper into the barracks. Lyrien watched them until they disappeared, then waited a few moments longer to see if anyone else was coming. Finally, when he was satisfied that they were alone, he turned back to a cabinet he had noted upon first entering.

He began to rummage through the cabinet and was rewarded with fresh towels and linens. He hurriedly cleaned his various minor wounds, then used some of the fabric to wrap a thin bandage around his waist to protect the worst of them, the clean slice across his ribs. When he was satisfied with his medical handiwork, he turned back to Jezindi.

The poor woman had slumped completely over on the bench and was sprawled on her side, eyes closed in a stupor. Shaking his head, Lyrien moved beside her and tried to roust her. She stirred, but he could not get her alert enough to talk to him. Sighing, he scooped her up and flung her over his shoulder again, grunting under her weight. He turned back to the doorway and made one last peek before emerging from the bathing room.

As quickly as he could with his burden, Lyrien scurried back toward the main hall. There, he stole a glance out into the passageway and saw that it was clear. He stepped out and considered which way to go.

One route's probably as useless as another, he thought, but I might as well keep going the way I was. Maybe something will look familiar.

The captain stumbled on, hoping against hope that he would either find his way out or else discover some abandoned section of the palace where he could hole up until Jezindi recovered enough to be more self-sufficient. Ezeria was going to start worrying soon, he realized. And once Mabon realized Lyrien wasn't where he was supposed to be and pieced everything together—if the bloodlord hadn't already deduced that, the captain thought dismally—the half-elf's time would be short.

Run, Ezeria, he willed. Take Gade and just get out. Use your magic.

Working through all of the challenges in his head as he ran, Lyrien was beginning to get that out-of-control feeling again. Everything began to spin faster and faster in his mind, and he could sense the vertiginous terror about to wash over him.

At that moment, he spotted a pair of guards stationed near a doorway further down the hall. Lyrien stopped and moved quietly against the wall, hoping they hadn't seen him, but his luck had run out. One of them shouted, and from around a corner near them, several more of Mabon's sentinels appeared and began to trot toward him.

Cursing, the captain spun and retreated the way he had come, and when he heard a shout drifting forward from behind him, calling for him stop, he quickened his pace. Soon, he could hear footsteps running toward him.

I'll never make it like this, Lyrien realized, coming to an intersection and turning a corner just to get out of sight for a moment. Gasping for breath, he set Jezindi down along one side of the new passage and stepped out into the middle of the floor, scimitar in hand. It was no rapier, but it was the most comfortable weapon he had managed to get his hands on since he had arrived.

Let's put it to good use, the captain thought, bouncing on the balls of his feet.

The first of the guards came around the corner too fast to react, and Lyrien cut him hard across the middle before the fellow knew what had happened to him. Side-stepping that first opponent, Lyrien spun and swiped upward with his blade at the next sentinel, one of the rooster-headed creatures he had seen his first day. A haze, Gade had called it.

The haze managed to parry Lyrien's blow and struck back, and the ring of steel on steel echoed through the halls as the creature and Lyrien exchanged attacks. A third and fourth guard arrived a moment later, one human and one a green-skinned creature of the same species as Gertroll the priest. They pressed themselves against the wall, trying to flank Lyrien and finish the fight quickly, but the captain managed to hold all three of them at bay, though he was almost purely on the defensive by then.

Lyrien might have actually enjoyed the fight under other circumstances, but he was already tired from the battle with the undead guardian in the throne room and the subsequent lugging of Jezindi about, and he could also feel the wound in his side beginning to bleed again. Every moment he wasted skirmishing with those three diminished his chances of escaping. Fortunately, the guards did not seem to be masters of their craft, for Lyrien began to spot openings in their defenses. On impulse, he focused his attention on his own senses, began to feel just how surefooted and balanced he was as he fought. He realized that the Forge was giving him an advantage, and he was going to take it.

Blocking a high strike from the guard on his left, Lyrien dropped to one knee and sliced at the haze's leg. Blood spurted and the creature staggered backward. Lyrien could hear the thing screaming, not a true sound, but some sort of voice in his mind. He tried to shake the intrusive imaginary sound, blocking a poorly aimed shot at his head from the middle guard. He realized that the remaining two soldiers must have been affected by the mental screams as well, and he capitalized on their distraction, rolling first to his left and then forward, coming up behind the pair of them.

The two sentinels spun around to face Lyrien again, but he was too fast. The heightened senses he was experiencing made time seem to move more slowly. He was able to sense each move his opponents made before he should have, and it became a simple matter to parry their strikes and counterattack with deadly accuracy. In the span of three breaths, all of the guards lay dead.

Sighing with weariness, Lyrien slid his blade free from his last opponent, turned to collect Jezindi, and noticed that the woman was awake again, sitting up and leaning against the wall. Lyrien moved over beside her. "Can you walk?" he asked.

Jezindi nodded. "I think so," she said, pushing herself off the stone floor.

The captain helped the woman to her feet and then held her arm as she tried to walk a few steps, and when he was certain she would not topple over, he began to lead her down that new hallway, looking for some place to get out of sight for a while. He needed to rest, to collect his thoughts, and though he regretted delaying any further, it was unavoidable. "I've got to find the route back," he muttered, half to himself. "Or find Ezeria and Gade."

"I saw him, you know. Last night. He was brought to Lord Mabon in his harem. He has an important part to play in this affair too."

"What do you mean?" Lyrien asked, uneasy at the prophetic, yet cryptic, statements.

"I'm not sure. I just tell what I know; I don't do interpretations," she replied, moving slowly, woozily.

"But you could see that by looking at him?"

"Yes," Jezindi replied, using one hand against a wall to keep herself steady as they walked.

"How accurate are these visions of yours? Are they certain to come to pass?" Lyrien asked as they advanced. As much as he wanted to find an odd corner for refuge, an out-of-the-way cubbyhole where he could recuperate and figure out his next step, it was not to be. The hallway led instead into a large, open chamber, some sort of great hall that was long rather than square, possibly a staging area for gathering troops, or perhaps a mess hall. It was large enough to do both at once. The tunnel they had followed to that massive chamber deposited the pair along one side of the room, behind a row of heavy, thick columns that partially obscured them from the vast open area beyond, where a number of guards either moved through the chamber or milled about, conversing casually in small groups. Lyrien cursed and ducked back into the shadows of the hallway itself.

"They aren't 'visions,'" Jezindi replied in a whisper, crouching unsteadily down beside Lyrien, "they're more like an awareness. They don't happen all the time. Sometimes, when I look at someone, I simply *know* something about that person."

"Well, do you *know* which way we should go to either get back to my chambers or else to find my friend Gade?" Lyrien asked, eying both the hallway behind them and the great chamber ahead. He hated to backtrack, but he had no notion of how to get through the chamber unseen, nor any clue which of the numerous passages lining the walls to follow once they had slipped past.

"No, but it doesn't matter," Jezindi replied, apparently taking Lyrien's rhetorical question as literal. The captain turned to look at her, and saw that she was pointing at something in the hall itself. He followed her gaze with his own and saw a cadre of guards moving through the vast room, cutting across it lengthwise. Their path was taking them toward a wide ascending staircase set in the wall to Lyrien's right, but what had drawn Jezindi's attention, and then caught his, was that they were escorting a prisoner. It was Gade, though the dover was shuffling rather than walking, as his hands and feet were restrained in manacles.

"Once in a very great while," Lyrien breathed, immensely relieved and worried at the same time, "I *do* get lucky." He turned to Jezindi. "Can you keep up?" he asked her. "Otherwise, I'll chase him down alone and come back for you."

In answer, the woman pushed herself up with the aid of the wall, her black eyes flashing defiantly with the first hint of fire that Lyrien had seen. She gestured for the captain to lead the way.

Lyrien gave his companion one careful, measured look, then turned and slipped into the chamber. He turned immediately to the right so as to follow the wall and stay behind the line of columns in an effort to stay out of sight from the rest of the room's occupants as much as possible. Glancing once behind him, he saw Jezindi padding along, continuing to keep one hand on the wall for support. Satisfied that she would be able to stay reasonably close, he turned back to his quarry, wondering how he was going to be able to pull the rescue off. He studied the troupe of guards, assessing their potential as foes.

There were four guards in the group, three humans and one of the pale-skinned, four-eyed lunars. All four were armed with scimitars, and Lyrien could see that a couple also had small, curved daggers. In addition, the one nearest to him had a lightweight crossbow slung over his back. Of course, those four weren't the captain's biggest problem; even with the element of surprise, Lyrien doubted he could defeat them all before reinforcements arrived from the other end of the great hall. In order for it to work, he realized, he would have to drop the four escorting Gade and get out of there quickly. Unfortunately, even in her improved condition, he doubted Jezindi could keep up.

The captain darted from column to column, staying out of sight while continuing to shadow his quarry, looking for some sort of advantage. The four soldiers and their prisoner were almost to the steps now. If he waited until they were well up the stairs and out of sight of their associates below, he might have a chance, but it was also a risk, since he had no idea what was at the top of the steps.

For all I know, Lord Mabon is up there with a whole mob of his goons, ready to execute Gade.

In desperation, Lyrien made the decision to act right then, where he knew the risks and could better account for them. He lunged out from behind the last column, slicing his scimitar across the neck of the nearest guard before the man realized what had happened. The soldier collapsed in mid-stride in a strangled cry of anguish, but Lyrien was already beyond him, bringing his blade to bear on the next soldier. Quickly, two of the guards began to fan out, weapons drawn, to deal with the surprise attacker. The third, the lunar, whipped out a dagger and placed it at Gade's throat, keeping his prisoner between himself and the captain, using the dover as an unwilling shield.

"Lyrien!" Gade cried out, recognizing his would-be rescuer. The captain risked a brief glance and smile for his companion, feeling a sense of gladness well up inside him at the sight of the dover. His smile faded again just as quickly, though, when he saw the haunted, anguished look in his companion's eyes. Then there was no more time to consider the meaning behind that troubled gaze, for the other two were spreading out, attempting to flank Lyrien and shouting for assistance at the same time.

Lyrien tried to ignore the weariness in his limbs as he turned toward one of his two main opponents, his bloody scimitar raised high as though to drive the guard back by brute force. At the same time, the captain kept half an eye on the other soldier, who was quickly moving around behind him. Lyrien knew he would have to make quick work of both of those two; at least half a dozen more soldiers were jogging toward the skirmish near the stairs, raising more shouts of warning and calls for aid. Squaring his shoulders, he began to attempt to drive his first opponent back as rapidly as possible, wanting to separate the two of them from the rest of the group.

The guard in front of Lyrien brought his scimitar up to fend off the apparent overhand strike the captain seemed to be aiming at him, but at the last moment, Lyrien reversed his swing and brought the blade down and under the man's defenses. As the soldier quickly yanked his own blade down to counter the stroke, Lyrien practically leaped to close the distance, swinging a wild punch with his off hand in hopes of rattling his foe with his unorthodox methods.

The blow only clipped the man's chin, but it was enough to cause him to stagger backward wide-eyed, flailing with his own arm to fend off other punches, unsure of what Lyrien was going to do next. Lyrien swung his scimitar wildly again, this time trying to strike at the soldier's own weapon, rather than get inside his defenses. With a harsh clang, the captain succeeded in snapping the man's weapon and arm back, causing him to stumble backward several more paces.

Lyrien didn't wait for his opponent to recover. Bounding in once more, he jerked his blade up to deflect an awkward counterstroke and then planted his left foot firmly while he swung his right leg up and around, delivering a solid kick into the man's ribs with a resounding crack. The soldier grunted as his breath left him, doubling over and bringing his arms in protectively. The captain snapped his left knee up into the guard's face, whipping the man's head up and shattering his nose with a spray of blood. As the soldier stumbled back yet again, Lyrien delivered a quick slash across the man's throat, finishing him.

The captain spun around, dropping into a defensive crouch as he did so, not certain what to expect. The whole series of strikes against the first guard had taken only a moment, but he had been forced to turn his back on his other foes in order to finish the man so quickly.

The second soldier was staring at Lyrien as he took a couple of tentative steps in the captain's direction, but he had an odd look on his face, one of confusion and perhaps a little dismay. The guard took another step, but it was unsteady, and he staggered to the side and then dropped to one knee, peering up at Lyrien with an anxious look in his eyes. Then he slumped down and pitched forward, sprawling onto his face as his blade clattered free and slid to within a step or two of Lyrien's feet. A thick feathered bolt protruded from the soldier's back.

Lyrien followed the logical path of the missile back, focused his attention to the columns beyond, where he saw Jezindi kneeling over the body of the very first guard the captain had slain. She held the man's crossbow in her hand, still looking down its sight in his direction, though now she began to let the weapon sag in her unsteady grasp. She had dropped the third guard before he could reach Lyrien.

That's twice I owe her, Lyrien thought.

The captain could see that the last guard, the paleskinned lunar who had maintained his grip on Gade, had turned to see who had fired the weapon. With a snarl, the lunar shoved Gade to the floor in a heap and spun toward Jezindi, who shrank back from him, retreating into the shadows of the columns. The four-eyed humanoid began stalking after her, scimitar in hand.

Lyrien did a quick search of the nearest guard's body, hoping to find keys with which to free Gade. There were none, but Lyrien snatched up a dagger and tucked it into his pants. "Which one has the keys?" Lyrien demanded as he scampered over to where Gade was struggling to sit up. He gestured toward the locked restraints around the dover's legs, wrists, and waist.

"Don't worry about me," Gade replied, jerking his head toward some unseen point behind Lyrien. "More company!"

The captain turned in time to confront three more guards approaching at a brisk trot, weapons out. One of them aimed a crossbow at him. At the same time, there was a high-pitched shriek from beyond the row of columns, from the direction Jezindi had fled. The frightened cry was just distracting enough to draw the soldiers' attention that way, giving Lyrien the opening he needed.

Lyrien whipped the dagger he had just pocketed free, flipped it around so that he was palming the blade, and flung it at the chest of the crossbowman in one smooth motion. As soon as he had released the dagger, he lunged to the side. In his haste, though, Lyrien's throw was not completely true, and the blade whirled through the air and embedded itself in the crossbowman's bicep. The soldier elicited a howl of pain and reflexively fired his weapon before dropping it and staggering away, holding his arm in agony.

Time seemed to slow down as Lyrien made his frantic leap to get out of the way of the oncoming missile. His lunge carried his torso out of harm's way, but he wasn't quite fast enough to get completely clear of the bolt, which pierced his calf. Lyrien's dive lost its gracefulness as the metal head bit deep into the soft flesh of his leg, and he went sprawling across the stone floor. He skidded to a stop on his side, breathless and grasping at his leg, which felt like it was on fire. The two remaining guards, a human and a haze, approached him warily, brandishing their weapons.

"So, even Tempest can't stop a crossbow bolt, huh?" the human one said as they drew near. "How about a scimitar?" he asked, raising his weapon high overhead.

Chapter 16

Lyrien slashed out, desperately blocking the killing stroke aimed at his head. The captain tried to roll to one side to get out of range of the next attack, but the crossbow bolt in his calf made that both impossible and painful. He was forced to defend himself from where he lay, struggling to keep the flurry of slashes and pokes clear of himself. As the human guard kept up his flood of attacks, the haze circled around, looking for a way to come at Lyrien from the opposite direction, to divide his attention and weaken his already strained defense. Very quickly, the captain's arm began to sag, as weariness and loss of blood took their toll. It was clearly a losing battle.

The haze darted in just as Lyrien redirected yet another swing from the human in front of him, and the captain could not completely avoid the strike the sinewy humanoid aimed at his shoulder. Though he managed to roll enough to keep the haze's blade from penetrating deeply, the attack still made contact, drawing a spurt of blood and cry of pain from the captain. The human saw the wound and stepped in again, smiling unpleasantly as he aimed a slash toward Lyrien's legs. Lyrien barely managed to wriggle out of the way.

The pair of guards were timing their attacks now, forcing Lyrien to contend with both of them at once. As they swooped in again, he swung wildly, knocking both blades away from his body, but he realized the mistake as soon as he had made it. The maneuver overbalanced him and he sprawled onto his side.

That's it, Lyrien thought as he rolled all the way over, grimacing when the maneuver jarred the bolt in his leg. Even as he brought his good knee up underneath him and slashed out at the human, he knew to expect the killing blow from the haze behind him. Make it quick, he prayed.

But the strike never came. Lyrien couldn't wait to see what had happened, though, for the guard in front of him was pressing the attack more fervently now, and it required every last bit of effort and concentration on the captain's part just to keep the man at bay. All the while, he felt a shiver all up and down his back as he waited for that inevitable stab.

Suddenly, the human in front of Lyrien grunted and spun away, stumbling off balance as a crossbow bolt blossomed in his shoulder. At the same time, the haze let out a mental cry of anguish and pain that radiated through Lyrien. He risked a quick glance back over his shoulder and saw that the haze had completely turned away from the captain, retreating from some new threat, its weapon arm sagging and bloody.

Lyrien spotted Gade opposite the haze, blade in hand, steadily advancing, sending quick and accurate strikes from all angles at the perimeter of the guard's drooping defenses. A few paces further away, Ezeria cocked a crossbow, watching the human she had apparently just winged with her last shot. The captain exhaled in relief, then tried to get to his feet, despite the throbbing fire in his calf. He managed to rise briefly, but the pain was too sharp, and he gingerly sank back down to one knee and watched as Gade feinted a high strike at his opponent, then came back around and underneath the guard's defenses with a cut across the haze's thighs. The thing went down with another mental scream of pain and terror, causing everyone in the fight to wince.

Ezeria, meanwhile, was taking aim at the other guard, who had turned and was running back the way he had come, his wounded shoulder sagging. The half-elf let loose the bolt, striking true. The human stumbled as the missile struck him squarely in the back. He went sprawling across the floor and came to rest at an awkward angle, feebly reaching over his shoulder with one hand, as though he were trying to remove the bolt. His arm trembled, and then relaxed, and the guard didn't move again.

Lyrien turned back to stare at Ezeria, who was dressed again in a set of his shirt and pants. "Your timing is impeccable," he said. "Jezindi and I got lost, and I didn't think I'd ever find my way back. It was dumb luck that we saw Gade being marched through here," he exclaimed, beaming in effusive relief and breaking into a big grin. "How did *you* manage to find him?"

"You still have a lot to learn about magic, don't you?" Ezeria answered, grinning back at him. "When the alarm was raised and all the guards began to act like they were hunting for something, I knew you were in trouble." Then she turned to the dover as she said, "You must be Gade. I'm Ezeria. Grab him and catch up; we've got to get out of sight." And with that, the half-elven woman turned and sprinted across the open floor of the great hall in the direction Lyrien had last seen Jezindi.

"Ah, the reknowned Ezeria," Gade replied as he finished wiping his newfound blade on the dead haze's tabard. "It's damn good to meet you," he called after the retreating concubine. Then the dover stepped to Lyrien's side and threw the captain's arm around his shoulders. "You want to talk about impeccable timing," the dover said, "I can't tell you how glad I was you appeared when

you did. Thank you for coming for me," he added, looking Lyrien squarely in the face as they passed the dead
guards.

Lyrien spotted the pile of chains and manacles that
had held Gade initially. He shook his head in wonder.
"How did you escape?" They moved between the columns to the side of the chamber, back toward where
Ezeria had vanished.

"Oh, that," Gade said, smiling, though the grin didn't
quite reach his eyes. "I managed to filch the keys off my
jailor while he was busy using me as a shield, thanks to
your timely distraction. I slipped out of the manacles
while you were dealing with those other three guards."

"Ah," Lyrien replied. "Glad I could be of service."

There was a shout from back over the captain's left
shoulder at that moment, and he looked past Gade's head
and in that direction. A whole host of guards had descended the large stairs, accompanied by none other than
Oderic Salas. They had been spotted.

"Damn," Lyrien muttered under his breath. "Run,"
he said, trying to quicken his pace. It was difficult with a
large hunk of wood protruding through both sides of his
calf, but with Gade's help, they scrambled as fast as they
could out of sight and down the hall. "We've got to find
Jezindi," the captain said as they hurried along. "She was
in trouble; that lunar who had you in a head lock spotted
her and gave chase. We've got to catch up before he skew-
ers her."

"I already did," Ezeria said, appearing suddenly from
a doorway to one side. Quickly, she stepped to Lyrien's
other side and together, she and Gade lifted the captain
completely off his feet. Then she began steering the three
of them back into the doorway. "She's fine."

Lyrien rode along between his two companions, glancing behind them occasionally for signs of pursuit. This
doorway fed into a large kitchen. They had entered from

the far side of a large set of double doors that Lyrien surmised must lead back into the great hall. At the moment,
there was no one else in the kitchen, though several fires
were burning in large hearths, sizzling and juice-drip-
ping meats slowly roasting over them. As well, there were
countless pots, pans, and kettles strewn about on long
trestle tables, where half-prepared meals sat waiting for
the cooks to return to them.

Lyrien looked at Ezeria quizzically. "Where is everyone?" he asked softly as the half-elf steered them around
a corner and to a large pile of flour sacks. Jezindi lay curled
up on the pile, an empty potato sack thrown over her like
a blanket. She was half-awake, though pale, and Lyrien
could see that she had a nasty gash across her forehead.

"I used a little magical trickery to send the cooks running," Ezeria explained with a sly grin. Then the grin
faded. "But it won't keep everyone away for long," she
added.

Lyrien could see the lunar slumped near one of the
fireplaces, very obviously dead, his chest a smoking series of blackened holes. He looked like he had been hit by
grapeshot from a cannon, Lyrien thought, though he had
yet to see such a weapon anywhere in the palace, or in all
of Blackwall, for that matter.

"What did you do to him?" the captain asked as Ezeria
and Gade set him down beside the seer.

"I'm good for more than a roll between the sheets,"
Ezeria replied, leveling a quick gaze at Lyrien. "Let that
be a lesson; don't cross me." Her eyes glittered as she said
this, and the smile on her face lent credence to her humor.

The captain nodded. "That's good to know," he said,
giving Gade an exaggerated sidelong glance of mock
worry.

The half-elf ignored the little jibe as she bent down to examine Jezindi. "We can't stay here long," Ezeria said, "but first, these two need healing."

Lyrien could see that Jezindi had drifted back out of consciousness again, and he wondered just what sort of toxins and drugs Mabon had been force-feeding her while she had been caged.

Gade dropped down beside the captain after helping him to the floor. The dover took a look at the bolt, which passed right through Lyrien's boot, into the fleshy part of his calf, and then back out again. Finally, he nodded and took hold of the missile. "Hold still, now," he said, and then quickly snapped the head of the bolt off from where it jutted out through the flesh.

Lyrien yelped in pain. He swallowed once, then nodded at Gade's questioning look. "I'm all right," he said. "Go ahead and pull it out."

Gade nodded back and gently but firmly pulled the remainder of the bolt back out in one smooth motion. Lyrien gritted his teeth but said nothing. "That needs to be looked at by a healer," the dover said, tossing the two halves of the bolt away.

"Cadmus can take care of it," Ezeria said, tearing the hem of the oversize shirt she was wearing off and then into strips. Gade helped Lyrien work his boot off. The inside was squishy with blood.

"Once I get this wrapped, I doubt you'll be able to get that back on," the dover said.

Lyrien shrugged. "I'll make do," he replied.

Ezeria began handing bandages to Gade who tightly wrapped them around the puncture wounds. As she worked, she said, "I can't believe you managed to free her," gesturing down at Jezindi. "That's remarkable." Then she eyed the bloody bandages wrapped around the captain's waist, and the crusty gash on his shoulder. "I see you ran into some other trouble," she added.

Lyrien nodded. He reached behind himself and removed the dagger from the waistband of his trousers. "Yes," he said. "Some *thing* was left to roam in the throne room to keep watch over her. If it hadn't been for her," he added, gesturing toward the unconscious girl, "I never would have made it. After that, there was no way I was leaving her there or—" He simply shook his head, not finishing the thought. "Anyway, I guess I won't be needing this anymore," he said, tossing the black blade down to the floor.

"There," Gade said, stepping back and admiring his handiwork with the bandages. "That ought to keep you from bleeding to death until this nobleman, Cadmus, shows up." Lyrien, noting that the astute dover had overheard the nobleman's name amongst the chaotic din and was already putting the pieces together, nodded in thanks and tried to stand up in order to test it. "Easy, there," Gade said, frowning. "You're in no condition to be walking on that."

Lyrien shook the dover off and got to his feet, slowly, gingerly. "I'll be all right," he said. "Hopefully, I don't have to go too far."

Ezeria bent and picked the dagger up and tucked it away inside her clothing. "No sense leaving this lying around for someone else to find," she said. "We'll return it to Effron."

Lyrien shrugged in acquiescence, not wanting anything more to do with the malignant weapon. Then he peered back through the doorway of the kitchen. "We don't have time to waste."

Ezeria got Jezindi up while Gade put an arm around Lyrien. In pairs, the four of them began to make their way across the kitchen toward what appeared to be a large walk-in pantry on the opposite side.

The dover frowned. "You're not leading us into a dead-end, are you?" he called ahead to Ezeria.

The half-elf shook her head. "I don't know. But if you have a better idea of where to go, then I'll gladly defer."

"No, keep going," Gade replied. "I would just hate to end up trapped in there," he said.

"Too late," Lyrien said as he spotted guards appearing on the opposite side of the room, entering through the same doorway the four of them had used. "Hurry!" he said as triumphant shouts rose up. He and Gade ducked inside the pantry just as a crossbow bolt clacked off the stone of the doorway. The pantry itself was a huge place, as large as Lyrien's main room had been back in his suite. Shelves lined every wall and sat in rows through the middle of the room, too. There were enough foodstuffs in barrels, sacks, and wooden bins to feed an army.

I guess the guard contingent in the palace is an army, Lyrien realized.

Gade released the captain to lean against the inside wall and flattened himself on the opposite side of the doorway, setting aside a crossbow he had grabbed off one of the dead guards. "Help me," he urged Ezeria as he moved to a large table covered with dried herbs standing next to the doorway. The half-elf nodded and lowered Jezindi to the floor, along with a second crossbow and some bolts she had been carrying. As the two of them tipped the table on its side and slid it into place across the doorway, Lyrien peered around the corner to see what was happening.

At least a dozen guards were streaming into the room, threading their way through the trestle tables, coming in his direction. Oderic Salas was among them, the captain saw. The four of them were trapped. Two more guards raised their crossbows and fired from the opposite side of the room, forcing him to duck back out of sight. "They're coming!" he said, motioning for Gade to defend their makeshift wall.

Gade scooped up the crossbow again and quickly cocked it, then loaded a bolt from the quiver he had managed to scrounge from their foes. "I'm awful with these things," the dover muttered as he brought it up, preparing to return fire.

"Give it to me," Lyrien said as he reached for the weapon. "Load the other one," he added, nodding in the direction of the one Ezeria had. Then, careful of his wounded leg, the captain leaned out a bit and saw four guards almost upon them. One of the guards saw Lyrien and raised his own crossbow, but the captain was too fast. He fired off the shot and struck the man in the gut, then ducked back around before anyone else could shoot at him.

Next to the captain, Ezeria began a casting, and then she gestured out into the kitchen. Instantly, three blinding darts of glowing fire sprang from her fingertip and made a beeline for one of the closest guards. The three magical missiles slammed into the man's chest, rocking him back and leaving three smoking craters in his torso.

Ah, Lyrien thought. Mystery solved.

Gade already had the second crossbow loaded. Quickly, they switched weapons, Lyrien handing off the first one to be re-cocked.

"How many more bolts?" he asked as he got ready to fire again.

"Nine left," Gade responded.

Lyrien grimaced. Not many at all, he thought. Make them count, he told himself and ducked back around.

The guards had wised up after watching the fugitives drop two of their number and had taken refuge behind the trestle tables. Salas was now in the rear. The slavemaster was apparently more interested in commanding than leading—and in protecting his own hide. One of the guards fired at Lyrien, but it was a rushed shot that went wide. Lyrien ducked low and saw a gap through the bottom of the trestle table where a guard's leg was exposed. He stuck his head out more than he would normally, hoping to draw some fire and buy some time of his own. A second later, two other guards rose up out of their crouches and fired simultaneously. Lyrien ducked back inside just in time. Both missiles flew through the doorway and struck the back wall.

That was what Lyrien had been waiting for. He lunged back out, bringing his own weapon up. He sighted down the length of the bolt, aiming at the bit of exposed thigh that he could see under the table. Squeezing the trigger, he watched in satisfaction as the bolt slipped right between the frame of the table and plunged directly where he'd aimed it. The guard leaped up in pain, then dived out of sight again, groaning. Quickly, Lyrien exchanged weapons with Gade again and took a peek.

After the captain's demonstration of marksmanship, though, Mabon's thugs were much more cautious, despite severe cajoling from Master Salas. They refused to move any closer to the pantry or expose themselves to any more crossbow fire until the odds were more in their favor. Lyrien nodded in satisfaction, though he knew that, unless they could get out of there, it wouldn't matter how many of them he shot.

Lyrien took another peek out into the kitchen. He could see the edge of Oderic's blue robes sticking out from behind a large cabinet at the far end of the room. It was a risky shot and wouldn't do much damage, but Lyrien decided to take it.

Keep him cowering a little longer, the captain decided.

Taking careful aim, Lyrien fired again, watching long enough to see the missile rip a large gash in the rich material of the robe. Salas jumped when the bolt shattered against the wall next to him, yanking himself the rest of the way out of sight.

Lyrien grinned smugly. "They think they're pinned down," he said softly, turning back from the doorframe. "Ezeria, can you do your thing so we can get out of here?"

The half-elf nodded and began to cast a spell. As she gestured, she whispered something too soft for the captain to pick up on. When she finished, Lyrien could see no visible effect. "Well?" he asked, growing nervous.

Ezeria gave him a reassuring smile. "I just sent a special message to Effron," she explained. "He'll find us and we'll all leave together." When Lyrien still didn't understand and cocked his head to one side to show his confusion, she gave his arm a light pat. "I can't move us all by myself; I can only do one other person at a time, and I don't have enough magic left to leave and come back for each of you. Effron has something much better; you'll see."

Lyrien nodded, comprehending at last. "Well, let's hope he arrives soon," the captain said, peering into the kitchen again. "We won't be left alone for much longer. Our luck's going to run out."

At that moment, a shimmering doorway of blue appeared, hovering in the air in one corner of the pantry a few feet from Ezeria. As if he had heard the captain's concern, Effron Cadmus appeared, stepping through. When he saw the four of them and their surroundings, his eyes widened a bit. Then he recovered and smiled warmly. "You did it!" he exclaimed, pointing to Jezindi. "I didn't think you'd actually manage to free her." He moved closer to the unconscious woman, kneeling down to examine her. "What a blessing," the nobleman said, smiling back up at Lyrien. "This is such a boon for—"

Ezeria charged toward Lyrien suddenly, the black dagger unsheathed and held high. She came so quickly that the captain simply stared at her, shocked, for a full heartbeat. She closed the distance in two strides, ready to strike. In his injured state, he was off-balance, all his weight on his good leg. He barely had time to get his scimitar up before she was at him, and then she was past. He swung awkwardly at her with the flat of his blade with the intention of knocking the dagger free, but when she didn't try to plunge it into his chest, his stroke was off, and he merely smacked her across the back of her shoulder as she dived past him.

The captain spun to see Ezeria plunge the dagger into a guard who had somehow crept up on their position, unseen and unheard, and was in the process of climbing across the barricade they had erected. The man had his own weapon upraised and appeared to have been ready to drive it into Lyrien's back, but Ezeria interceded, and her strike was true. But when the weapon impacted with the man, he did not cry out in pain. There was no wound blossoming with blood. Instead, a roiling wave of malignant essence radiated outward from the dagger. In the blink of an eye, both the guard and Ezeria were swallowed by this darkness that seemed to hover, enveloping them, and then it recoiled again, sucked back into the dagger itself. As the last of the inky vapor receded, the dagger fell to the floor, and Lyrien could see that neither Ezeria nor the guard were still there. They had disappeared, somehow magically vanishing.

Lyrien simply stood there for several long moments, shifting between shock and anger. Then realization struck him. *That would have been me, if I had slain Jezindi with it,* he thought, horrified. *Like Cadmus wanted me to,* the captain understood then, cold hatred filling him.

Just as Lyrien was about to turn back and confront the nobleman, two more guards lunged up, scrabbling to climb over the barricade. Their efforts caused the table to scoot back a foot or so, and he was nearly knocked over. Quickly, he stepped back and exchanged blows with the pair. Even though he was outnumbered and hobbled, his fury made Lyrien's strokes rapid and sharp. Quickly,

Gade was beside him, helping to repel the small assault. In only a moment, one lay dead at their feet and the other had been driven back to the opposite side with a nasty wound.

Lyrien did a quick check to see if any other guards were on the prowl, then he turned back toward the nobleman, gripping his scimitar with white-knuckled fingers. Effron Cadmus had Jezindi with him, one arm snuggly around her neck, the other supporting her at the waist. He was staring at Lyrien and Gade, all pretense of kindness gone now.

"You bastard," Lyrien said, seething, trying to take a single step toward the nobleman. He nearly fell and had to draw up short as Gade reached out a hand to stabilize him. "You lied. That was supposed to be me! You never expected to whisk us away from here, because you knew I'd be *dead!*" He tried to shrug off Gade's grip in order to take another step, but the pain in his leg was too great. He sagged down to his good knee. "Who the hell are you?" He said viciously, in a near-whisper. Gade began to advance himself, his scimitar still dripping blood from the guard he had slain.

But instantly, Effron Cadmus reacted to the threat, snapping his fingers. The dover froze in mid-step, and Lyrien knew all too well that his friend had been magically held in place. He snarled in rage and tried to rise to his feet again, but Cadmus gestured quickly in his direction. Lyrien tensed, waiting to see what sort of wizardry the nobleman was using against him, but he felt nothing. Instead, the dagger shot forward across the stones, right between him and the dover's still form. The captain tried to snatch it up when he realized what Cadmus was doing, but he was an instant too slow. The dagger glided past and slipped itself into the scabbard, which rested right near the nobleman's foot where Ezeria had apparently dropped it.

Cadmus scooped the sheathed weapon up. "She's not dead," he said threateningly, presenting the dagger to Lyrien as though it were some sort of proof. "But she will be, if you take try to take one more step toward me."

Lyrien froze, not wanting to trust this treacherous man, but not daring to disbelieve him, either. "What are you talking about?" he asked coldly, flexing his fingers on the hilt of his scimitar. "Where is she?"

"Oh, she's safely tucked away inside the dagger," Cadmus replied, "and that's where she stays, too. Now, drop your blade. I won't ask twice."

Lyrien glowered, hesitating. He used his anger to focus on the blade in the nobleman's hands, seeking some proof that there was any truth in Cadmus's words. Sure enough, a strong emanation of magic glowed around the dagger and sheath. Unlike the blackish-blue glow he remembered from before, it was a bright, almost white emanation at that point. Though he had no idea whether that meant Ezeria was really trapped inside or not, he wasn't going to risk her life calling the man's bluff. He carefully placed the scimitar on the floor near his feet.

"Good," Cadmus said. "Now, back away."

Lyrien wanted to scream in frustration, but he carefully limped backward, keeping the pressure off his wounded leg. He took one step away from both his blade and the man who had betrayed him, then another.

"Excellent," Cadmus said smugly. "See? You *do* know how to be a good slave. Now, I'm going to leave you here, but I'm taking both the dagger and this whore and her visions with me. She ought to prove quite useful in my overthrow of Mabon. If you do anything that looks like an attack, I will banish Ezeria's soul to a demiplane of nightmares forever. Do you understand me?"

Lyrien grit his teeth and nodded. He eyed the distance between himself and the nobleman, but he realized he could never reach Cadmus in time to stop him, not on only one good leg.

Effron began to back up, toward the shimmering blue door from which he had appeared, pulling the still-limp Jezindi with him. "Good luck making your way out past all those guards," he said smugly. Then, with a callous smirk on his face, Effron Cadmus began to turn and step through his magical portal.

Lyrien began to rise to his feet again, unwilling to let the man escape, which drew Cadmus's attention immediately. The nobleman raised an eyebrow, looking at the captain in a scolding manner. Lyrien wanted something, anything, to heave at the traitor. He longed to have the dagger back in his grasp, wished that he had never tossed it away for Ezeria to claim, but then of course, he would simply be the one sucked inside it, he realized.

It was at that moment that Jezindi reacted, planting both feet firmly on the ground and shoving upward. She rammed the crown of her head into the nobleman's jaw with all her strength. It wasn't much, but it was enough to cause Cadmus to let go of her and stagger, shocked at the attack. Then Lyrien was lunging toward Gade.

The captain could not get a good first step, with his leg already in bad shape, but he didn't need to go far. He heaved himself in the direction of his friend, focusing every last bit of his attention on the magic surrounding the immobile dover's body. As he kicked off, Lyrien reached out and balled his leading hand into a fist, which he used to pile-drive into the mystical glow.

The magic shattered in a million sparks of light to his eyes, and in the next instant, Gade was lunging forward again, leveling the scimitar at the man's chest. Cadmus, who had expected Lyrien's attack to be at him, had side-stepped out of the way, but when the captain's lunge carried him toward Gade instead, the nobleman stood rooted to the spot where he stood, unable to cleanly dodge the dover's charge. Gade ran his scimitar into Effron Cadmus's gut, eliciting a surprised gasp from his mouth and a crimson spray of blood from his midsection. Both dover and nobleman staggered toward the blue door, Gade driving the blade deeper into his foe.

Effron flailed out with his hands, grunting in pain and surprise at the attack. He began wordlessly muttering something now, blood flecking his mouth. His hands trembled as they feebly wrapped around the hilt of the scimitar, vainly trying to pull the weapon free.

"Don't let him escape!" Lyrien cried out, already rolling to one side after he tumbled to the ground, groaning in pain. He was now on his back.

But Cadmus was a little too quick for either of them, and in the next instant, he planted a foot against Gade and gave a good shove, pulling himself off the scimitar and falling back through the doorway. In the blink of an eye, the doorway vanished, leaving behind a pool of blood.

Chapter 17

"Damnation!" Lyrien shouted at the top of his lungs. He sagged against the hard stone of the pantry, laid his head back, and closed his eyes in despair. Beside him, Gade nearly toppled over from the shove Cadmus had given him.

"I'm sorry," the dover said softly, dismally, regaining his balance. "I wasn't fast enough."

Lyrien snarled, pounding his fists into the floor on either side of himself. Another betrayal. Another moment of clarity, when Lyrien could see at last that there was no one to trust. When it was too late. He was beginning to understand his father a little bit better.

Regaining his composure, the captain sat up. "It's not your fault," he said to his friend. "He got lucky." Then, looking around himself, Lyrien shook his head. "But he was our way out. Little hope remains," he said, feeling the vertigo of helplessness begin to wash over him.

The dover nodded. "We've still got a chance," Gade said firmly. "And if nothing else, we'll die with our blades drenched in the blood of our enemies," he added, looking directly at Lyrien.

The captain nodded. "To the end, then," he said. Silently, he added, I swear this isn't over. Effron Cadmus, you *will* get yours. "And when we get out of here, the first thing we're going to do is find Ezeria, if she's still alive."

"She is," Jezindi said, sitting crosslegged where Cadmus had dropped her during the scramble.

Lyrien turned to the girl, open-mouthed in surprise. "How do you know? Another reading?"

"No," the seer said, lowering her eyes. "I wasn't always a slave." When Lyrien said nothing, she looked at him intently. "But I know."

"Then the first thing we do if we get out of here—" Lyrien began.

"Don't you mean *when* we get out of here?" Gade said, beginning to rummage around on the body of the dead guard, gathering a few things from the corpse. He looked over at Lyrien, giving the captain a meaningful stare.

Lyrien nodded. "Yes," he said, remembering a similar conversation from a long time previous, in the slave pits. He needed that determination once more. "*When* we get out of here, the first thing we do is find her and free her." He turned to Jezindi and asked, "Can she survive like that? What if she is dying, or unable to breathe? How much time—?"

"If it's the sort of confining spell that I think it is," Jezindi said, interrupting, "then she is none of those things. She's safe for now, and will be until the noble uses a counterspell to free her from the dagger."

"And then she has a whole new set of problems," Lyrien said vehemently, his fury at Cadmus Effron boiling to the surface once more. "All right," he acknowledged. "One problem at a time. First, we've got to find a way out of this damned palace."

"All right, then," Gade said, standing. "Jezindi, since you know so much about this imprisoning magic, maybe you have some other tricks at your disposal, too. Perhaps some healing magic?"

Jezindi didn't answer for a long time, turning away and swallowing several times. Lyrien could see great anguish cross her face. Finally, she shook her head, and when she spoke, her voice was husky with emotion. "I don't do that anymore."

Gade started to speak, presumably to ask the seer why not, but Lyrien caught the dover's attention first and gave a warning shake of his head.

Now isn't the time, the captain thought, willing Gade to understand.

The dover looked at him curiously for a few seconds then shrugged and nodded.

Lyrien told the dover, "Unless there's another way out of here, we'll find ourselves in chains, or worse. See what you can find," he said.

"Right," Gade said and began to slink away. "Gather what supplies you can," he said, handing a small sack to Lyrien as he passed. "We might need some provisions before the day is done." The he was moving deeper into the pantry, leaving the two crossbows for Lyrien to contend with. The captain hoped that he and Jezindi would be sufficient to hold the assault off long enough for Gade to discover something useful.

With cold hatred now percolating in the pit of his belly, Lyrien struggled over to Jezindi and knelt down beside her. Her eyes seemed clear for the moment, and she looked up at him with sorrow in them.

"I'm sorry," Jezindi said. "Cadmus Effron is a deceitful man."

"Did your foretelling reveal that?" Lyrien said, instantly regretting the words as soon as he spoke them. He was taking his frustration out on one of the few people who wasn't responsible for any of this mess.

"I don't need a foretelling to tell me that, but yes," Jezindi replied, trying to rise to her feet. "I've seen his evil before, every time he's come into the court. Lord

Mabon has never asked me to read the man, but I knew. I also don't need a foretelling to see you're hurting over the loss of your beautiful friend, nor do I need one to realize that we're in a lot of trouble. I am more than my gift, warrior."

Lyrien realized that the woman's eyes were sparkling in anger, and his guilt deepened. "I'm sorry," he said, trying to help Jezindi to her feet. "I am angry, but not at you. I just—" he paused, not knowing what to say. "I know you're more than your gift. That's the very reason I couldn't just leave you behind, or . . . or—" Put you out of your misery, he finished silently. Then he grimaced, thinking of the trick Cadmus had intended to play on him with the dagger. "Although Effron had no intention of letting you die. *He* certainly doesn't see you as anything more than a gift, as a tool to be exploited." The captain squared his shoulders. "Regardless, it's not over between Effron Cadmus and me, not by any means. I *will* track him down and get Ezeria back."

Jezindi nodded but said, "Perhaps. You have another role to play before your stay here is complete, though."

Lyrien looked at the girl sharply. He started to ask her to once and for all tell him what she meant, but he never got the chance.

At that moment, the barricade thudded with a resounding thump, sliding back several feet. Three more guards slipped around the ends of the overturned trestle table and rushed at the three fugitives. Lyrien scrambled to his feet, wincing at the pain, and tried to go for his scimitar, which was still on the floor. Behind the first guards, several more were slipping into the gaps, crossbows in hand. The pantry was being overrun.

"All right, all right!" Lyrien said earnestly, feeling his heart sink in despair as he put his hands up high in the air and stepped between Jezindi and the oncoming thugs. "We surrender! No more!"

The guards slowed slightly, eyeing the captain warily, but they still advanced toward him. "One wrong move, and you're finished," the closest one said. "Don't even blink funny," he warned. "Get down on your belly, nice and slowly."

Lyrien gave the guard a measured look, but when the brute pulled his scimitar back to strike at him, the captain gestured for patience and then slowly, laboriously, dropped first to his knees and then began to lie down.

Lyrien's throat felt thick with emotion. He had not expected it to wind up like that. It seemed as though everything he had counted on was letting him down. The people he had trusted, his own wounded leg, all of it. And the frustration was only exacerbated by the knowledge that that same sense of hopelessness must have been exactly what his father had felt watching the king surrender Ilnamar to Lord De'Valen.

And how Iandra must have felt, watching her father stop fighting for his kingdom, the captain realized. Sooner or later, everyone reaches their limit and gives up. Is this my limit?

A creaking groan was the only warning the guards got that they were in danger, and none of them reacted in time to avoid the shelf that came crashing down among them. Lyrien spotted it in time to roll backward, out of the way, grabbing at Jezindi to pull her clear, as well. The large wooden shelf had been piled with jars of foodstuffs, and it was tall, as well. As it tumbled into the force of Mabon's thugs, the guards cried out and disappeared beneath a small avalanche of pottery and glass. The resultant cascade of foodstuffs, along with the shelf itself, effectively sealed the passage back into the kitchen for the time being.

On the opposite side of where the shelf had stood a moment before, Gade was picking himself up. "Hey," he said, sidling back over to Lyrien and Jezindi. "Thought you might need a hand." Lyrien couldn't help but grin. "There's a set of back stairs over there," the dover said, jerking his head in the direction from which he'd come. "It only goes down, though."

"We've got no choice," Lyrien said, and laid a hand on Jezindi's shoulder. The girl turned and looked back at him, and he could see she had been crying. "Can you walk?" he asked, ignoring her tears for the moment, wanting only to get her focus back on then and there. "We've got to go," he said when she simply stared at him. "Can you walk by yourself?" he repeated.

Finally, hesitantly, Jezindi nodded. "I think so."

"Then come on," the captain insisted, scowling in discomfort as he forced his weight onto his wounded leg. "We've got to get away from here before they figure out a way past that," he finished, jerking his head toward the pile of ruined shelving and food.

"Grab what you can," Gade said, scooping up the sack he had tossed down next to Lyrien before. "Don't know if we'll get a chance to use it, but you never know."

"It's good to be thinking ahead," Lyrien said in mild admiration. "You'd make a decent officer in the military."

Gade shrugged. "Spend enough time in the maze, you learn to scavenge anything you can."

Quickly and quietly, trying to gain as much distance as possible before the guards realized they were no longer there, the three companions hobbled their way through the pantry and to the stairs. As they went, Gade began to toss a few more things into the bag, grabbing items off of shelves or out of barrels as he led the other two along. When it was full, he handed the sack to Lyrien and grabbed a second one, dumping flour on the floor to empty it. The dover continued to gather anything that looked useful as he led them to the back wall.

The flight of stairs was a spiral staircase, steep and narrow, and unlit, to boot. The going would be tricky with two of them lame. Lyrien fetched a single torch to help the trio see by. It glowed warmly and flickered, but it was plenty bright enough to make out the immediate surroundings. Gade spotted a stack of extra, unlit torches on another shelf and shoved them into his sack, too. They set out, working their way quickly but cautiously down the stairs.

The steps descended a long way, continuously turning in a steep corkscrew. When they finally came to the lower end of the staircase, they had to have dropped seven or eight levels, Lyrien surmised. The chamber at the egress was a dark and gloomy place, stretching out as far as they could see, but with huge columns as wide as a chamber at regular intervals. In fact, once they had stepped out from the doorway, the captain saw that the staircase descended through one of the columns, and that they were somewhere in the middle of the vast chamber. Despite its dimensions, the ceiling overhead was not very high.

"This must be the very bottom of the palace," Gade muttered, overawed. "We're down where the ground used to be; I wonder if there are ways into the maze from here." He took the torch from Lyrien, then turned and began to pace around the column through which the stairs had descended, looking beyond the limit of the faint light source.

A sound from inside the staircase caught Lyrien's attention, an almost inaudible thud that made him pause.

"Lean on me," Jezindi said. The seer took hold of Lyrien's arm and together, they made their way toward Gade. There was another noise from inside the staircase, and that time, the captain was certain he could hear voices.

No time for this, he thought in dismay.

"Hey," Gade called from not too far away. "This place is huge!"

"Shh!" the captain admonished, moving toward the dover. "They're on their way down! It's time to go!" Lyrien insisted, his whisper as loud as he dared make it, though he had no idea which way to flee. They were trapped, he realized, but running still felt better than just sitting down and waiting for their doom.

From the opening into the column, the captain was then certain he could hear footsteps and soft voices. "Here!" Lyrien said. "Help me," he gestured, indicating to Gade that the dover should prop him up on the other side. Quickly, Gade handed the captain the torch to hold again, then slipped under Lyrien's other arm. Together, the three of them hobbled away from the entrance to the stairs.

"I know what this place is," Gade said suddenly, softly, as they kept moving, trying to put some distance between themselves and the column that would disgorge more of Mabon's soldiers at any moment. "I think this is where they house some of the nasty things they release into the maze. I'll bet this butts up against the side of the pedestal."

"Shh," Lyrien said again, very softly. "Keep moving," he added, listening intently. There were no sounds at the moment, but he had no doubts that their pursuers were closing in on them. The light of the torch seemed feeble in that great hall, and the whole weight of the palace looming over their heads made Lyrien feel as though he were suffocating. He fought against the sense of panic, of vertigo, that was swirling around him. "Gade," Lyrien whispered. "You said you think this leads into the maze."

"Right," came the soft reply.

"If we find a way into the maze, can you get us to the surface from there?"

"I can sure as hell try."

Lyrien hesitated. He was wary of getting trapped again, but he didn't see that they had any other choice. A part of his mind kept trying to tell him that it didn't matter what they did; they were going to get caught in the end. He shoved that voice down deep, refused to listen to it. "Are you sure?" he asked the dover.

"Look," Jezindi cut in, whispering fiercely. "It's a lot better than sitting down right here and waiting for them to find us. I say we try."

Lyrien looked in surprise at the woman. Her eyes glittered passionately in the torchlight. Her jaw was set determinedly. He was remembering what Ezeria had told him, about how the seer had been so anguished upon arriving, an anguish that eventually sank into despondency. The half-elf had even said that Jezindi probably would have killed herself, if Lord Mabon had given her the chance. Looking at the woman now, the captain wondered how true all of that was.

Jezindi seemed to sense the captain's scrutinizing stare, seemed to understand his unspoken question. "For the first time since I was brought here, to this world, I have a sense that I have something worth fighting for," she said. "I can't explain it, but I know that I have to go with you and help you."

"And then?" Lyrien asked.

Jezindi shook her head. "I don't know," she whispered solemnly. "Maybe I can—" a cloud of emotion passed over her face then, and she swallowed hard, unable to complete the sentence. "Maybe I can find some peace. But only if we keep trying. Only if we fight to survive, to be free, even when it feels like there is no point. I lost that somewhere along the way, but in you, I've found it again."

The hurt so plain on Jezindi's face made Lyrien think of Iandra. He wanted to ask her what she had lost that could cause such pain, but he knew that was a question for another time. "All right," he agreed finally, turning back to Gade. "Which way?"

"We're already headed in the right direction," the dover said.

"Then lead the way," Lyrien urged. Together, the three of them began to silently limp further away from the staircase.

For a long time, there was nothing but the passing of time and the columns sliding endlessly by. The immensity of the chamber stunned the captain. He wondered if the distances in every other direction were just as impressive. If that was the foundation of the entire palace, as Gade claimed, then it made a certain sense, but still, the scale of the chamber dazzled Lyrien.

Eventually, Lyrien began to make out…something… ahead of them. After a dozen or so additional steps, he realized what it was: the glow of magic. The trio reached one side of the chamber a short time after that, and the captain saw what it was that he had detected.

Where there should have been a solid wall, instead there were only the broken and crumbling remnants of one. Where the divider was missing, Lyrien could see tons of rubble beyond, layers of ancient buildings, squashed tightly together and stacked one atop the next, like pancakes on a stack. It was the edge of the pedestal, just as Gade had predicted.

The dover let out a long, low, soft whistle, staring up at what he could see in the light of the torch. "It's the foundation of the world."

To Lyrien's eyes, a great, glowing surface of magic resonated in front of that immense pile of rubble. Someone had placed a magical barrier to hold it back, keep it stable to prevent it from collapsing. He, too, was stunned.

Finally, the captain shook himself out of his reverie. "So, where do we go?" he asked.

Gade peered ahead and then pointed. "Look. Right there," he said, and when Lyrien gazed in the direction the dover was indicating, he could see a large valve, a door of metal set into the wall. It was barred from the near side with thick, heavy beams of iron. It would take the three of them all of their strength, he thought, to lift them out of the way.

With Gade on one side, and a wounded Lyrien and woozy Jezindi on the other, they began to work. The lowest beam was easy. The middle one, they struggled with. The high one, they could not move.

"Maybe we can slide it out of the brackets," Gade said.

Lyrien frowned. "That will make a lot of noise, draw attention to us," he said.

"I don't see any other way to try it," the dover replied. "It's not as if we're really hidden here, anyway, with that torchlight."

"All right," Lyrien finally agreed. "Nothing to lose." Together, they heaved on the iron beam, but it still wouldn't budge. It was simply too heavy.

"It's no good," Lyrien said despondently, sliding down to the floor to give his leg a rest. The wound throbbed. "I think we're done," he lamented.

"We're not," Jezindi insisted, trying feebly to get Lyrien to stand once more. "Try again," she pleaded. "Don't let them put me back in that cage," she added, fear making her eyes wide.

Lyrien shook his head, but he got to his feet. "One more try," he said. Together, the three of them shoved on the massive metal bar, and they actually managed to move it a little bit, to the accompaniment of a loud scraping sound, but that was the extent of their success.

Exhausted, Lyrien collapsed again, panting. "It's just too heavy," he said. The sense of weight overhead, the claustrophobia, was closing in.

From behind them, the captain could hear voices clearly then, and when he looked back, the glow of torchlight was visible in the distance. Lyrien knew that if he could see that torchlight, they could see the trio's.

"Gladiator," came the call, echoing through the chamber. It was Master Salas, flanked by a dozen or so guards, many of them with crossbows out and loaded. "There is no escape from here for you three. You're trapped, as you must see by now. Please make this easy on yourselves. Surrender to us."

Lyrien's closed his eyes, near to capitulating finally to the despair that had been growing at the edges of his thoughts. No! he silently screamed at himself, taking up the crossbow and cocking it. Go down fighting, he insisted to himself silently. Fight for what's right, to the bitter end.

Lyrien clung to that emotion, that need to take the defiant stance until his very last breath. He saw his father, beaten down and broken, a man who had let his pride vanish when he had so foolishly backed down from Lord De'Valen. The pain in the captain's heart at that mental image made him utter one choking sob. He would not be his father. He couldn't.

But when Lyrien looked at his two companions once more, his resolve wavered.

Gade stood to one side, watching the approaching contingent of palace guards with trepidation, fumbling with his own crossbow. The dover's eyes had that same haunted look in them that Lyrien remembered from before. On the captain's other side, Jezindi pressed her back against the wall of the huge chamber, cowering. She had both of her hands up, subconsciously jerking on the thick metal collar that was still bolted around her neck. Her eyes were wide with terror.

"Gladiator," the slavemaster called. "We have . . . pets. Even if you think to escape into the maze, they will hunt you down and kill you. There are better ways to resolve this, you know. Come now, surrender quietly, and we will be merciful. We might even still find cause to spare your lives."

Lyrien realized suddenly that he was being selfish. *I can't ask them to do this*, he understood finally. *I can't ask them to keep the cause just for my sake, for my sense of duty. Their fear of dying is too great.* He shook his head and let it droop, holding it in his hands. *All of this effort, wasted*, he lamented. *So many depending on me, and I've let them down. But there's no other way. I can't ask them to sacrifice themselves for me, for my own sense of honor.*

Choking back another sob, Lyrien knew then what he had to do. To Oderic Salas he called, "Really? If we surrender now, you'll let us live?"

Master Salas smiled, stepping closer, his guards following suit. "There's always that possibility. You all can still be quite useful to Lord Mabon, you know."

"Then give us a moment to decide."

"Do not try my patience, gladiator," Salas replied, but he folded his arms as if to wait, at least for a moment.

"I think it's time to give up the fight," he whispered to his two companions. "We're out of choices."

"What?" Gade hissed. "No. We're all going down together, remember?"

"We can still get away," Jezindi agreed, panic rising in her voice. "We can still try. We agreed that trying was better than just giving up."

"I can't ask you to do that," Lyrien said. "I can't ask you to sacrifice yourselves just so I can die with my own self-esteem intact. If there's even a chance to live, that's got to be even better than dying." Gade began to protest, but Lyrien cut him off. "This is the one chance we have to survive, my friend. And that's the best hope we can have. I understand that, now."

"No," Jezindi begged, dropping to her knees, yanking desperately on the collar. "Please, let us try. I won't go back to that cage," she added, turning to Lyrien. "I won't drink any more of Mabon's poisons. I won't!" she screamed.

Lyrien was confused. He had thought to spare the two of them the pain of death, and yet they refused to take the opportunity. He looked back at their potential captors helplessly. Salas and his men still held in place, though they had their weapons aimed at the three fugitives. Even if Lyrien had a notion of changing his mind then, he realized, there was nowhere to run. It really was over. He looked back at Jezindi despondently, then at Gade.

The dover's eyes smoldered in anger. "How dare you," he said. "How dare you choose for us! What gives you the right to decide how we live and die?"

Lyrien winced at his friend's harsh words. "But I can't ask you to suffer for my cause," he said, trying to make the dover understand. "It's not right to make you die so I can feel superior to my own father."

"You're not asking us to do anything of the sort," Gade replied. "You're not asking us at all. You're taking away our choices as you make yours. You're as guilty as Lord Mabon, trying to choose for us."

Jezindi was sobbing, cringing away from Salas and his thugs, who were gathered in a semicircle around the trio. She crushed herself against Lyrien, tried to crawl behind him, babbling and pleading not to let them put her back in the cage. Lyiren ached for her, for her pain and suffering. He wanted to heal her and take her terror away, but he didn't know how.

"We told you we'd die with you," Gade said, dropping down beside Lyrien as the captain took hold of Jezindi and just hugged her. She sobbed again, laying her head down in his lap and burying her face in her hands. "Give us credit for staying true to what we believe in, just as you wish to stay true to your own beliefs. Ever since I met you, you've been trying to protect the whole world. You can't do that. You can only be true to your-self, and let everyone around you make their own path. You can't choose for us to live as slaves if we don't want to."

And suddenly, it all made sense to Lyrien. It was that one simple word: choose. His father had never given him the choice. He had never been given a chance to choose between watching his father fight for what he believed in, giving Lyrien something to be proud of, or watching him wither away, callus and bitter, ridiculing everything he had taught Lyrien to value. His father had given up and had left the king's side, not because he was a cow-ard, or because he no longer believed in what he had taught Lyrien to hold so dear, but because he was doing what he had thought was the best thing for his family, for his son. And all those years, Lyrien had grown angry and resentful because his father had taken away the boy's right to choose how he perceived his father.

The clarity of truth, the understanding, brought tears to the captain's eyes. The revelation was painful, but it brought with it a calmness and a serenity, that he had not felt in many years. It didn't change anything, he knew, but at least he understood. The anger and resentment were gone. What was left was . . . conviction, Lyrien decided. The same convictions as before, only without the need to throw it in the face of his father. Both men did what they thought was right, and there was no shame in that.

"We choose to go down together," the captain said at last, hugging his two companions close to him. "And we take them down with us," he added in a whisper. "Stay close."

The guards and their leader were perhaps fifteen paces away, eyeing their quarry warily, still brandishing their crossbows. Lyrien took a deep breath, looked Oderic Salas right in the eye, and said, "All right, we've decided."

"And?" the blue-robed man asked expectantly. "Will you be fools? Or wise?"

"We'll rid the world of at least a few bastards like you," the captain said, eyeing Salas defiantly, and he reached up with his hand and smacked at the huge magical barrier that sealed the pedestal off from the chamber. Then he grabbed hold of both of his companions and huddled with them, proud to know them both. He could not think of a better way to die.

For a heartbeat, then two, and then three, nothing happened. Several of the guards raised crossbows as if to fire shots, but to their eyes, nothing had changed, and they simply stared at the trio in confusion. Oderic sniffed in disdain. "Take them," he ordered. "They are still useful as—" He choked off the last of his sentence as the rumbling began. His eyes widened in alarm as he realized, at last, what Lyrien had done. For another moment, the slavemaster stood rooted to the spot, terror gripping him. Then he screamed and turned to run, but his robes got tangled around his feet, and he sprawled to the stones.

The other guards sensed then what was happening and they, too, began to flee, but by that point, great slabs of stone had begun to tumble down, filling the area with dust and debris. As the wall collapsed, several of them were crushed beneath the massive weight of eons of rubble cascading over them. Very quickly, Lyrien lost sight of the contingent of soldiers. He closed his eyes, bracing himself for the impact of tons of rock on him, knowing the end would be quick and painless. He felt the door buckle at his back, bending down and over him, and then something struck him in the head, and he drifted from consciousness.

* * * * *

The first thing Lyrien realized when he came to was that he was not dead, though he didn't understand why that should be such a shock. Everything was pitch black around him, and he was finding it difficult to breathe. The smell of dust was thick in his nostrils, and he felt stuck, trapped immobile at an awkward angle. Strangely, his mind drifted to thoughts of the womb.

Then, suddenly, the captain remembered what he had done. He should be dead. He had brought down the wall atop everyone. Why wasn't he crushed? Maybe he was, Lyrien thought, and he just couldn't feel it. He shifted slightly, struggling to free one arm, and he heard the trickle of gravel around himself. He was wedged and half-buried in the stuff. Tentatively, he moved his arm and found that there was solid stone only a few inches from his face. Somehow, the great collapse had settled around him, rather than on him. He was buried alive.

That thought panicked him, and he began to flail desperately. He did not want to die like that. It wasn't right. He had tried to depart this life nobly, on his own terms, and instead he was doomed to die in darkness, of thirst, of hunger.

His arm struck something soft. Hair. It was a head. No, not hair, fur. Gade was there. He felt around and discovered that his companion was still breathing. He didn't know if that was better or worse. Assuming the dover wasn't half-crushed and dying, they would have each other for company in their final hours. He regretted bringing that end to Gade, but then he remembered the conviction his friend had expressed of wanting to die free. This would have to do, Lyrien decided.

A sudden fit of coughing on his other side clued the captain in to the fact that Jezindi was alive, too. He felt her shift, move, and suddenly, he could feel some of the gravel that had him pinned sliding away, freeing a leg. He actually sank down several inches, settling as the gravel poured away. He briefly worried about getting dragged down into some sort of sink hole, but that was ridiculous, he decided. He was sitting on solid floor.

Jezindi moaned and struggled away from him. Somehow, there was some room where she was. Perhaps Lyrien could free himself. "Jezindi?" he called softly, and his voice echoed oddly in the cramped environment.

"You're alive!" the woman exclaimed, coming closer. The captain felt a hand brush against his shoulder, then it found his face. "I thought we were going to be crushed."

"That was sort of the plan," Lyrien replied as Jezindi began to dig him out by feel. Soon, he could roll away from the slab that was hanging over him, and he found that there was enough room to sit up.

"Is Gade—?" Jezindi asked timorously.

"Alive," Lyrien said, turning to find their companion and pull him free of the gravel. "I don't know what injuries he has, though," he added, finding a furry paw and pulling.

As he felt the dover's body shift and slide out of the gravel, Gade began to gasp and cough. He flailed around and the captain heard the dover smack hard against stone, which was quickly followed by a grunt of pain.

"What happened?" Gade asked, and Lyrien smiled in the darkness in relief. Even though they were all trapped and going to die here, he was thankful in an odd way that they were all safe right then.

"I don't really know," Lyrien said. "There was a magical barrier, and I destroyed it. I thought we'd all be crushed, but somehow, it missed us."

"We need light," Gade said, and Lyrien heard him fumbling with something in the darkness.

The torches, the captain remembered. All the supplies. He wondered what good they would do the three of them, but maybe there was hope.

A few sparks of light flashed in Lyrien's field of vision, and then suddenly, a torch flared to life, and the captain was forced to shield his eyes for a moment. When he finally had his vision adjusted, he peered at his two companions.

Save for a few scratches and bruises, everyone appeared unscathed. Overhead, a huge slab of rock canted down over them, shielding them from what must have been a massive pile of rubble overhead. The steel door was folded nearly to a right angle, and the massive iron bar that had blocked it from opening was acting as some sort of a pillar at the moment, though it was bent and looked like it might give any minute. The space where they had waited for the end had been spared, and it was roomy enough that they could gather in a small circle and face one another.

"We'll use up our air much faster with that burning," Lyrien said, pointing to the torch. "Do you want to die quickly with light, or slowly in the dark?" Neither choice seemed particularly preferable right then.

"I say neither," Gade replied with a smile, pointing at the ruined door. "There's a gap there just big enough to squeeze through, I think."

Lyrien and Jezindi leaned around to peer where the dover indicated. Beyond the twisted portal, the captain could see blackness, a tunnel receding from them. He wondered if it went back very far, or if it had collapsed, too.

"Where does it lead?" Jezindi asked worriedly.

"Only one way to find out," Gade replied, patting the woman on the arm. "But if it goes anywhere, I can take us there safely. We have a chance, now."

Jezindi smiled wanly, as though she was afraid to hope again after what they had just gone through.

"All right, rafter," Lyrien said, smiling at Gade. "Lead the way."

Gade nodded. "To freedom."

"To Ezeria," Lyrien added.

The other two looked at the captain and nodded solemnly, then filed through the opening and into the darkness beyond.

As he turned to follow the dover and the seer, Lyrien paused and looked back once at the pile of rubble that had come tumbling down around them. He wondered if it had spilled out far enough to crush Oderic Salas. The thought made him feel oddly warm, but he knew better than to count on it. Even of the slavemaster was dead, Galak Mabon still sat on the throne of Blackwall.

Lyrien squeezed past the gap in the passage and got to his feet in the tunnel beyond, thinking it strange that he had come full circle since arriving in Penance. The difference was, finding himself trapped in the maze now was actually a welcome thought.

The Queen's Blade Trilogy

Book 1
FORGED

Book 2
TEMPERED

(available Winter, 2004)

Book 3
HONED

(available Summer, 2004)

For more information on any of our upcoming
Oathbound novels, please visit:

www.bastionpress.com

Further Adventures in

Domains of the Forge

This 352-page, full-color hardcover tome provides a complete overview of the *Domains of the Forge*, complete with political overviews of the seven domains and the complex makeup of the massive city of Penance, home of the scheming Bloodlords and the Feathered Fowl known as Israfel, Queen of Penance.

BAS-1005; ISBN: 0971439265; $39.95

Plains of Penance

Beyond the bustling city streets and dangerous underground areas of the city of Penance are the sprawling plains. This rough and wild wilderness area contains new challenges for heroes, as well as political implications for the great city of Penance.

BAS-1008; ISBN: 097143929X; $29.95